PRAISE FOR

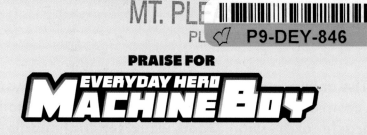

EVERYDAY HERO MACHINE BOY™

"Everyday Hero Machine Boy Hero is a fast-paced, hilarious adventure set in a post-apocalyptic world populated by humans and talking dogs. Tri and Irma's art is a treat to look at, and it's hard not to love Machine Boy, our hero with a heart of metal, and his adoptive, karate master grandma."
-KRISTEN GUDSNUK (*Making Friends*)

"I just loved it, what else is there to say? It's hilarious, drawn with a masterful touch, and rips through straight to your heart."
-TILLIE WALDEN (*Spinning*, *On a Sunbeam*, CLEMENTINE)

"The book is so rad! So funny and impeccably laid out colored... like a sugary modern twist on Toriyama."
-MATT FORSYTHE (*Pokko and the Drum*)

"Machine Boy's eccentricity and charm is undeniable...I laughed, choked back tears, and then cheered for this lovable android. This should be a perennial read for readers of all ages."
-FRANCIS MANAPUL (*Detective Comics*)

"...like *Mega Man* by way of Studio Ghibli! I read the whole thing in one sitting and found myself itching for more! MORE!!!"
-CHRIS SAMNEE (FIRE POWER, *Jonna and the Unpossible Monsters*)

"A charming and heartwarming tale of family and heroism."
-JORGE CORONA (*Middlewest*)

"The anime-inspired blend of martial arts, sf dystopia, and cosmic fantasy is energized by high-octane action and character expression. Good, weird fun that middle-grade readers will adore."

-BOOKLIST

"Spaghetti, karate, monster pets and superhero rock stars! Machine Boy is an 8-bit paradise that you will want to read every day."

-PABLO TUNICA (SEA SERPENT'S HEIR)

"Even though this comic has talking dogs, cool-headed super popstars, and a powerful grandma, you'll still end up wishing that Machine Boy was your best friend. I'm still not sure how he manages to consume spaghetti, but he brings fun and optimism to a fantastical and dangerous world full of robots and mystery. *Astro Boy* meets *Iron Giant*; Machine Boy is the kind of hero that more stories need."

-MICHELLE FUS (AVA'S DEMON)

"A boon for the misfits, screwballs, weirdos, outsiders, newcomers, and nonconformists. If you've ever felt like you don't check the right boxes, like you don't belong, or like you aren't good enough—and who hasn't?—Everyday Hero Machine Boy is for you."

-KELLY SUE DeCONNICK (*Pretty Deadly*, *Captain Marvel*)

"A charming book that chronicles the adventures only a boy who is also a machine could have. Delightful!"

-MAIRGHREAD SCOTT (SEA SERPENT'S HEIR)

"A gorgeous exploration of failure and forgiveness that made me grin, gasp, and cry. I loved this book."

-GREG PAK (*The Princess Who Saved Herself*, *Planet Hulk*)

For Ian, Cara, Jenna and Jasmine.
May the world you inherit be a kind place.
—IRMA KNIIVILA

Dedicated to Fern – for her patience, support,
and faith in both this project and myself.
—TRI VUONG

SKYBOUND
COMET

EVERYDAY MACHINES

IRMA KNIIVILA   TRI VUONG

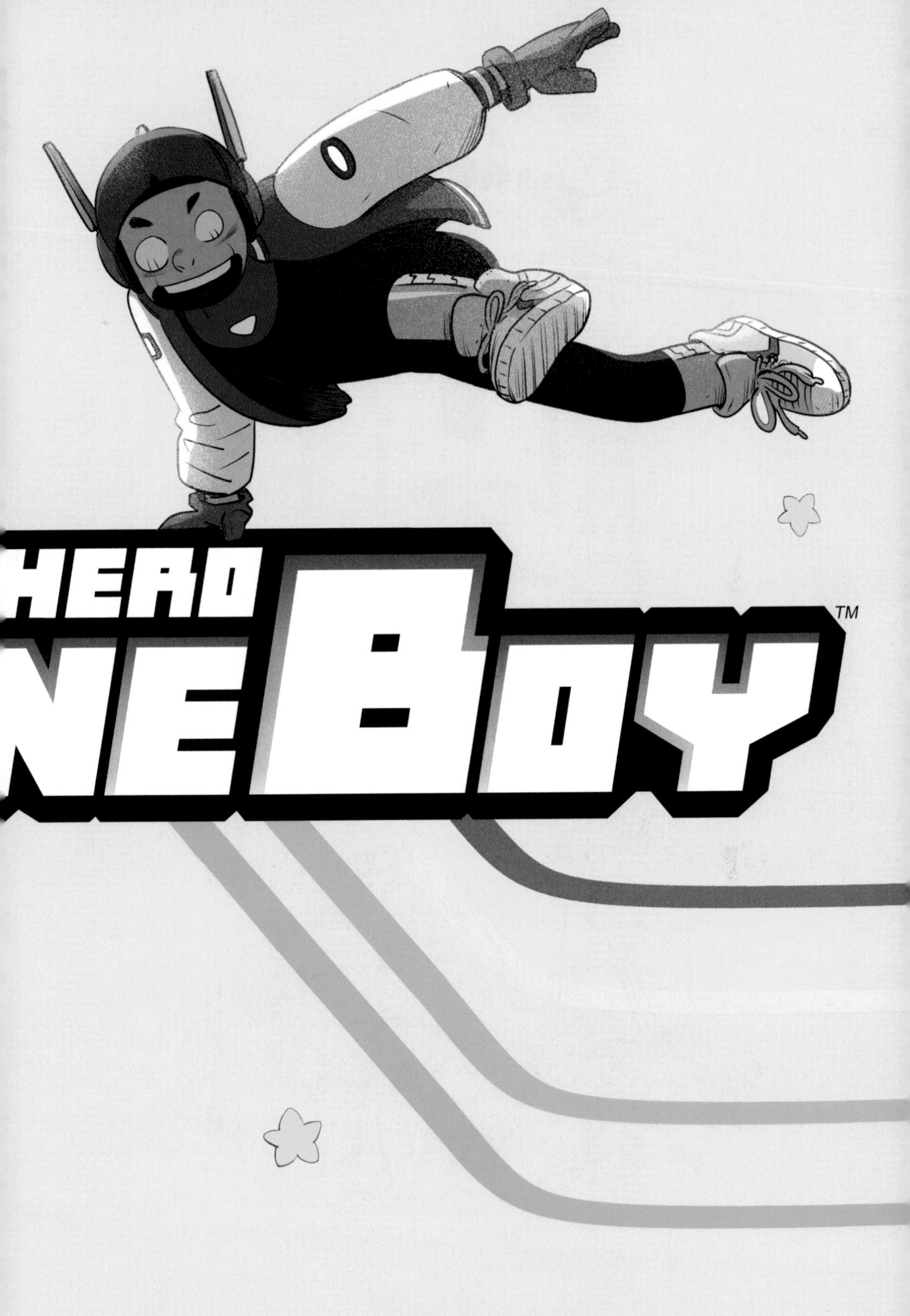
HERO
NE BOY
TM

CHAPTER 1

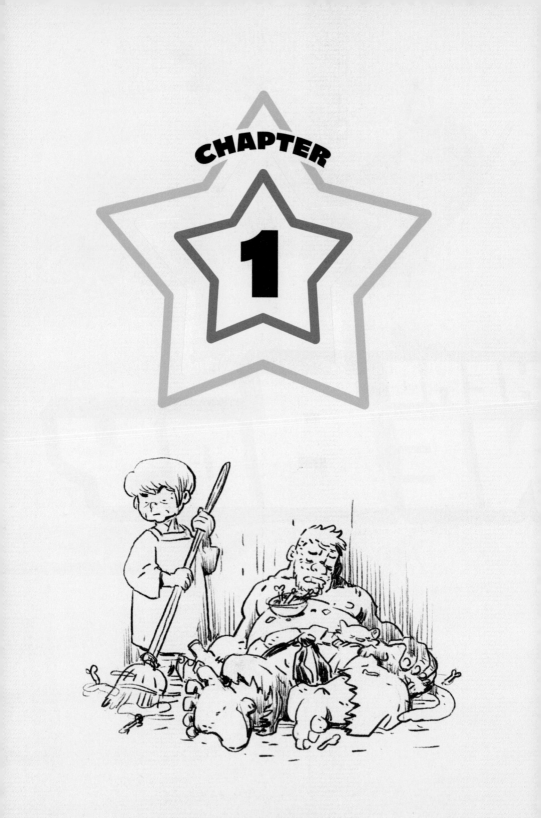

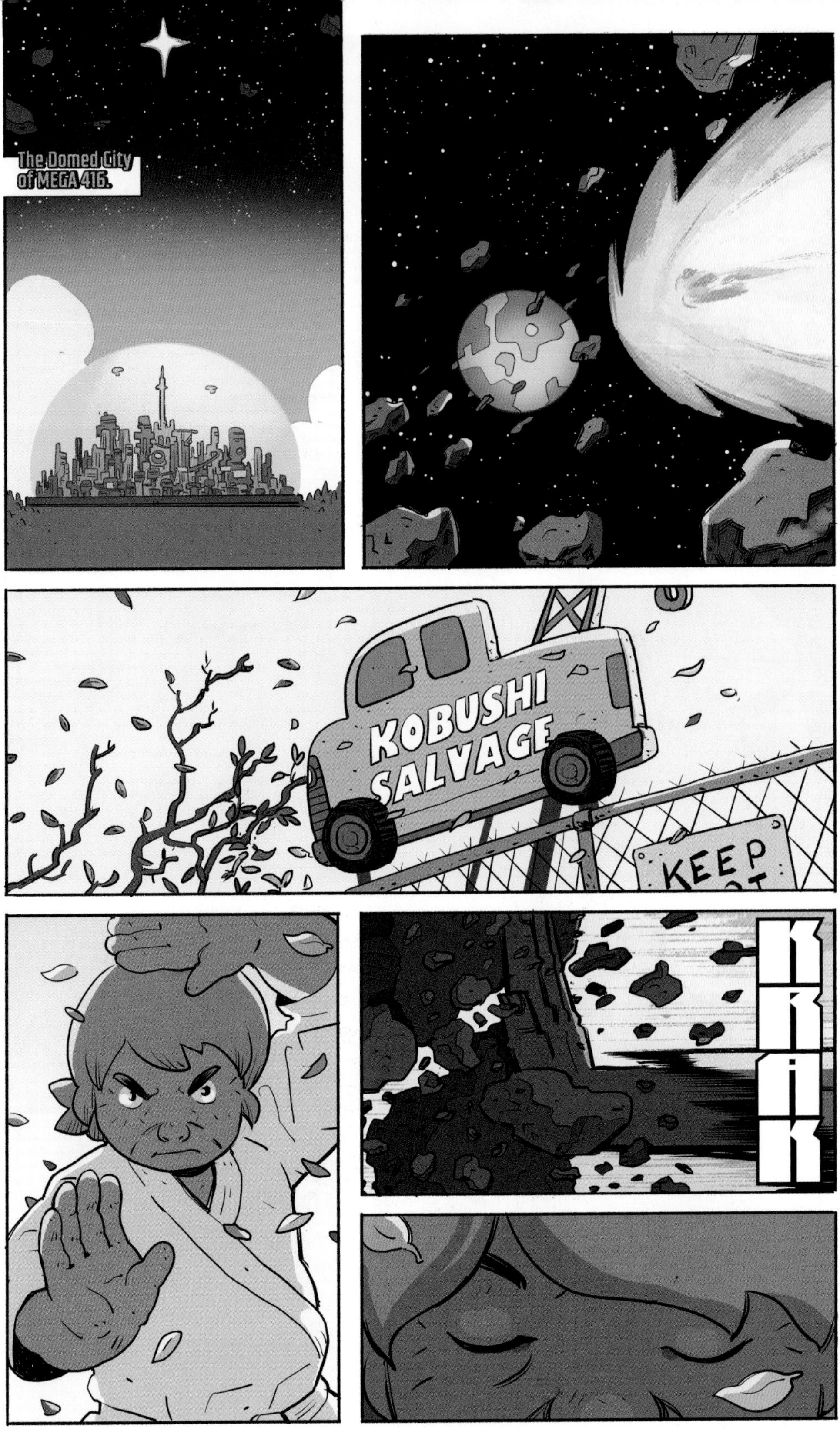
The Domed City of MEGA 416.
KOBUSHI SALVAGE
KEEP
KRAK

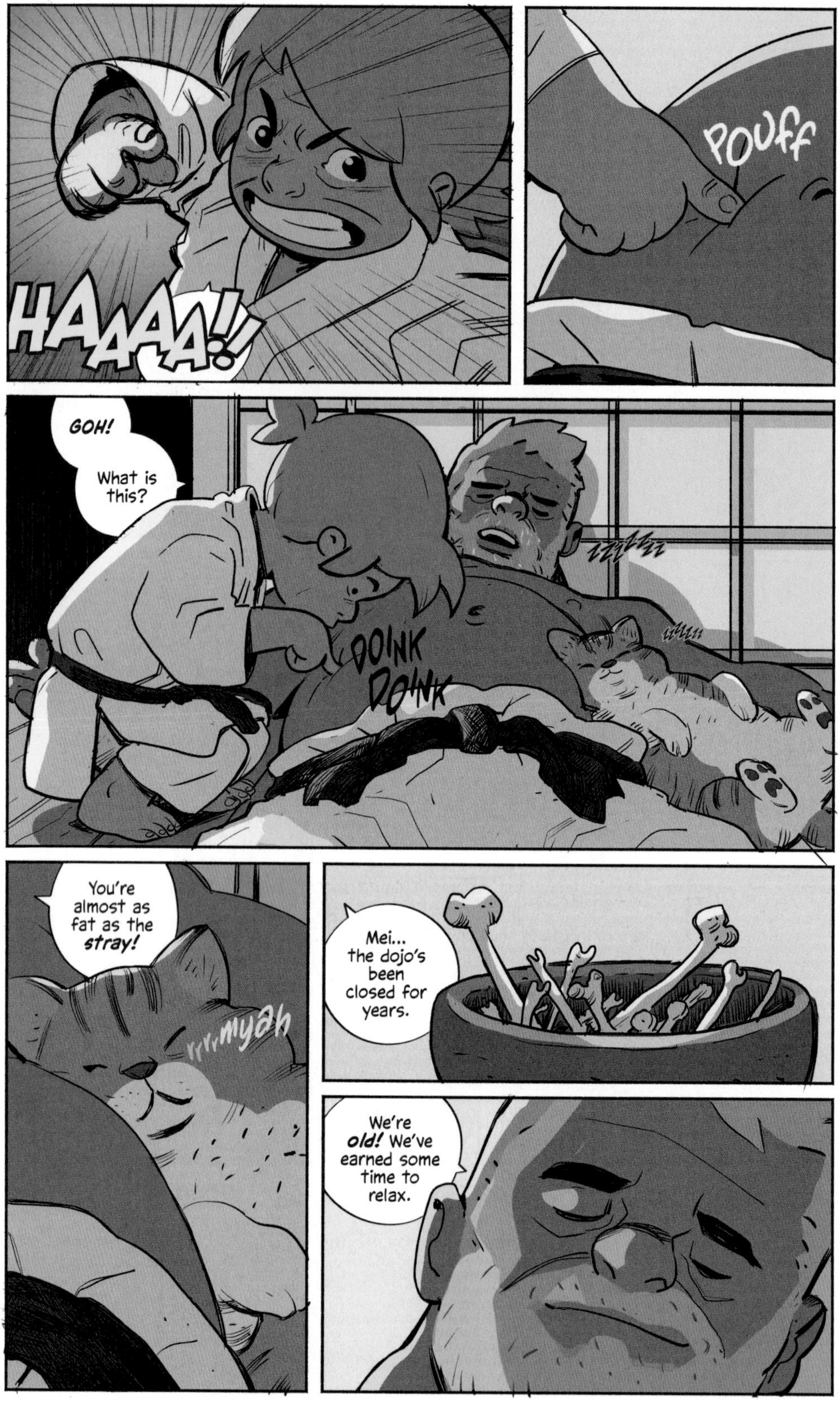
HAAAA!!!
POUFF
GOH!
What is this?
DOINK
DOINK
You're almost as fat as the *stray!*
rrrmyah
Mei... the dojo's been closed for years.
We're *old!* We've earned some time to relax.

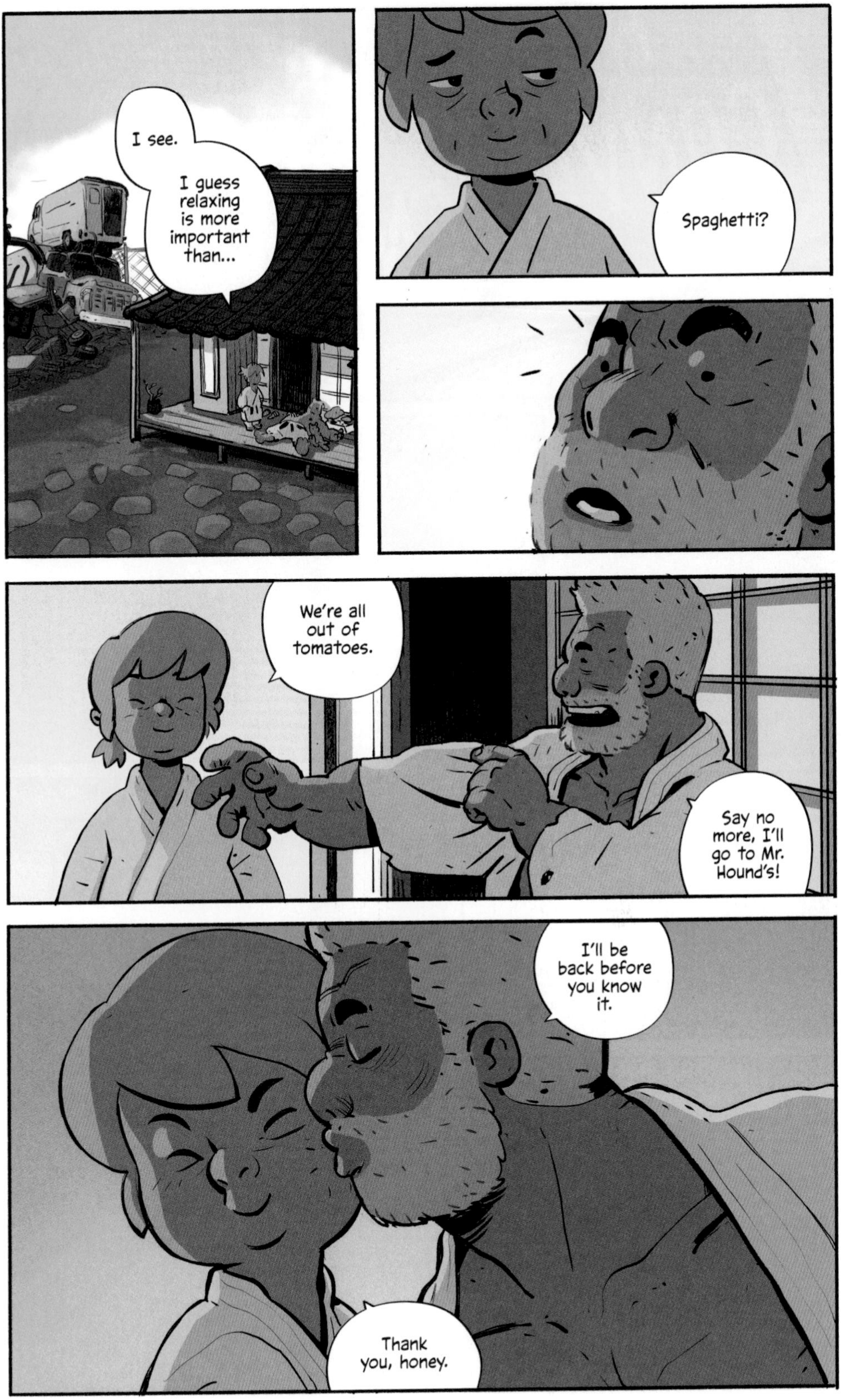
I see.
I guess relaxing is more important than...
Spaghetti?
We're all out of tomatoes.
Say no more, I'll go to Mr. Hound's!
I'll be back before you know it.
Thank you, honey.

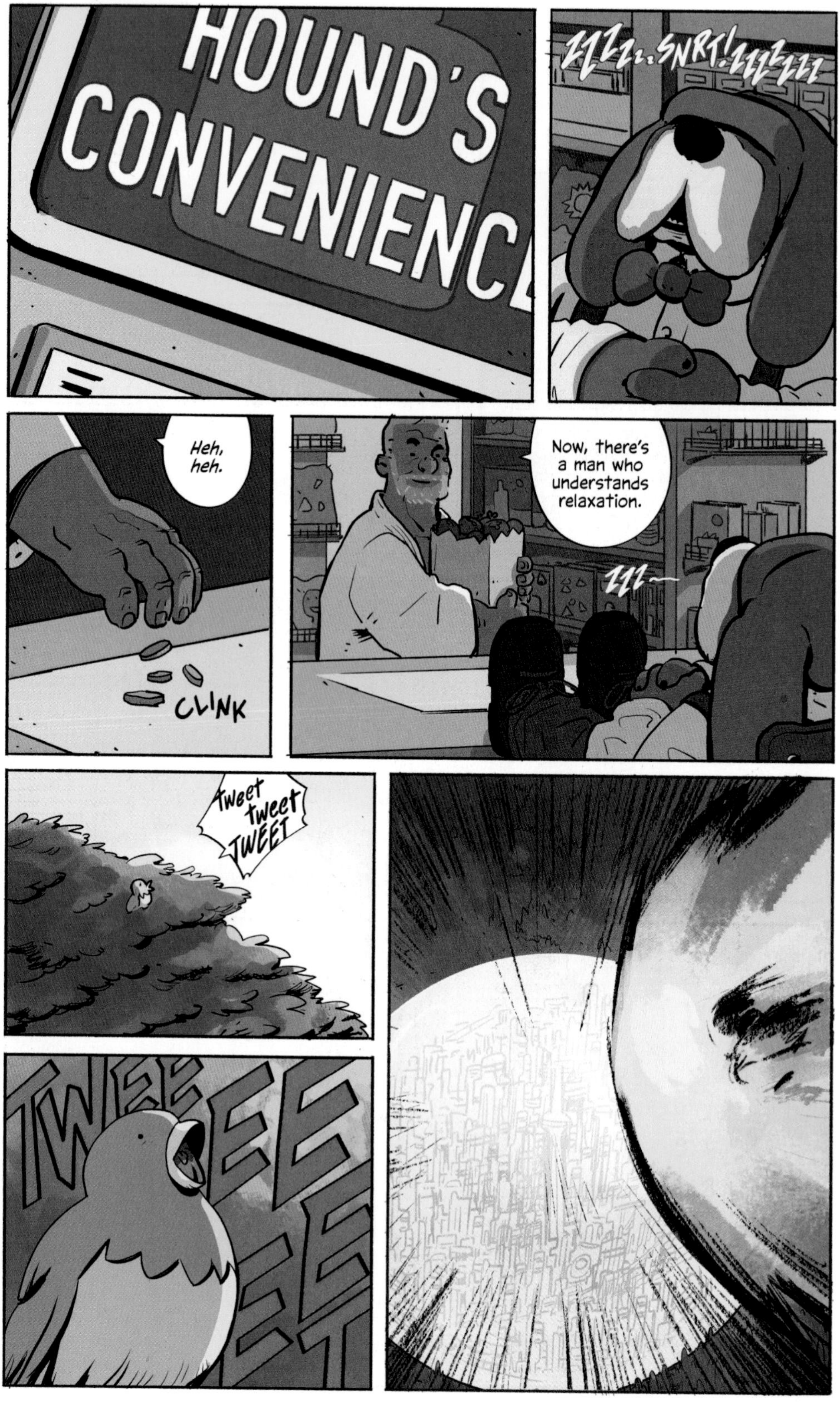
HOUND'S CONVENIENC
ZZZzz..SNRT! ZZZZZZZ
Heh, heh.
CLINK
Now, there's a man who understands relaxation.
ZZZ~
Tweet tweet TWEET
TWEEE

tweee~~

What in the world's got you all worked up?

SKASH

...

Oh.

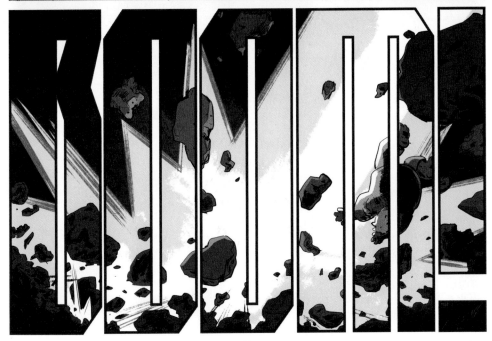

5

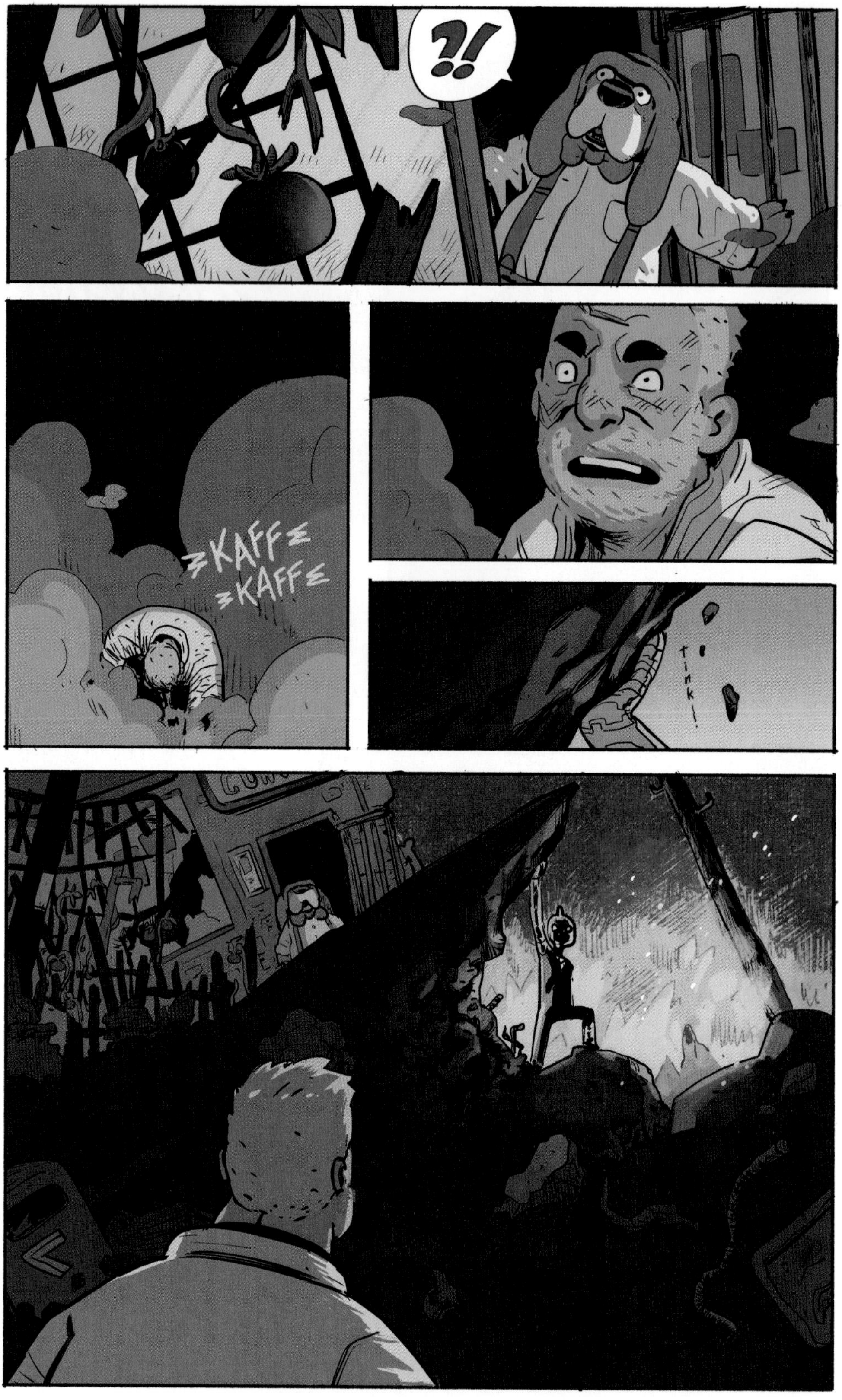
?!
KAFF
KAFF
tink!

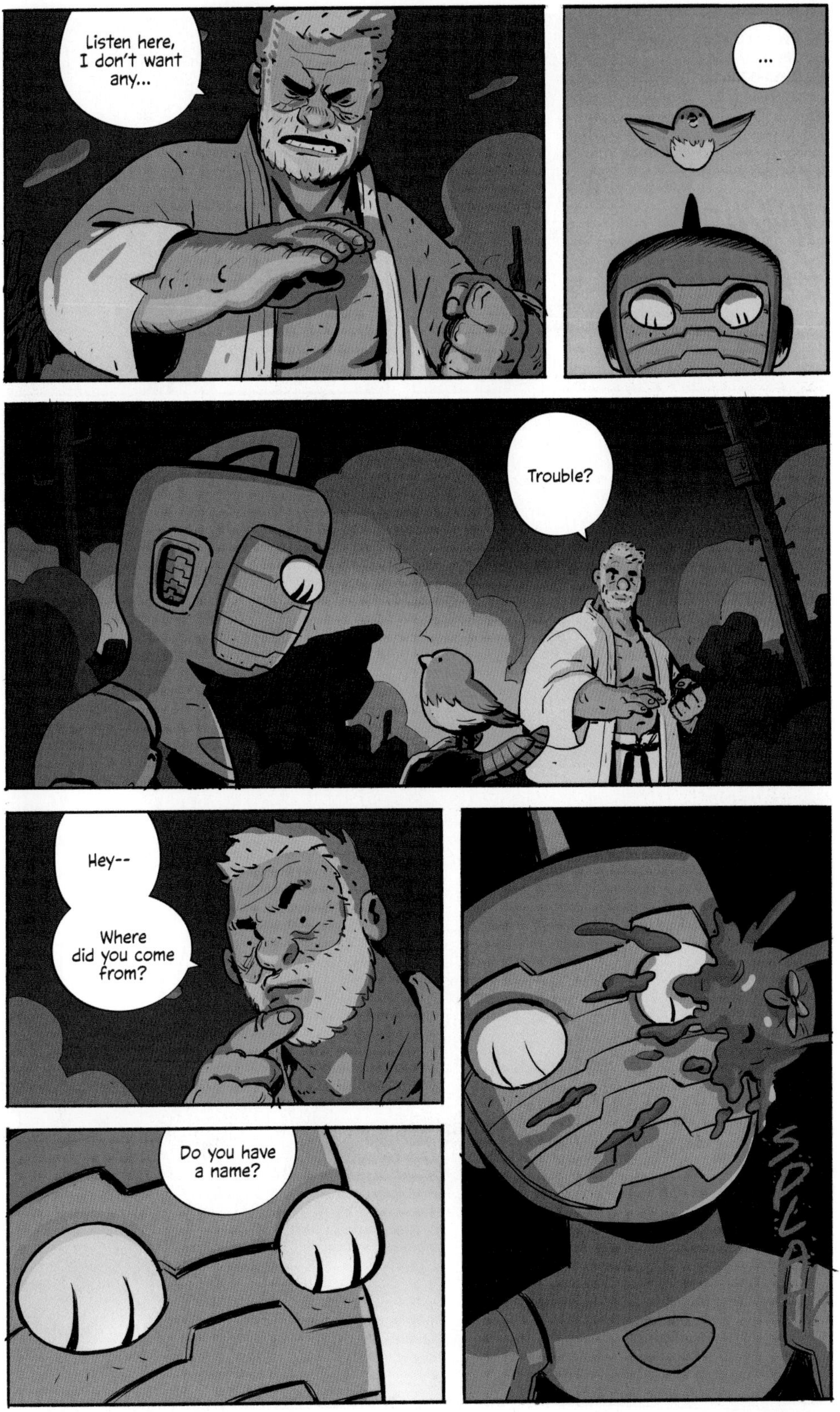
Listen here, I don't want any...
...
Trouble?
Hey--
Where did you come from?
Do you have a name?

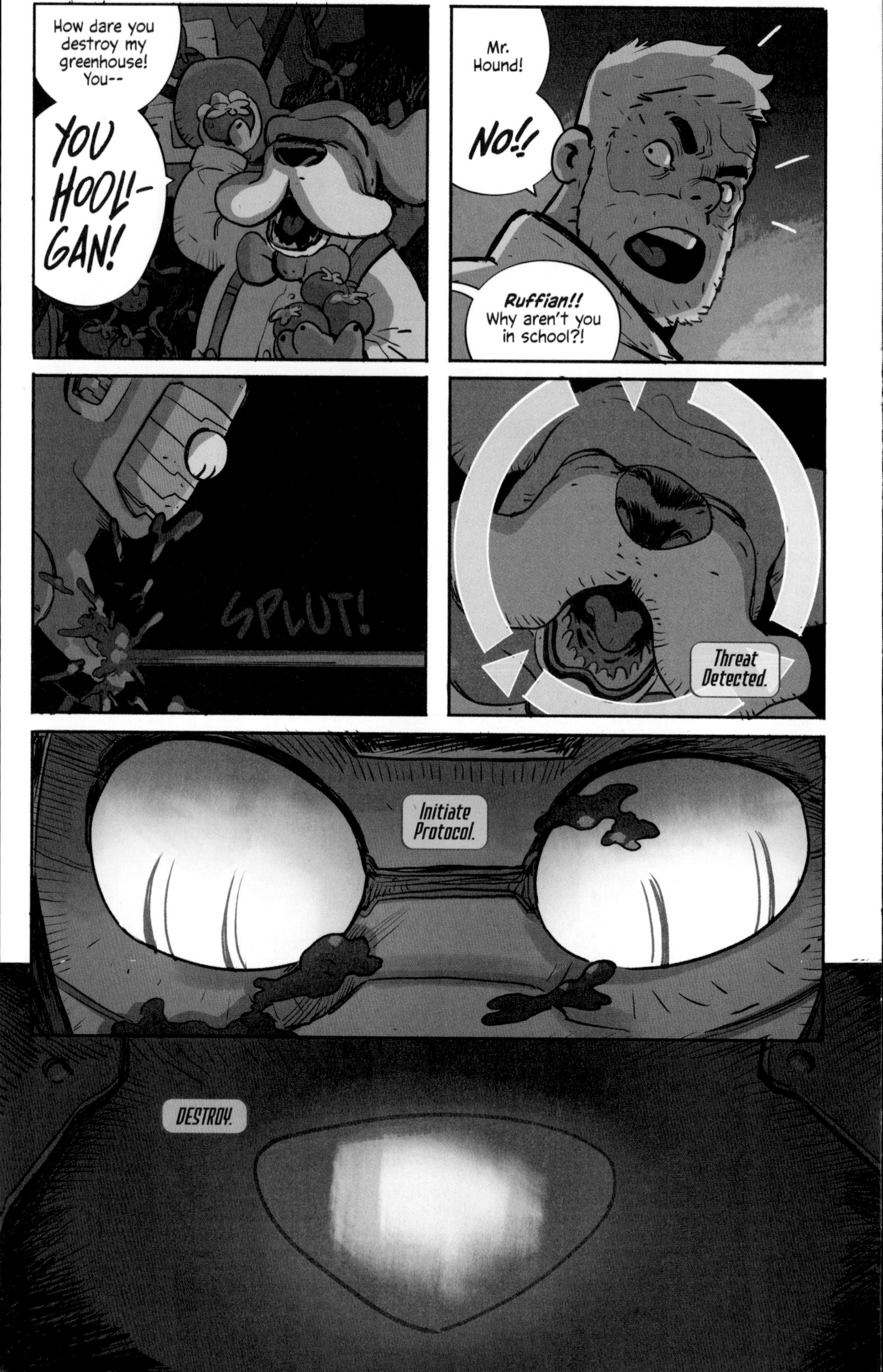
How dare you destroy my greenhouse! You--
YOU HOOLI-GAN!
Mr. Hound!
NO!!
Ruffian!! Why aren't you in school?!
SPLUT!
Threat Detected.
Initiate Protocol.
DESTROY.

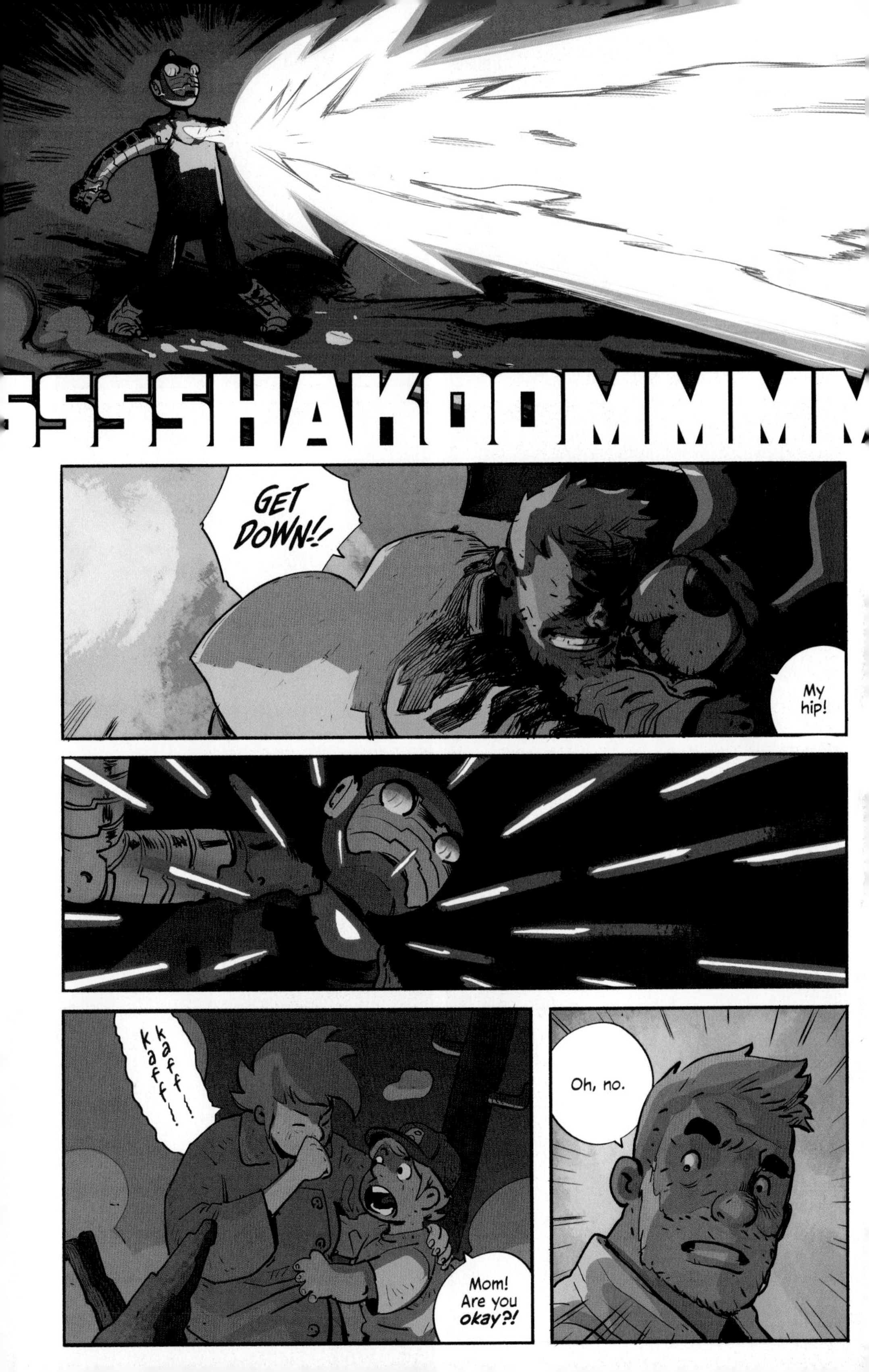

SSSSHAKOOMMMMM
GET DOWN!!
My hip!
kaff kaff!!
Mom! Are you *okay*?!
Oh, no.

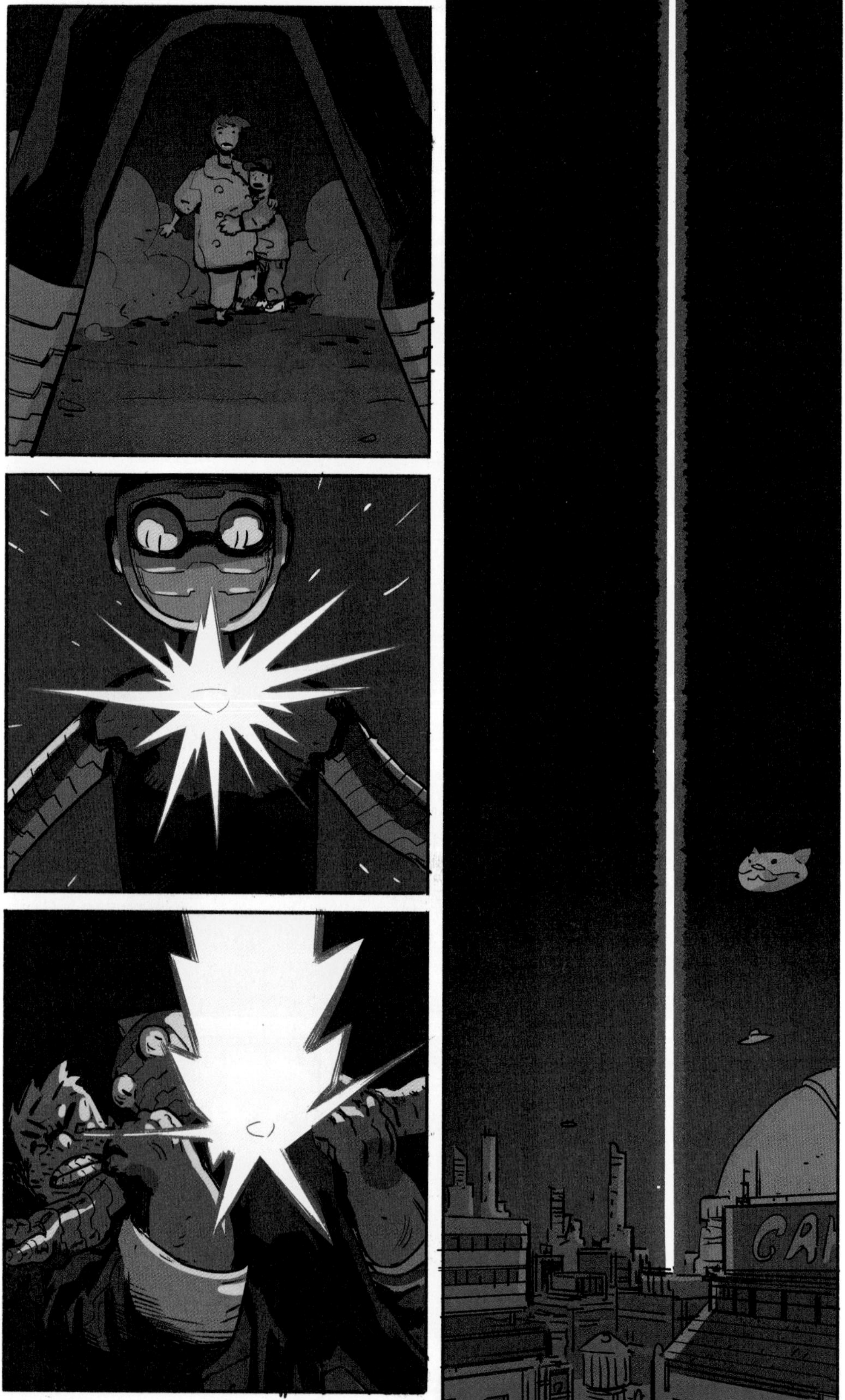

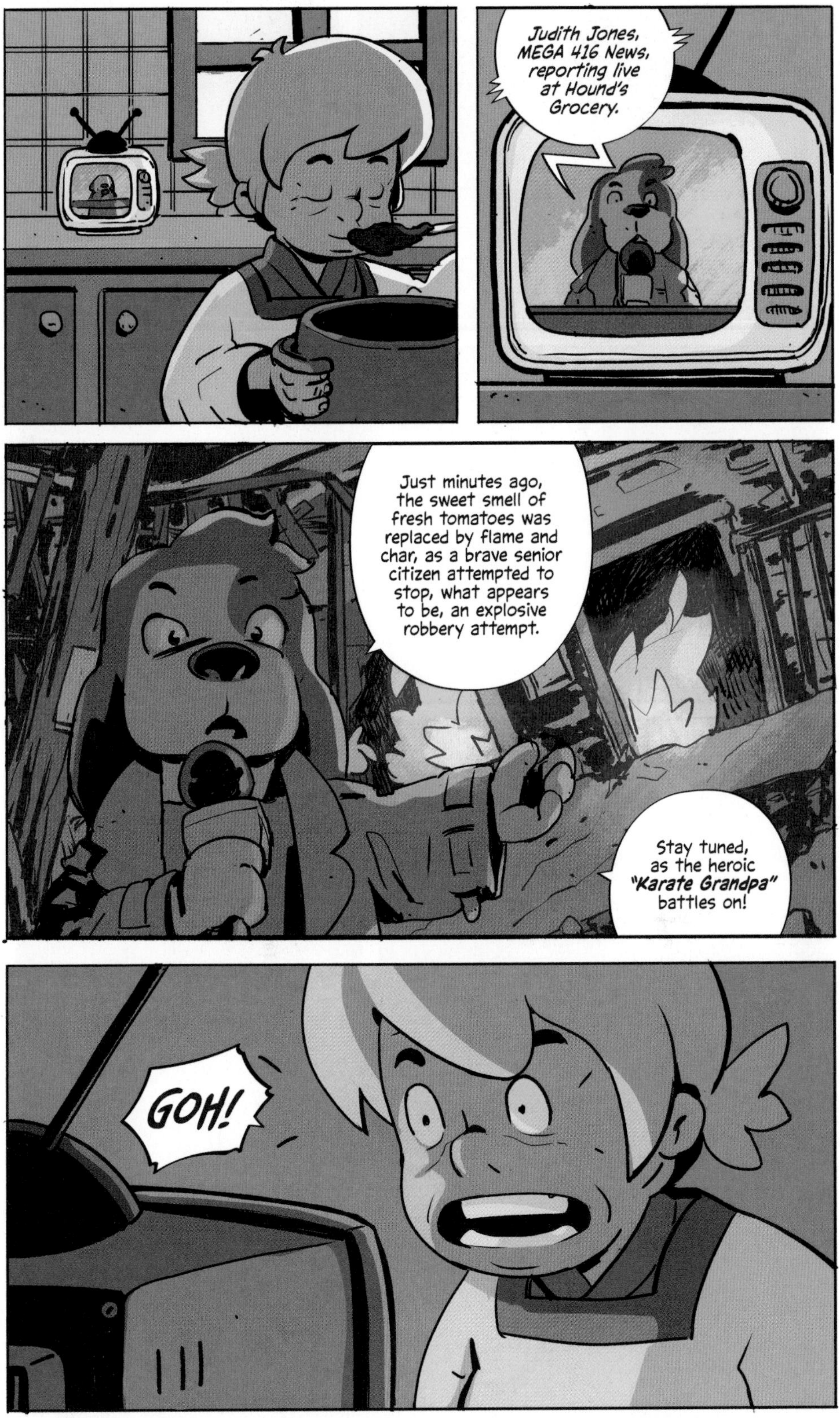
Judith Jones, MEGA 416 News, reporting live at Hound's Grocery.
Just minutes ago, the sweet smell of fresh tomatoes was replaced by flame and char, as a brave senior citizen attempted to stop, what appears to be, an explosive robbery attempt.
Stay tuned, as the heroic "Karate Grandpa" battles on!
GOH!

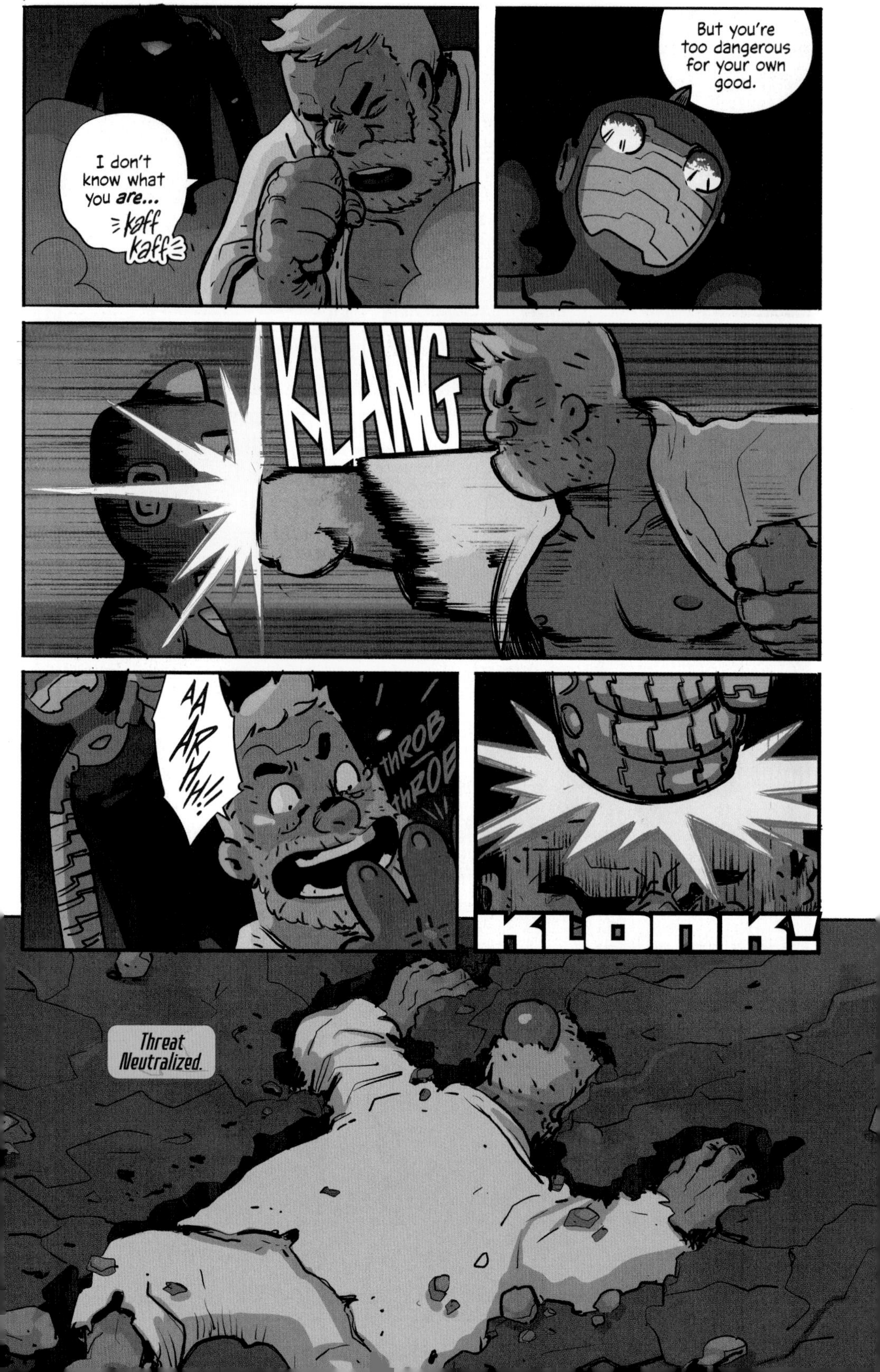
I don't know what you *are*...
kaff kaff
But you're too dangerous for your own good.
KLANG
AAARHH!!
throb throb
KLONK!
Threat Neutralized.

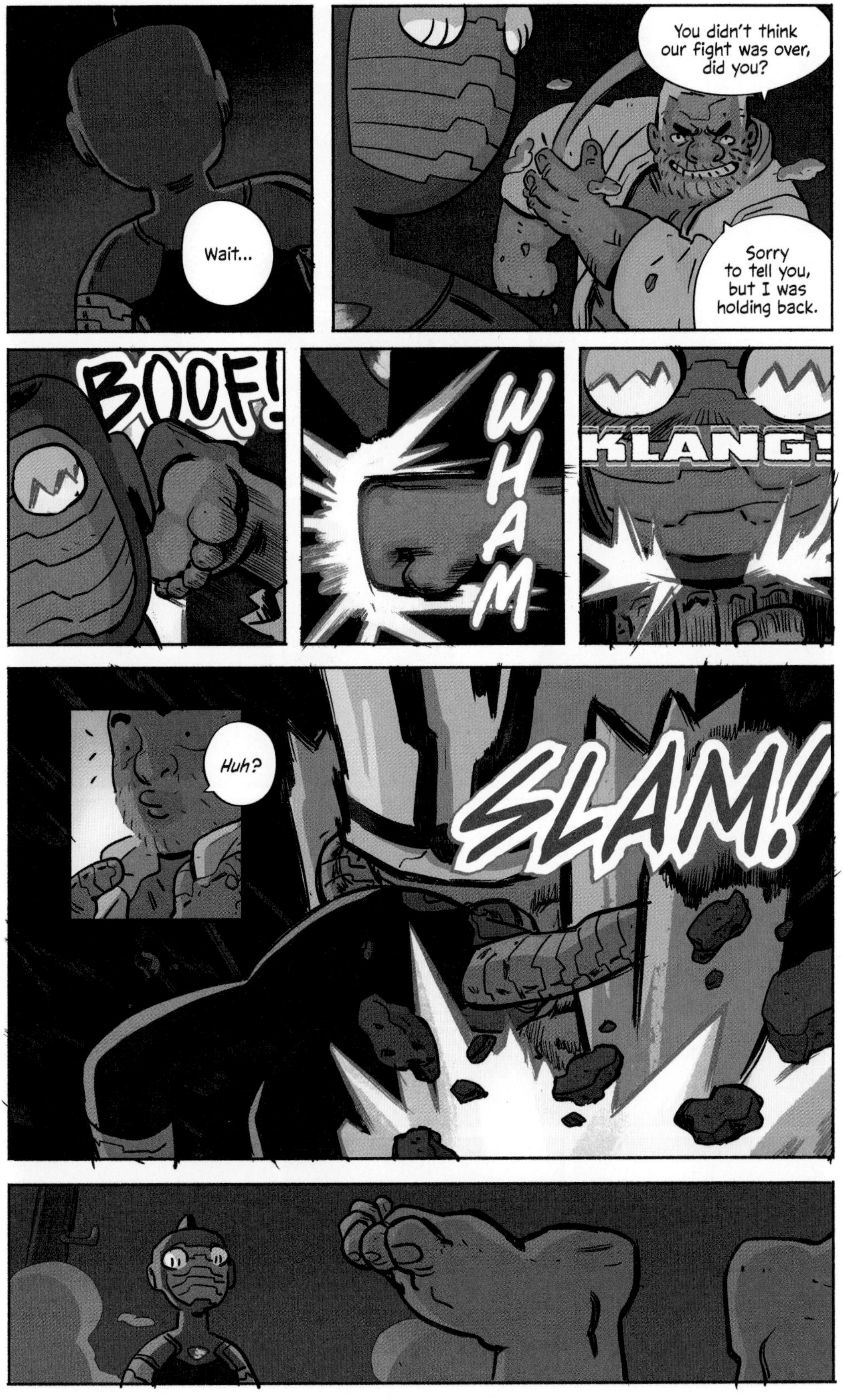
Wait...
You didn't think our fight was over, did you?
Sorry to tell you, but I was holding back.
BOOF!
WHAM
KLANG!
Huh?
SLAM!

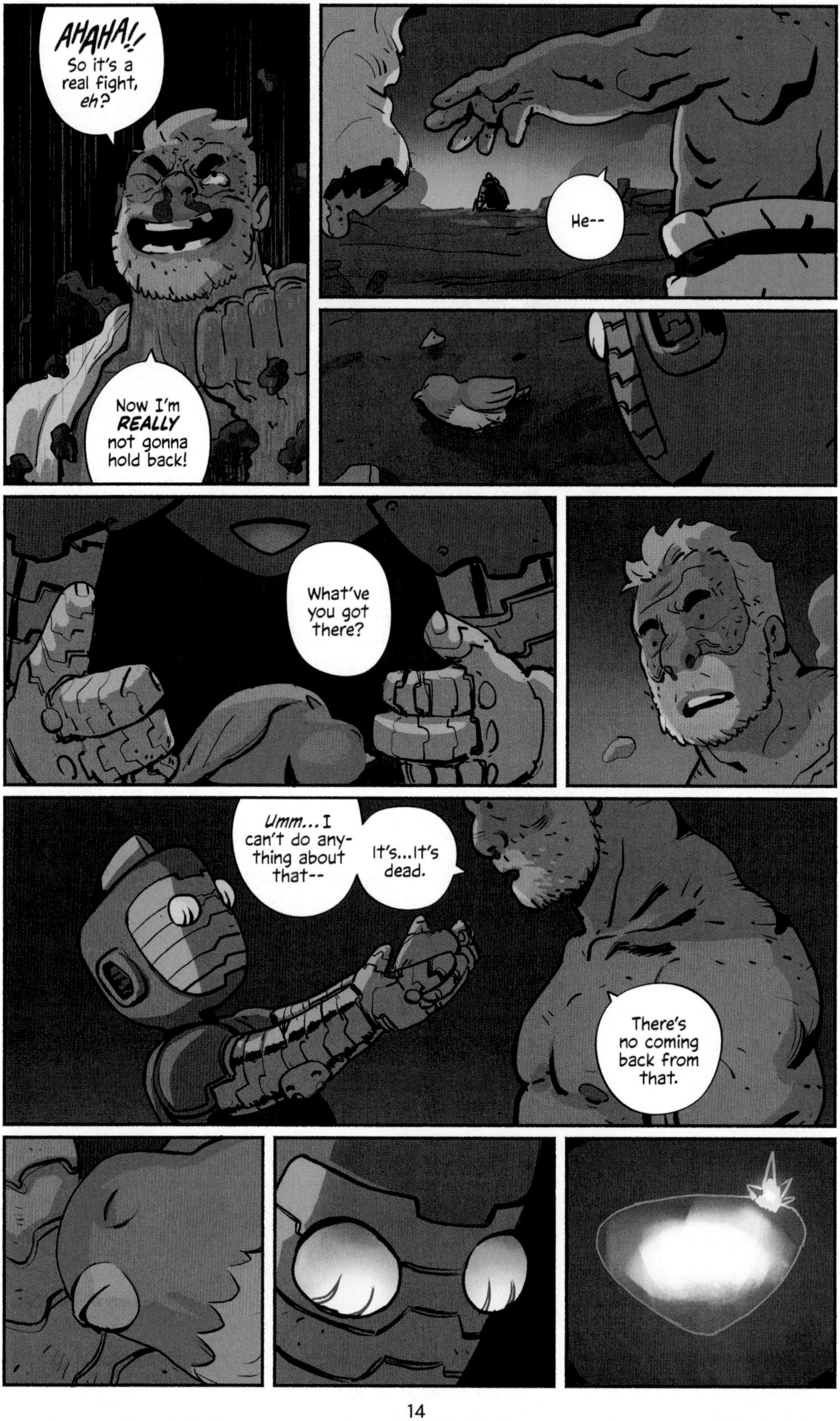
AHAHA!!
So it's a real fight, *eh?*
Now I'm ***REALLY*** not gonna hold back!
He--
What've you got there?
Umm... I can't do any-thing about that--
It's...It's dead.
There's no coming back from that.

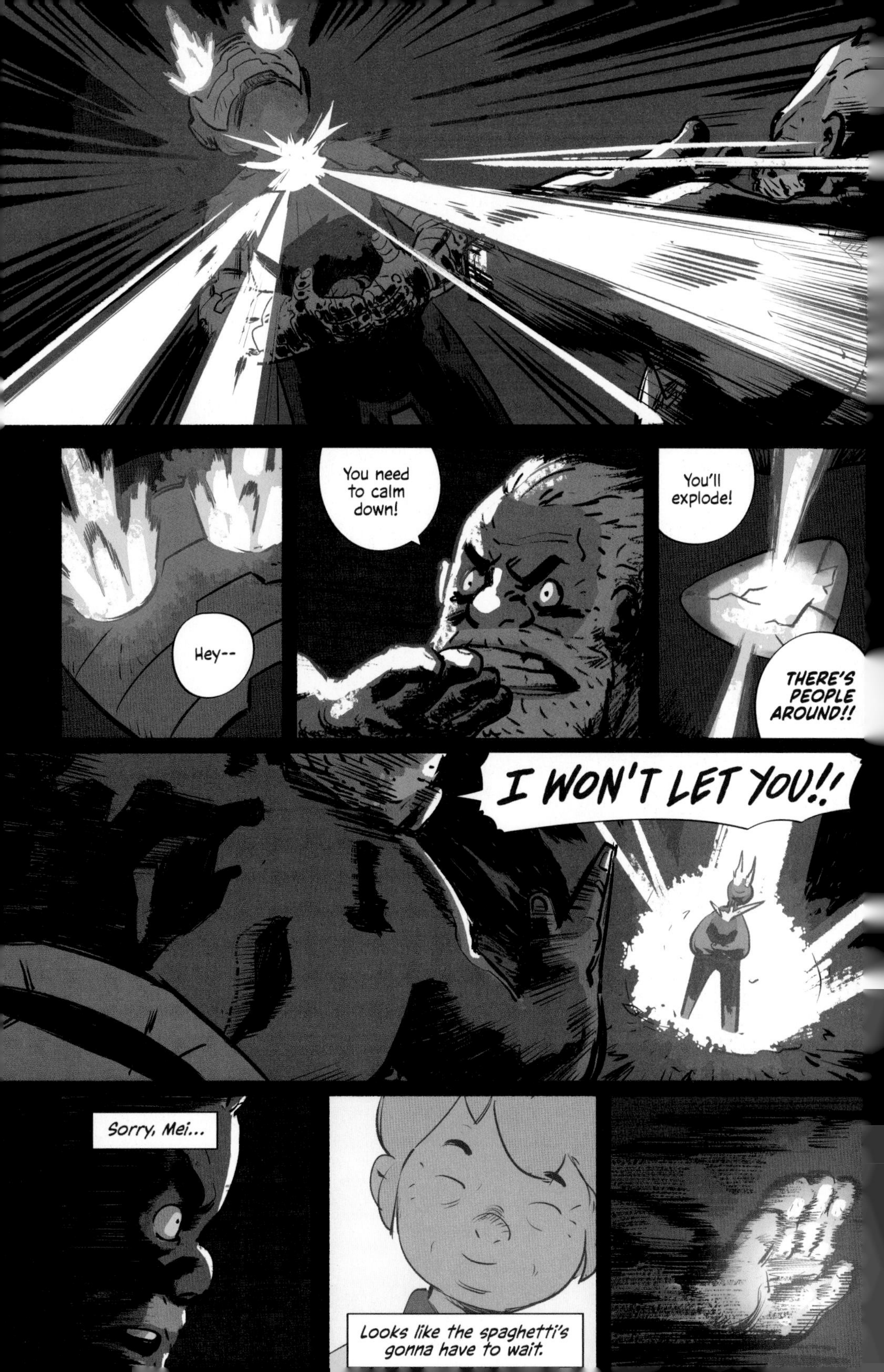
Hey--
You need to calm down!
You'll explode!
THERE'S PEOPLE AROUND!!
I WON'T LET YOU!!
Sorry, Mei...
Looks like the spaghetti's gonna have to wait.

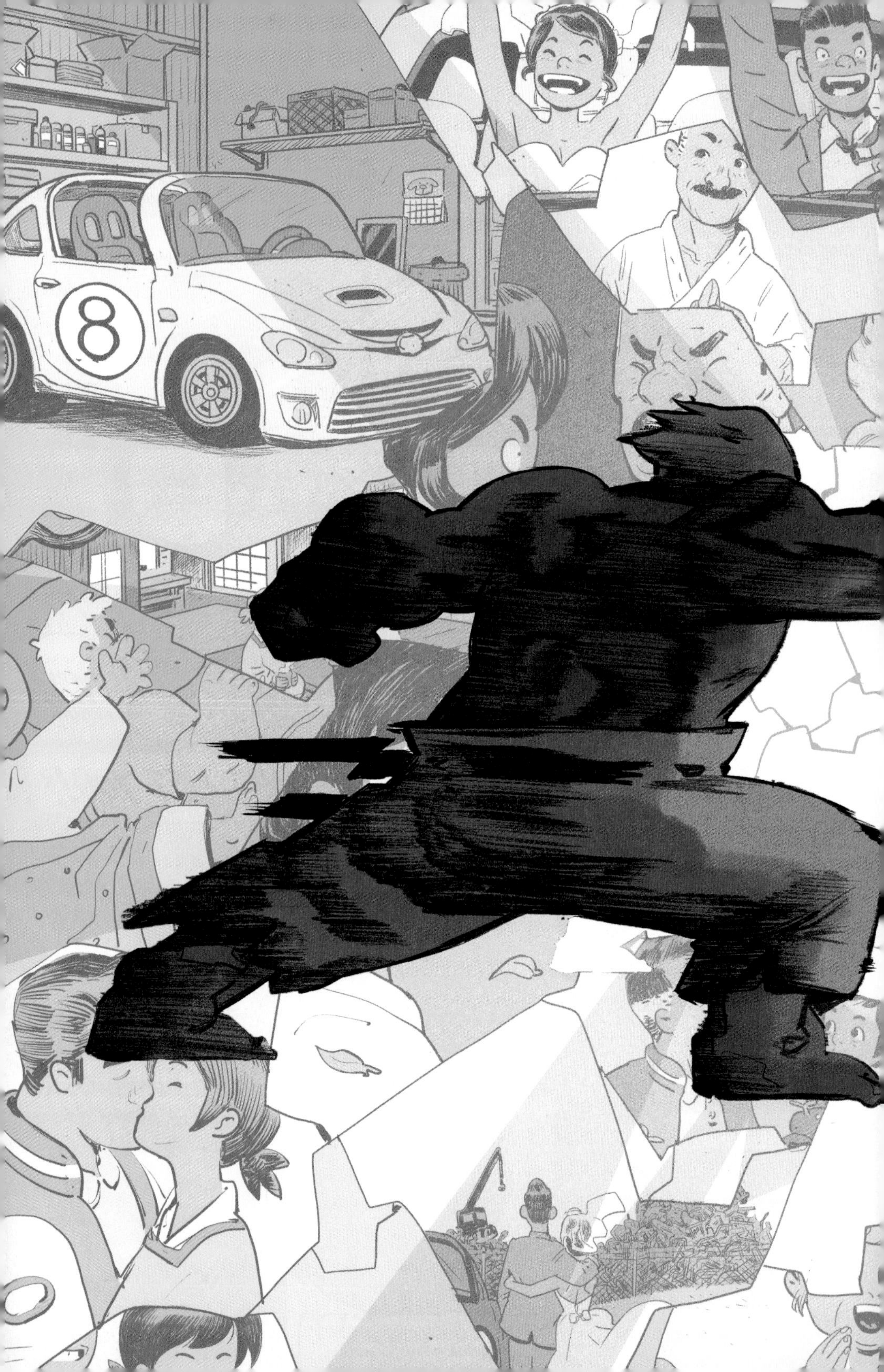

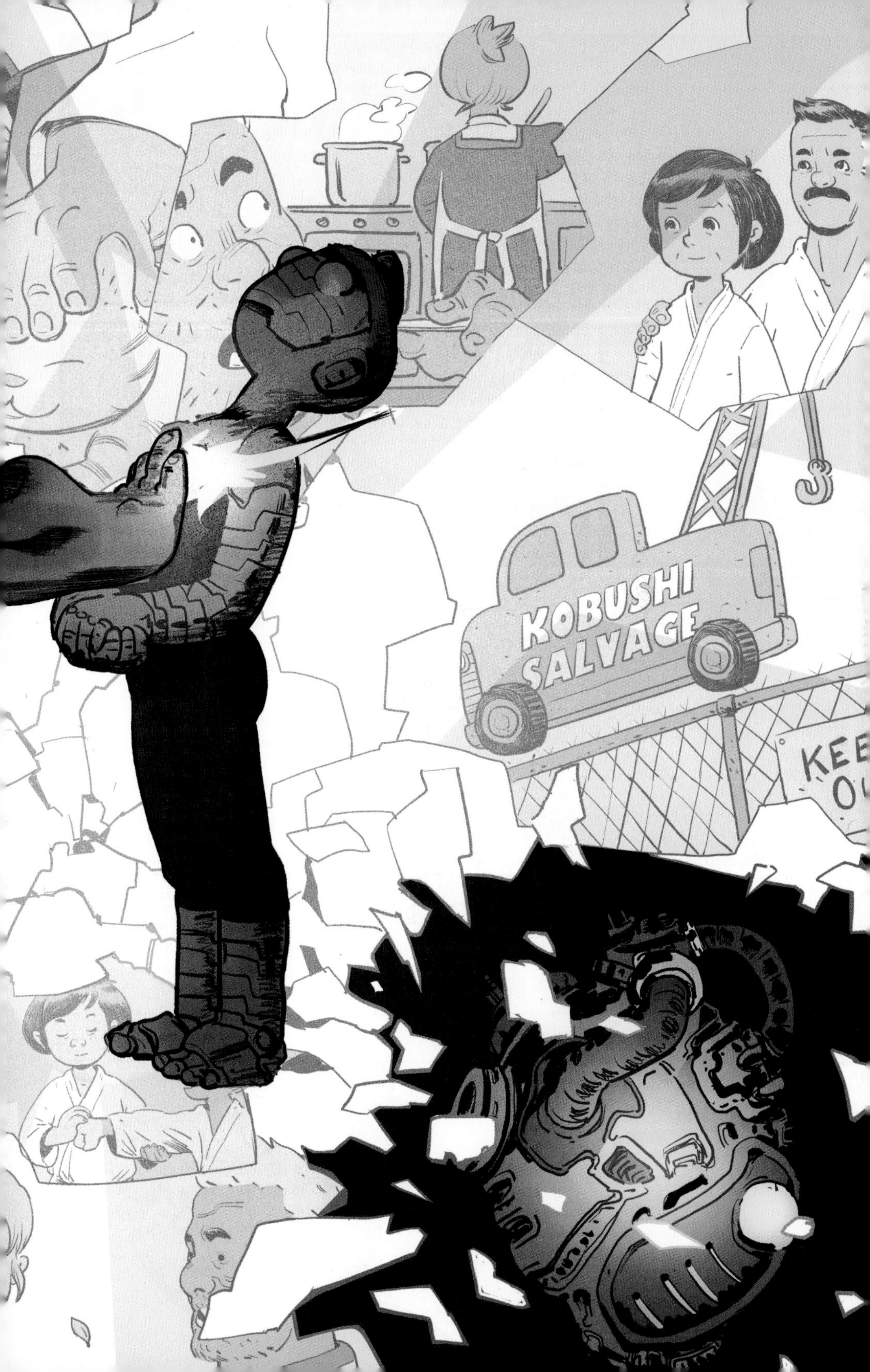
KOBUSHI
SALVAGE
KEE
OU

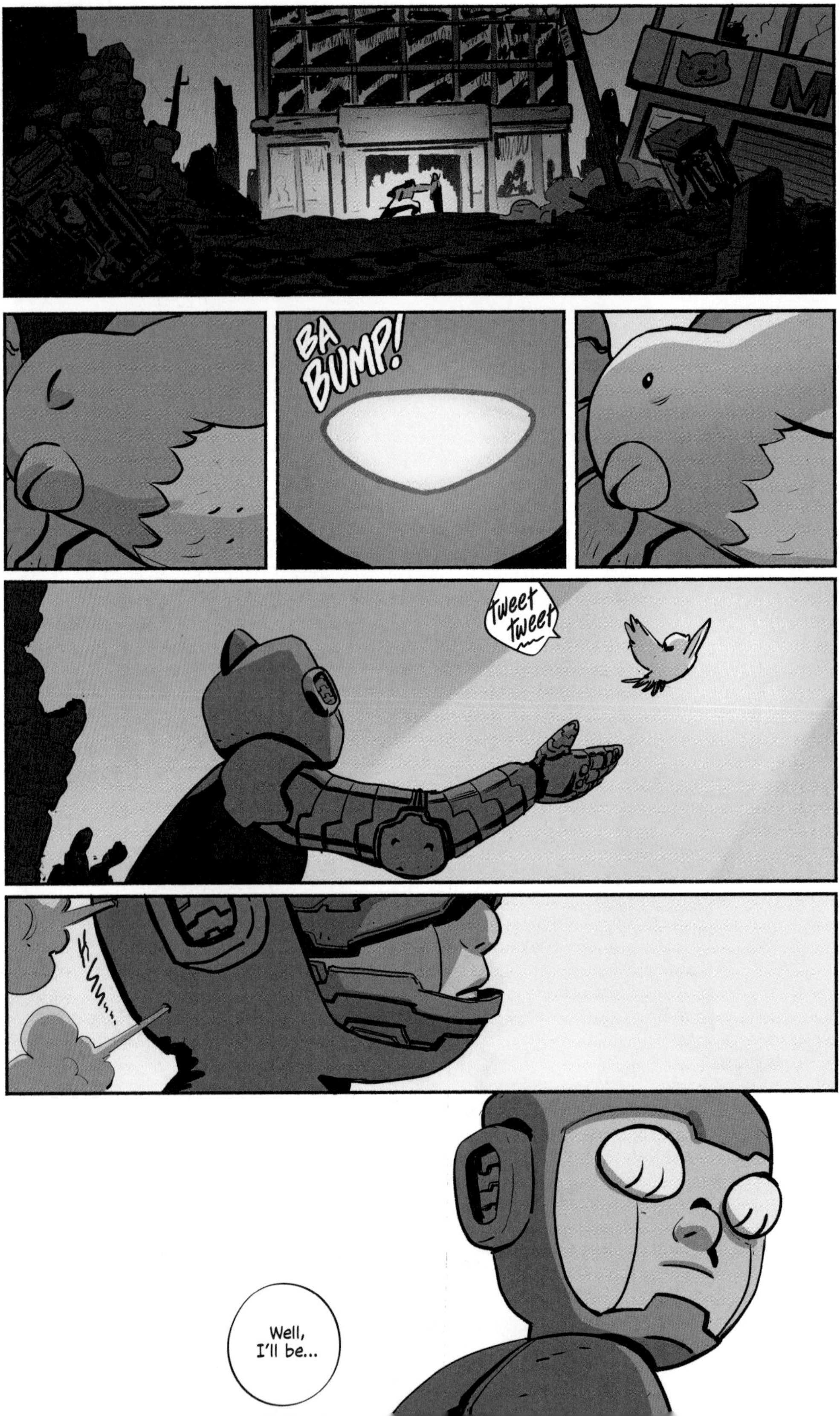
BA BUMP!
Tweet tweet
Well, I'll be...

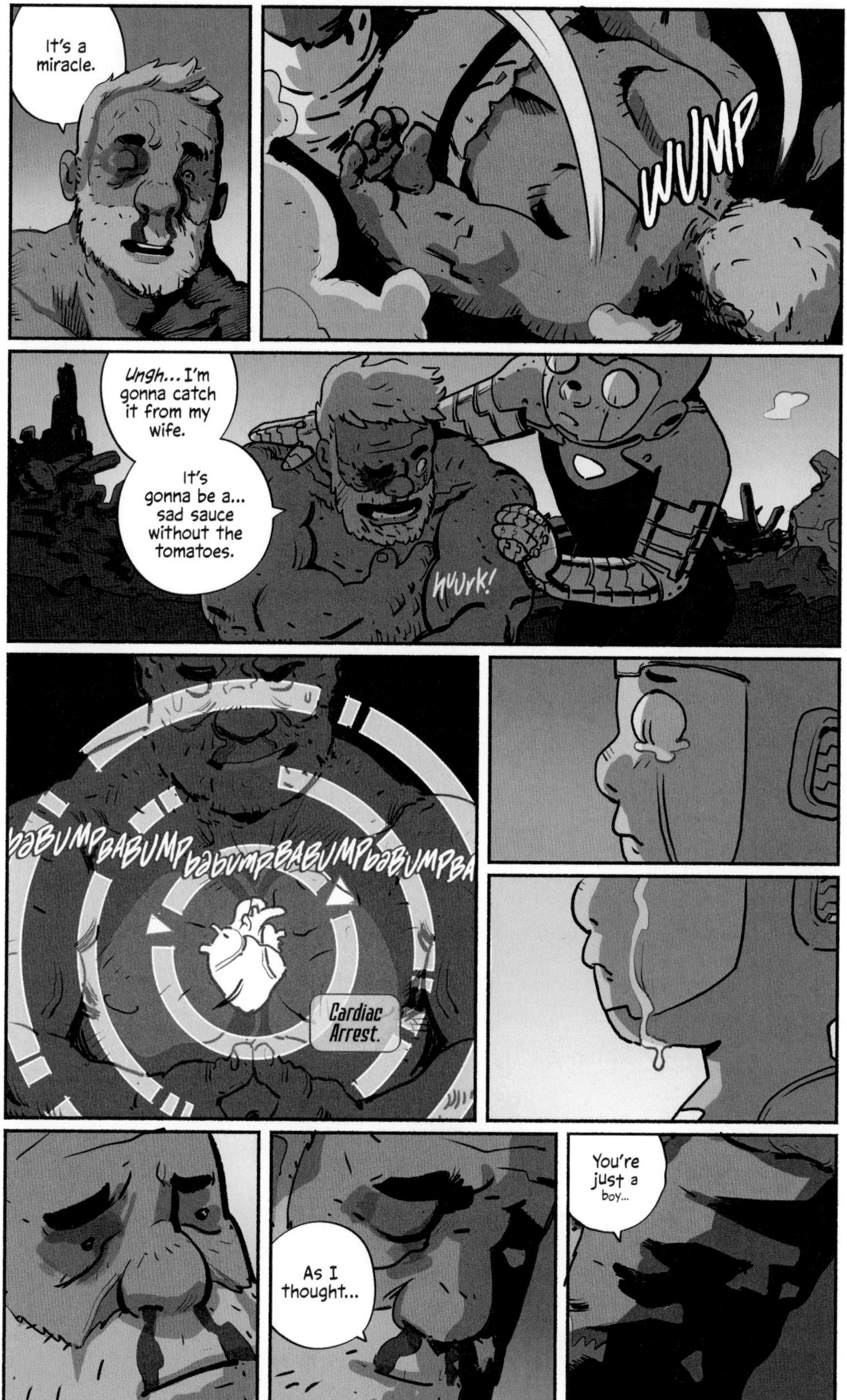
It's a miracle.
WUMP
Ungh... I'm gonna catch it from my wife.
It's gonna be a... sad sauce without the tomatoes.
hUUrk!
baBUMPbaBUMPbabumpBABUMPbaBUMPBA
Cardiac Arrest.
As I thought...
You're just a boy...

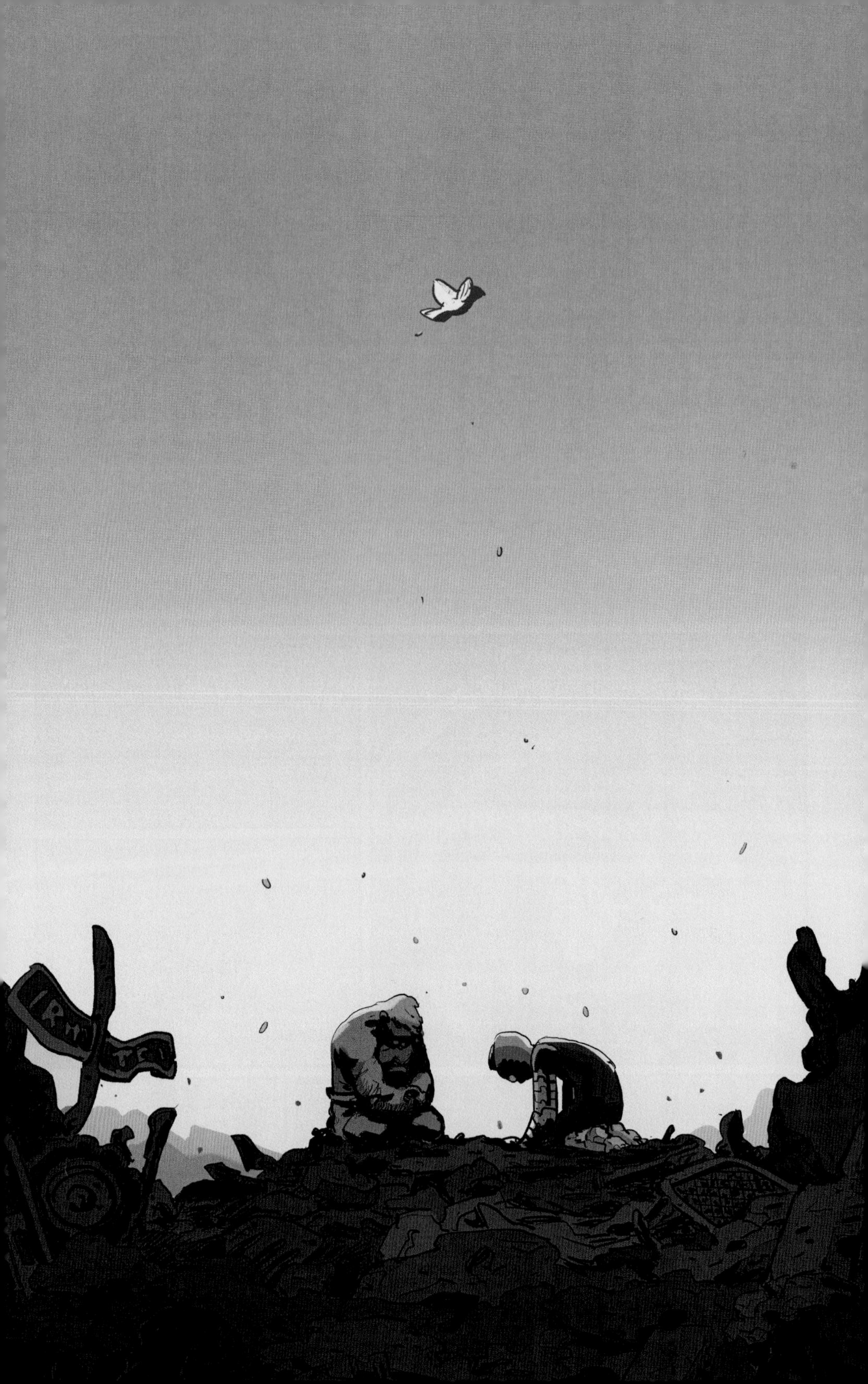

CHAPTER 2

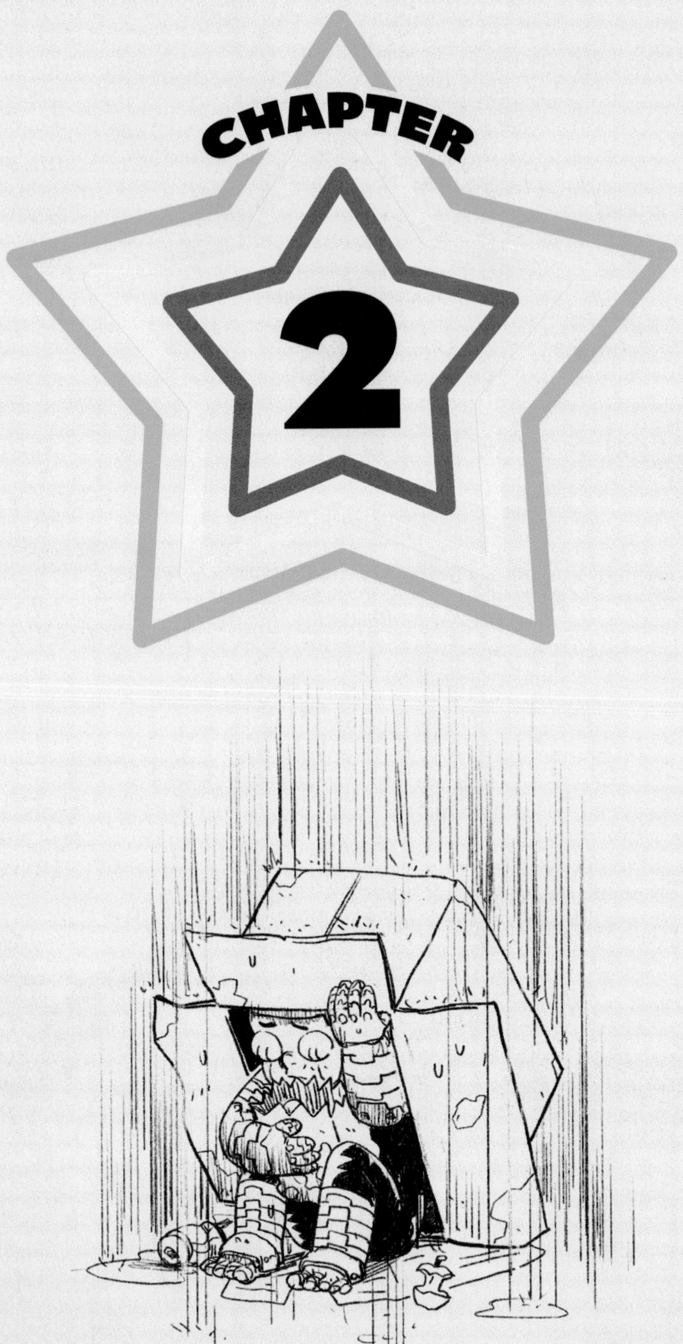

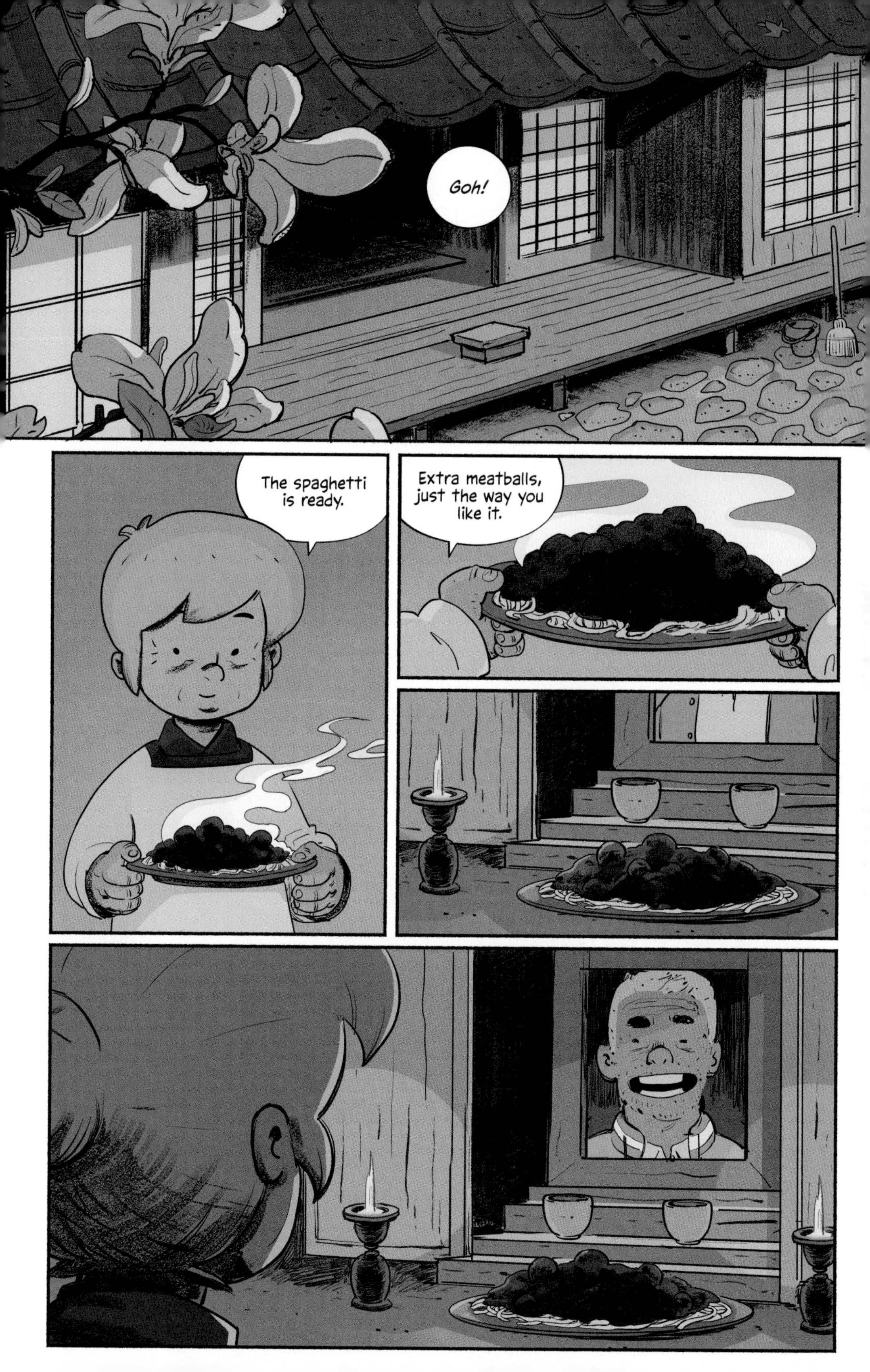
Goh!
The spaghetti is ready.
Extra meatballs, just the way you like it.

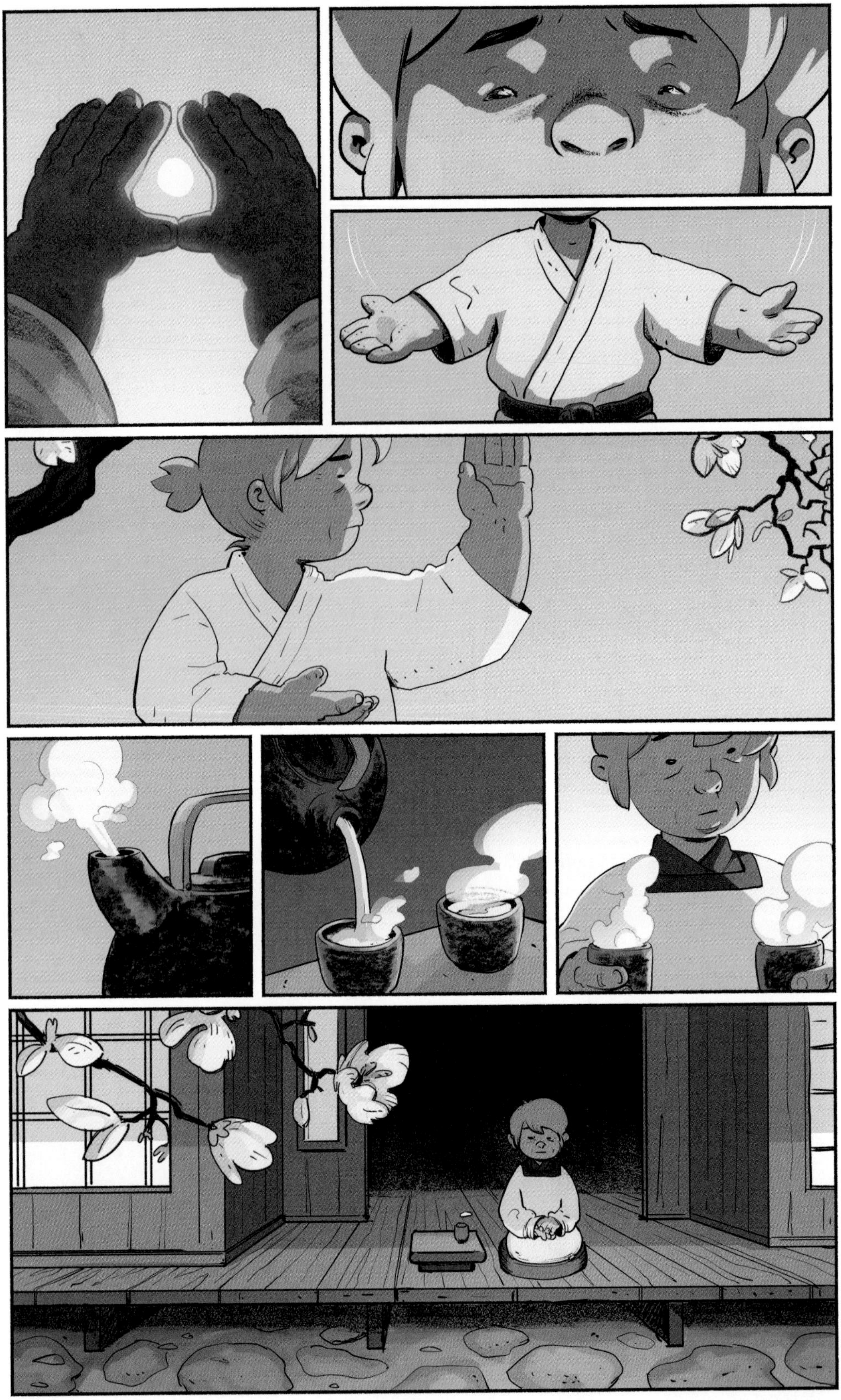

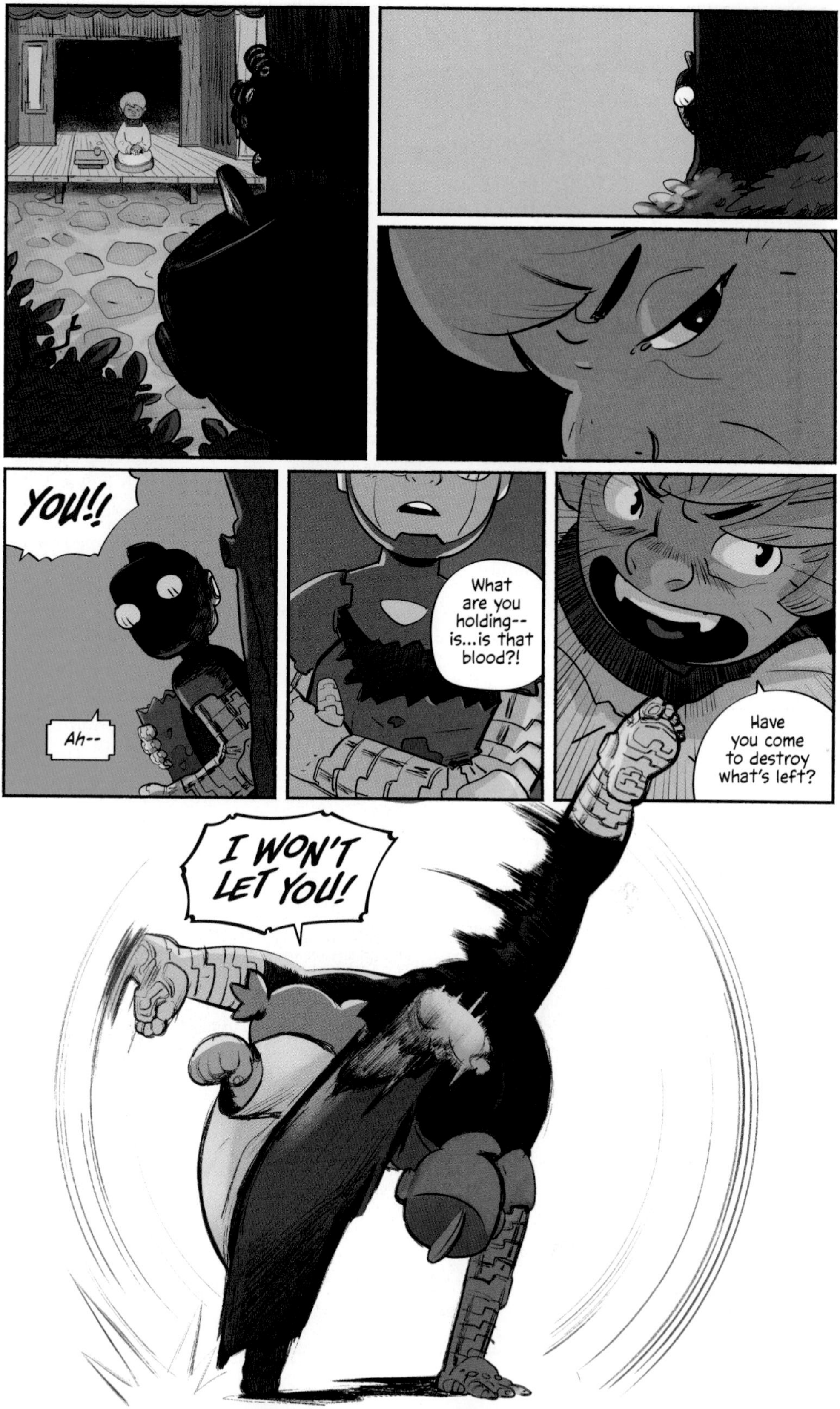
YOU!!
Ah--
What are you holding--is...is that blood?!
Have you come to destroy what's left?
I WON'T LET YOU!

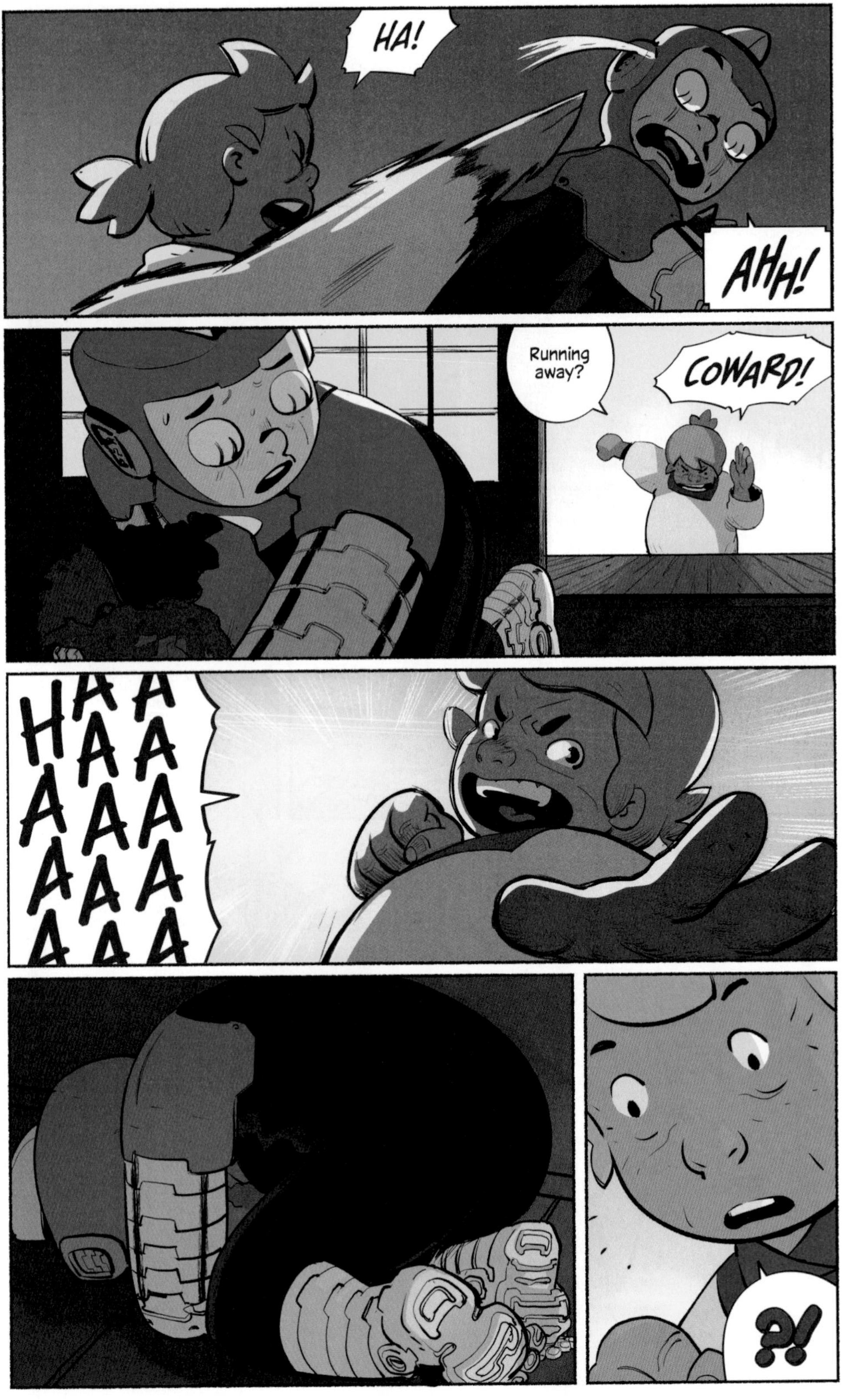
HA!
AHH!
Running away?
COWARD!
HAAAAAAAAAAAAAAAA
?!

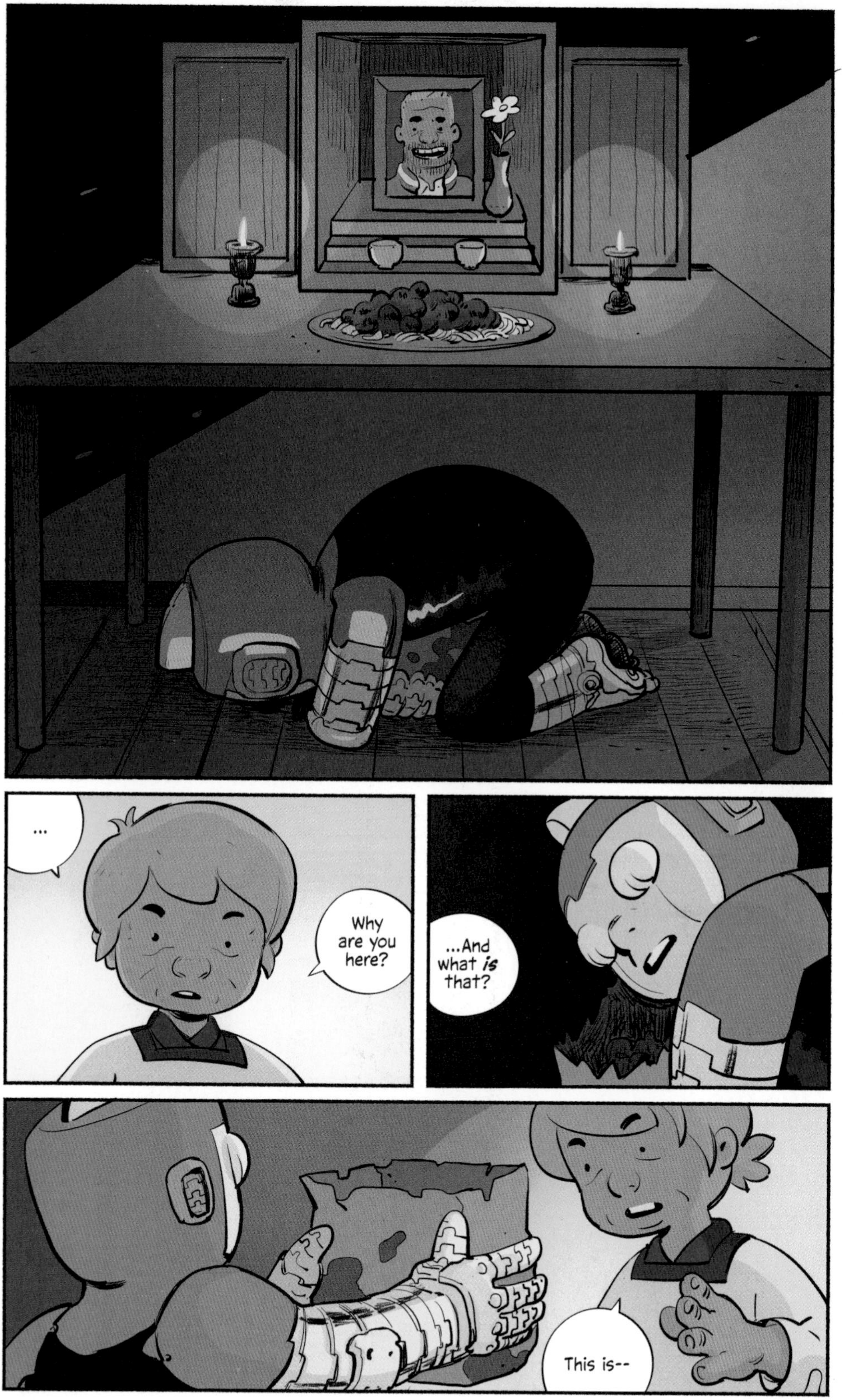
...
Why are you here?
...And what *is* that?
This is--

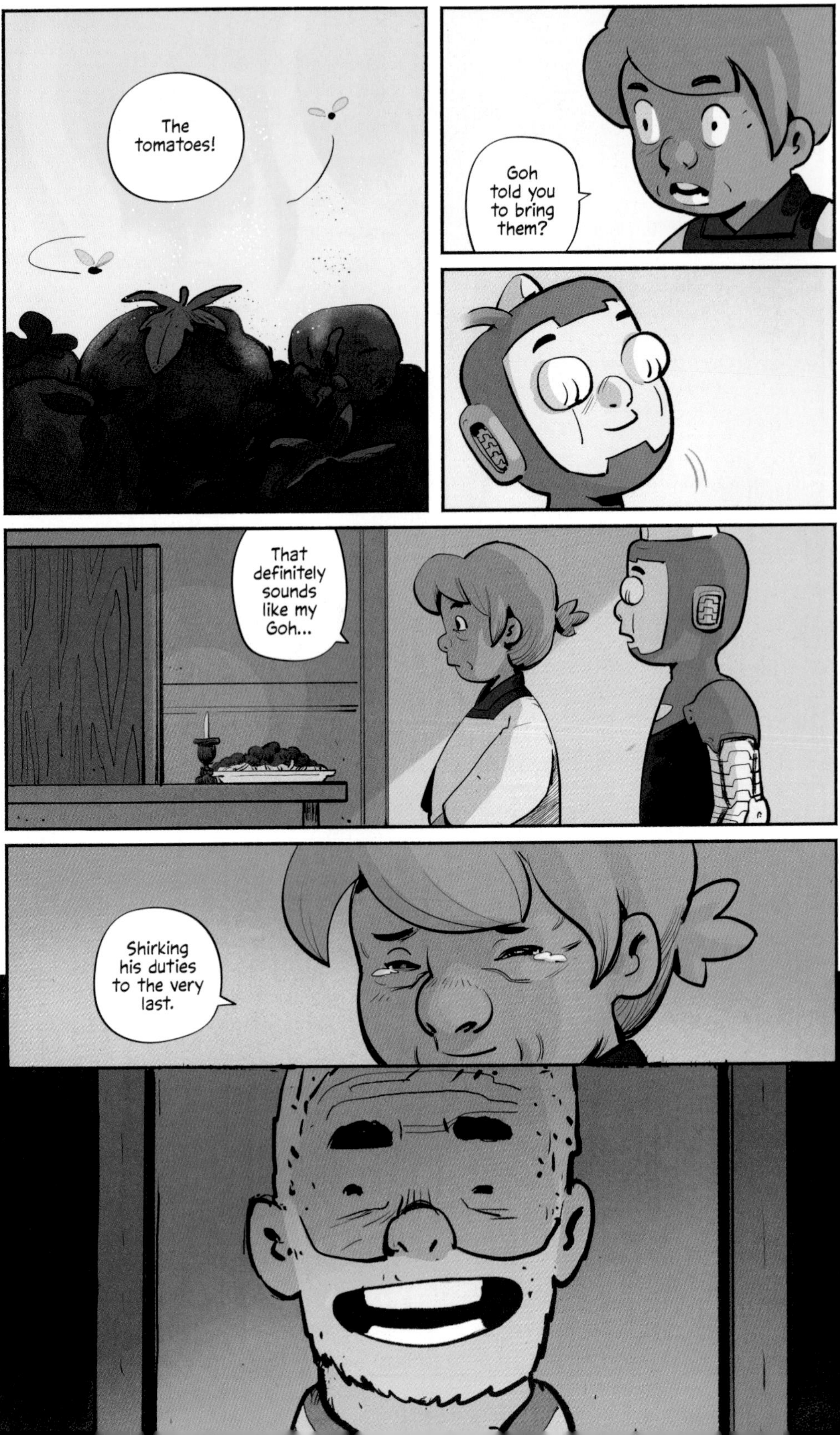
The tomatoes!
Goh told you to bring them?
That definitely sounds like my Goh...
Shirking his duties to the very last.

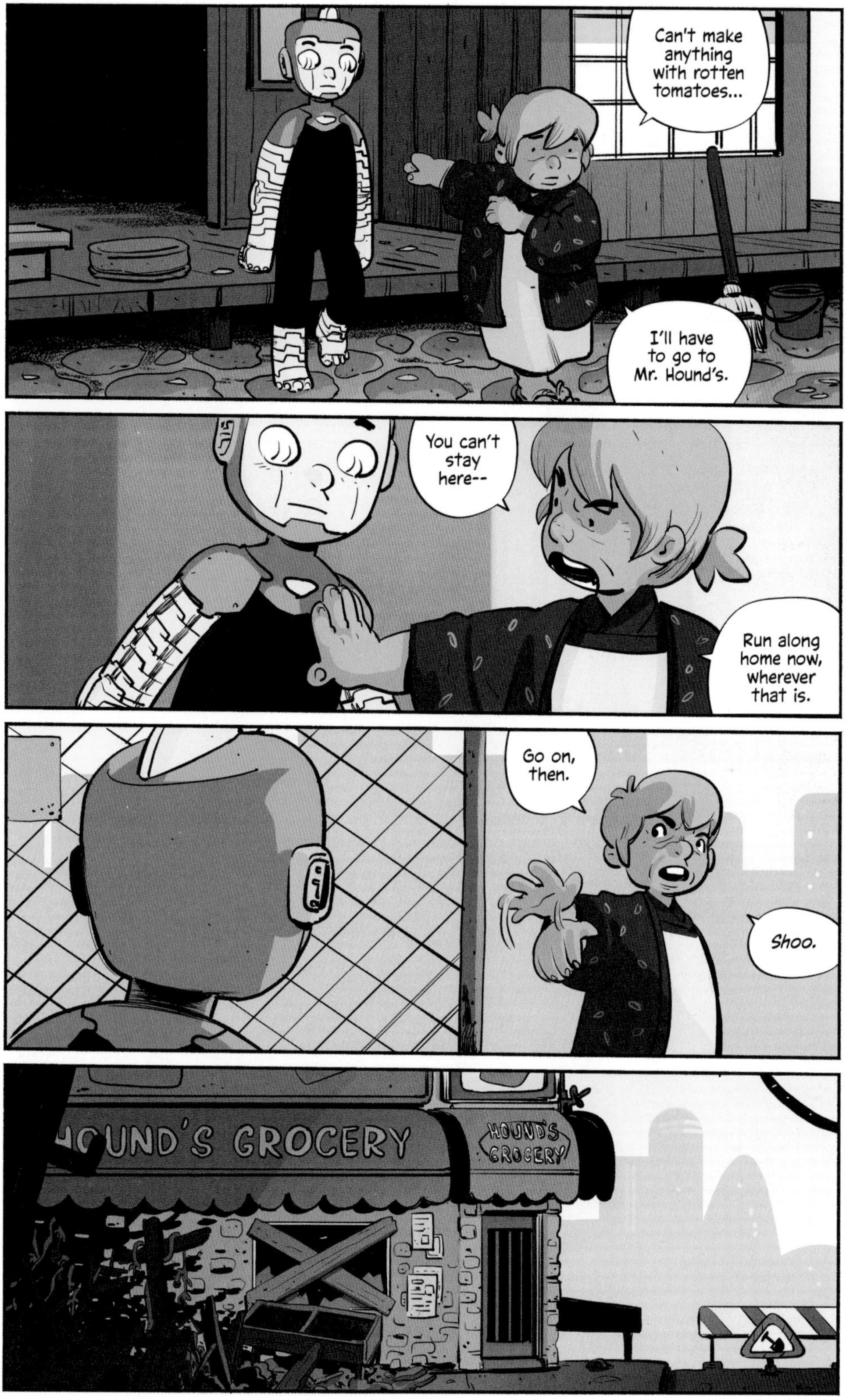

Can't make anything with rotten tomatoes...
I'll have to go to Mr. Hound's.
You can't stay here--
Run along home now, wherever that is.
Go on, then.
Shoo.
HOUND'S GROCERY
HOUND'S GROCERY

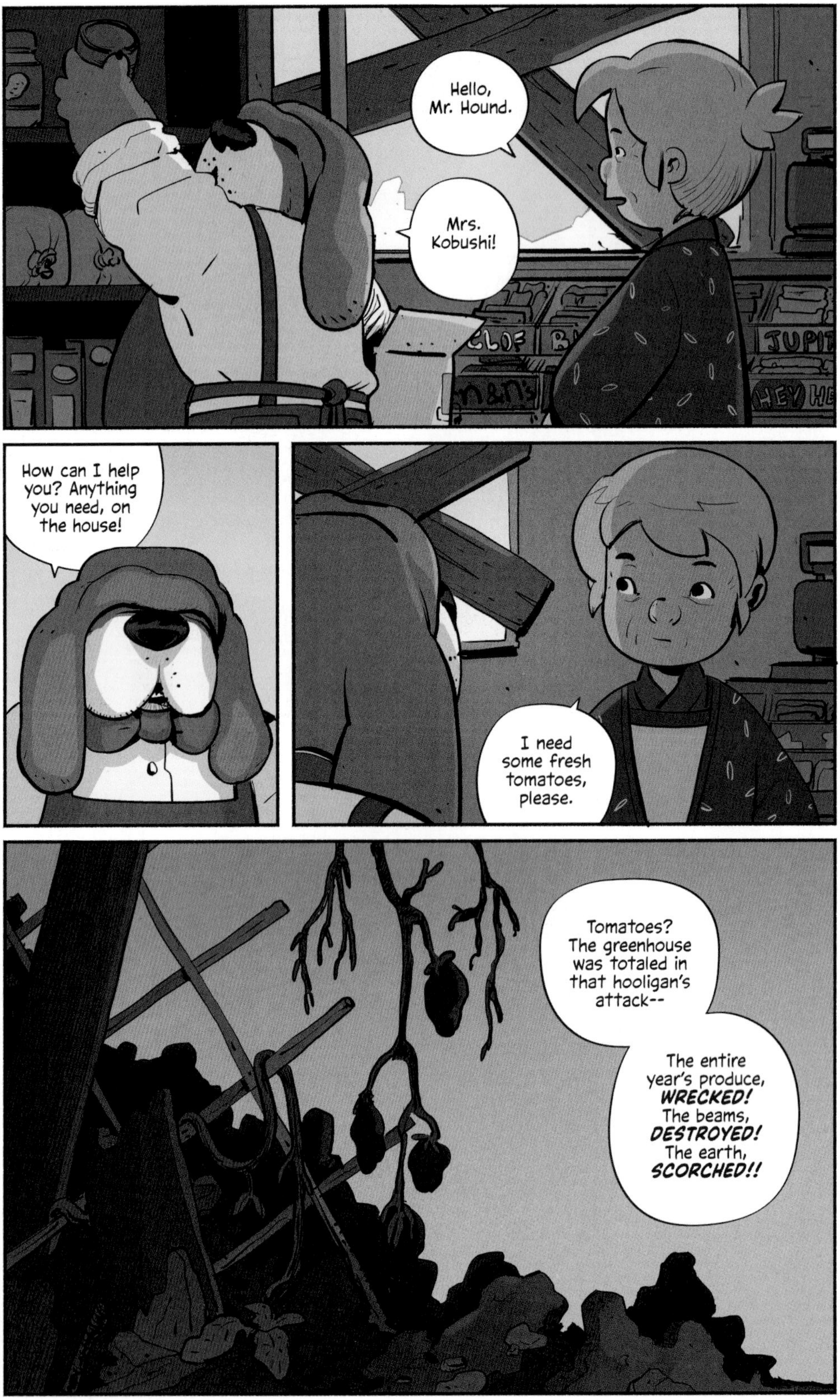
Hello, Mr. Hound.
Mrs. Kobushi!
How can I help you? Anything you need, on the house!
I need some fresh tomatoes, please.
Tomatoes? The greenhouse was totaled in that hooligan's attack--
The entire year's produce, ***WRECKED!*** The beams, ***DESTROYED!*** The earth, ***SCORCHED!!***

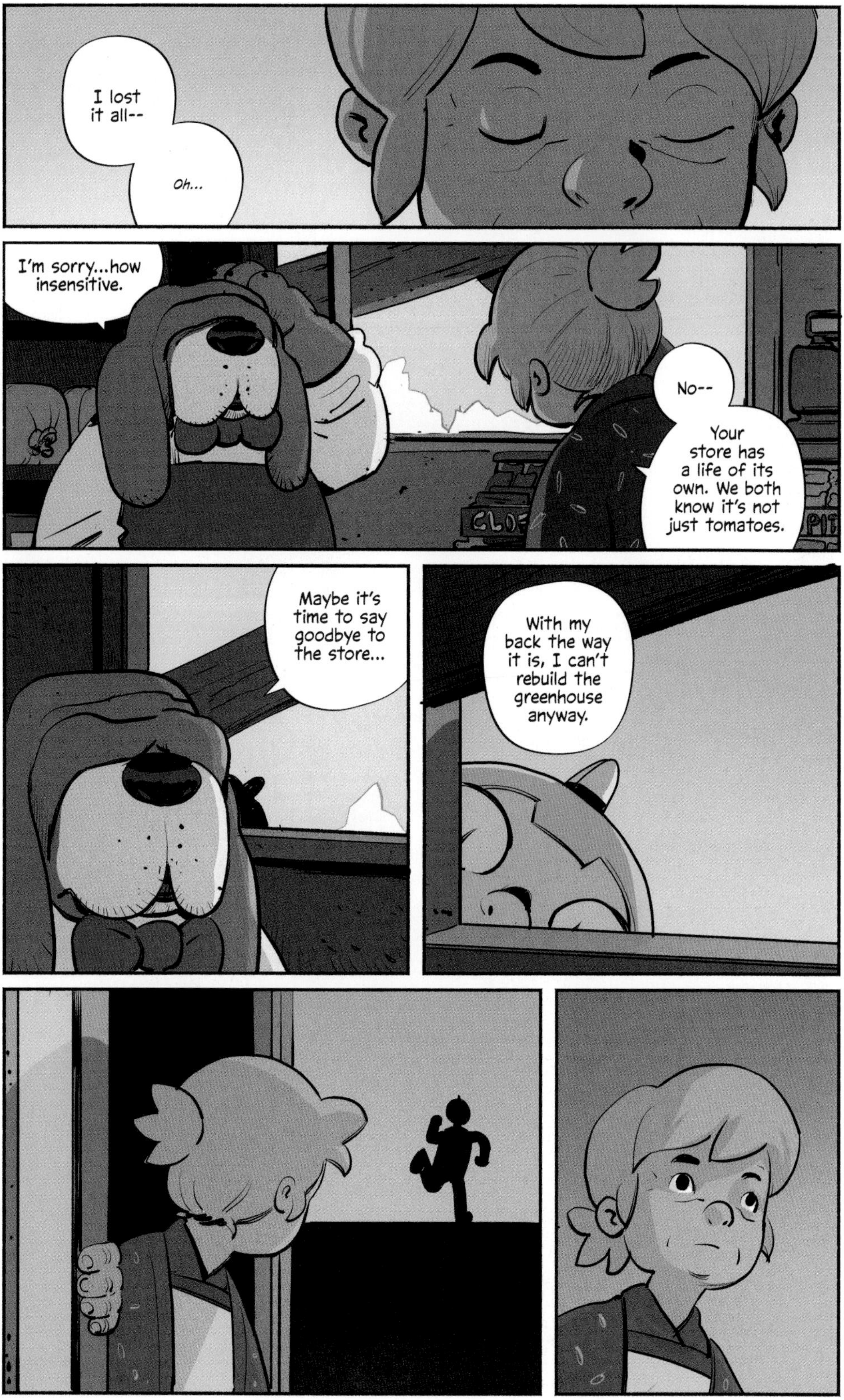
I lost it all--
Oh...
I'm sorry...how insensitive.
No--
Your store has a life of its own. We both know it's not just tomatoes.
Maybe it's time to say goodbye to the store...
With my back the way it is, I can't rebuild the greenhouse anyway.

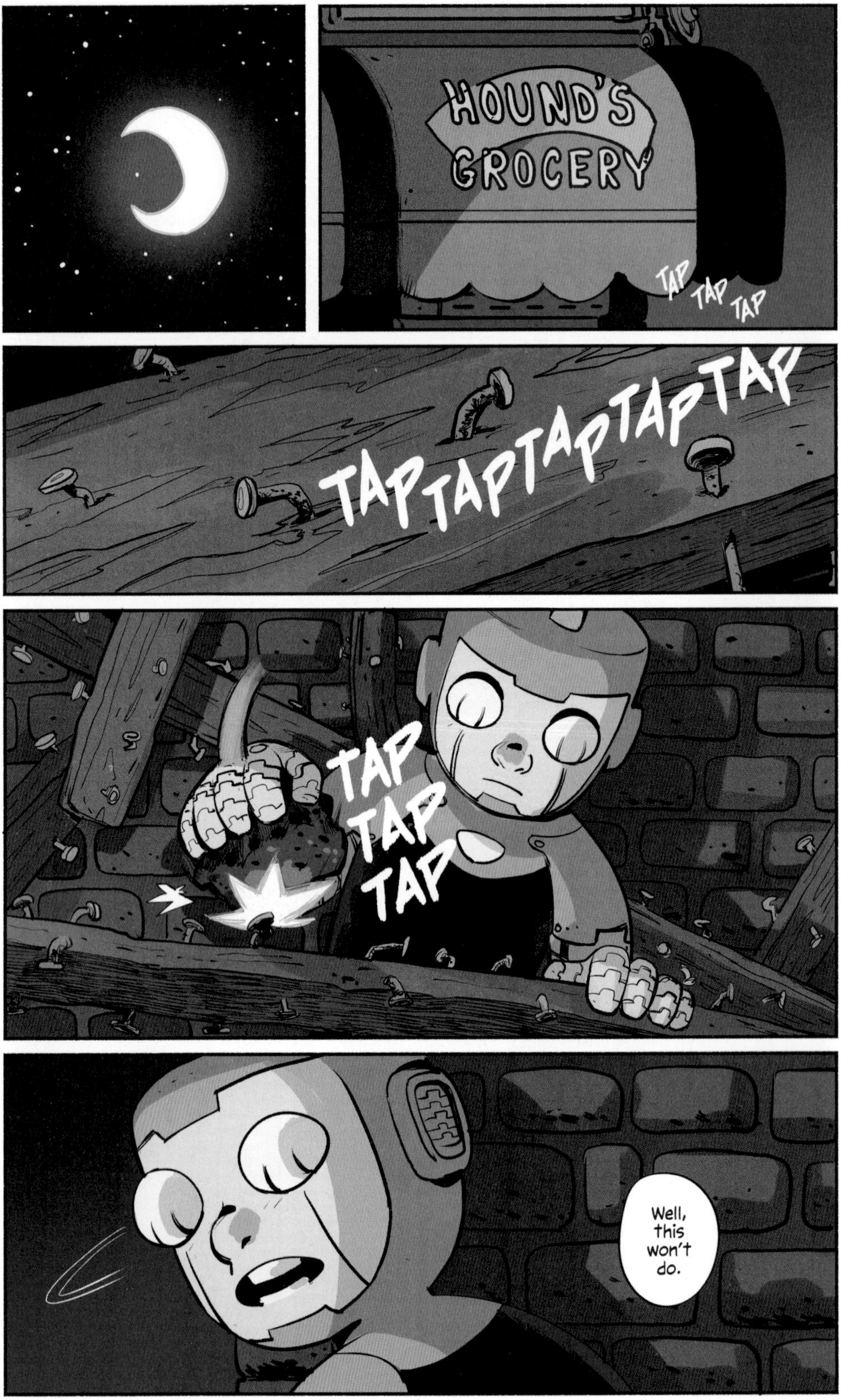
HOUND'S GROCERY
TAP TAP TAP
TAP TAP TAP TAP TAP
TAP TAP TAP
Well, this won't do.

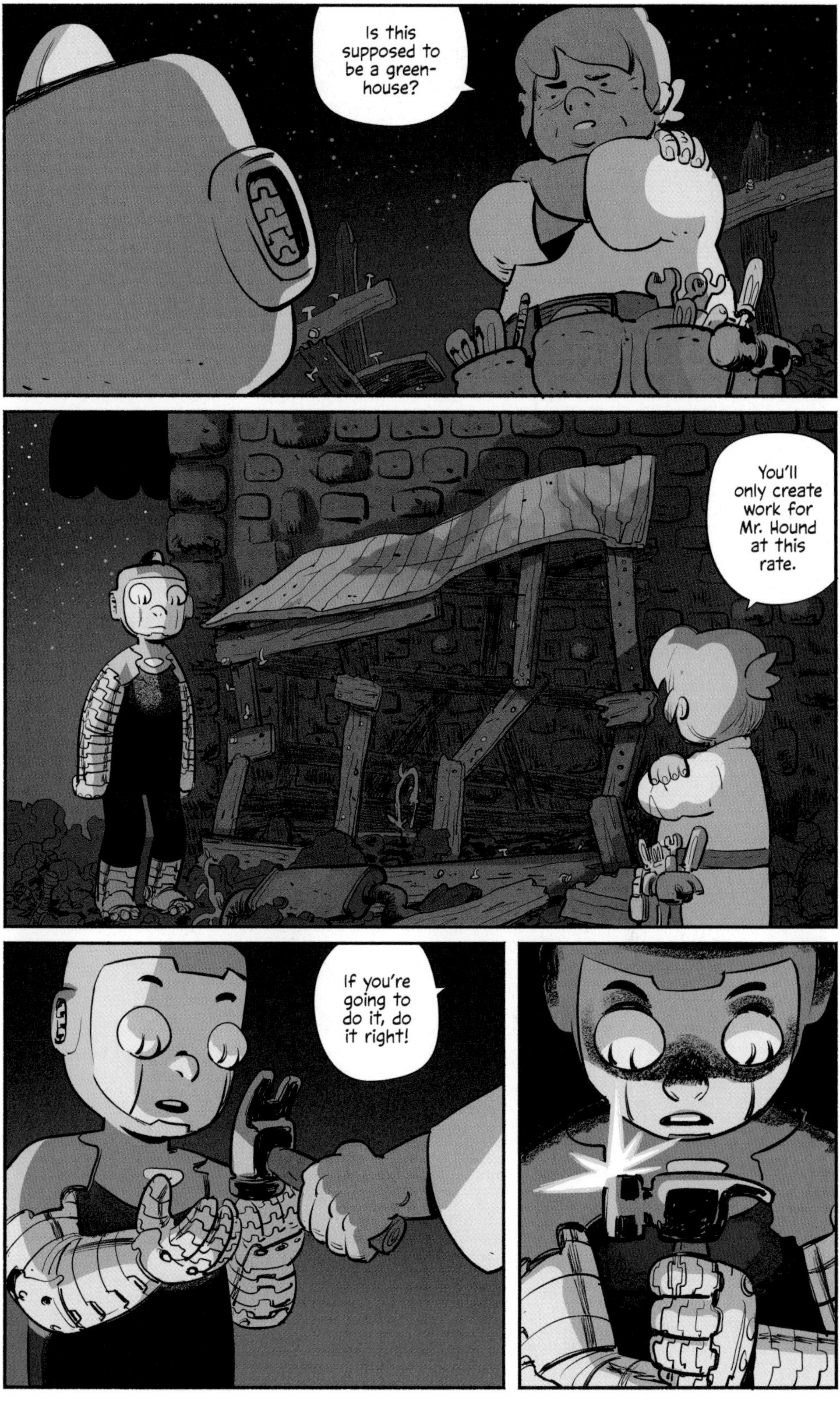
Is this supposed to be a green-house?
You'll only create work for Mr. Hound at this rate.
If you're going to do it, do it right!

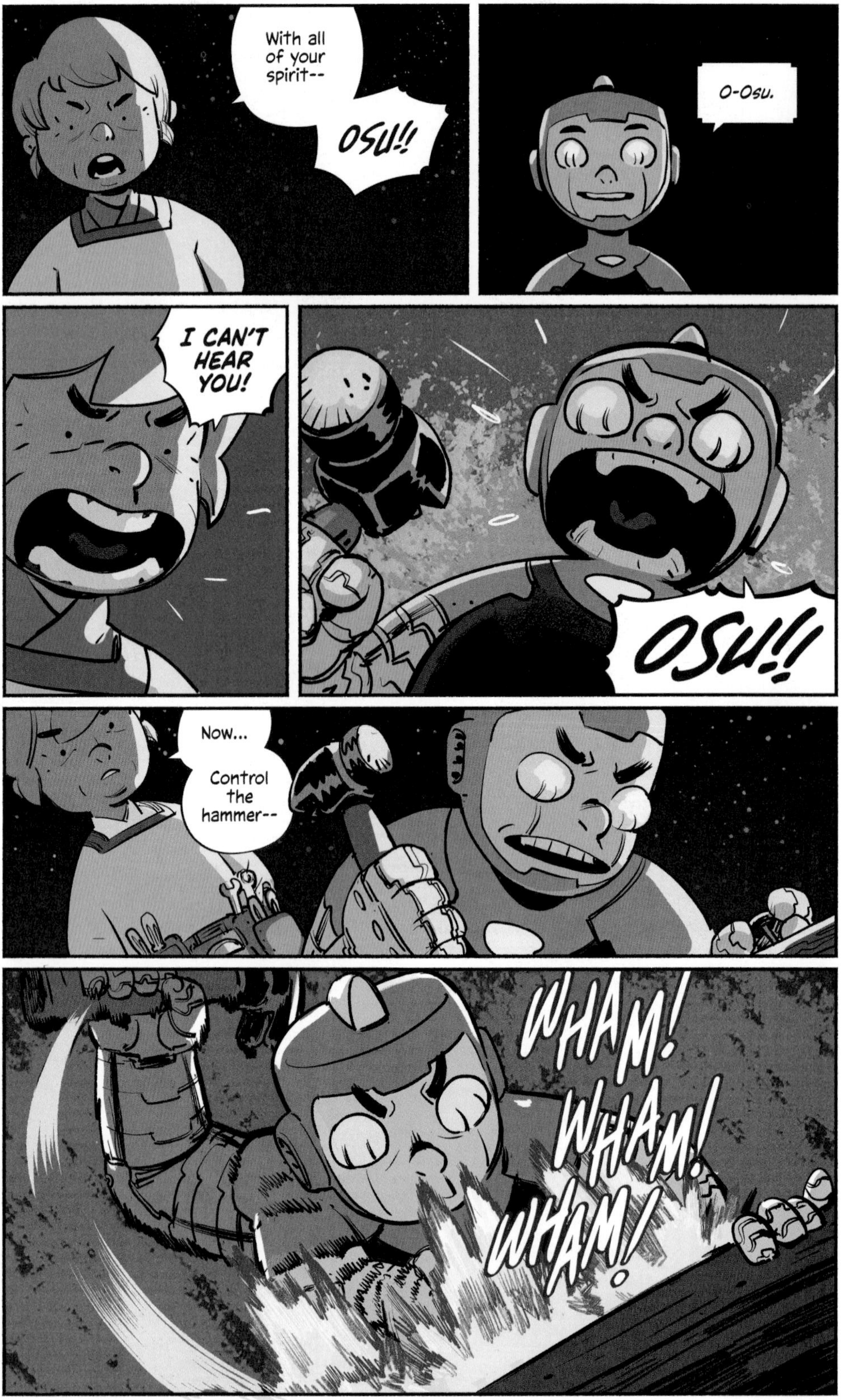
With all of your spirit--
OSU!!
O-Osu.
I CAN'T HEAR YOU!
OSU!!
Now...
Control the hammer--
WHAM!
WHAM!
WHAM!

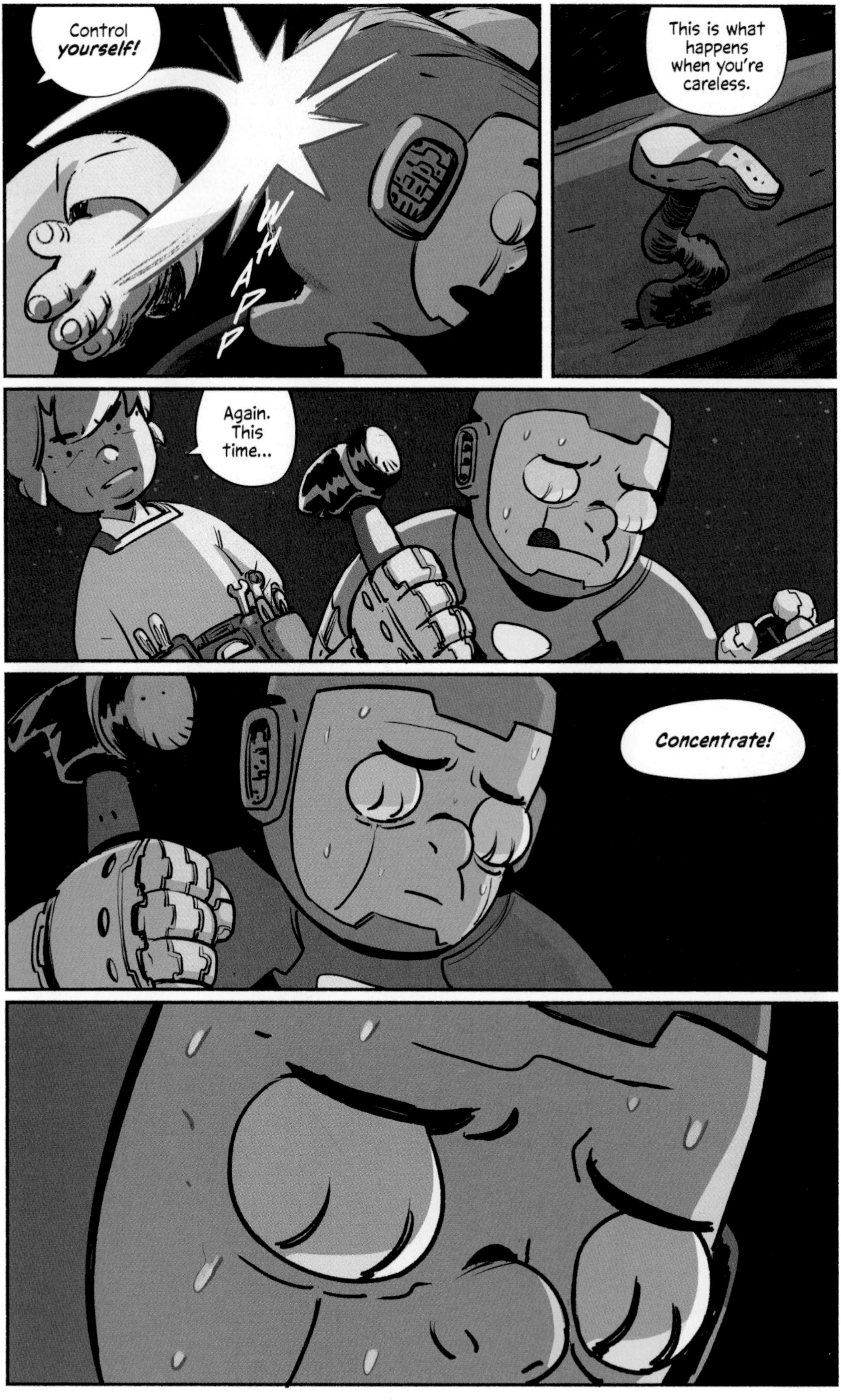
Control *yourself!*
WHAPP
This is what happens when you're careless.
Again. This time...
Concentrate!

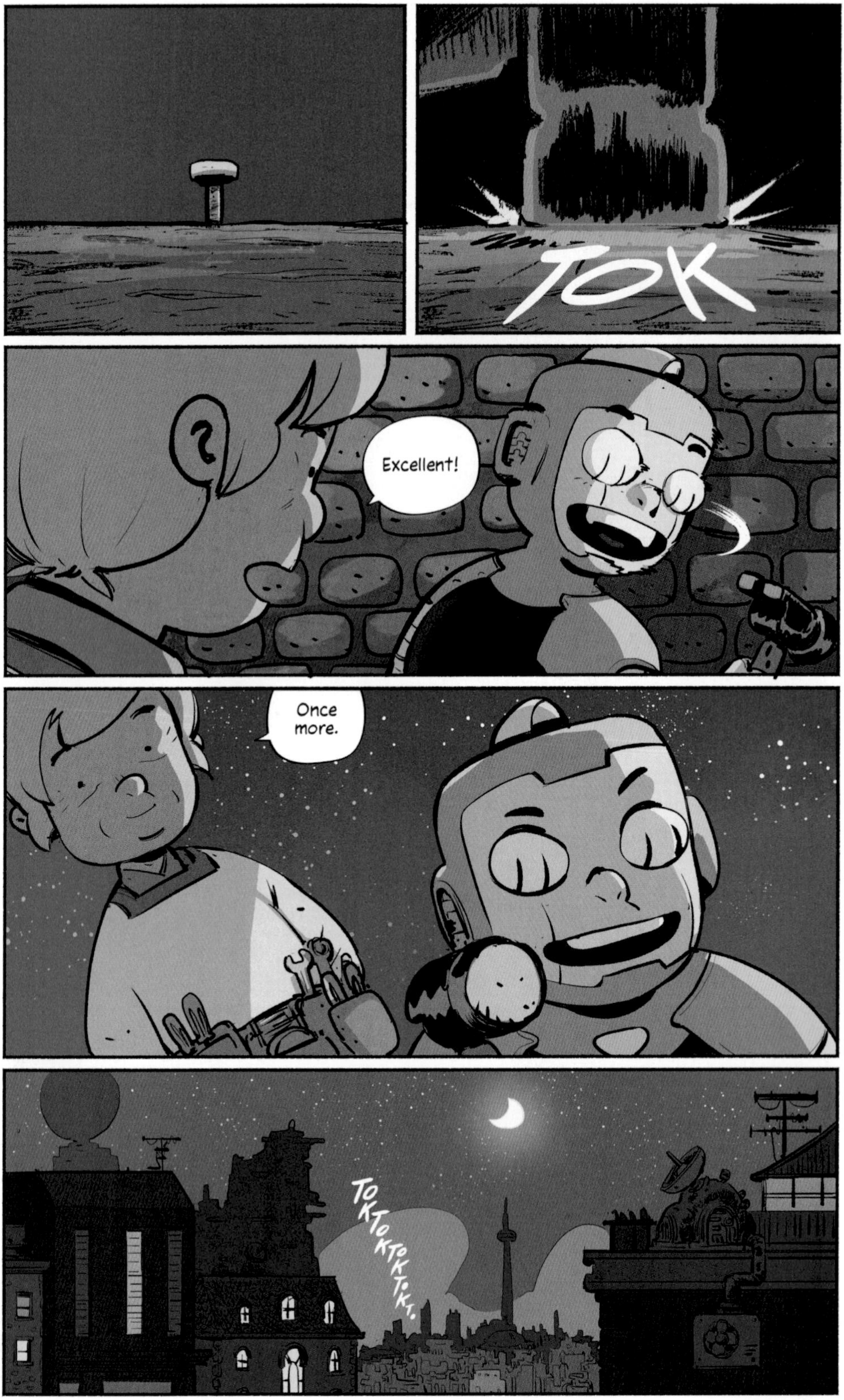
TOK
Excellent!
Once more.
TOKTOKTOKTOKTOK

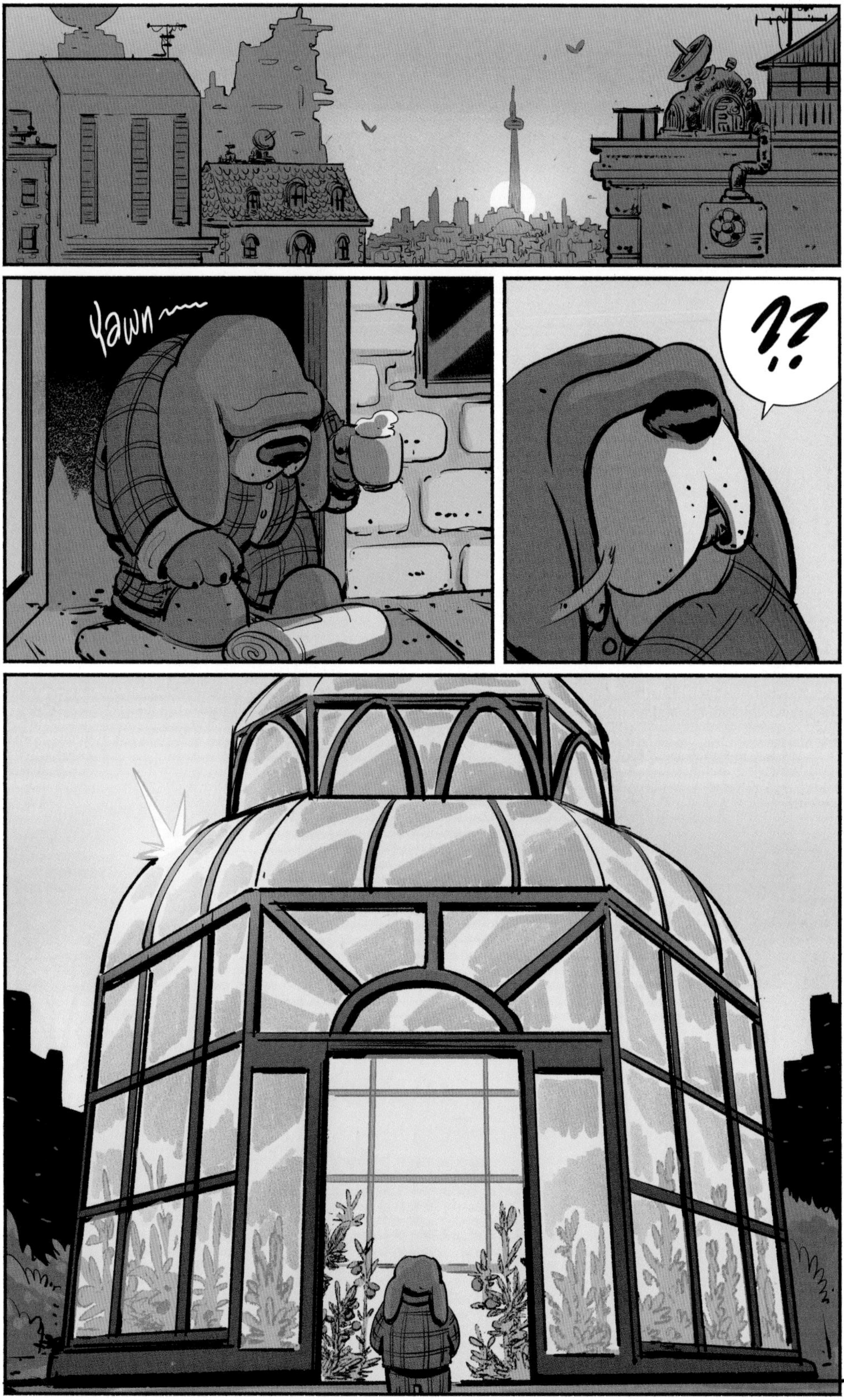
YAWN~~
??

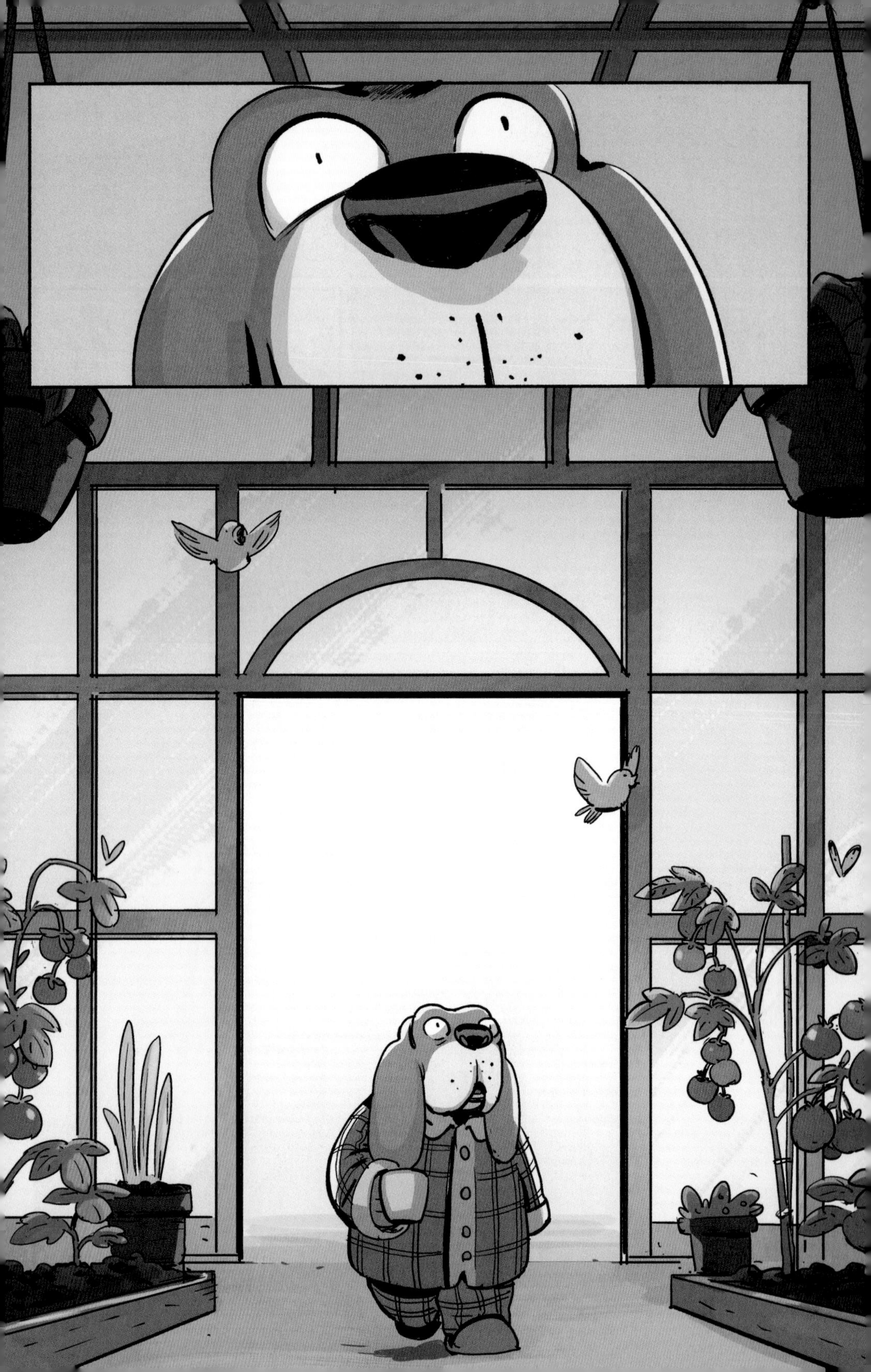

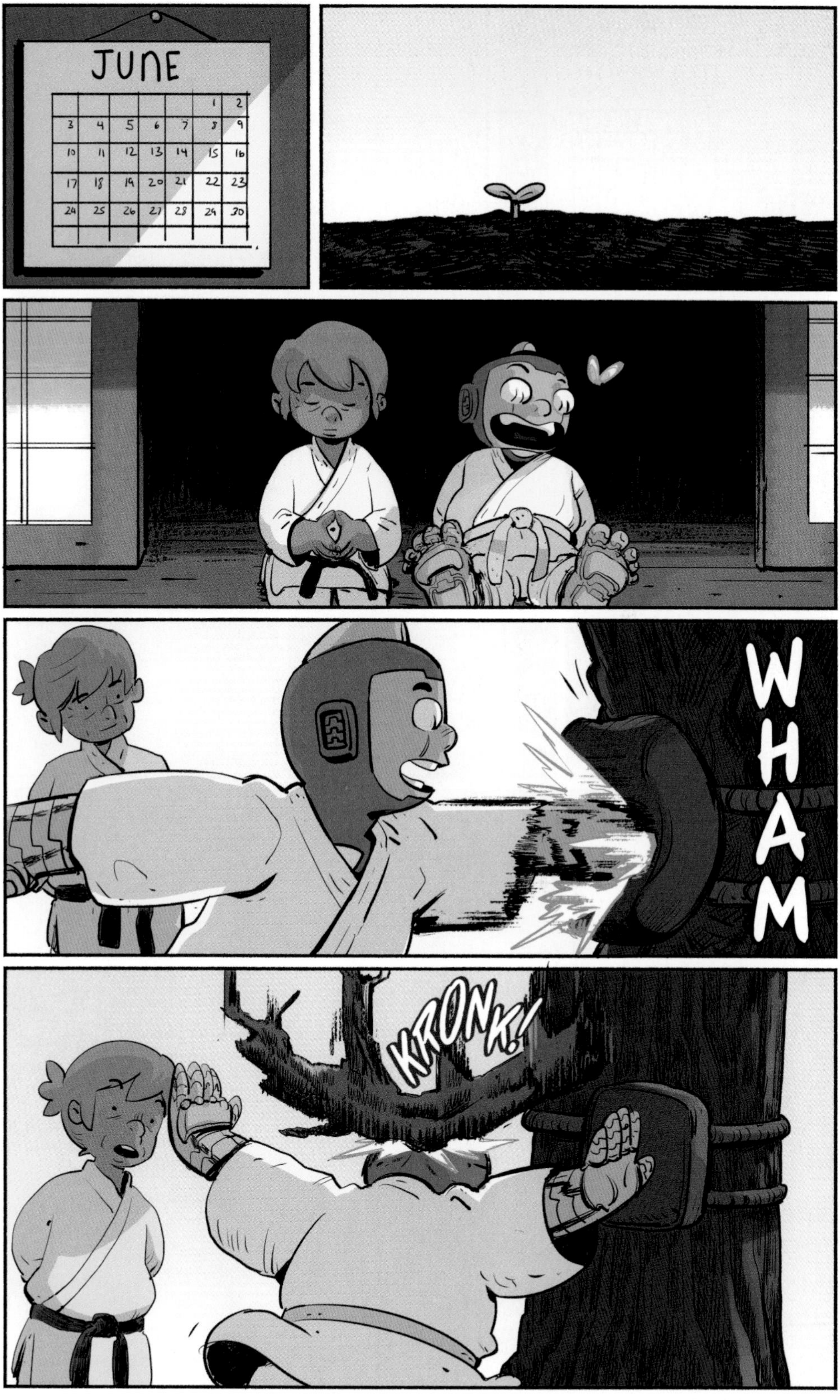
JUNE
WHAM
KRONK!

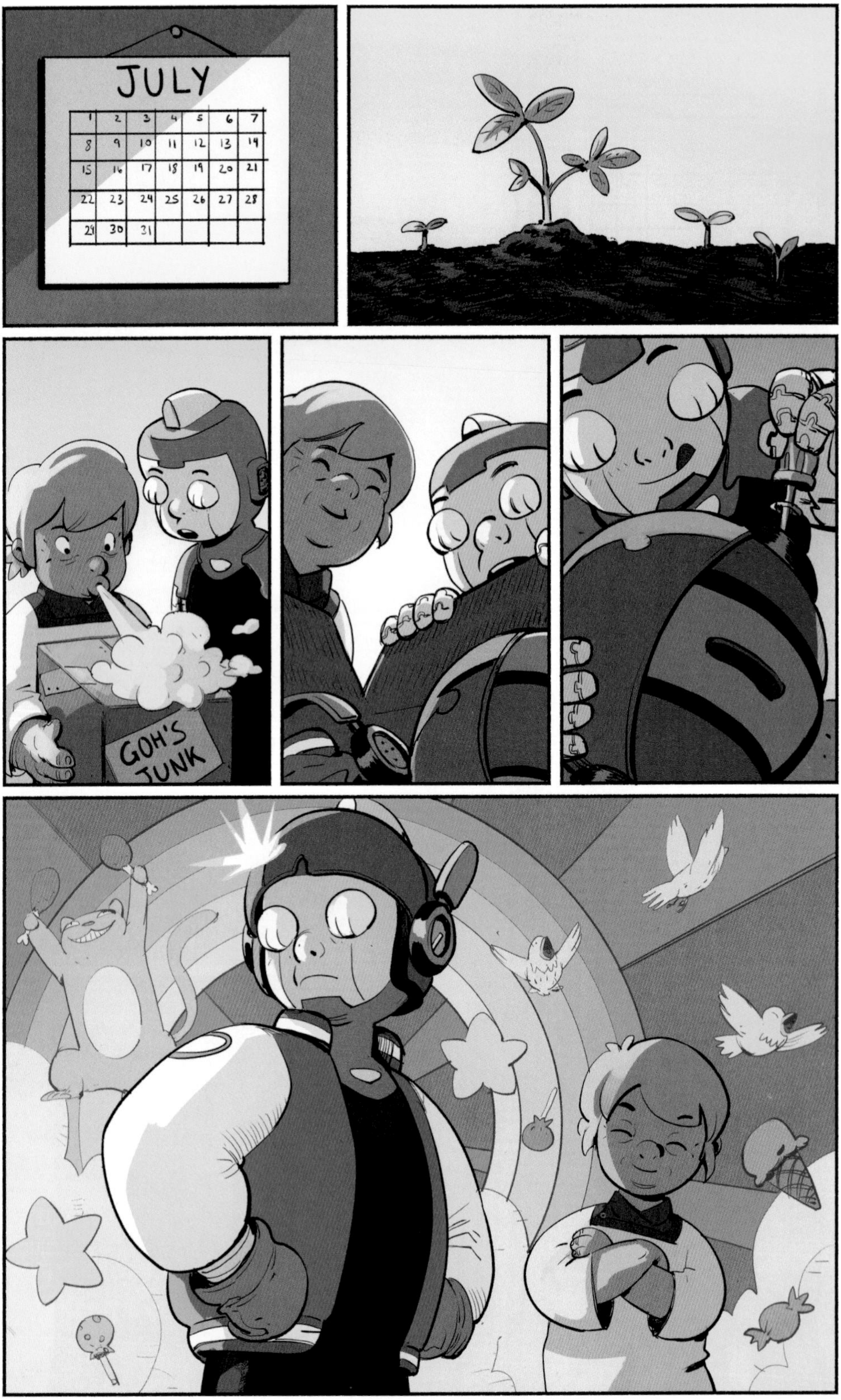
JULY
1 2 3 4 5 6 7
8 9 10 11 12 13 14
15 16 17 18 19 20 21
22 23 24 25 26 27 28
29 30 31
GOH'S JUNK

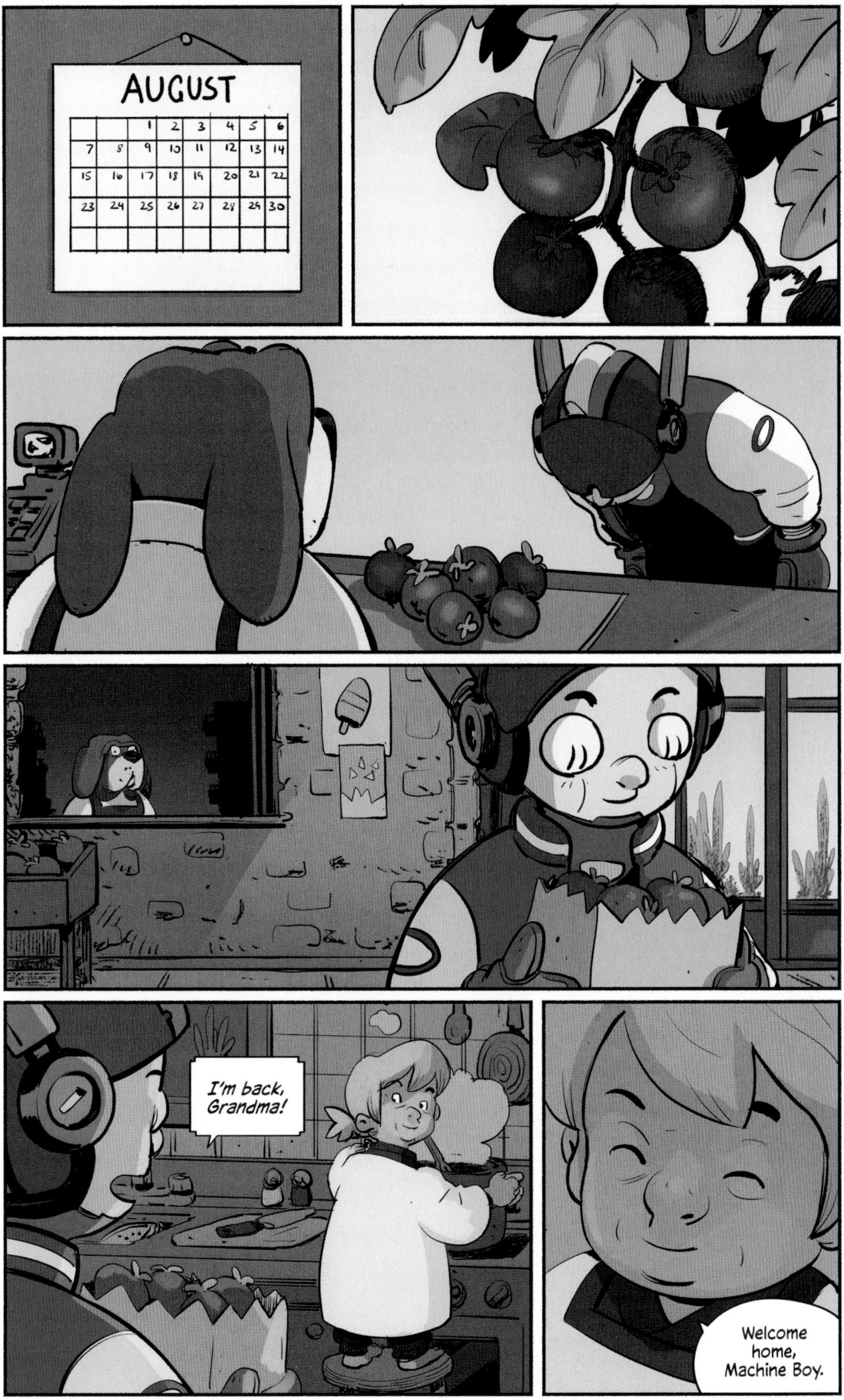
AUGUST
1 2 3 4 5 6
7 8 9 10 11 12 13 14
15 16 17 18 19 20 21 22
23 24 25 26 27 28 29 30
I'm back, Grandma!
Welcome home, Machine Boy.

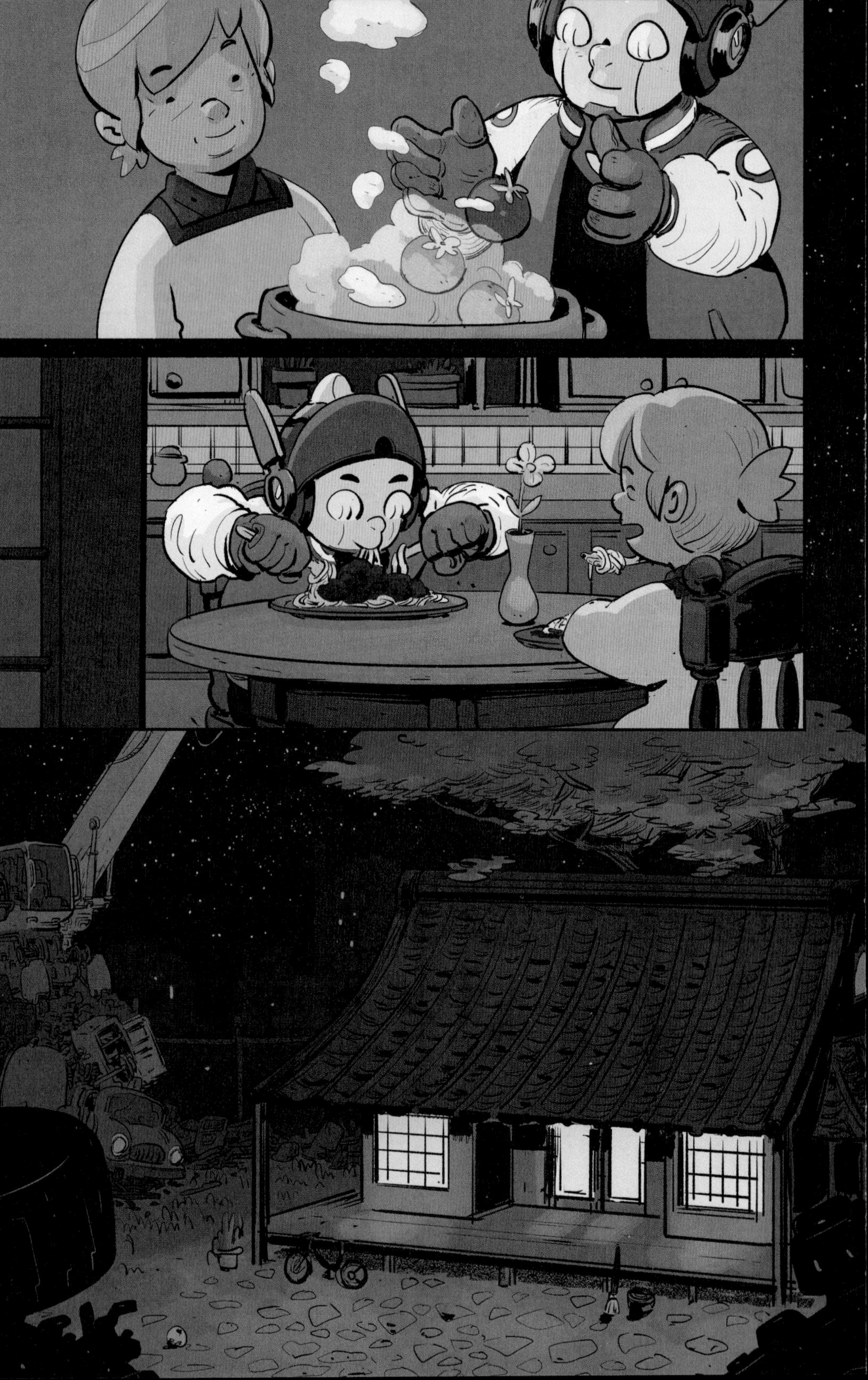

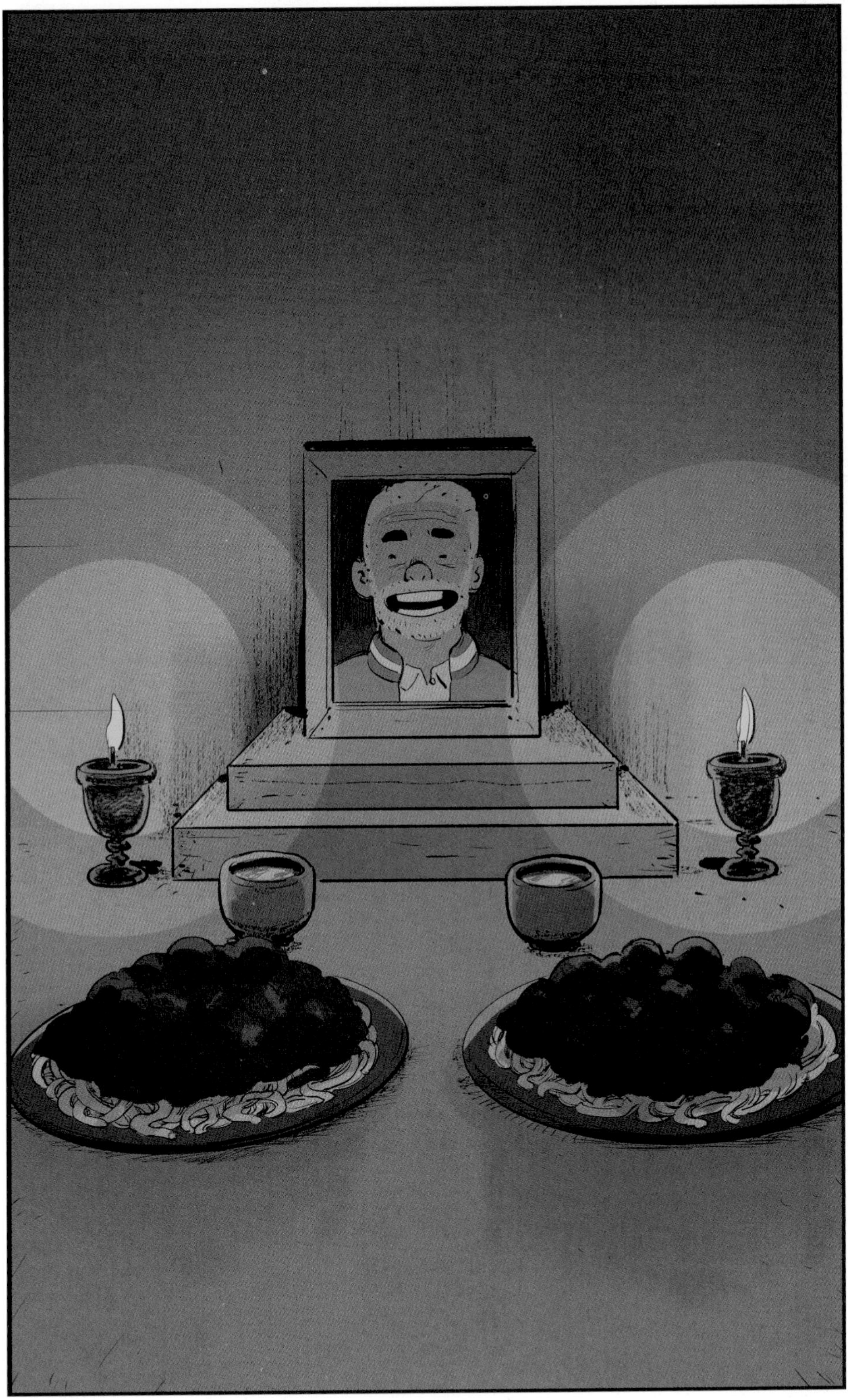

CHAPTER 3

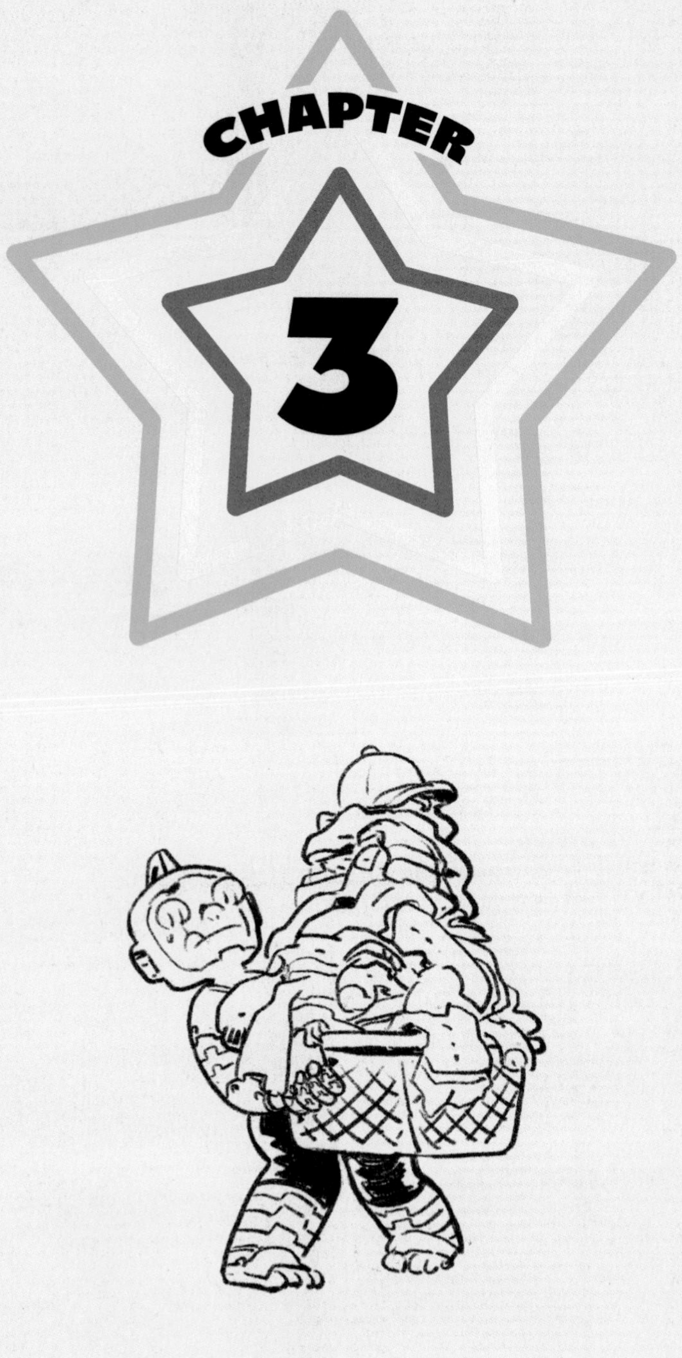

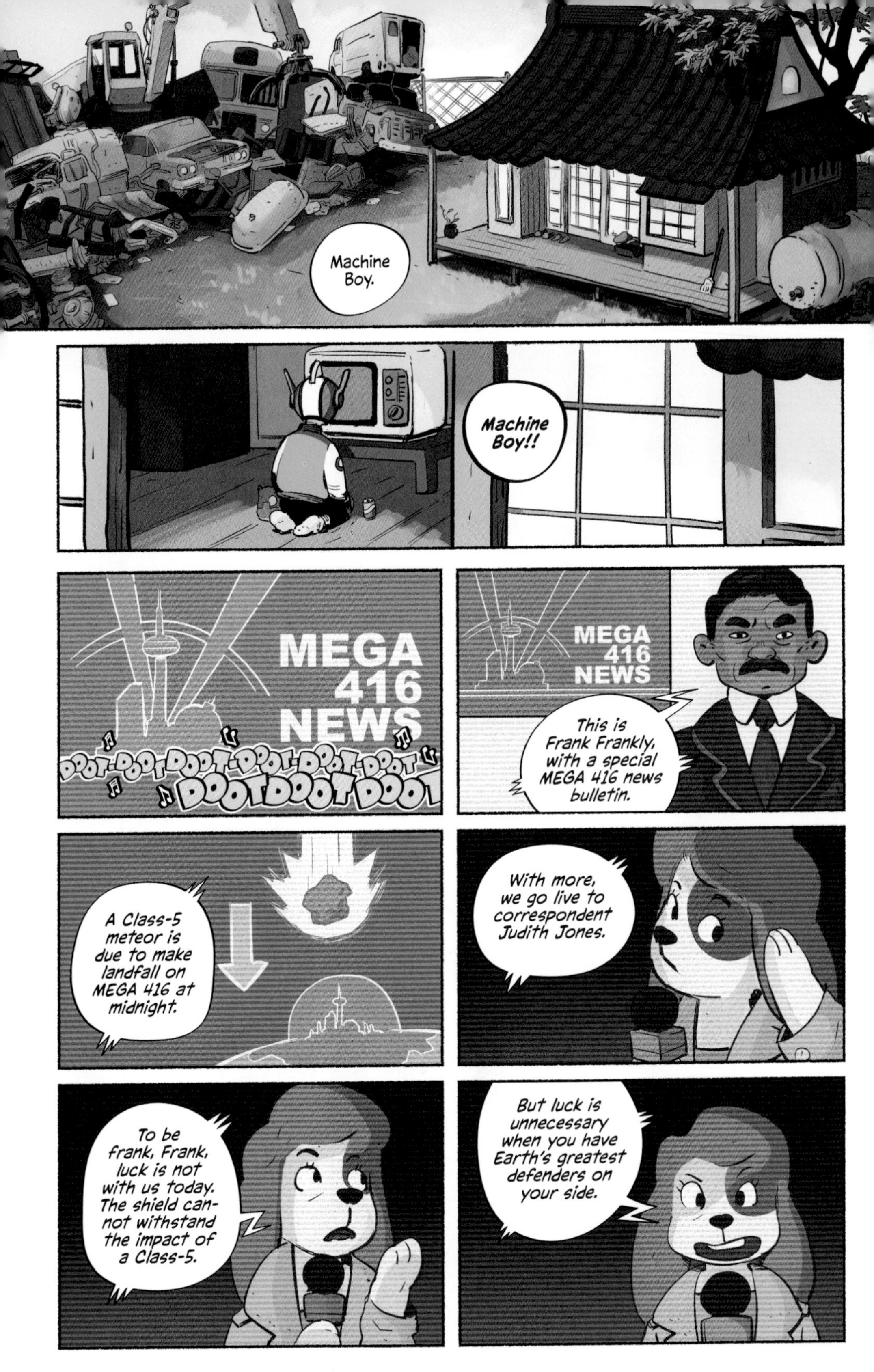
Machine Boy.
Machine Boy!!
MEGA 416 NEWS
DOOT-DOOT-DOOT-DOOT-DOOT-DOOT
DOOTDOOTDOOT
MEGA 416 NEWS
This is Frank Frankly, with a special MEGA 416 news bulletin.
A Class-5 meteor is due to make landfall on MEGA 416 at midnight.
With more, we go live to correspondent Judith Jones.
To be frank, Frank, luck is not with us today. The shield can-not withstand the impact of a Class-5.
But luck is unnecessary when you have Earth's greatest defenders on your side.

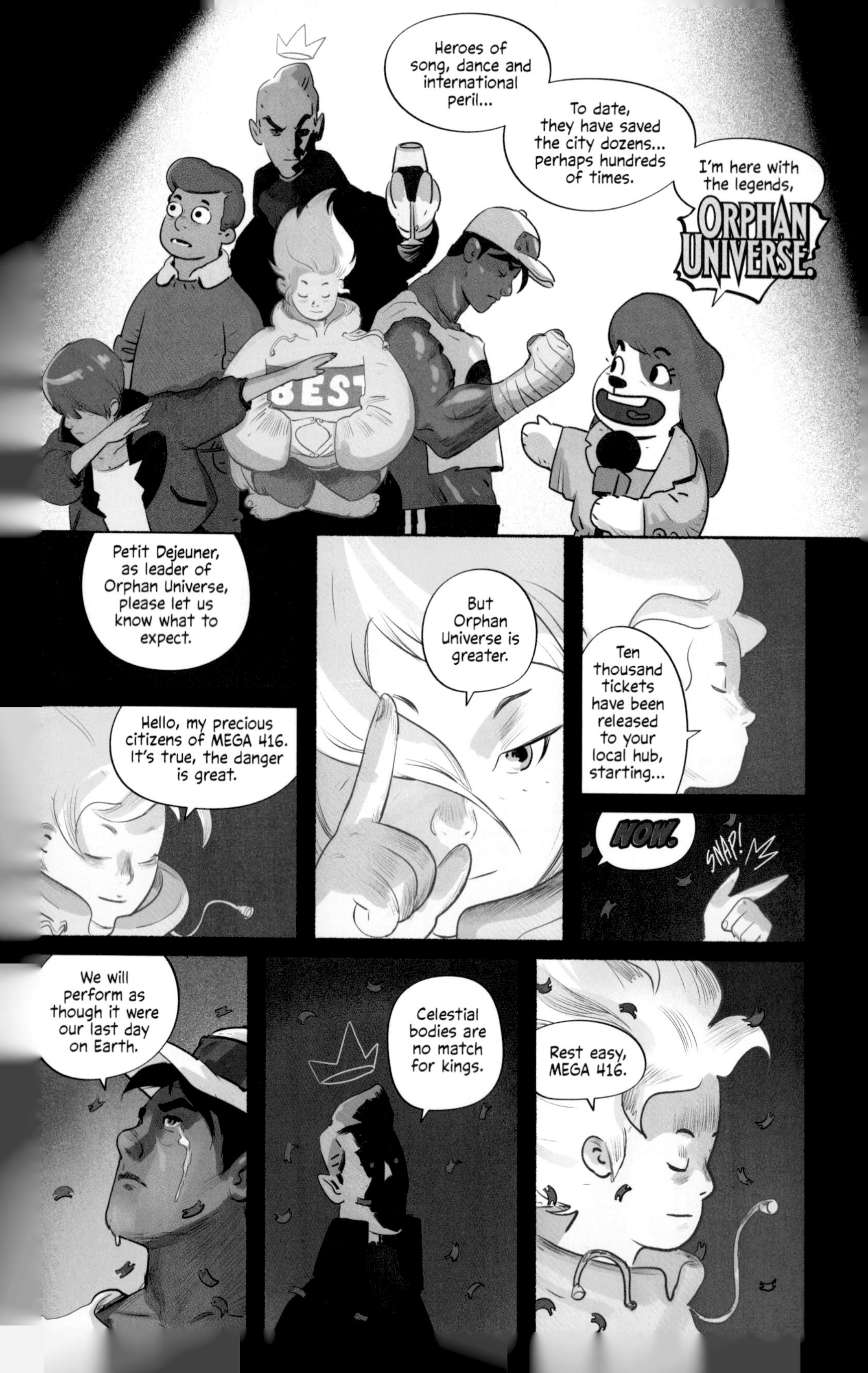
Heroes of song, dance and international peril...
To date, they have saved the city dozens... perhaps hundreds of times.
I'm here with the legends,
ORPHAN UNIVERSE!
BEST
Petit Dejeuner, as leader of Orphan Universe, please let us know what to expect.
Hello, my precious citizens of MEGA 416. It's true, the danger is great.
But Orphan Universe is greater.
Ten thousand tickets have been released to your local hub, starting...
NOW.
SNAP!
We will perform as though it were our last day on Earth.
Celestial bodies are no match for kings.
Rest easy, MEGA 416.

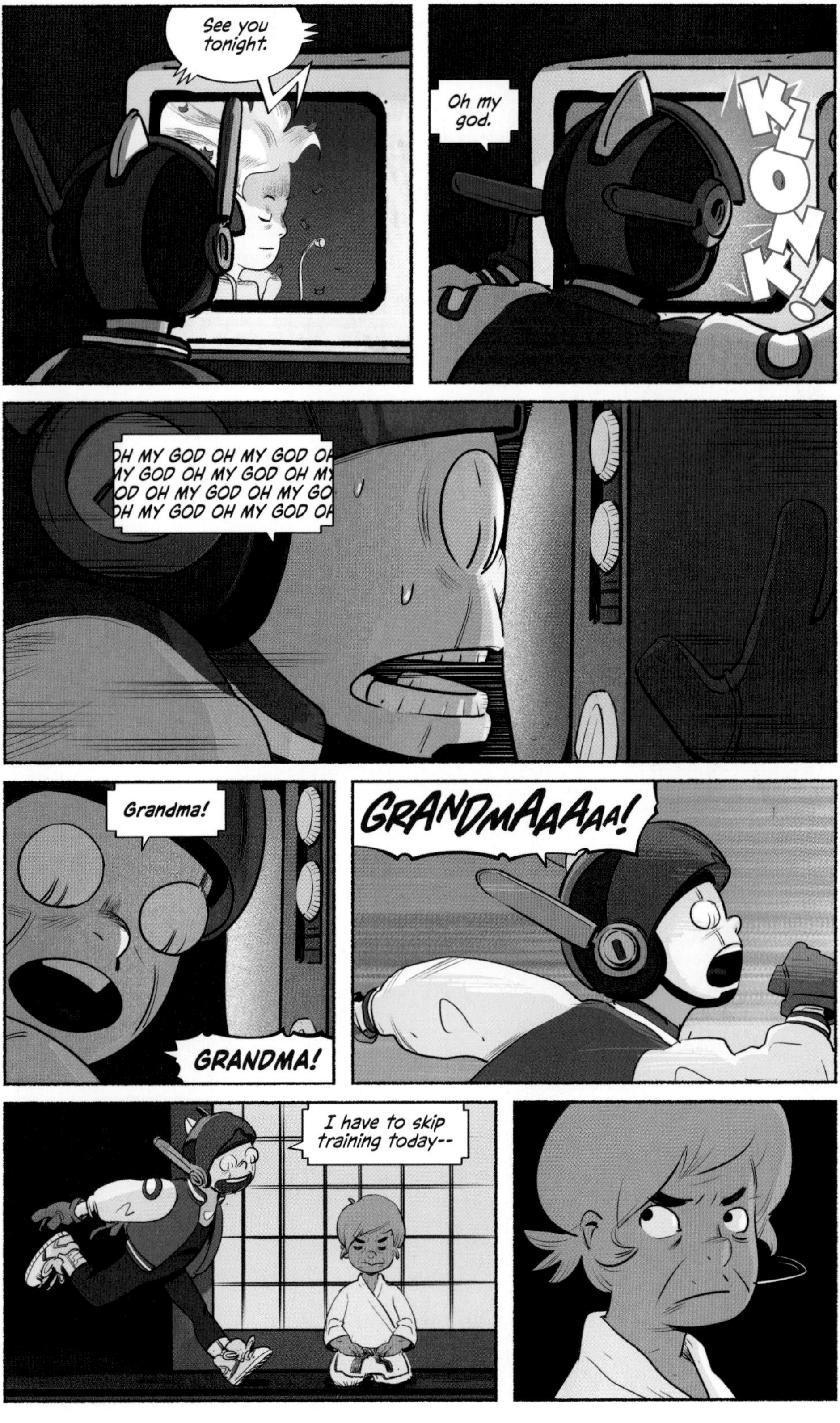
See you tonight.
Oh my god.
KLONK!
OH MY GOD OH MY GOD OH MY GOD OH MY GOD OH MY GOD OH MY GOD OH MY GOD OH MY GOD
Grandma!
GRANDMA!
GRANDMAAAAA!
I have to skip training today--

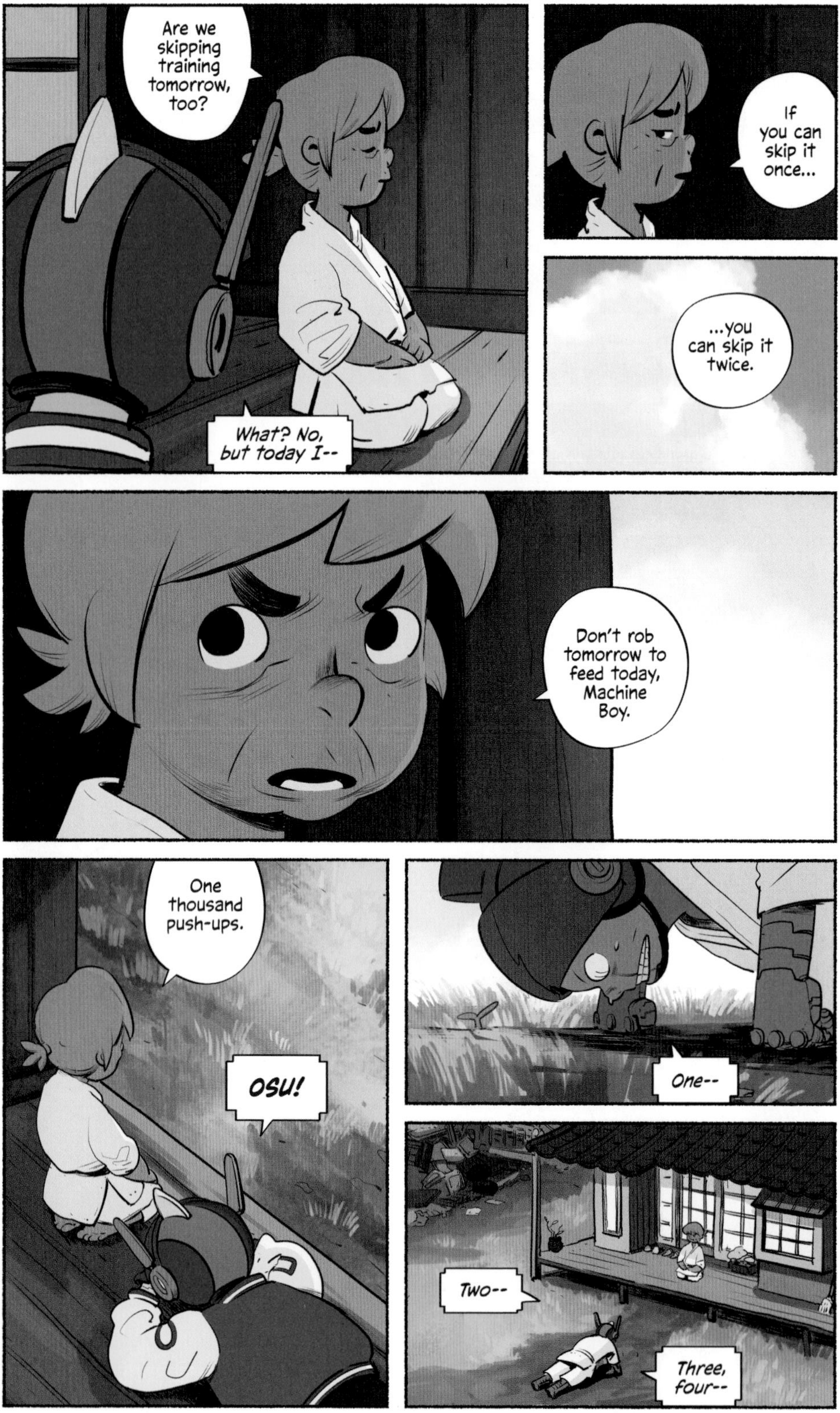
Are we skipping training tomorrow, too?
What? No, but today I--
If you can skip it once...
...you can skip it twice.
Don't rob tomorrow to feed today, Machine Boy.
One thousand push-ups.
OSU!
One--
Two--
Three, four--

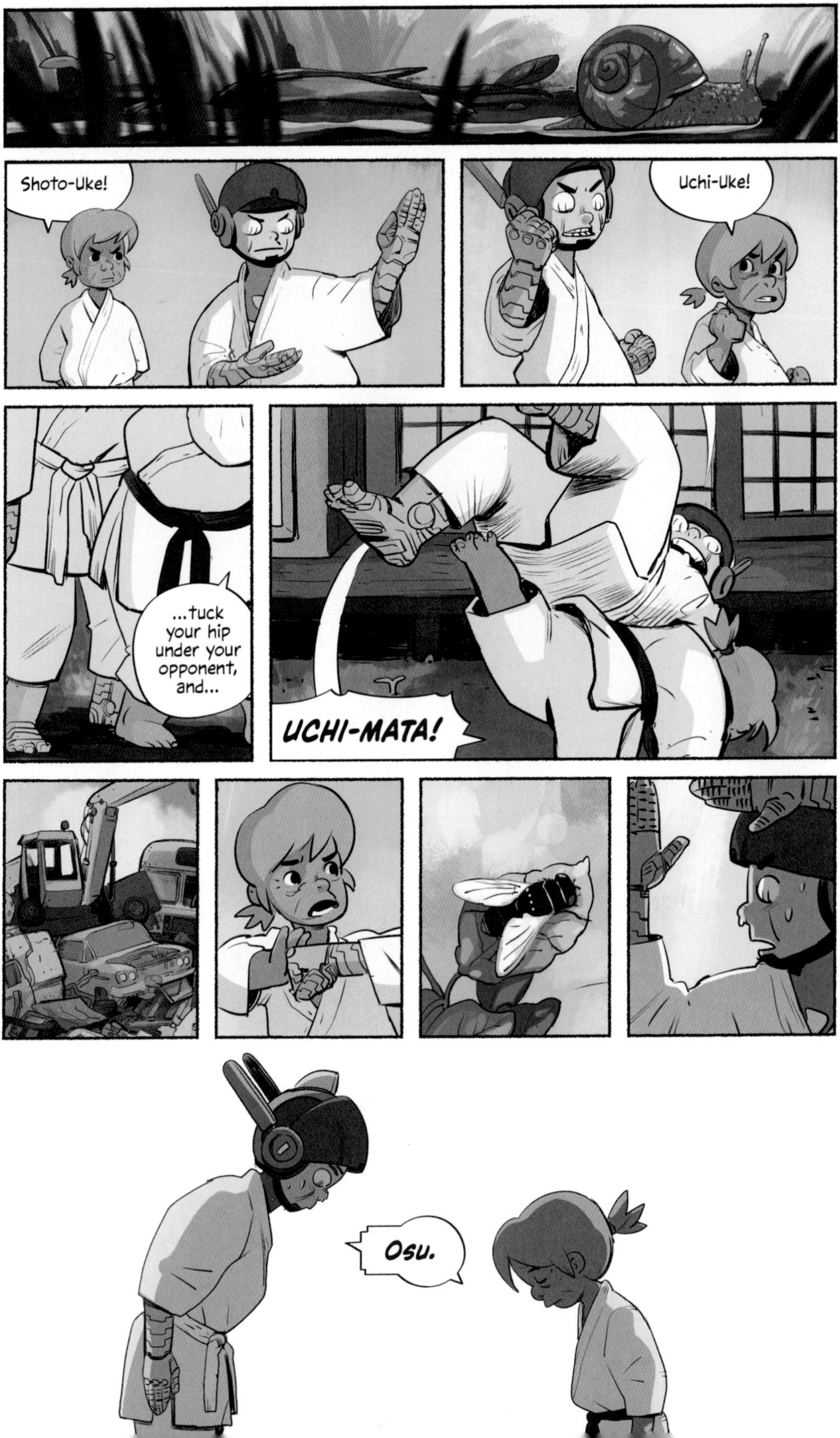
Shoto-Uke!
Uchi-Uke!
...tuck your hip under your opponent, and...
UCHI-MATA!
Osu.

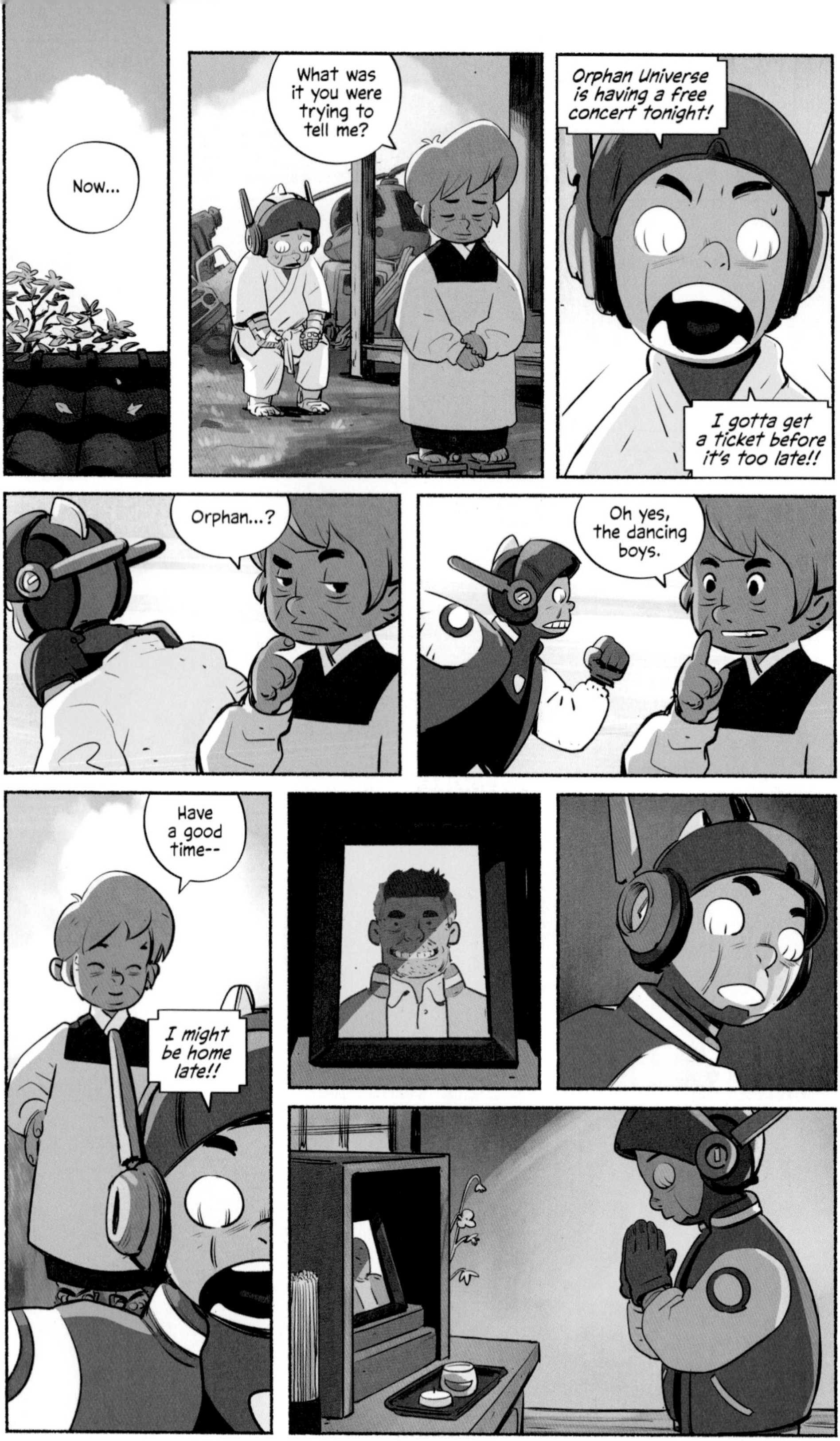
Now...
What was it you were trying to tell me?
Orphan Universe is having a free concert tonight!
I gotta get a ticket before it's too late!!
Orphan...?
Oh yes, the dancing boys.
Have a good time--
I might be home late!!

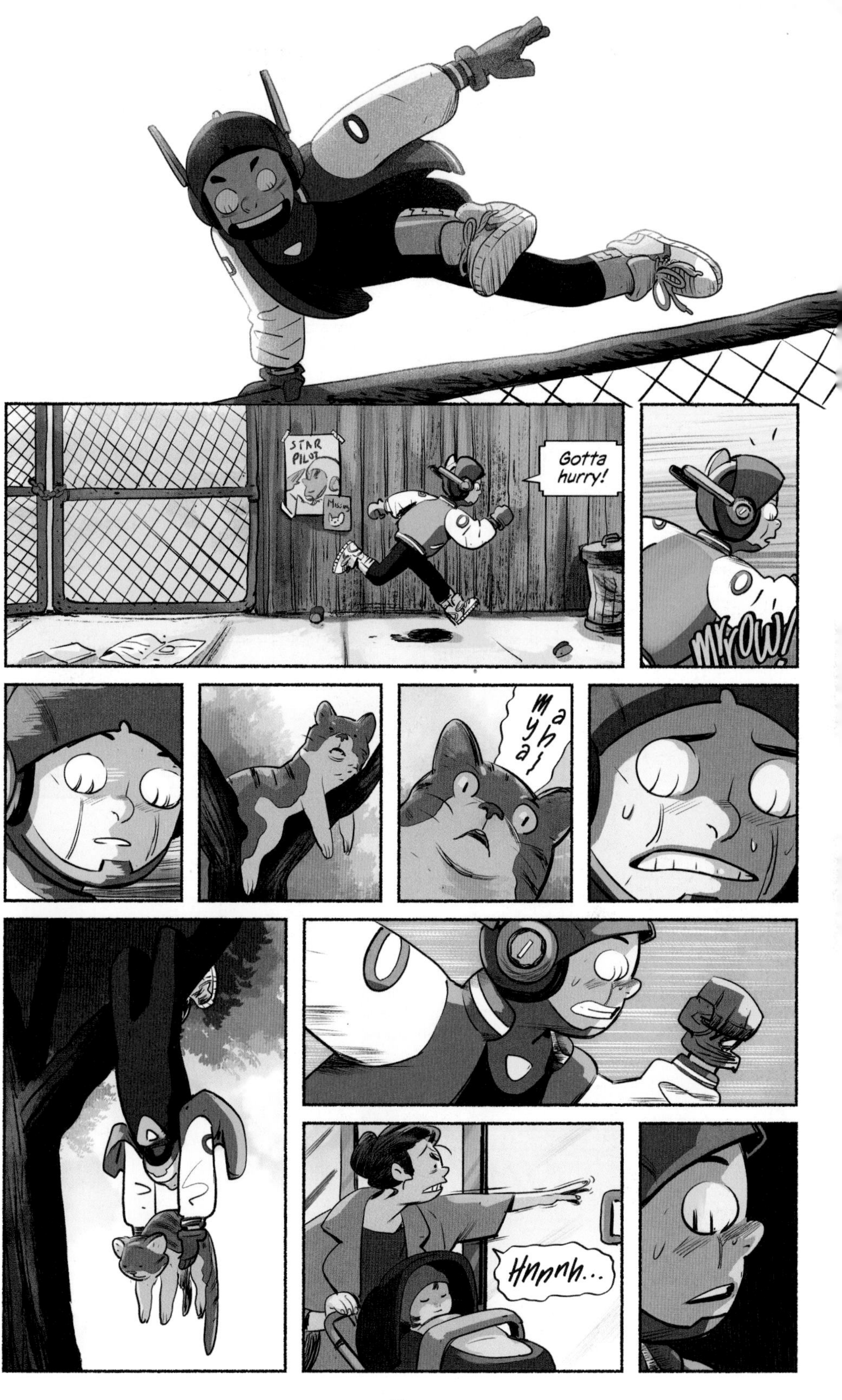
STAR PILOT
Missing
Gotta hurry!
MROW!
Mayhal
Hnnnh...

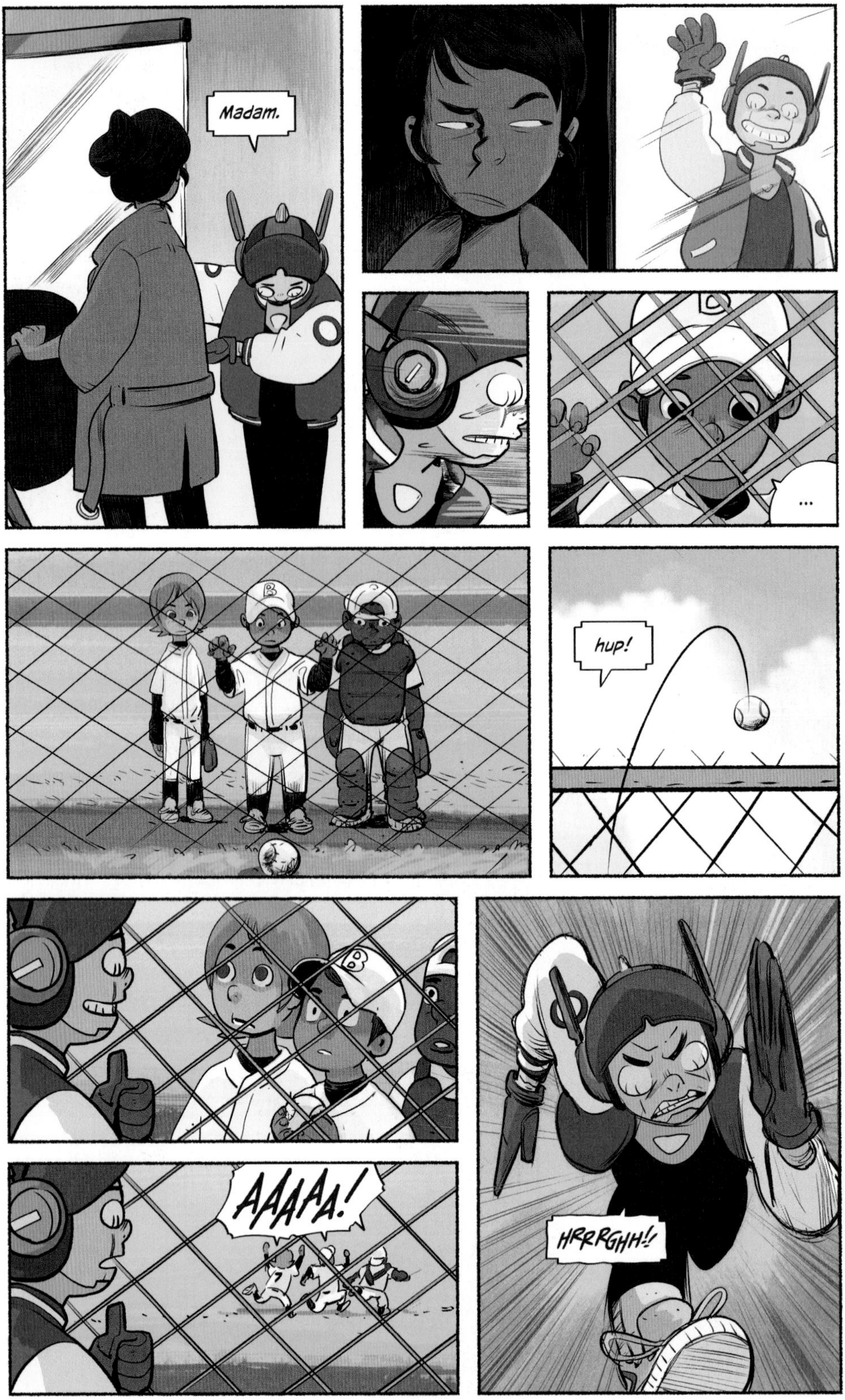
Madam.
...
hup!
AAAAA!
HRRRGHH!!

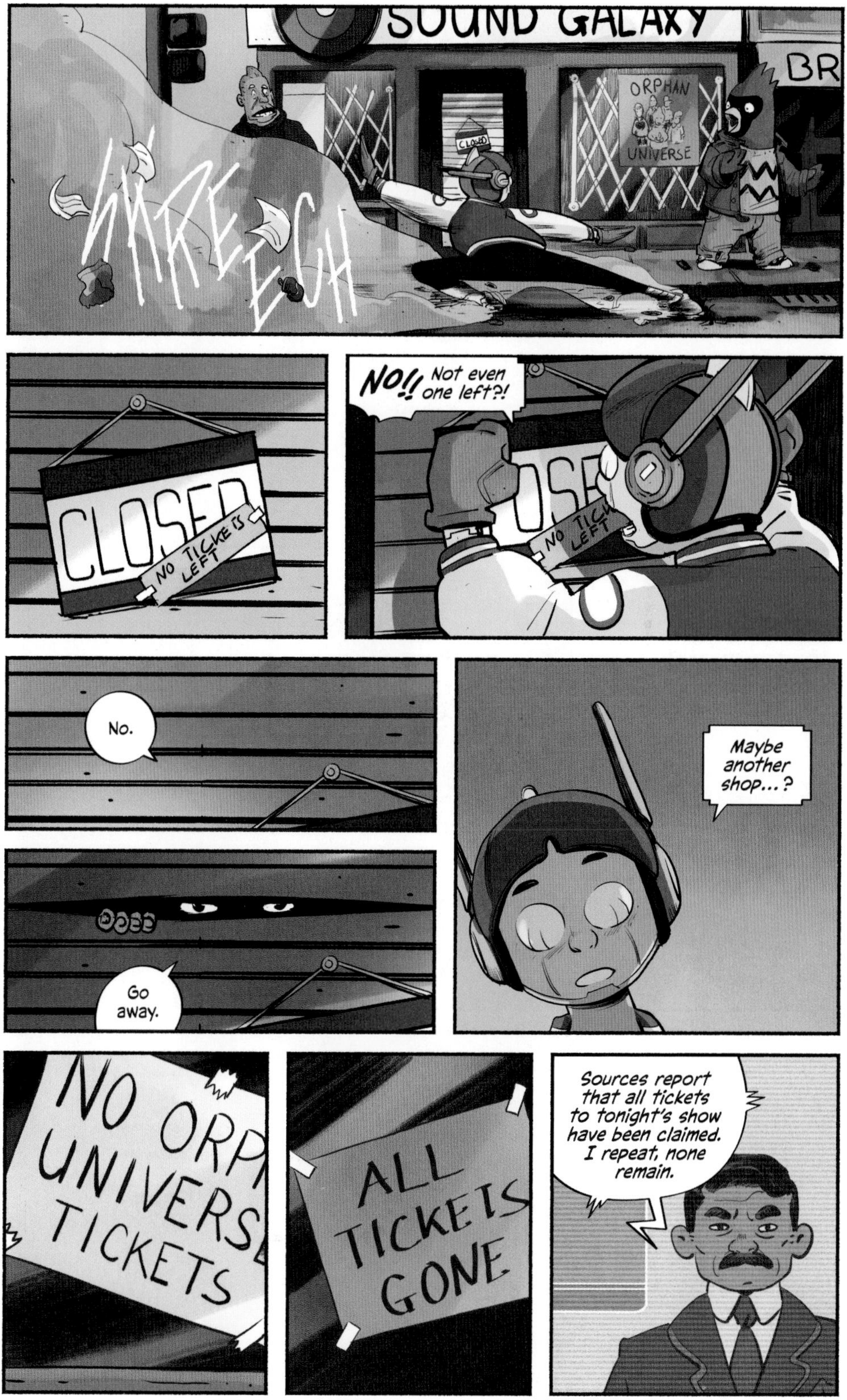
SOUND GALAXY
ORPHAN UNIVERSE
CLOSED
SKREEECH
CLOSED
NO TICKETS LEFT
NO!! Not even one left?!
No.
Go away.
Maybe another shop...?
NO ORP UNIVERS TICKETS
ALL TICKETS GONE
Sources report that all tickets to tonight's show have been claimed. I repeat, none remain.

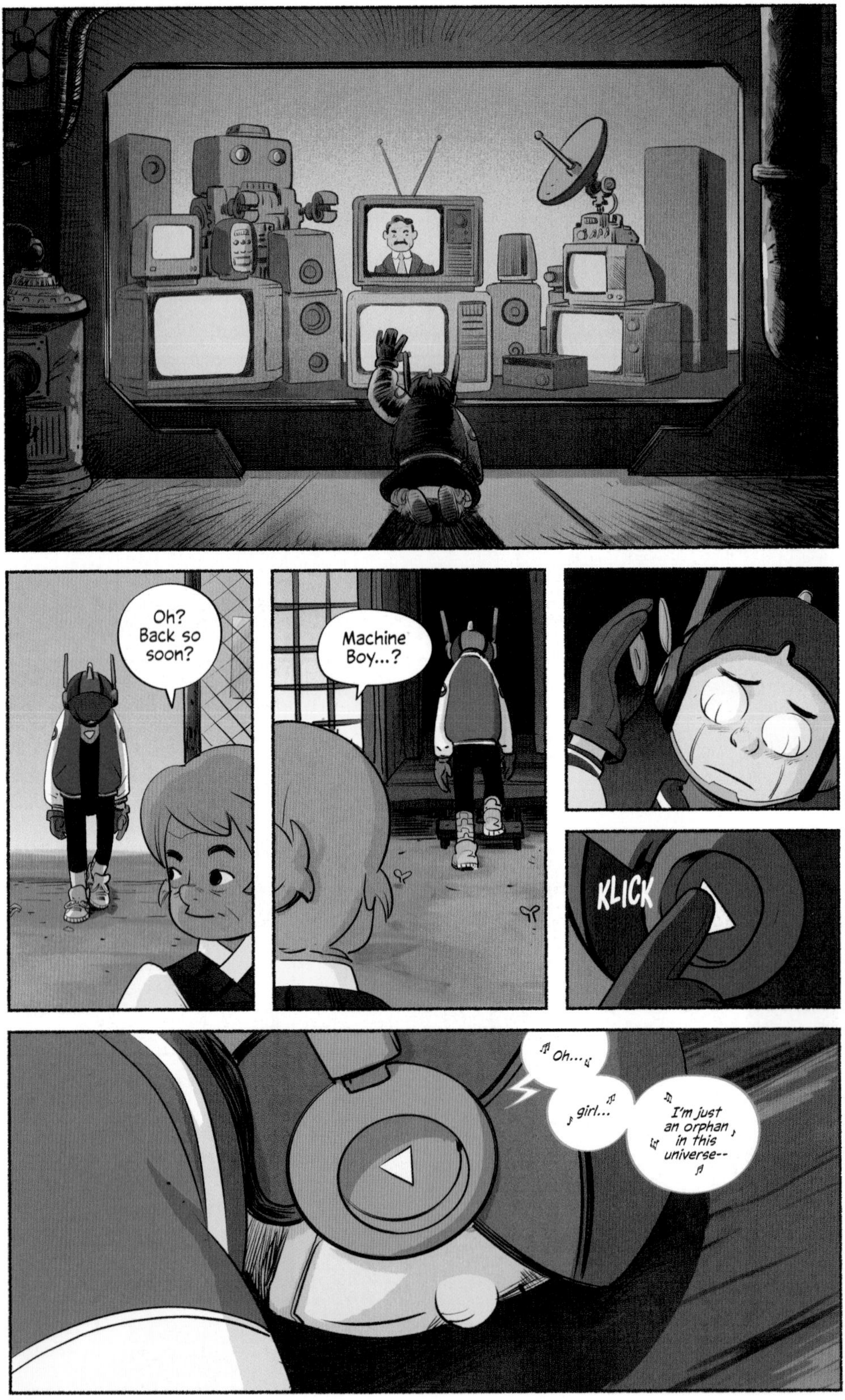
Oh? Back so soon?
Machine Boy...?
KLICK
Oh...
girl...
I'm just an orphan in this universe--

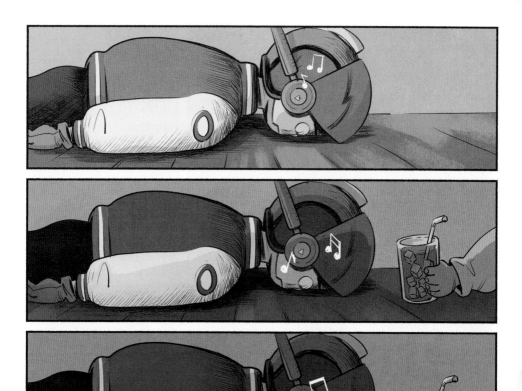

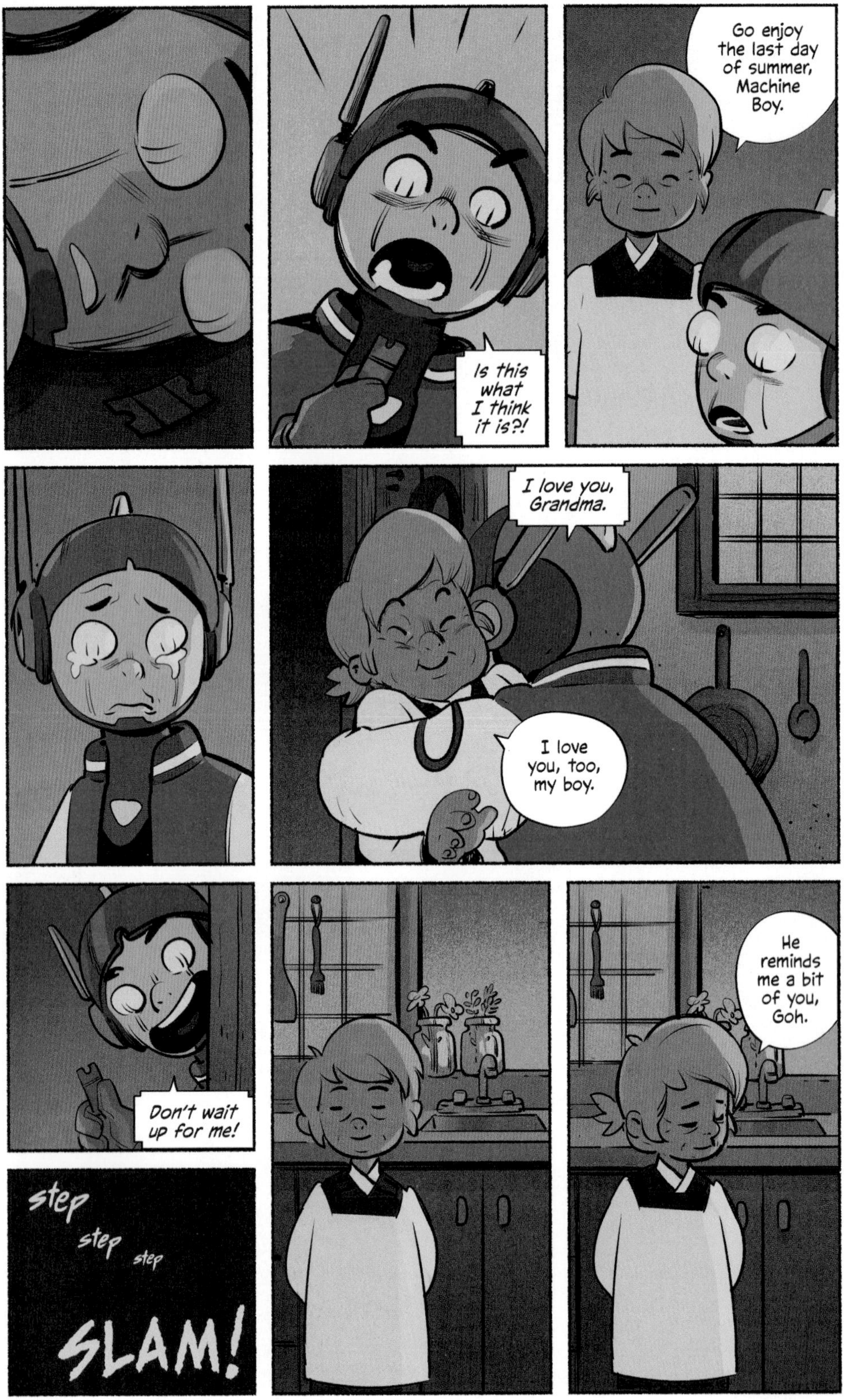
Is this what I think it is?!
Go enjoy the last day of summer, Machine Boy.
I love you, Grandma.
I love you, too, my boy.
Don't wait up for me!
step
step
step
SLAM!
He reminds me a bit of you, Goh.

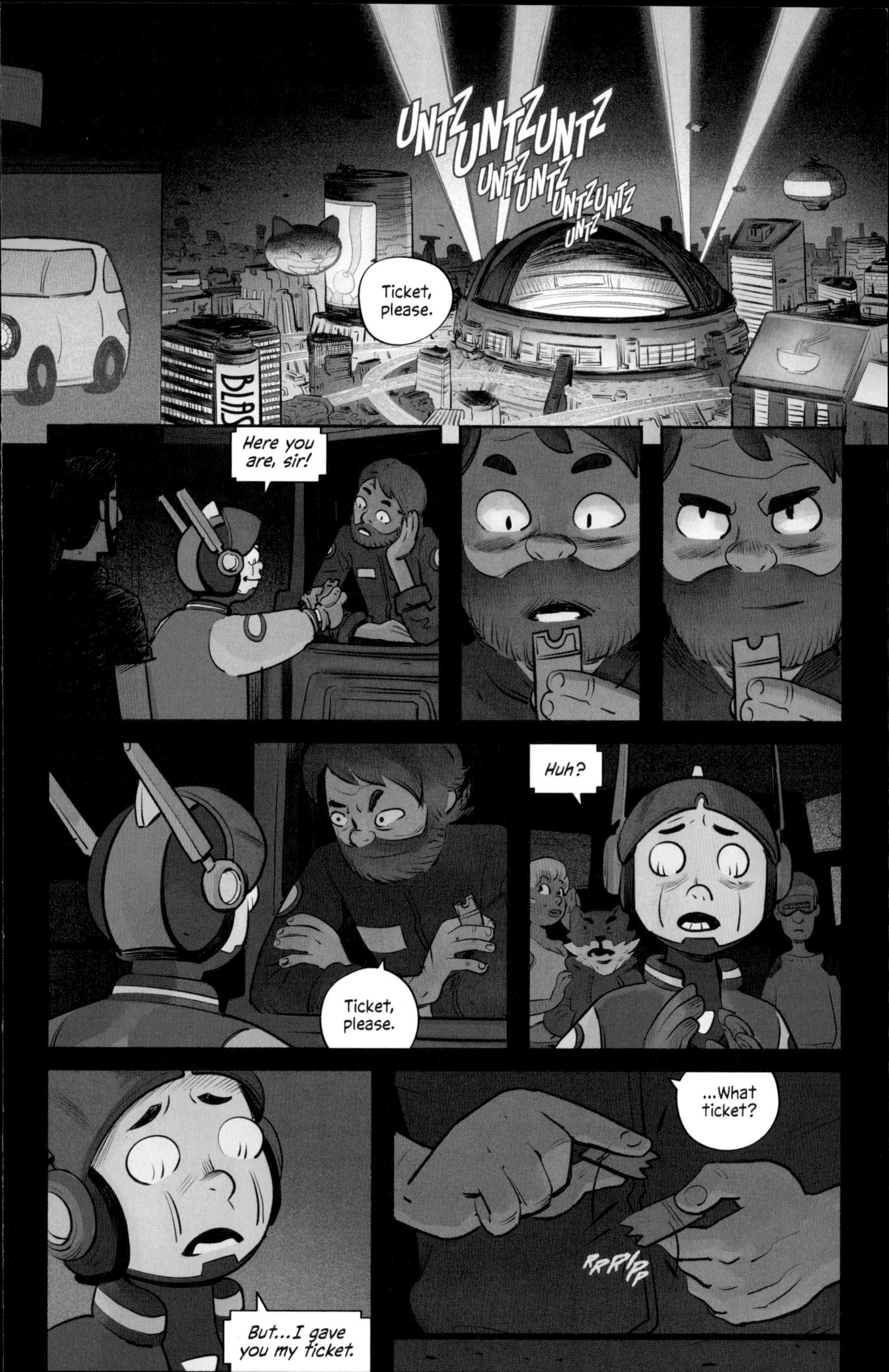
UNTZ UNTZ UNTZ
UNTZ UNTZ
UNTZ UNTZ
UNTZ
Ticket, please.
Here you are, sir!
Ticket, please.
Huh?
But...I gave you my ticket.
...What ticket?
RRRIPP

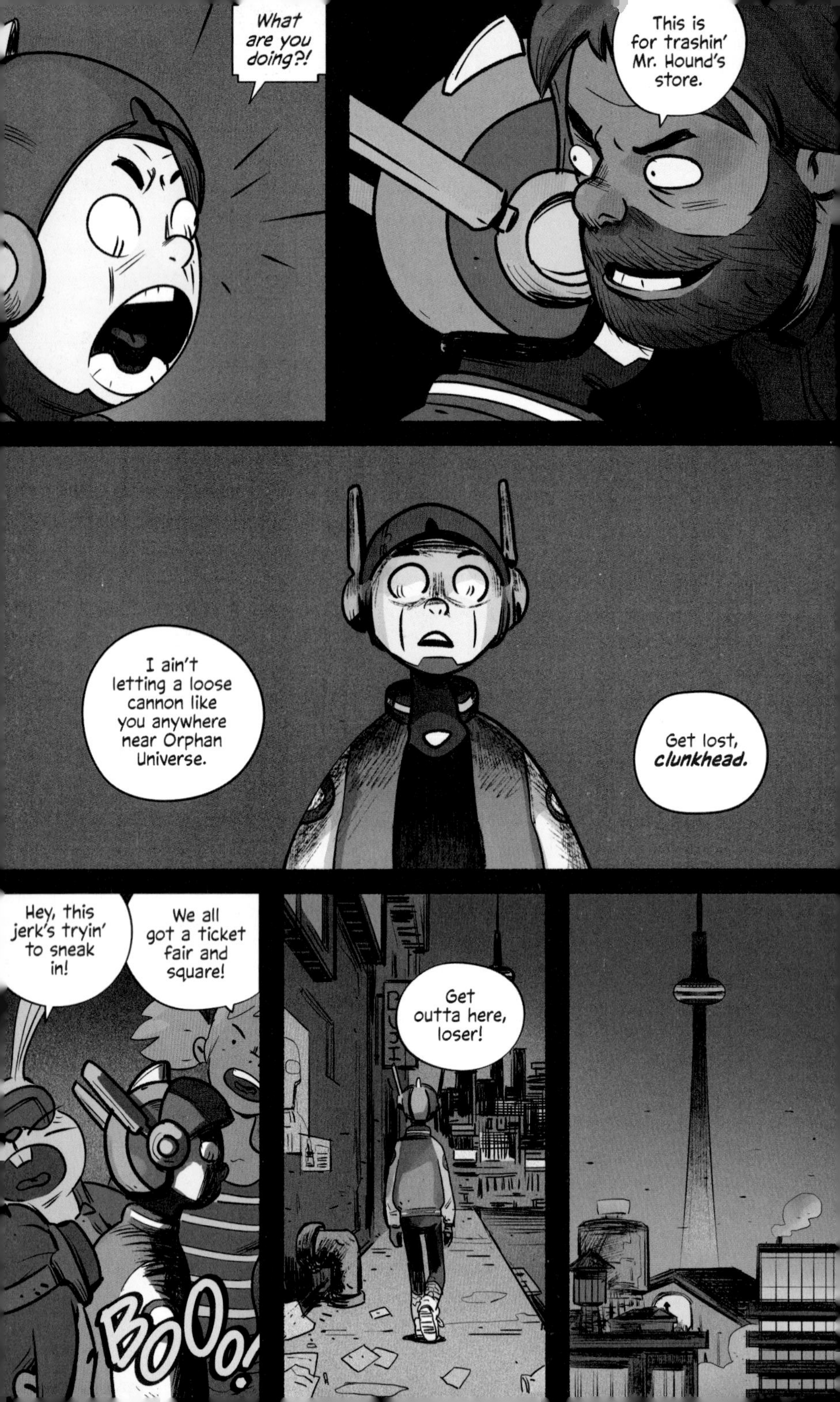
What are you doing?!
This is for trashin' Mr. Hound's store.
I ain't letting a loose cannon like you anywhere near Orphan Universe.
Get lost, *clunkhead.*
Hey, this jerk's tryin' to sneak in!
We all got a ticket fair and square!
BOOO!
Get outta here, loser!

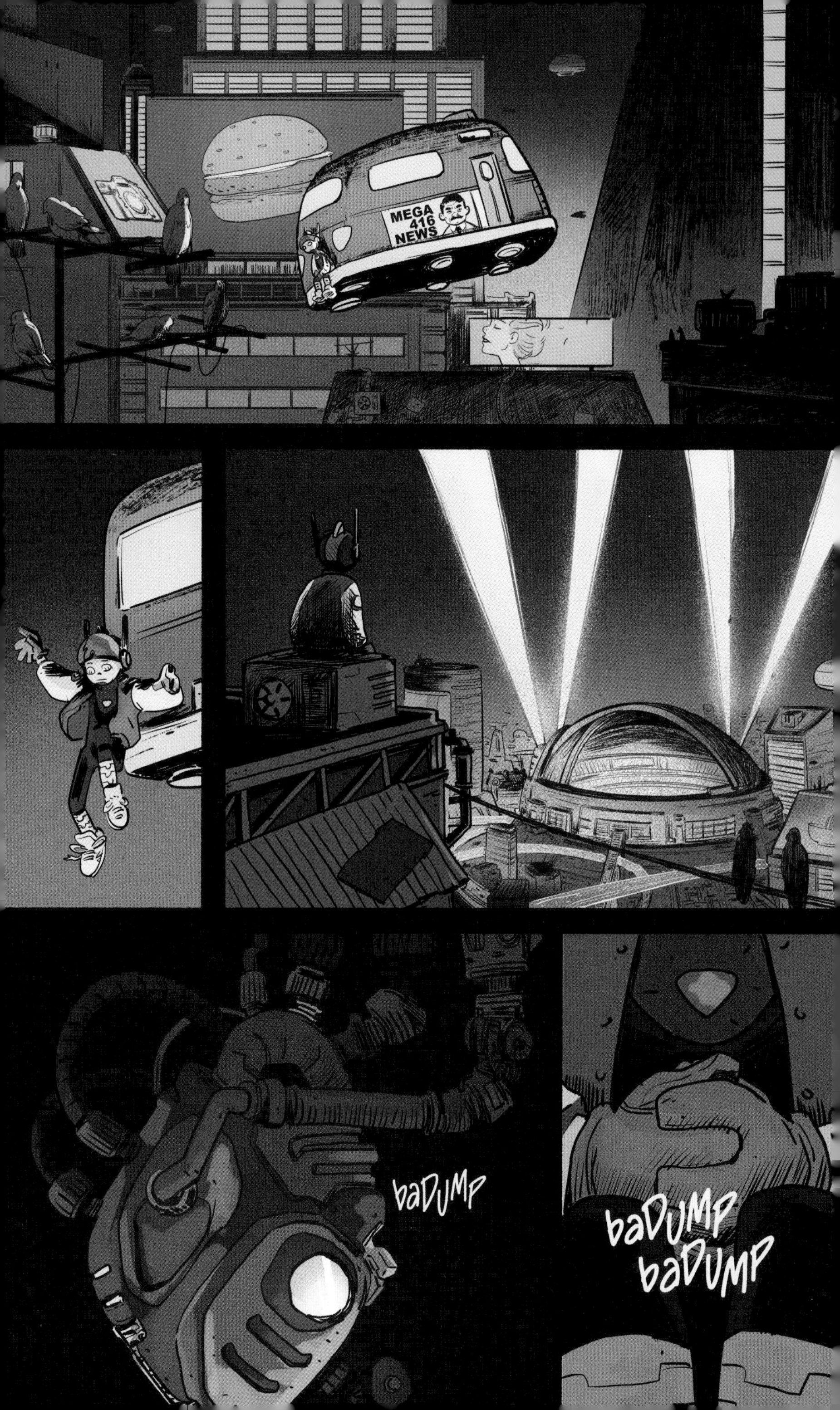
MEGA
416
NEWS
baDUMP
baDUMP
baDUMP

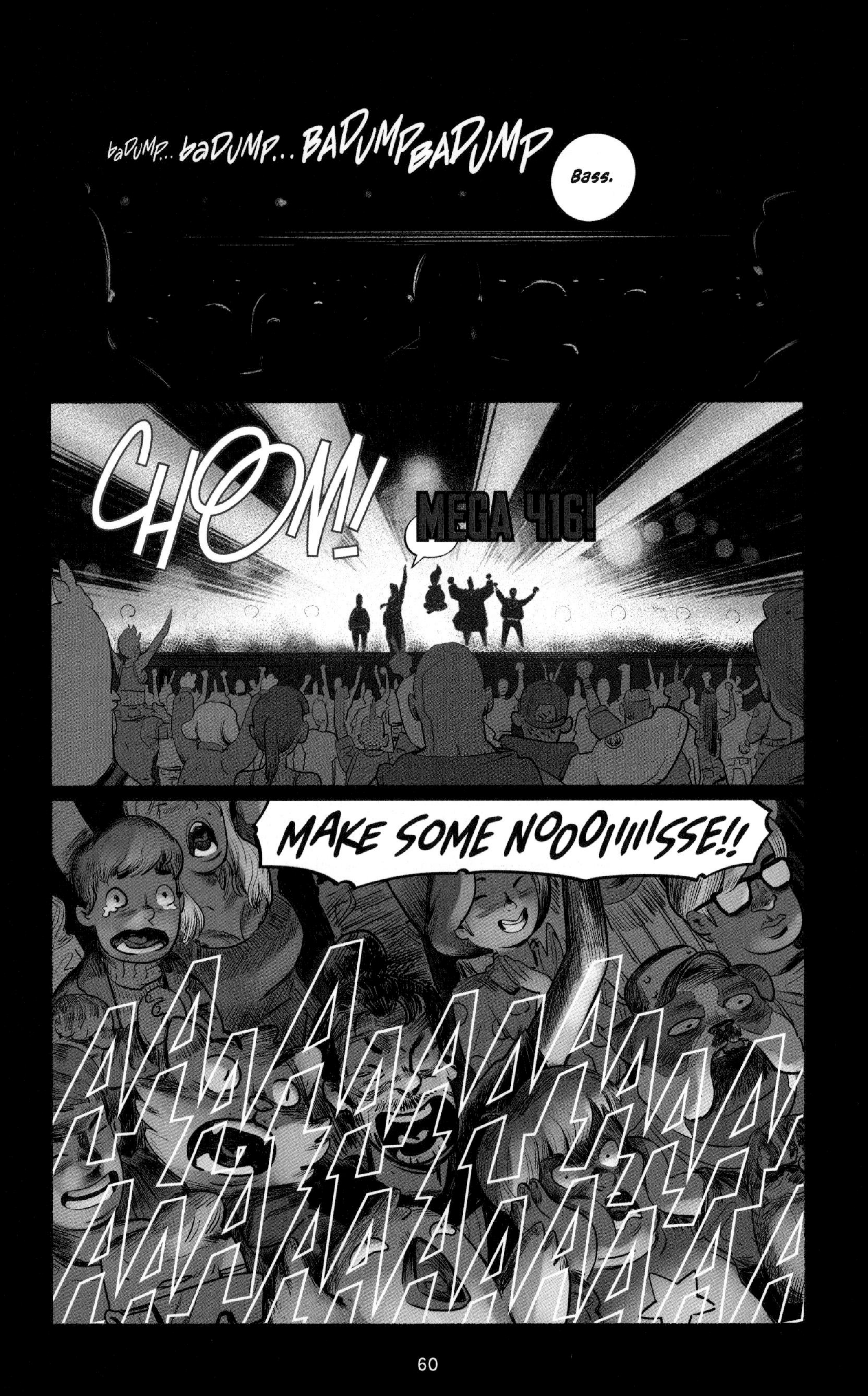

baDUMP... baDUMP... BADUMP BADUMP
Bass.
CHOOM!!
MEGA 416!
MAKE SOME NOOOIIIIISSE!!
AAAAAAAAAAAAAAAAAAAAAAAA

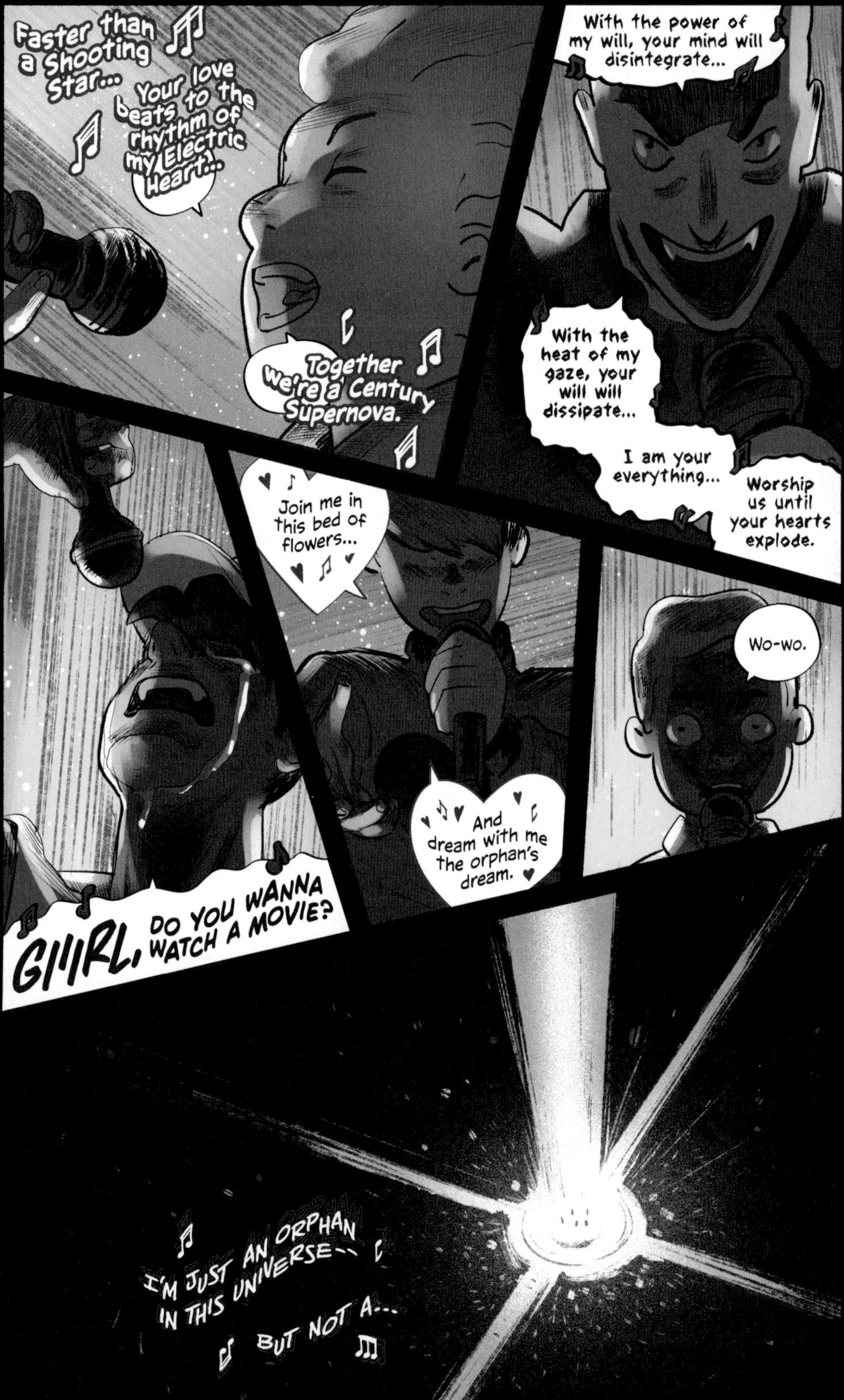
Faster than a Shooting Star...
Your love beats to the rhythm of my Electric Heart...
Together We're a Century Supernova.
With the power of my will, your mind will disintegrate...
With the heat of my gaze, your will will dissipate...
I am your everything...
Worship us until your hearts explode.
GIIIRL, DO YOU WANNA WATCH A MOVIE?
Join me in this bed of flowers...
And dream with me the orphan's dream.
Wo-wo.
I'M JUST AN ORPHAN IN THIS UNIVERSE--
BUT NOT A...

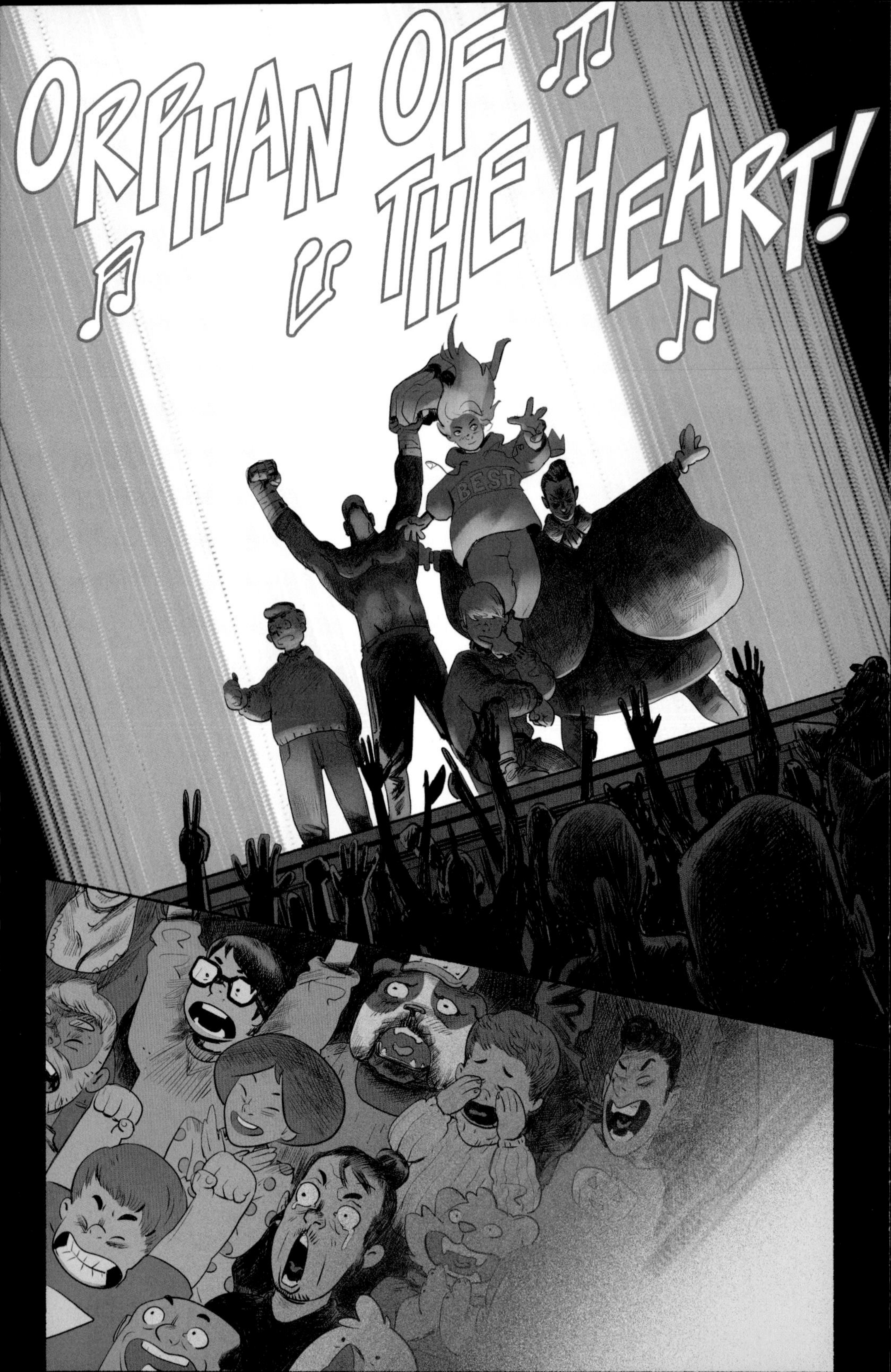
ORPHAN OF THE HEART!
BEST

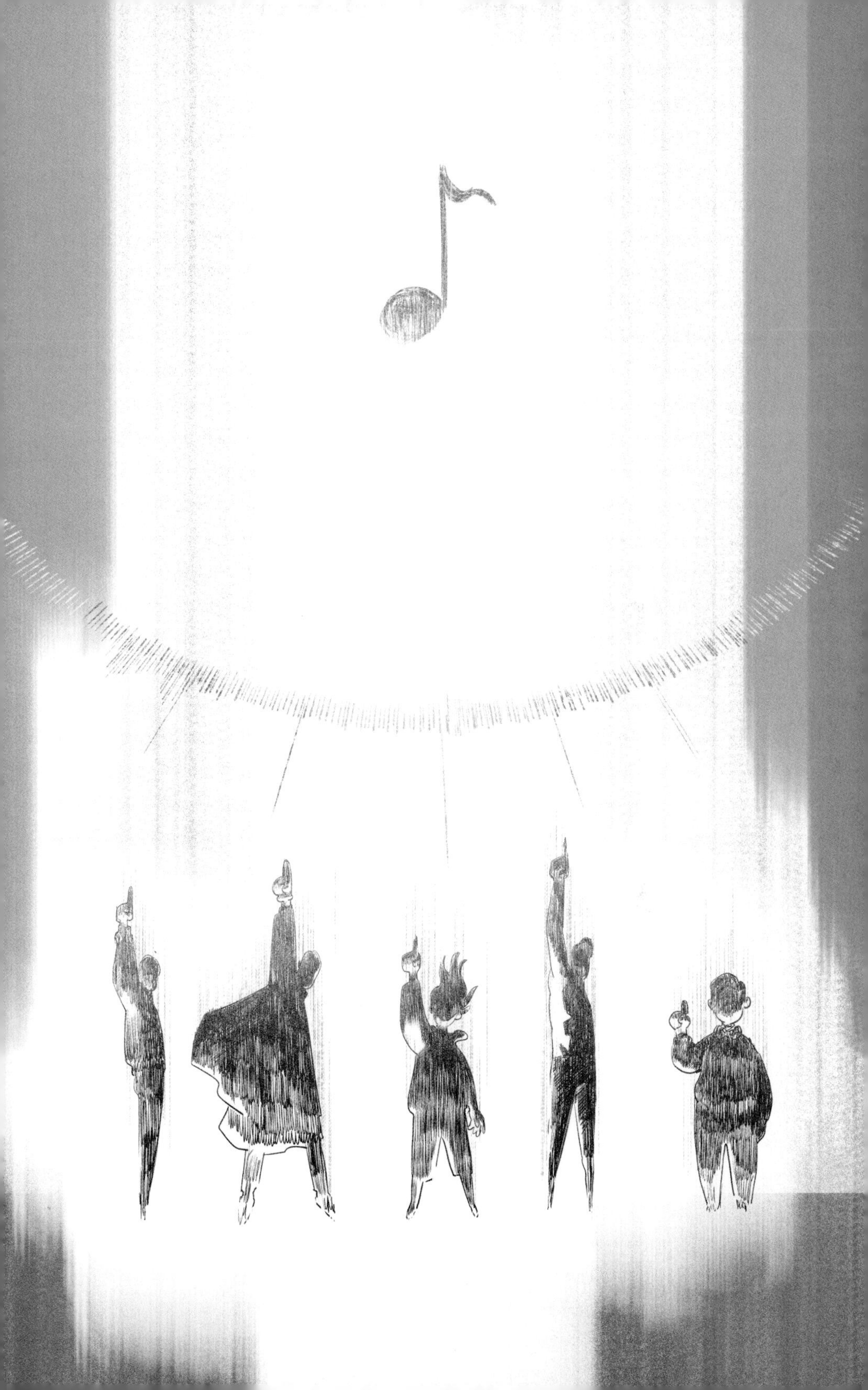

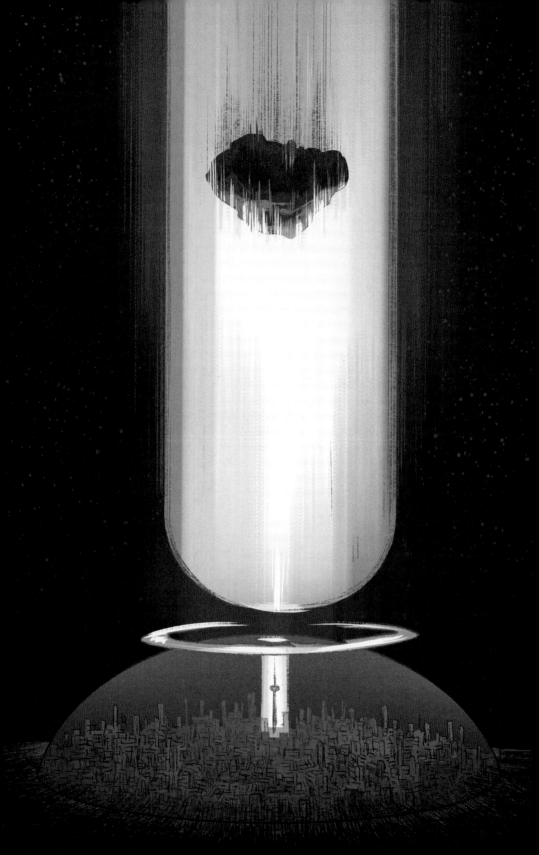

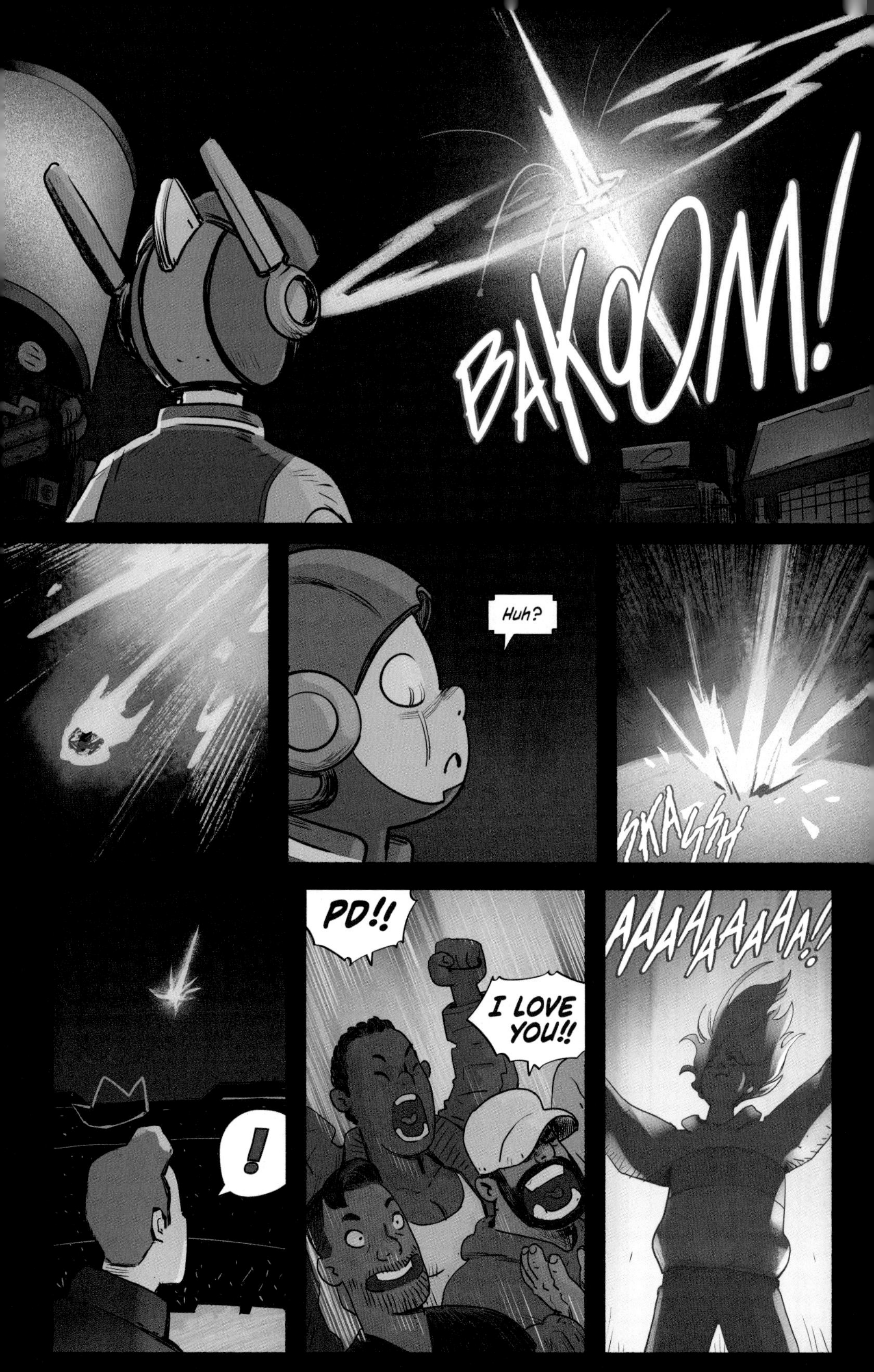
BAKOOM!
Huh?
SKASSH
!
PD!!
I LOVE YOU!!
AAAAAAAAA!

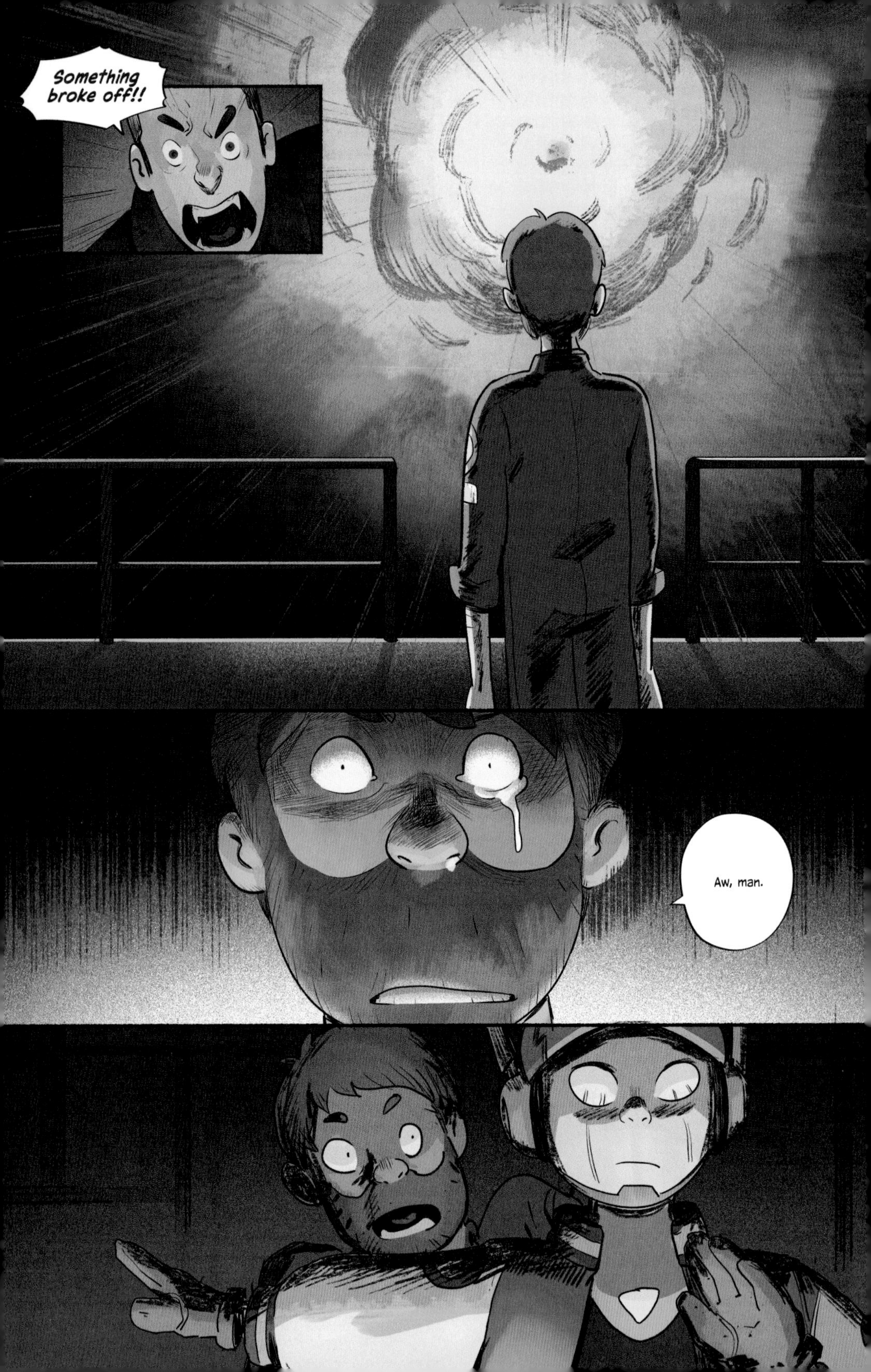
Something broke off!!
Aw, man.

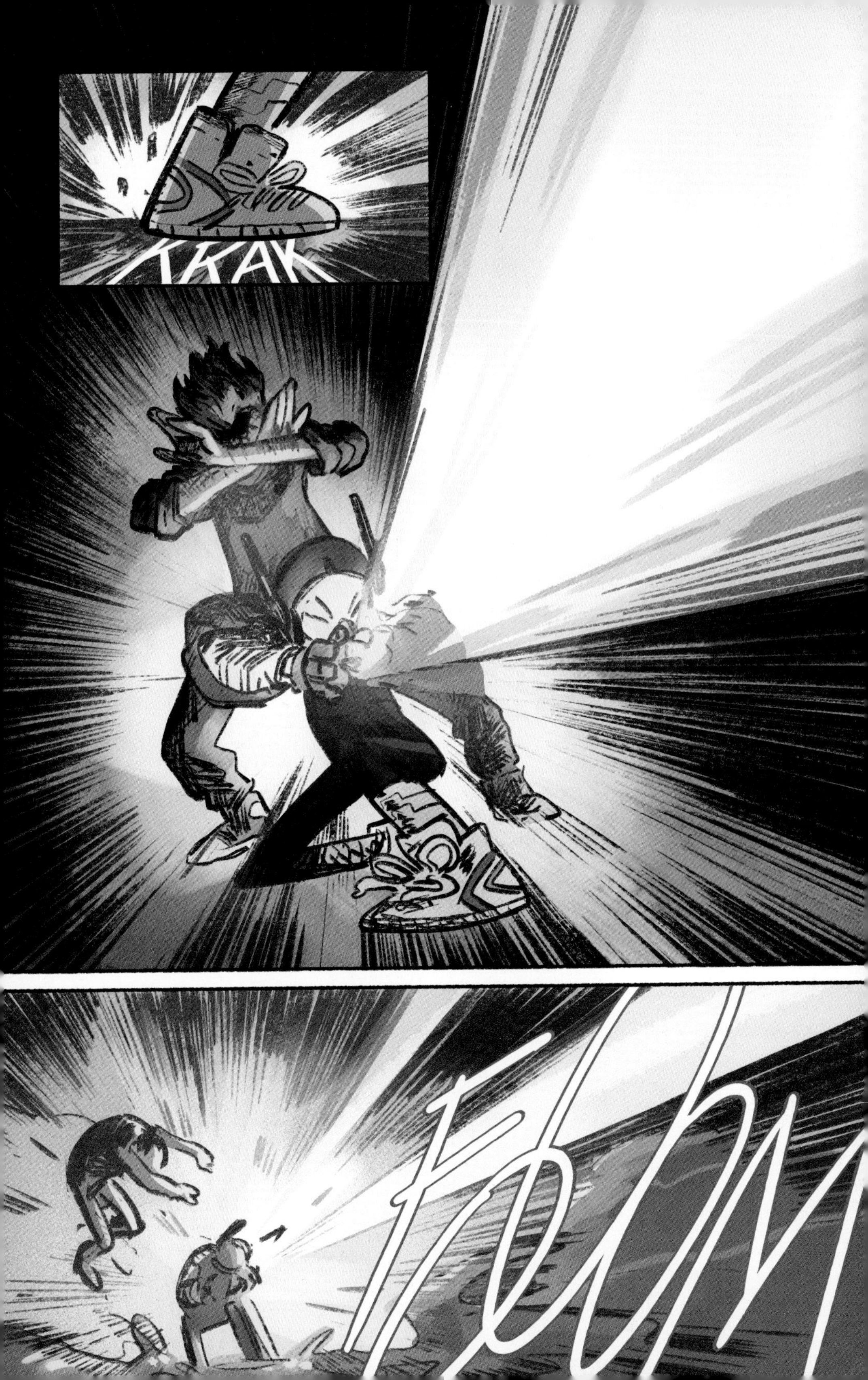
KRAK

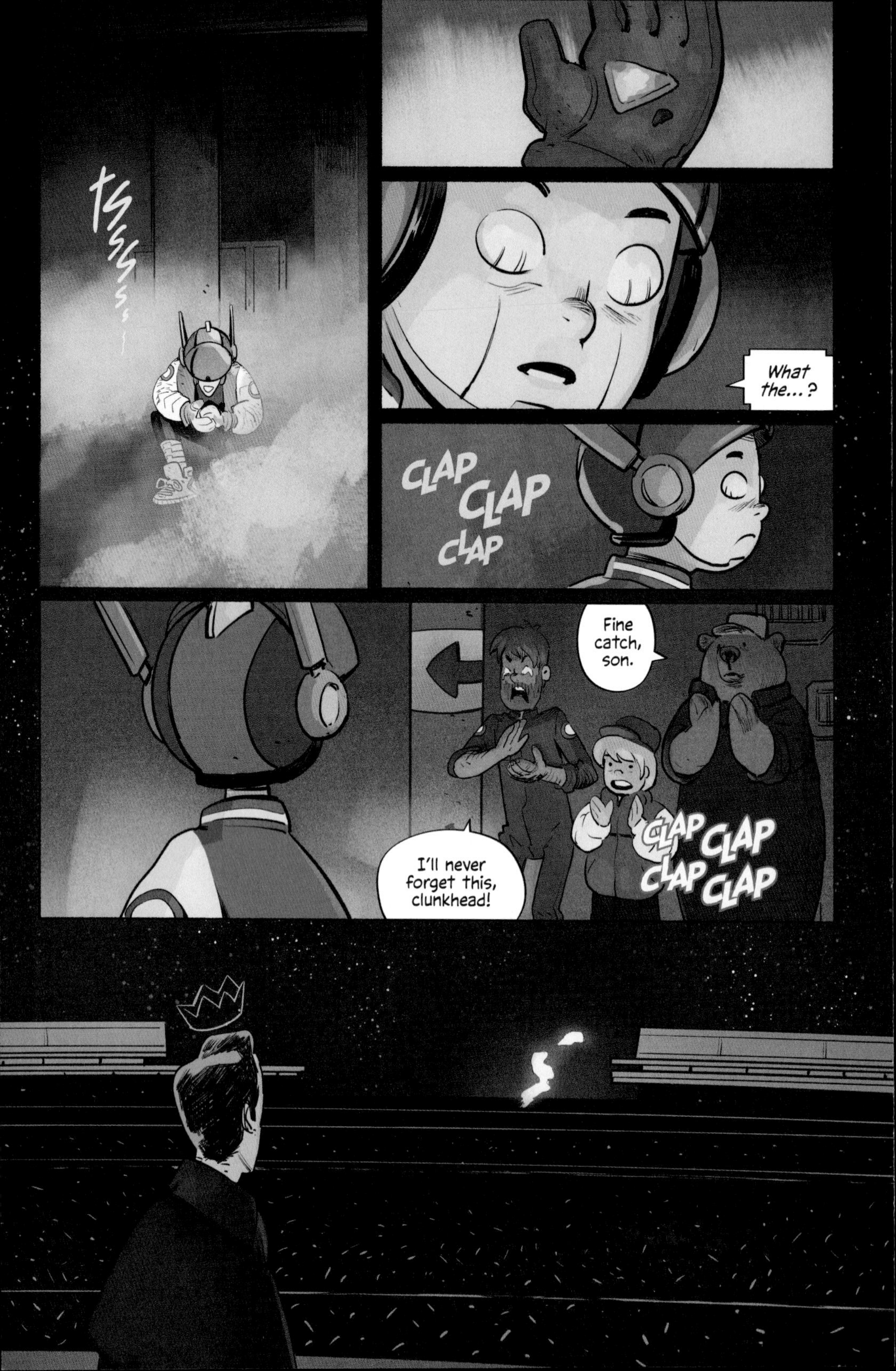

TSSSS...
What the...?
CLAP CLAP CLAP
Fine catch, son.
I'll never forget this, clunkhead!
CLAP CLAP CLAP CLAP

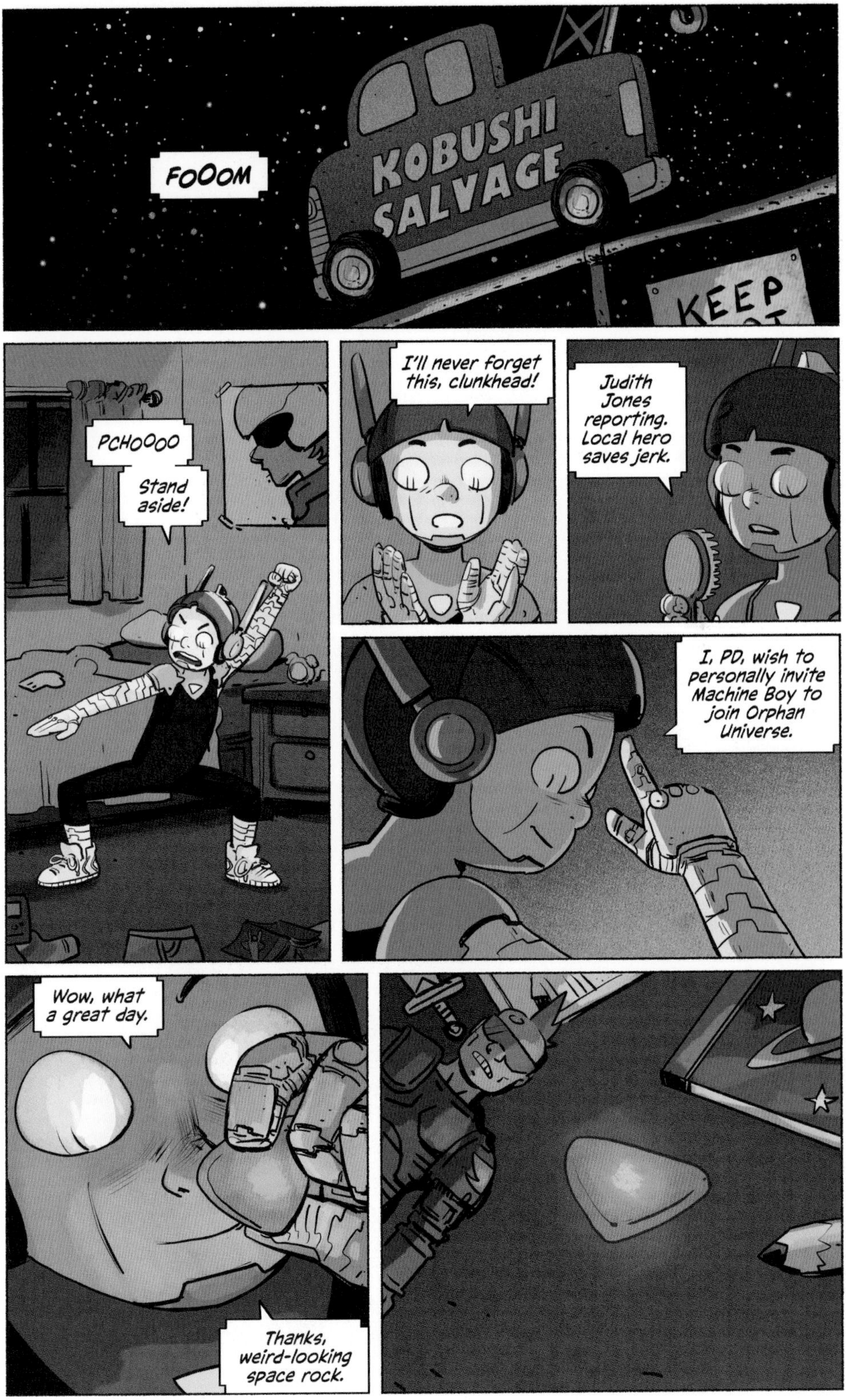
KOBUSHI SALVAGE
FOOOM
KEEP
PCHOOOO
Stand aside!
I'll never forget this, clunkhead!
Judith Jones reporting. Local hero saves jerk.
I, PD, wish to personally invite Machine Boy to join Orphan Universe.
Wow, what a great day.
Thanks, weird-looking space rock.

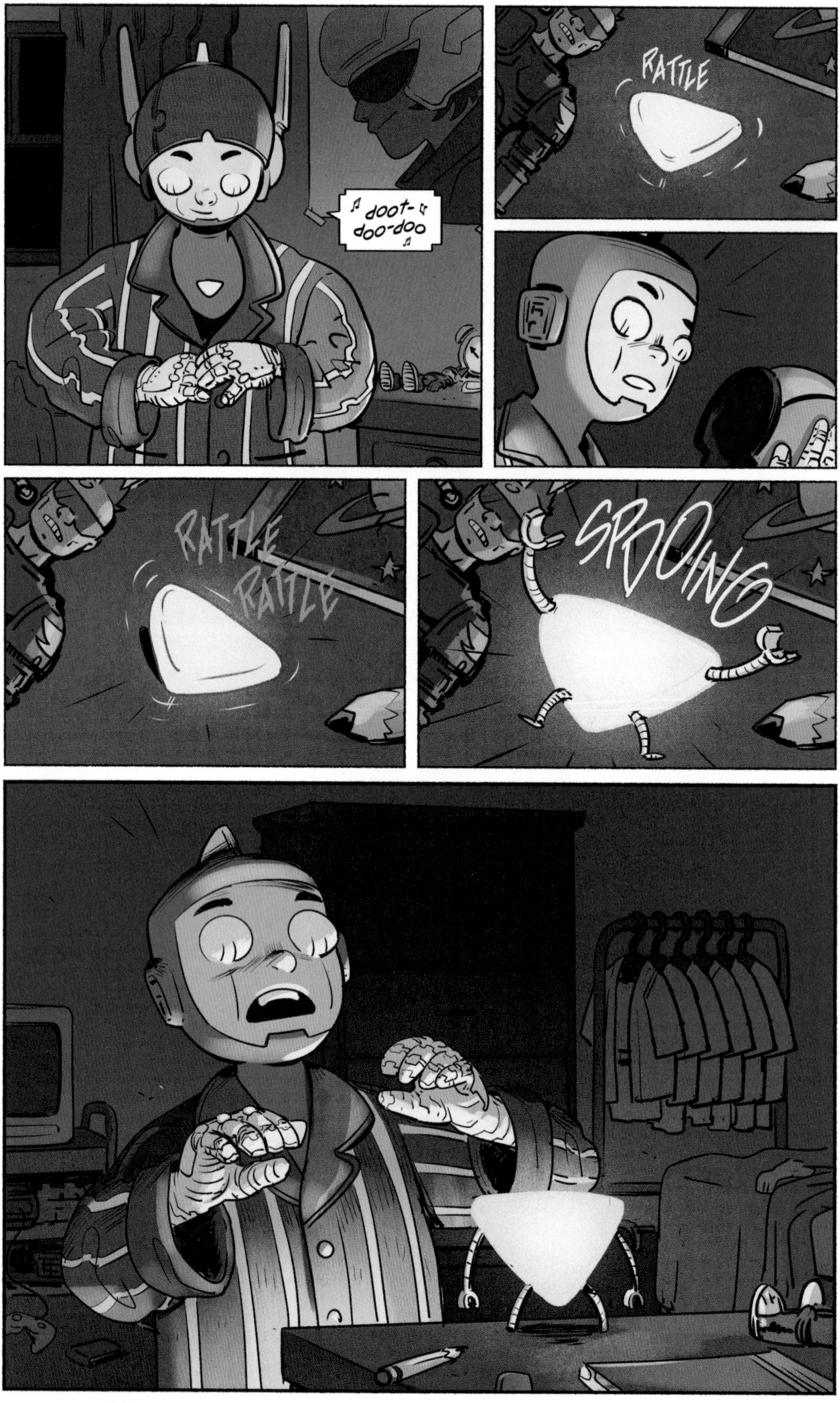
doot-doo-doo
RATTLE
RATTLE RATTLE
SPOOING

CHAPTER 4

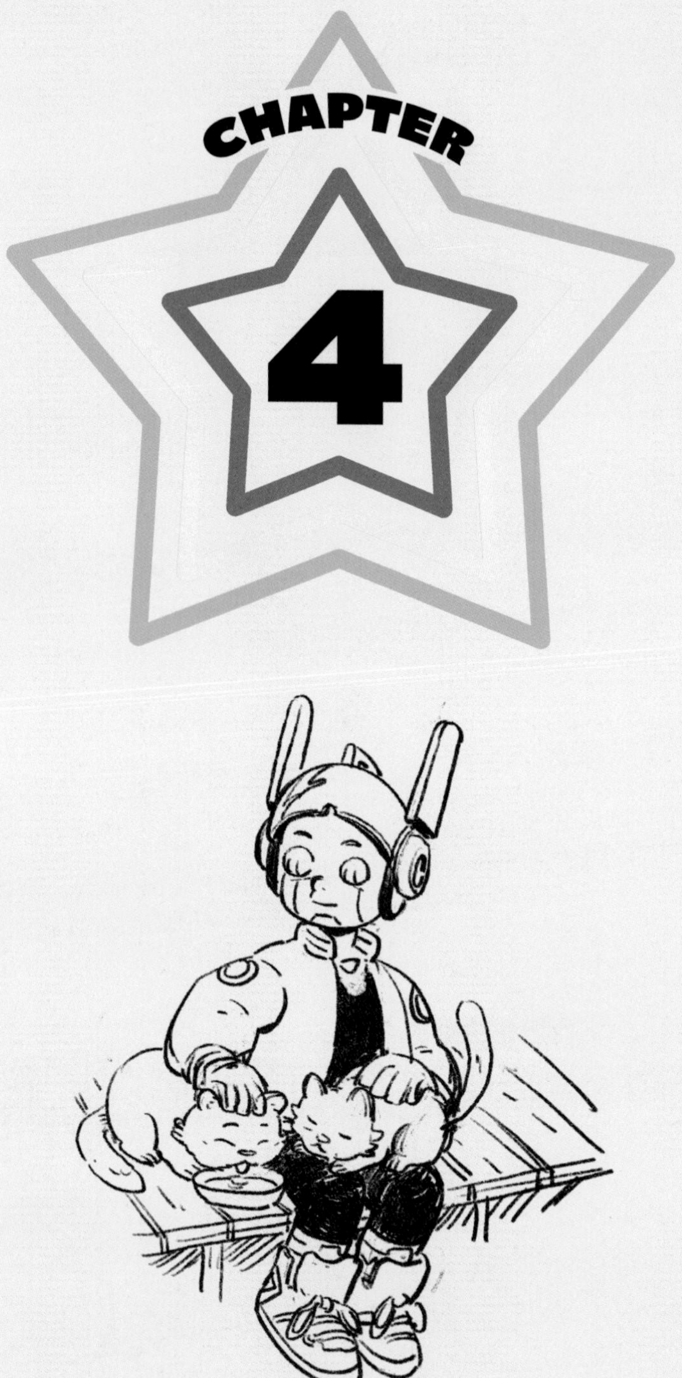

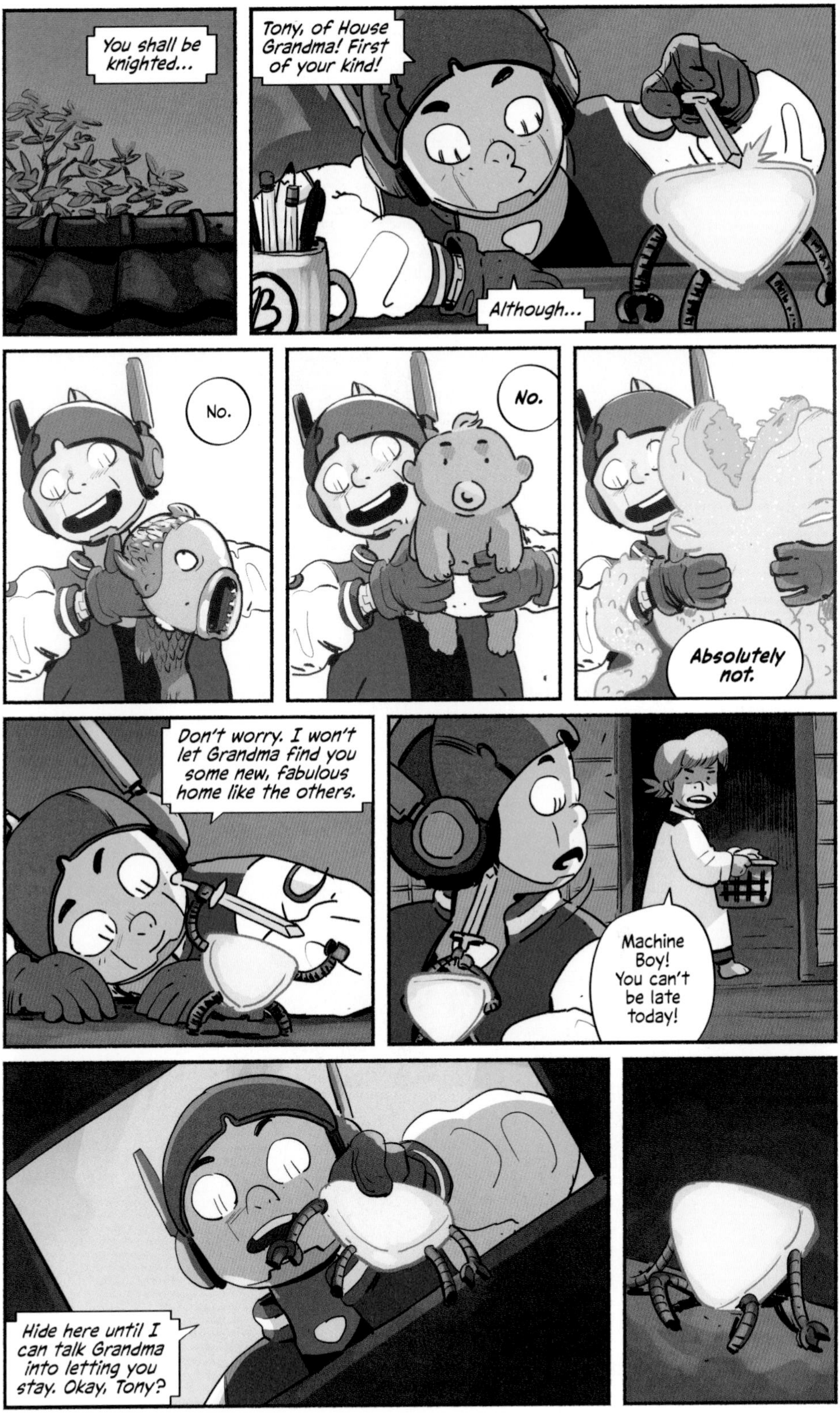
You shall be knighted...
Tony, of House Grandma! First of your kind!
Although...
No.
No.
Absolutely not.
Don't worry. I won't let Grandma find you some new, fabulous home like the others.
Machine Boy! You can't be late today!
Hide here until I can talk Grandma into letting you stay. Okay, Tony?

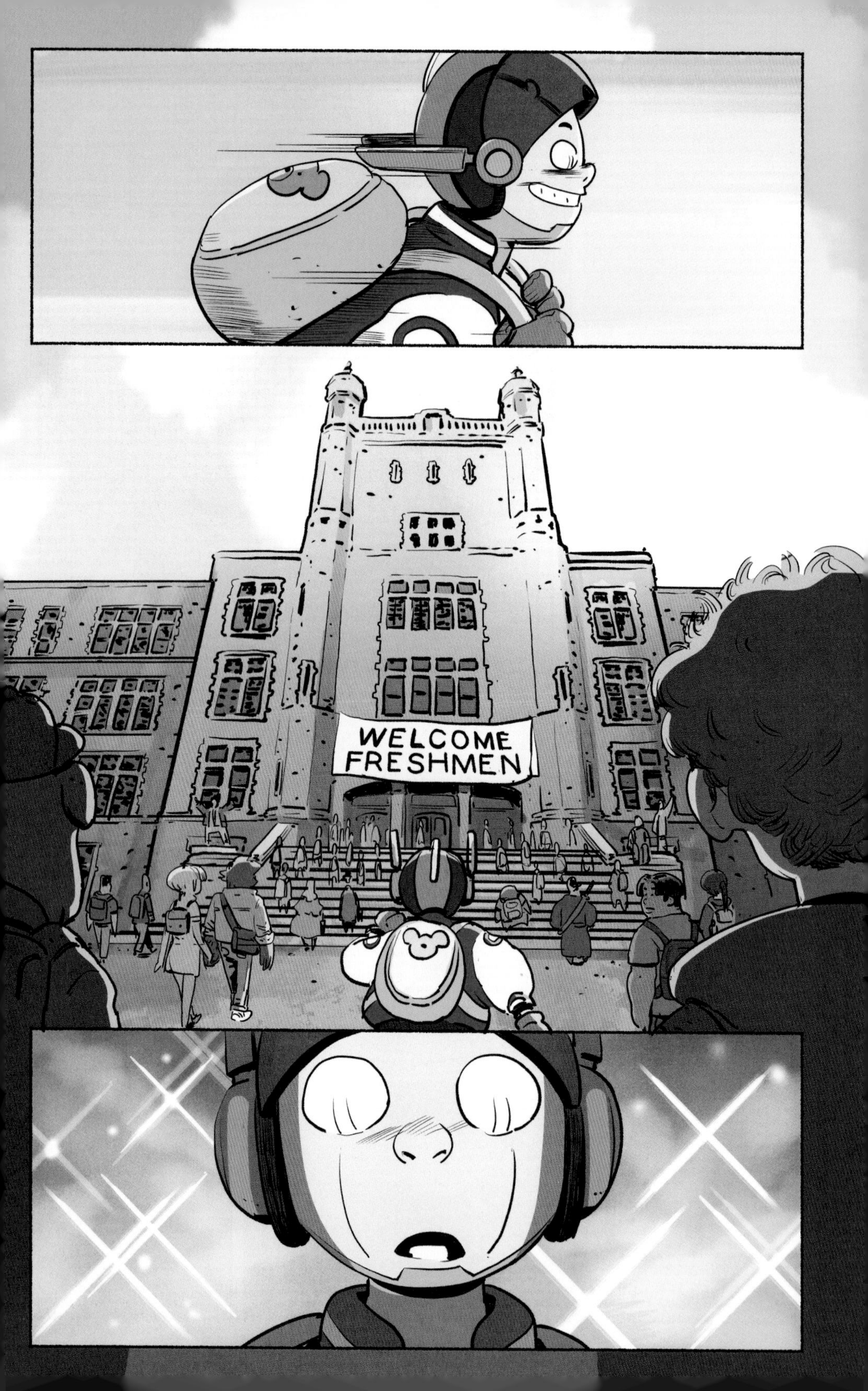
WELCOME
FRESHMEN

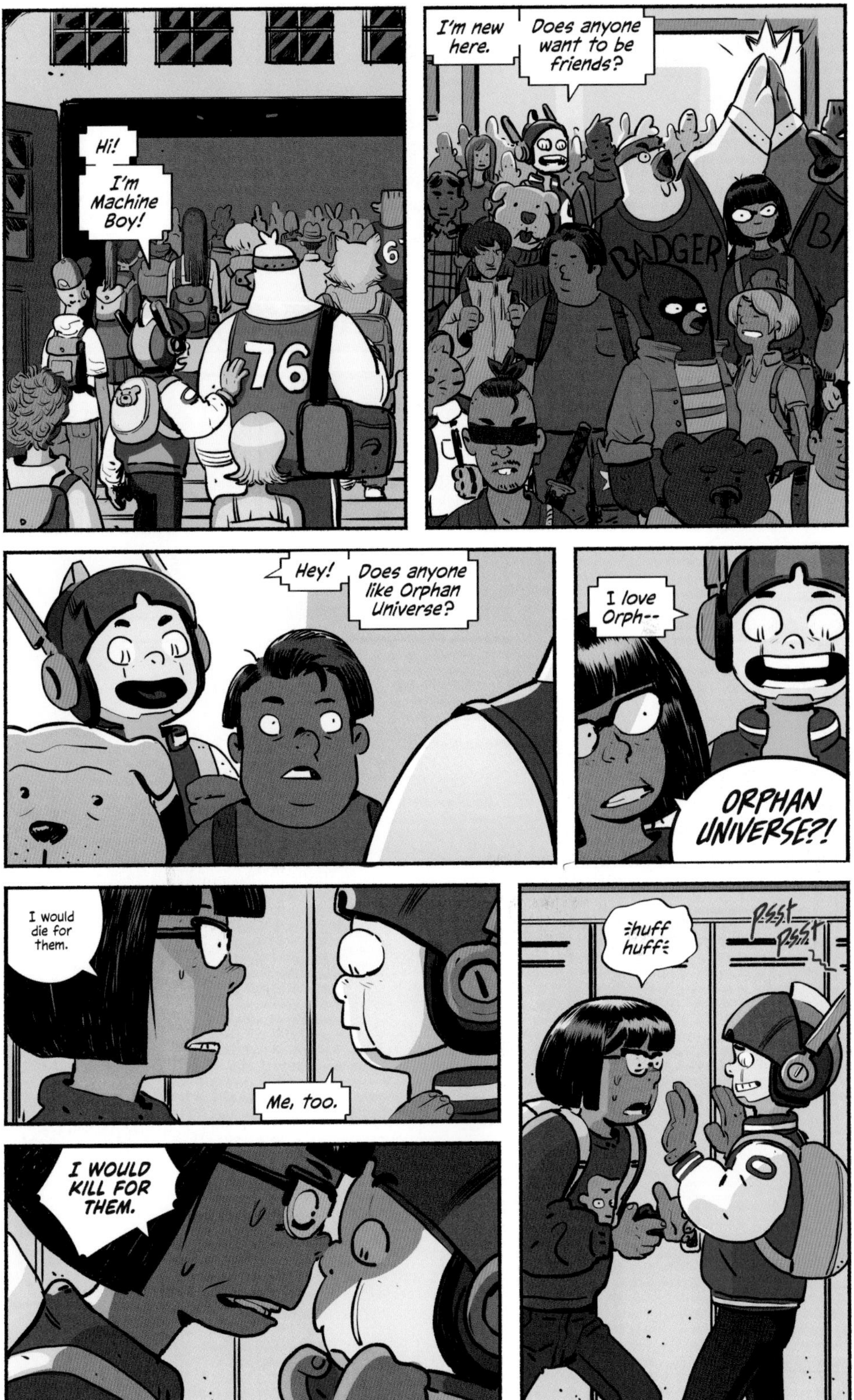

Hi!
I'm Machine Boy!
76
I'm new here.
Does anyone want to be friends?
BADGER
Hey!
Does anyone like Orphan Universe?
I love Orph--
ORPHAN UNIVERSE?!
I would die for them.
Me, too.
I WOULD KILL FOR THEM.
huff huff
PSST PSST

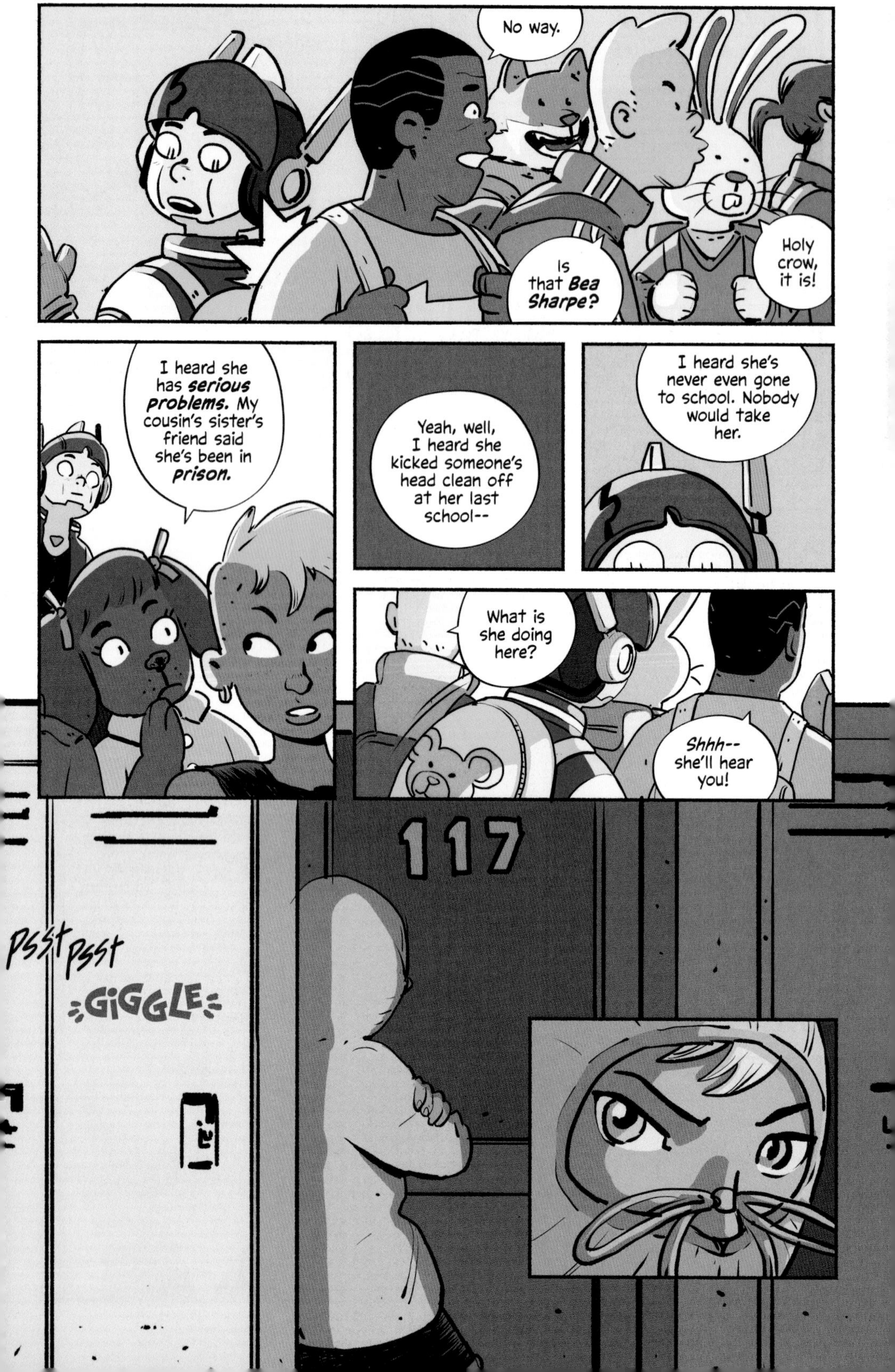
No way.
Is that **Bea Sharpe?**
Holy crow, it is!
I heard she has **serious problems.** My cousin's sister's friend said she's been in **prison.**
Yeah, well, I heard she kicked someone's head clean off at her last school--
I heard she's never even gone to school. Nobody would take her.
What is she doing here?
Shhh-- she'll hear you!
117
PSST PSST
GIGGLE

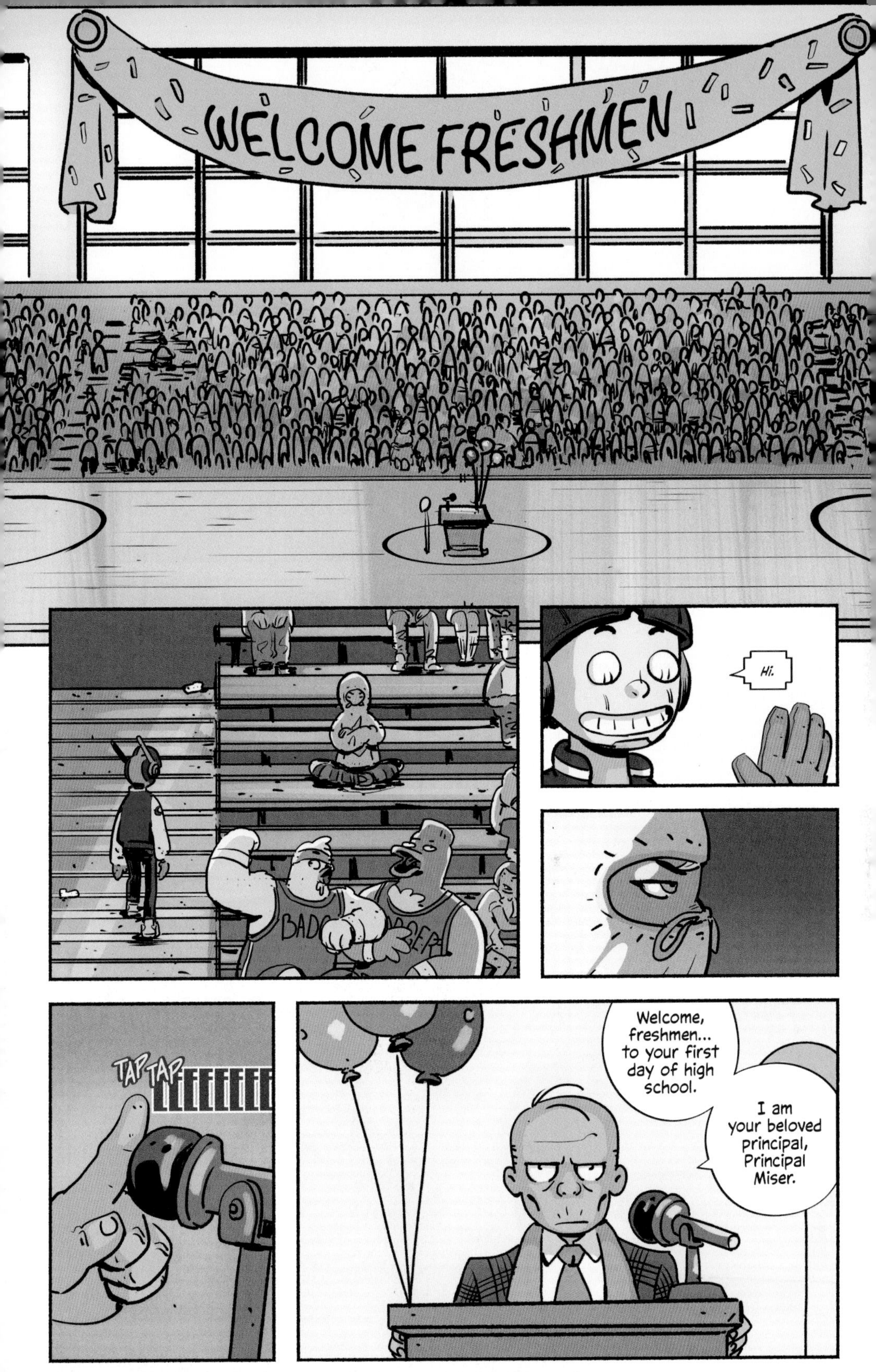
WELCOME FRESHMEN
BADGER
Hi.
TAP TAP
EEEEEEE
Welcome, freshmen... to your first day of high school.
I am your beloved principal, Principal Miser.

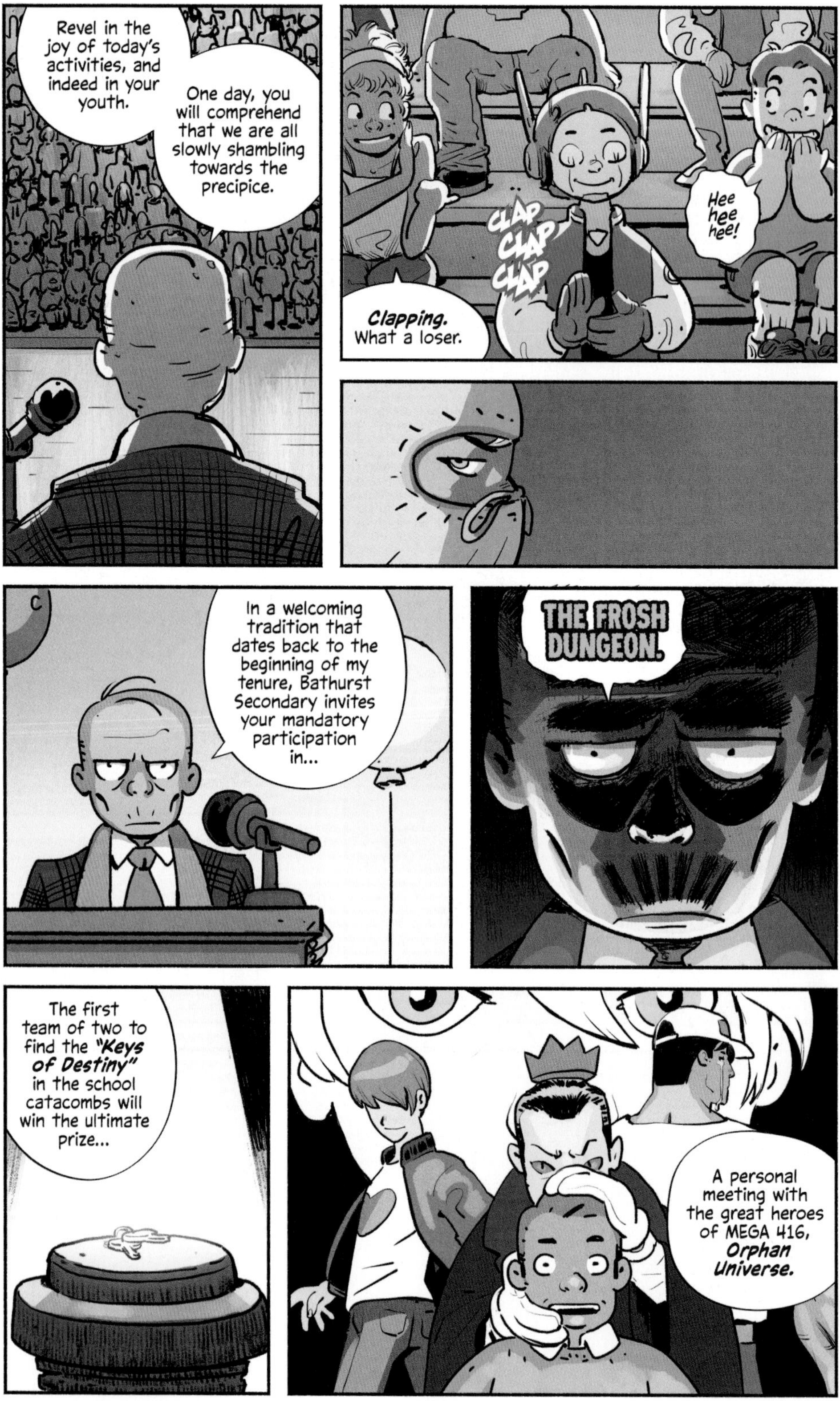
Revel in the joy of today's activities, and indeed in your youth.
One day, you will comprehend that we are all slowly shambling towards the precipice.
CLAP CLAP CLAP
Hee hee hee!
Clapping. What a loser.
In a welcoming tradition that dates back to the beginning of my tenure, Bathurst Secondary invites your mandatory participation in...
THE FROSH DUNGEON.
The first team of two to find the "Keys of Destiny" in the school catacombs will win the ultimate prize...
A personal meeting with the great heroes of MEGA 416, Orphan Universe.

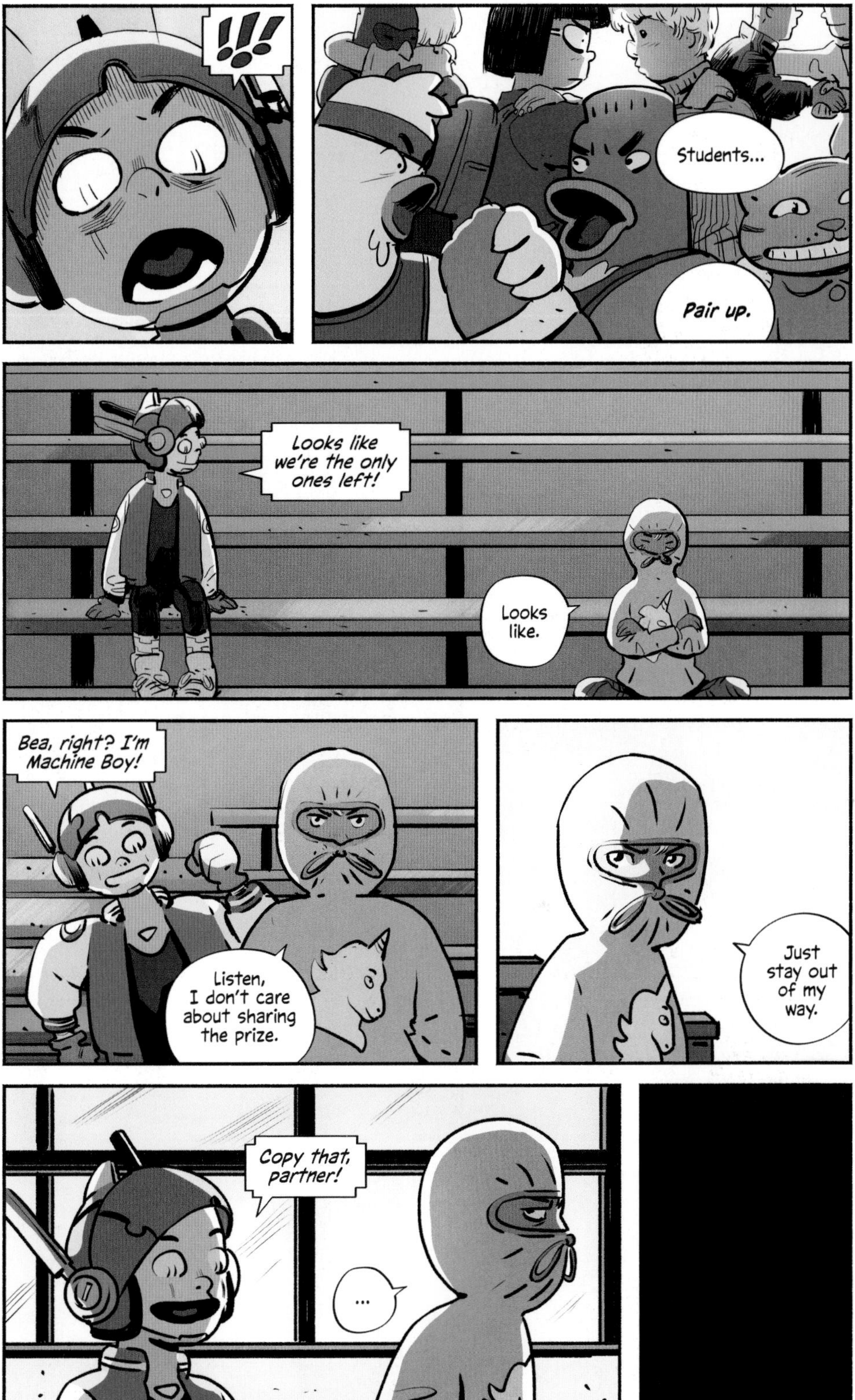
!!!
Students...
Pair up.
Looks like we're the only ones left!
Looks like.
Bea, right? I'm Machine Boy!
Listen, I don't care about sharing the prize.
Just stay out of my way.
Copy that, partner!
...

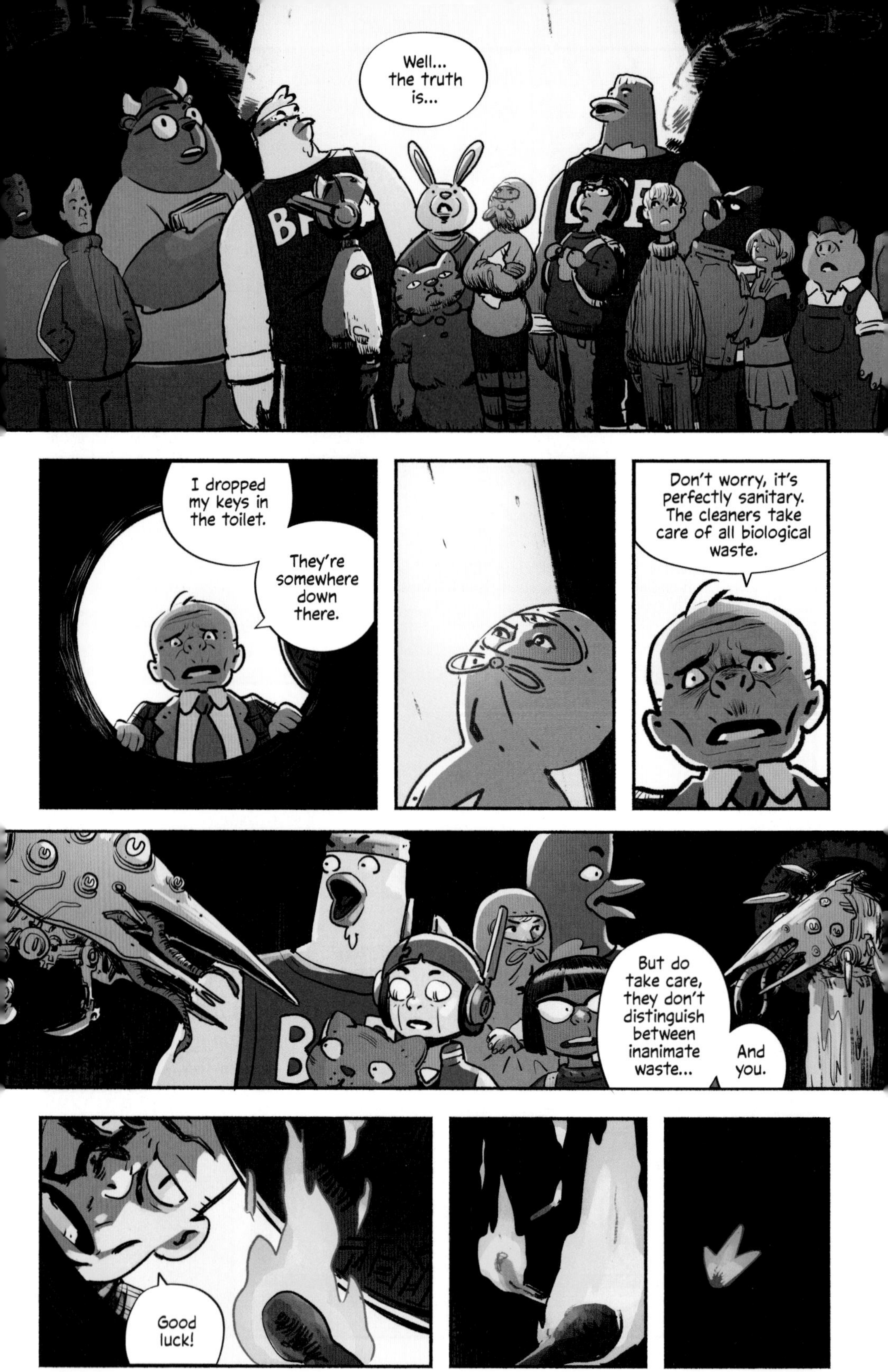

Well... the truth is...
I dropped my keys in the toilet.
They're somewhere down there.
Don't worry, it's perfectly sanitary. The cleaners take care of all biological waste.
But do take care, they don't distinguish between inanimate waste...
And you.
Good luck!

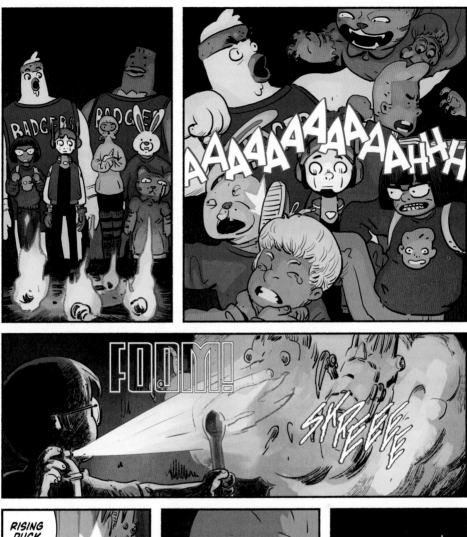

AAAAAAAAAAAAAAHHH

FOOM!

SKREEE

RISING DUCK FIST!!

DJ

Grand jeté.

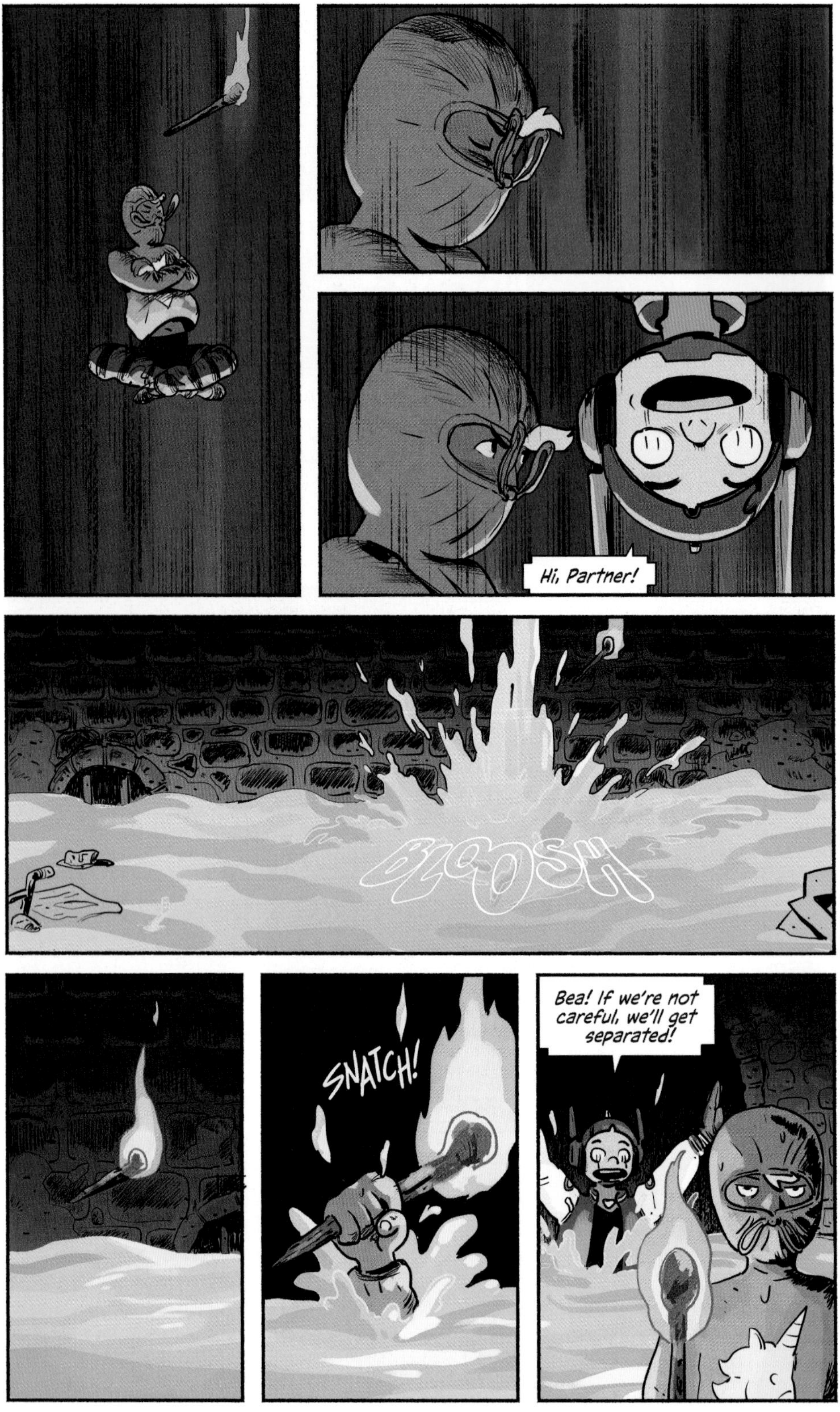

Hi, Partner!
BLOOSH
SNATCH!
Bea! If we're not careful, we'll get separated!

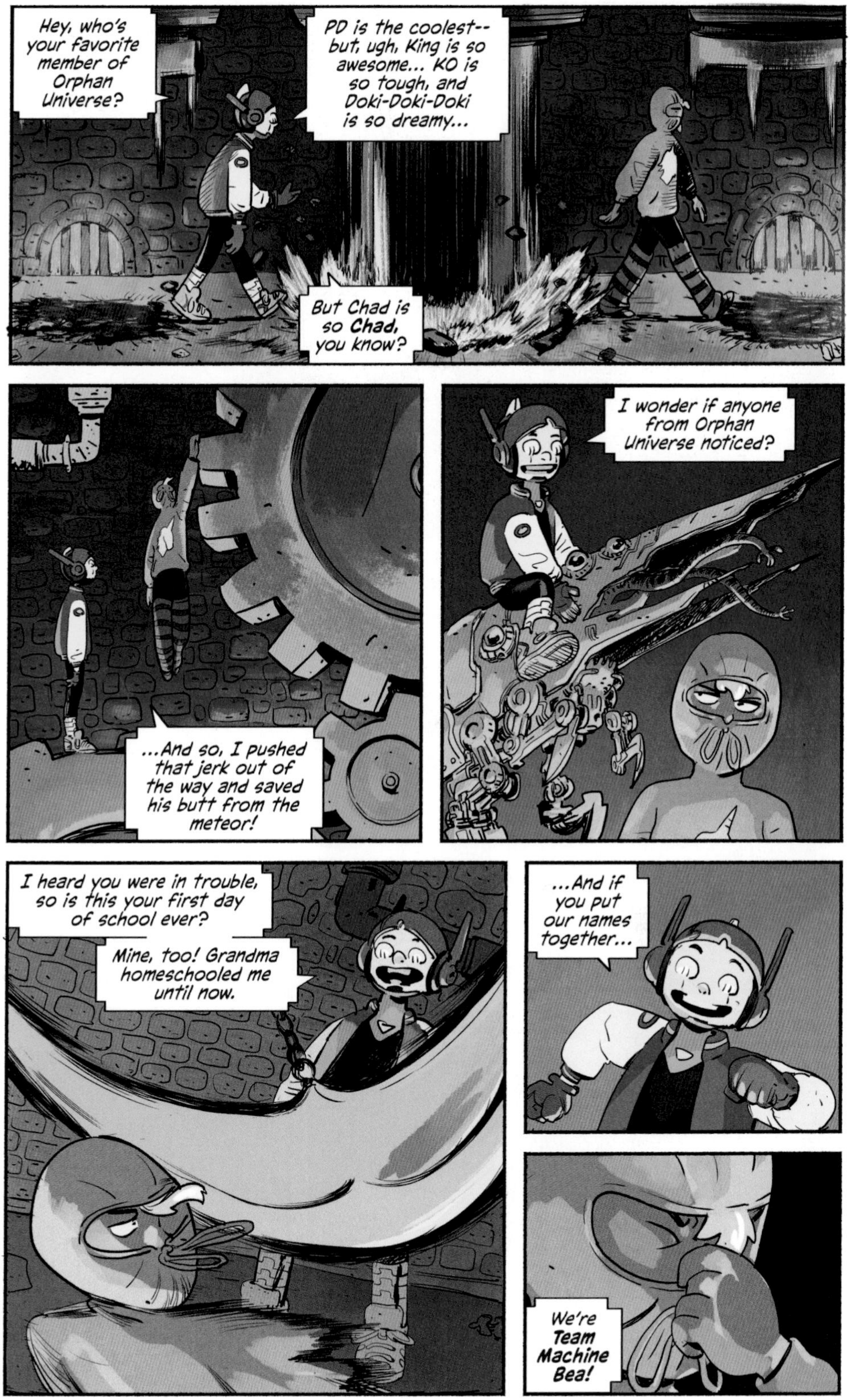

Hey, who's your favorite member of Orphan Universe?
PD is the coolest-- but, ugh, King is so awesome... KO is so tough, and Doki-Doki-Doki is so dreamy...
But Chad is so **Chad,** you know?
...And so, I pushed that jerk out of the way and saved his butt from the meteor!
I wonder if anyone from Orphan Universe noticed?
I heard you were in trouble, so is this your first day of school ever?
Mine, too! Grandma homeschooled me until now.
...And if you put our names together...
We're **Team Machine Bea!**

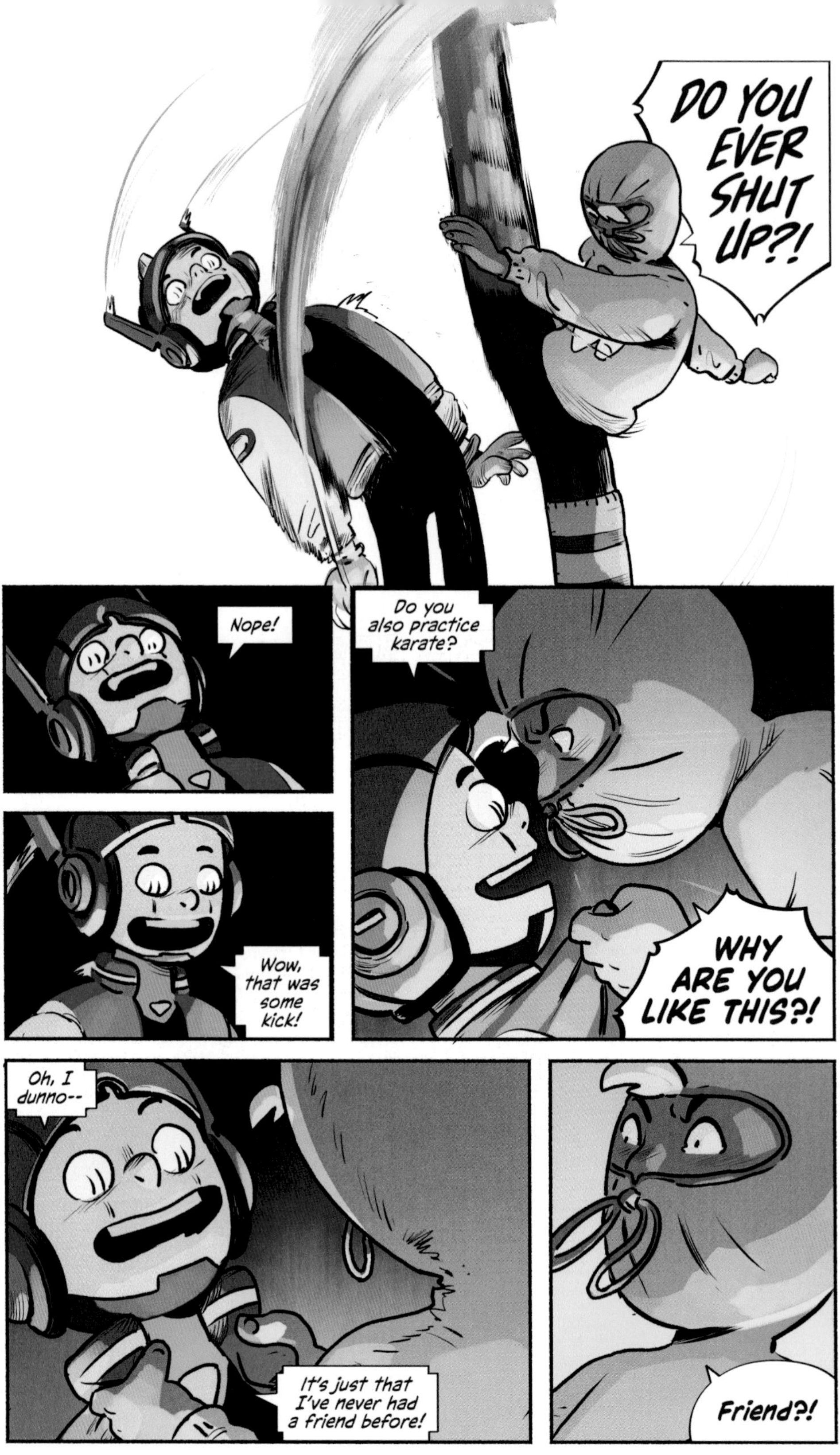
DO YOU EVER SHUT UP?!
Nope!
Do you also practice karate?
Wow, that was some kick!
WHY ARE YOU LIKE THIS?!
Oh, I dunno--
It's just that I've never had a friend before!
Friend?!

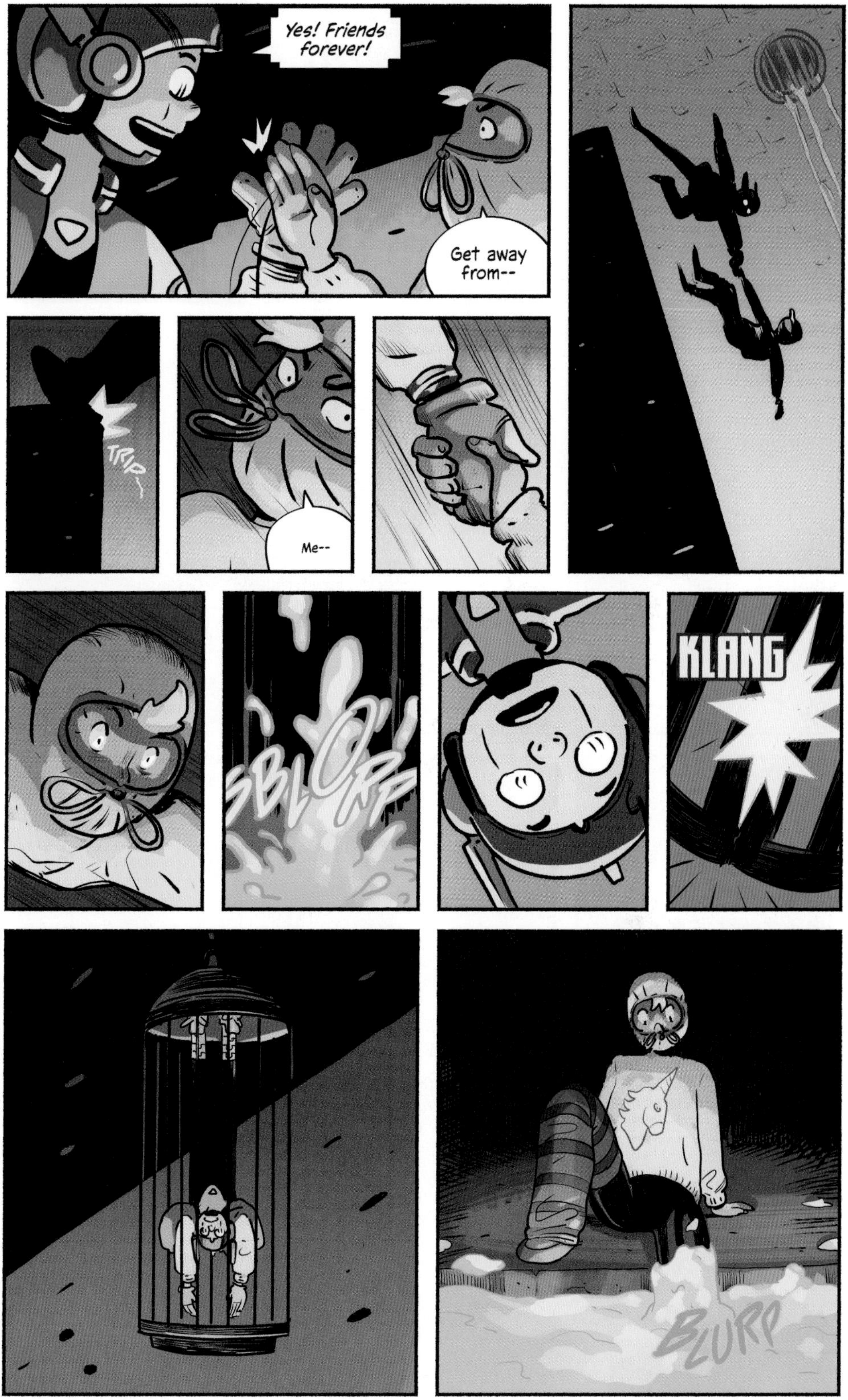
Yes! Friends forever!
Get away from--
TRIP~
Me--
SBLORP
KLANG
BLURP

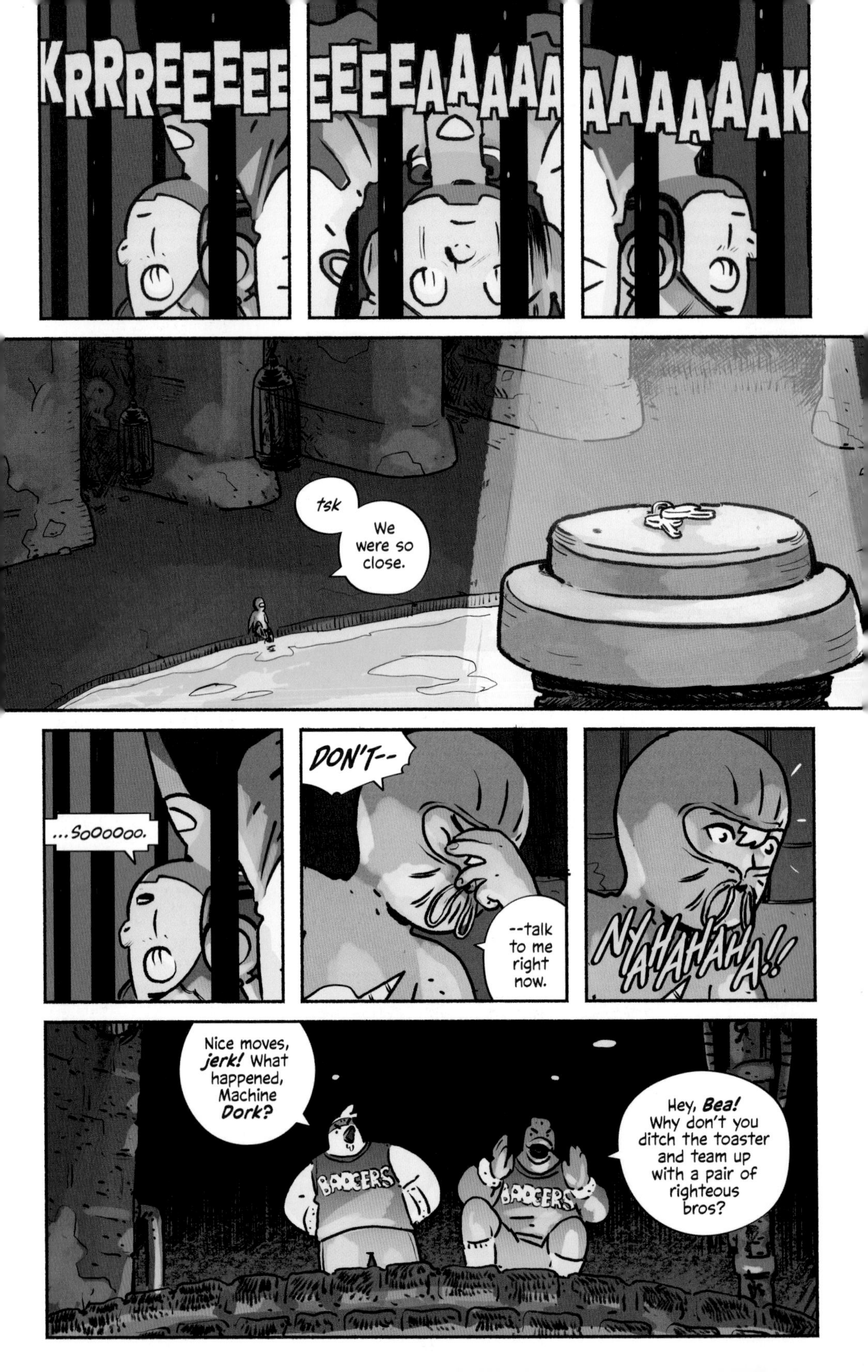
KRRREEEEE
EEEEAAAAA
AAAAAAK
tsk
We were so close.
...SOOOOOO.
DON'T--
--talk to me right now.
NYAHAHAHAHA!!
Nice moves, *jerk!* What happened, Machine *Dork?*
Hey, *Bea!* Why don't you ditch the toaster and team up with a pair of righteous bros?
BADGERS
BADGERS

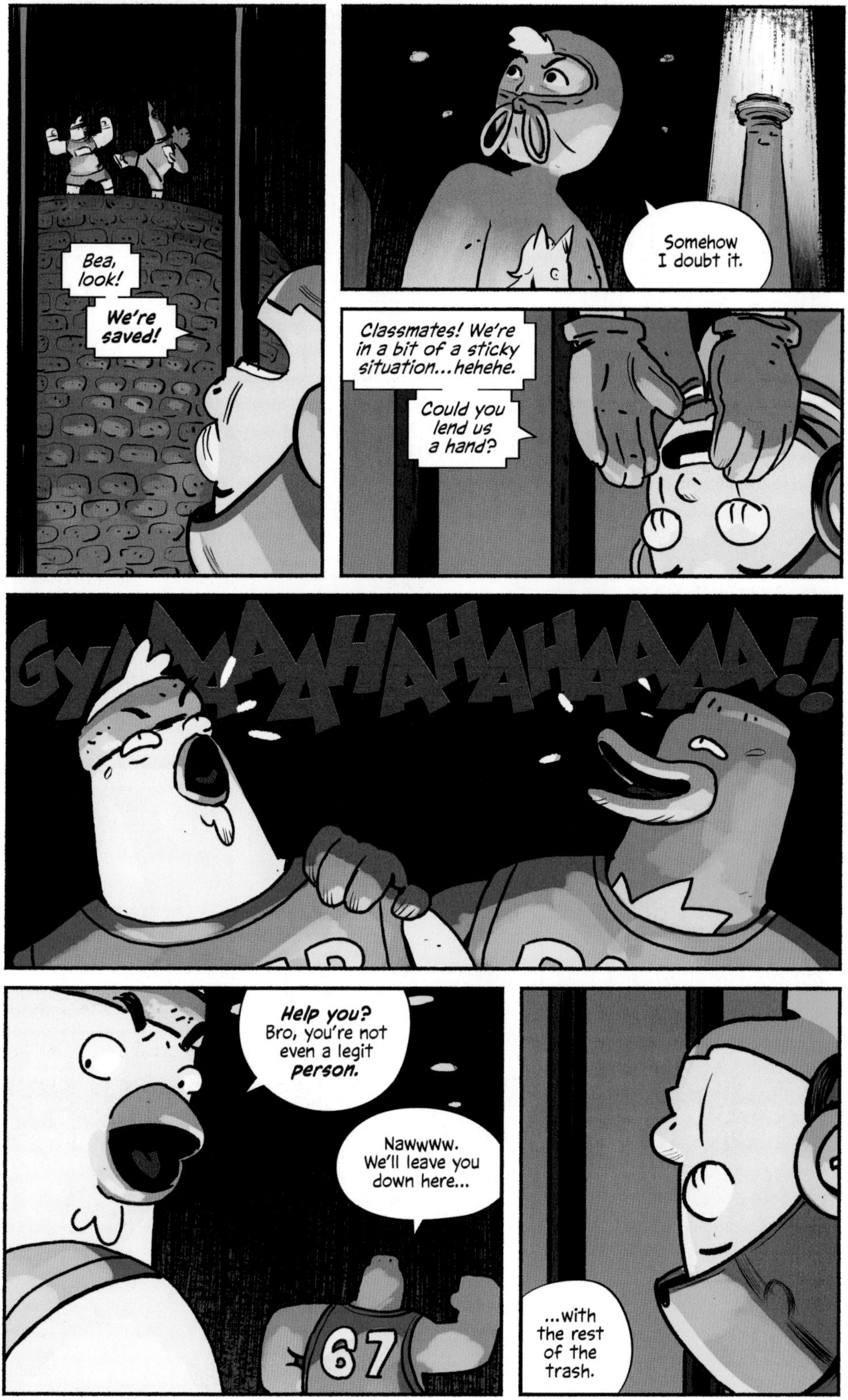
Bea, look!
We're saved!
Somehow I doubt it.
Classmates! We're in a bit of a sticky situation...hehehe.
Could you lend us a hand?
GYAAAHAHAHAHAAAA!!
Help you? Bro, you're not even a legit person.
Nawwww. We'll leave you down here...
67
...with the rest of the trash.

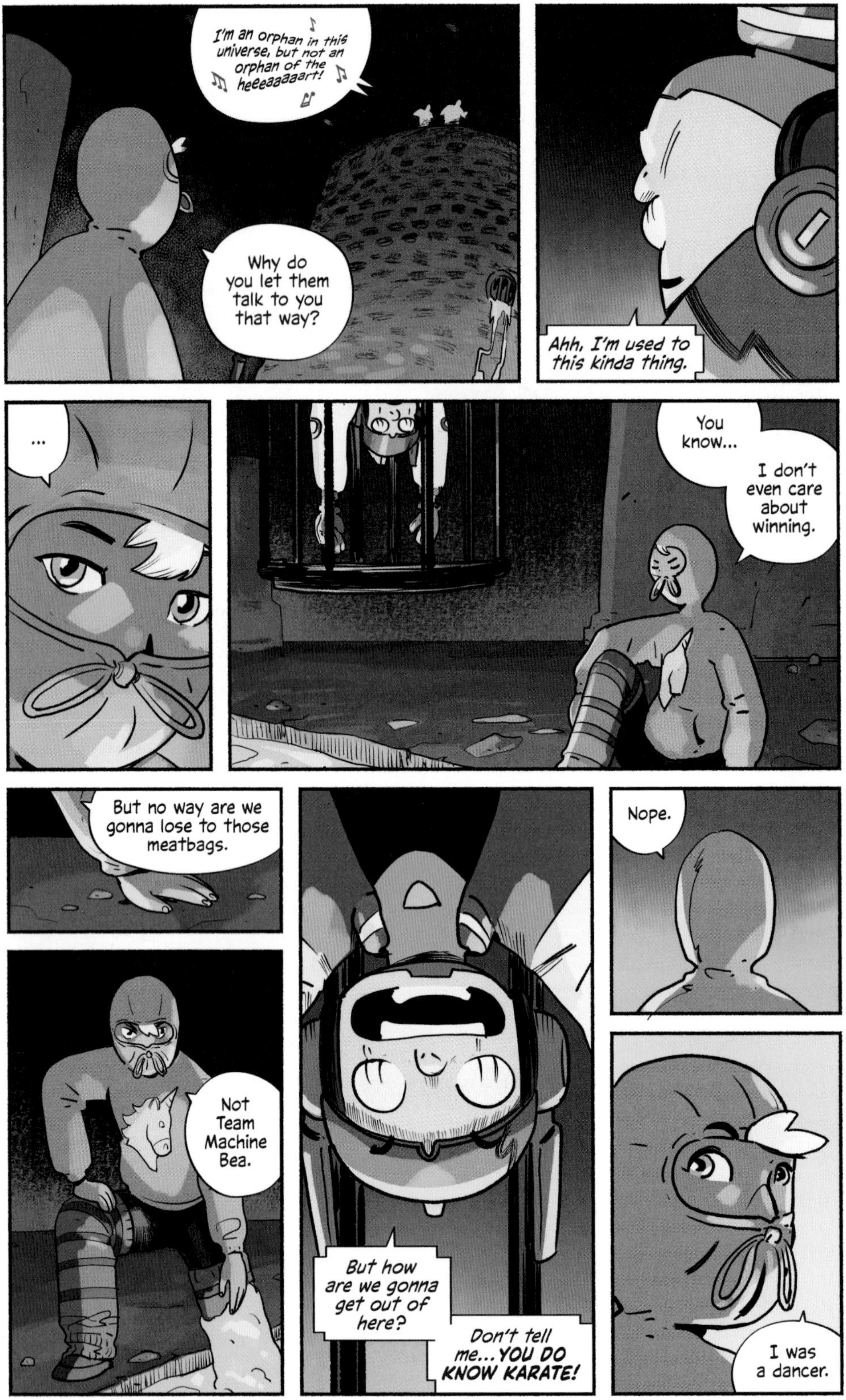
I'm an orphan in this universe, but not an orphan of the heeeaaaaart!
Why do you let them talk to you that way?
Ahh, I'm used to this kinda thing.
...
You know...
I don't even care about winning.
But no way are we gonna lose to those meatbags.
Not Team Machine Bea.
But how are we gonna get out of here?
Nope.
Don't tell me...YOU DO KNOW KARATE!
I was a dancer.

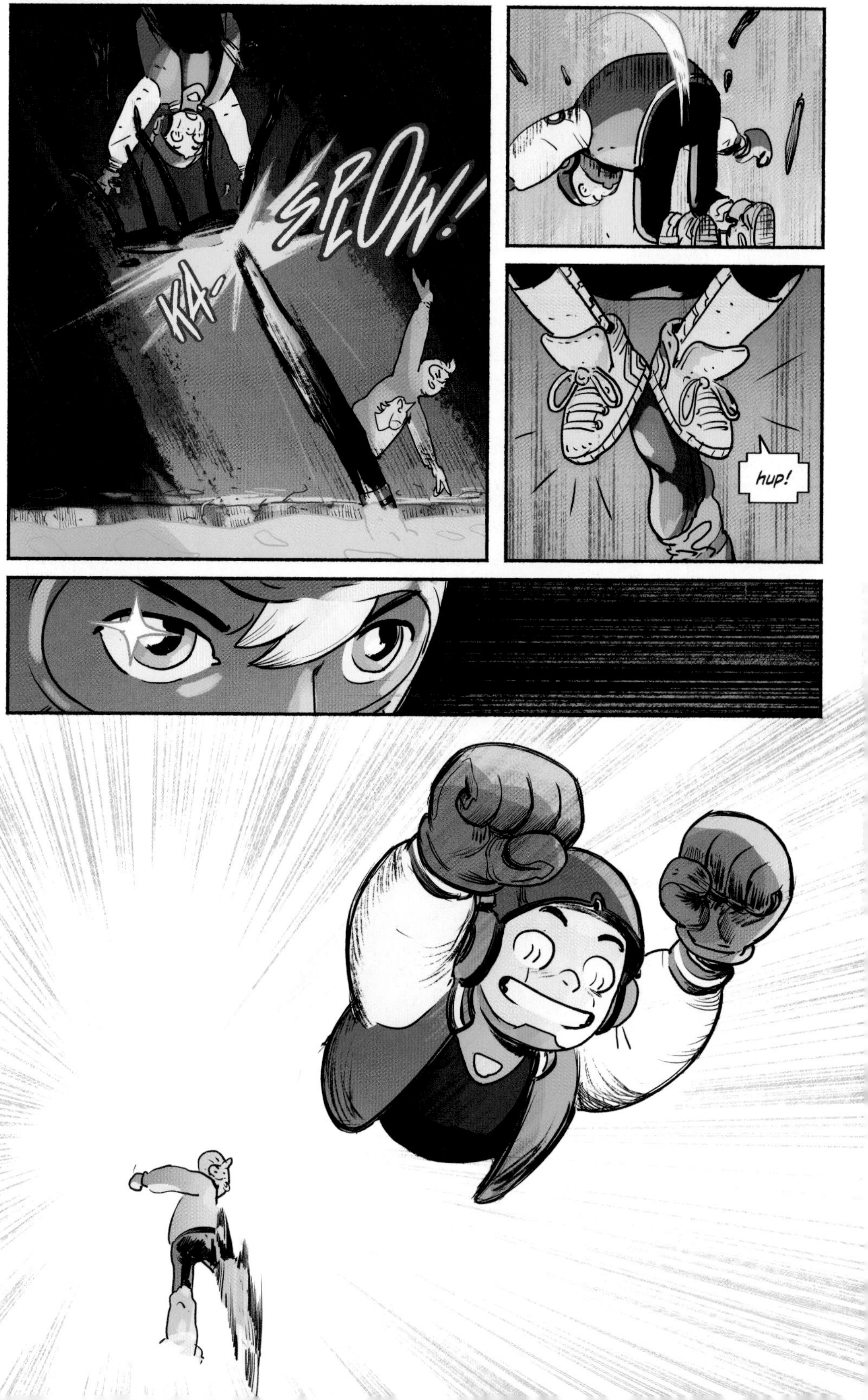
KA-
SPOW!
hup!

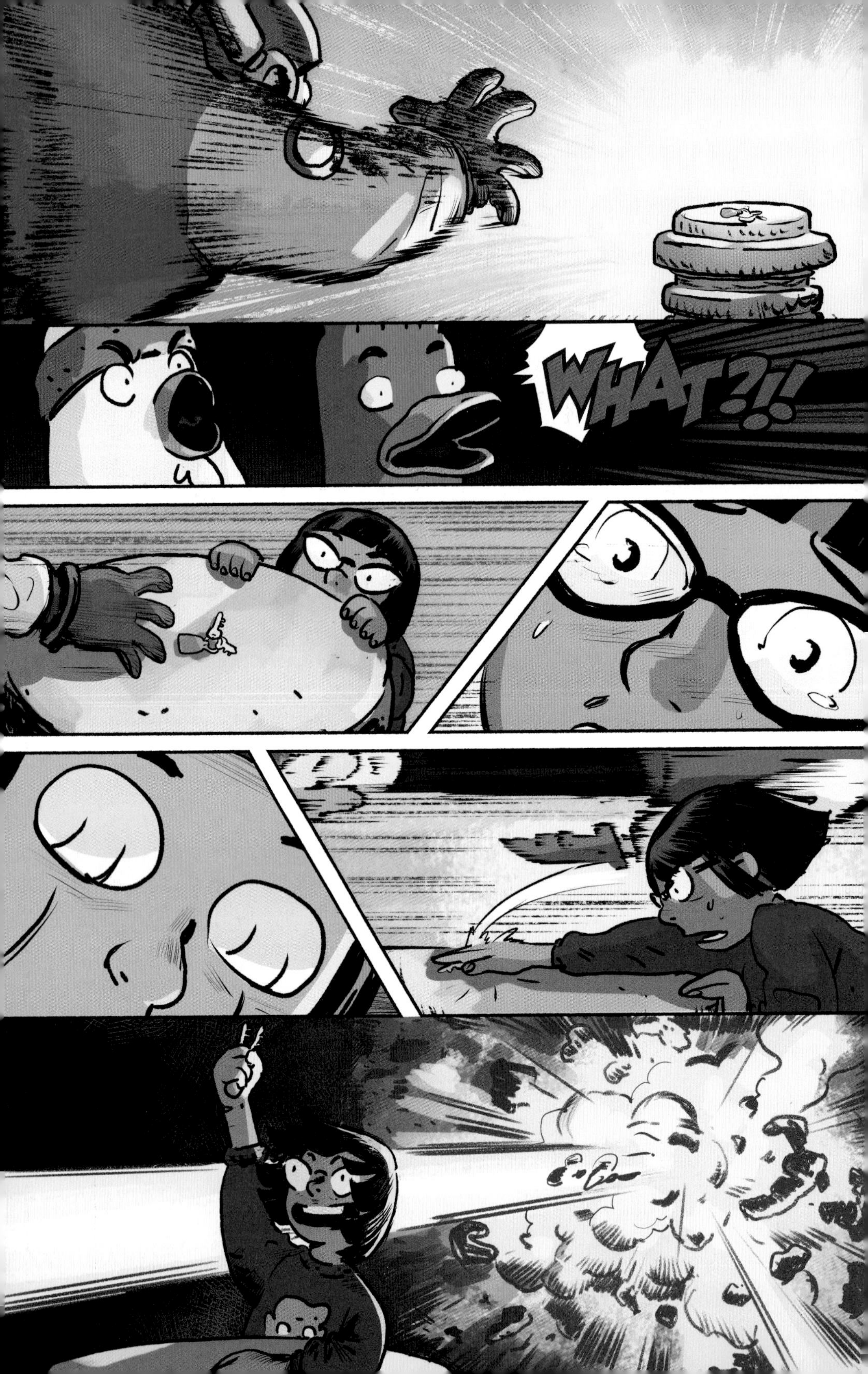
WHAT?!!

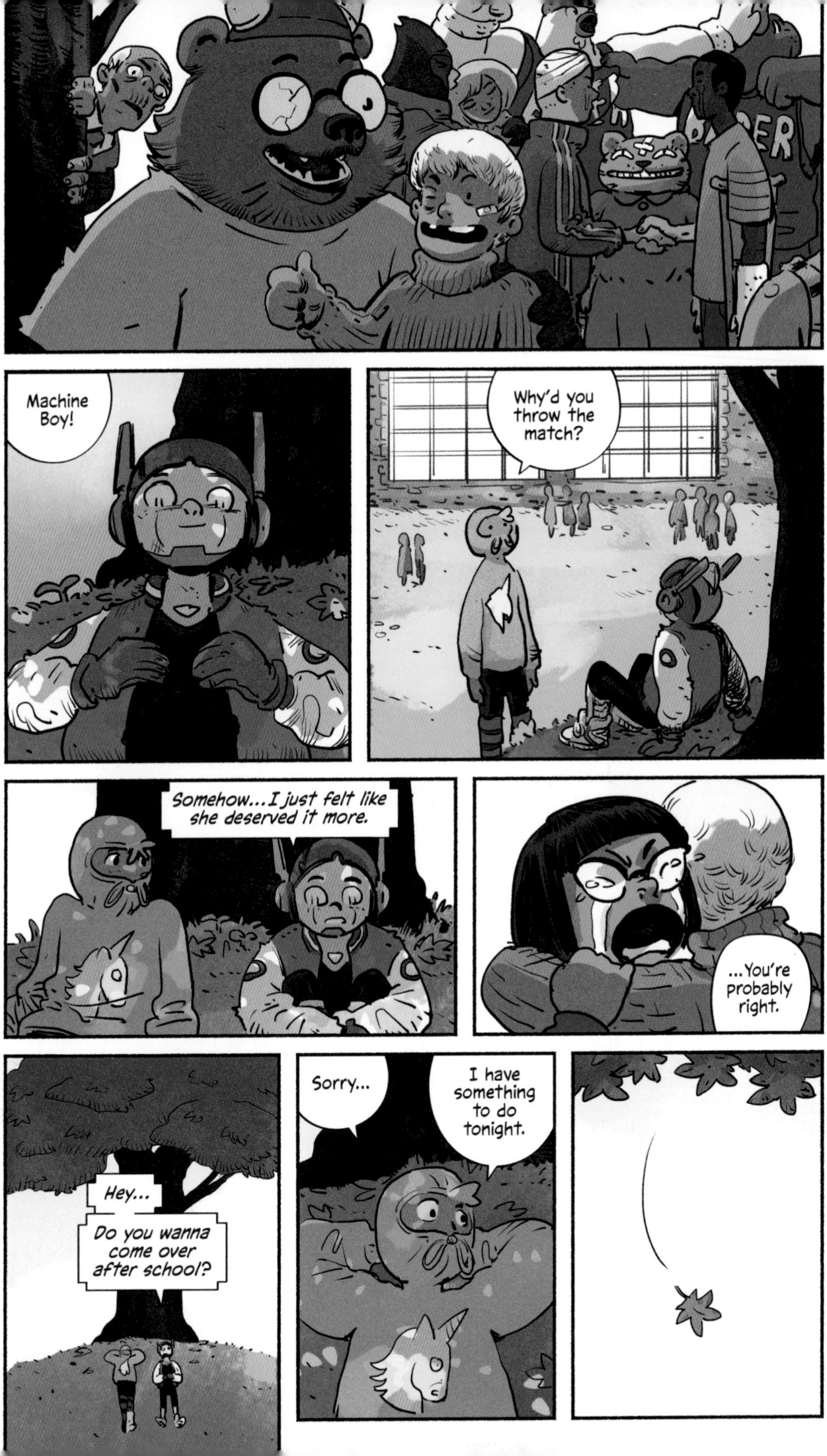
Machine Boy!
Why'd you throw the match?
Somehow... I just felt like she deserved it more.
...You're probably right.
Hey...
Do you wanna come over after school?
Sorry...
I have something to do tonight.

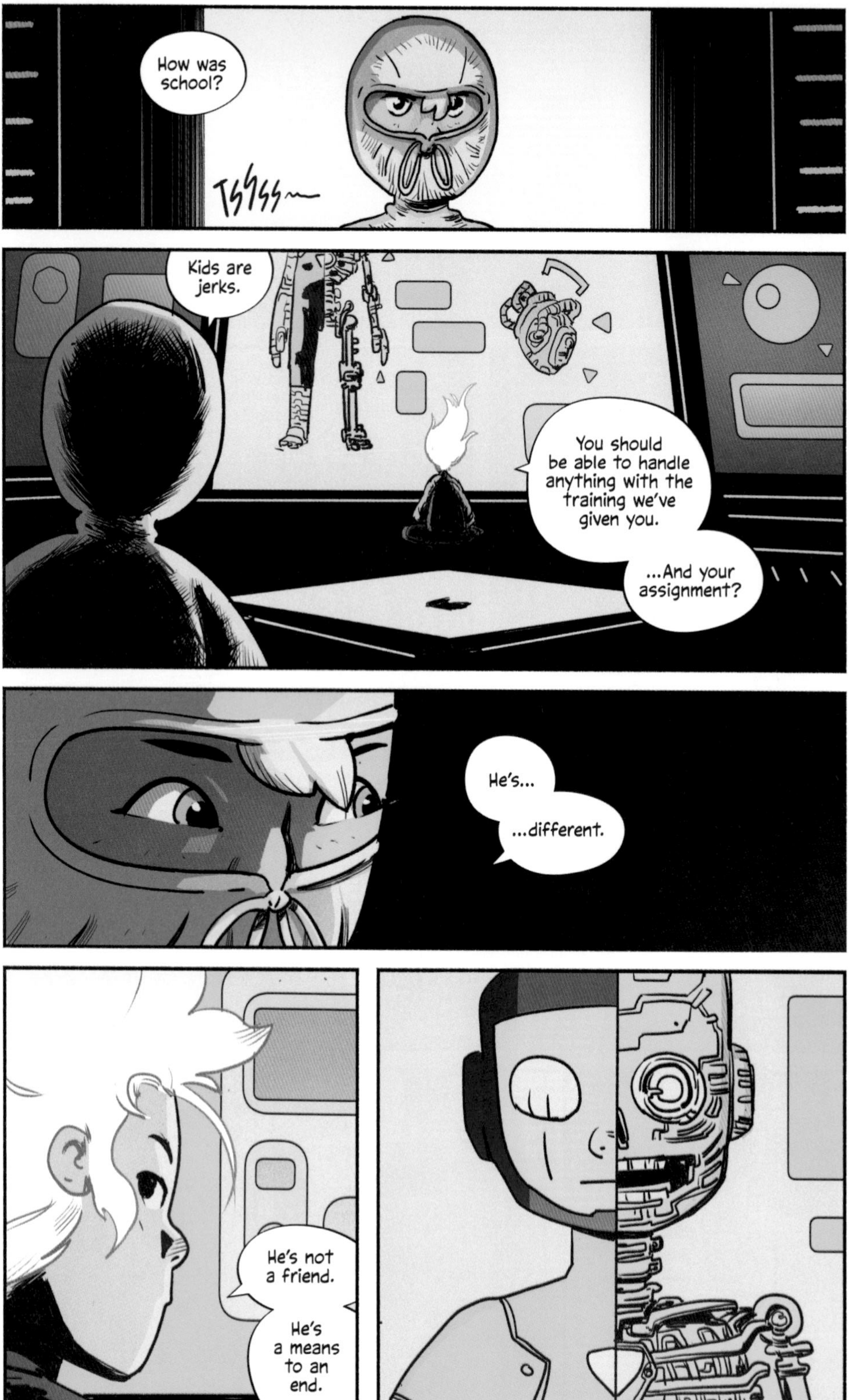
How was school?
TSSSS~
Kids are jerks.
You should be able to handle anything with the training we've given you.
...And your assignment?
He's...
...different.
He's not a friend.
He's a means to an end.

CHAPTER 5

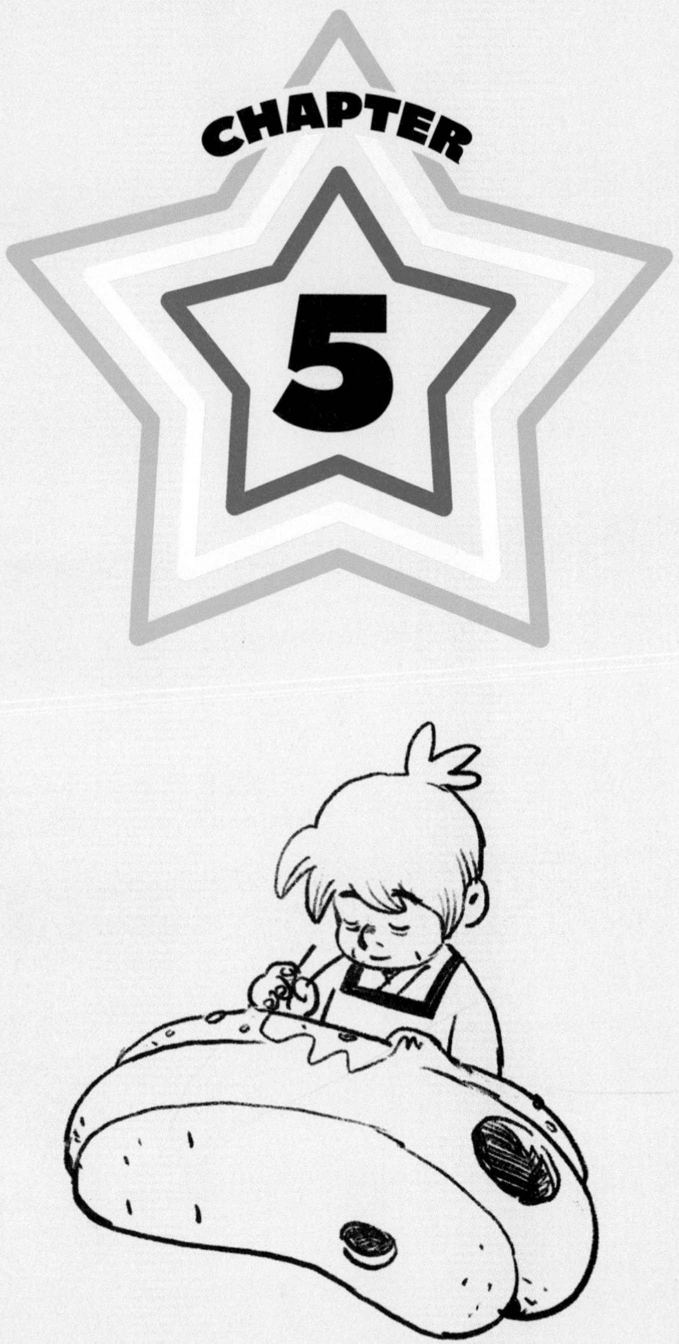

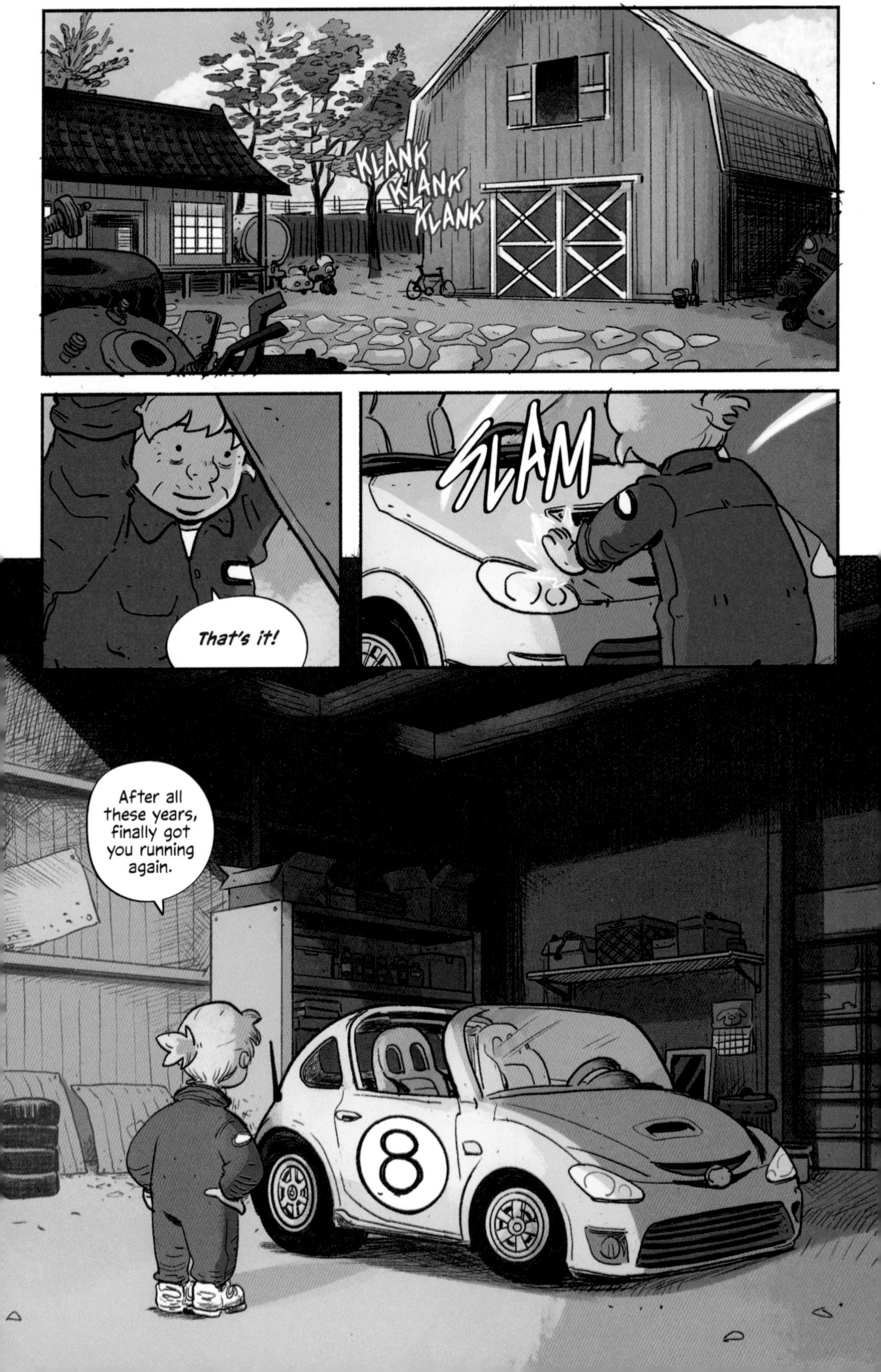
KLANK
K'LANK
KLANK
That's it!
SLAM
After all these years, finally got you running again.

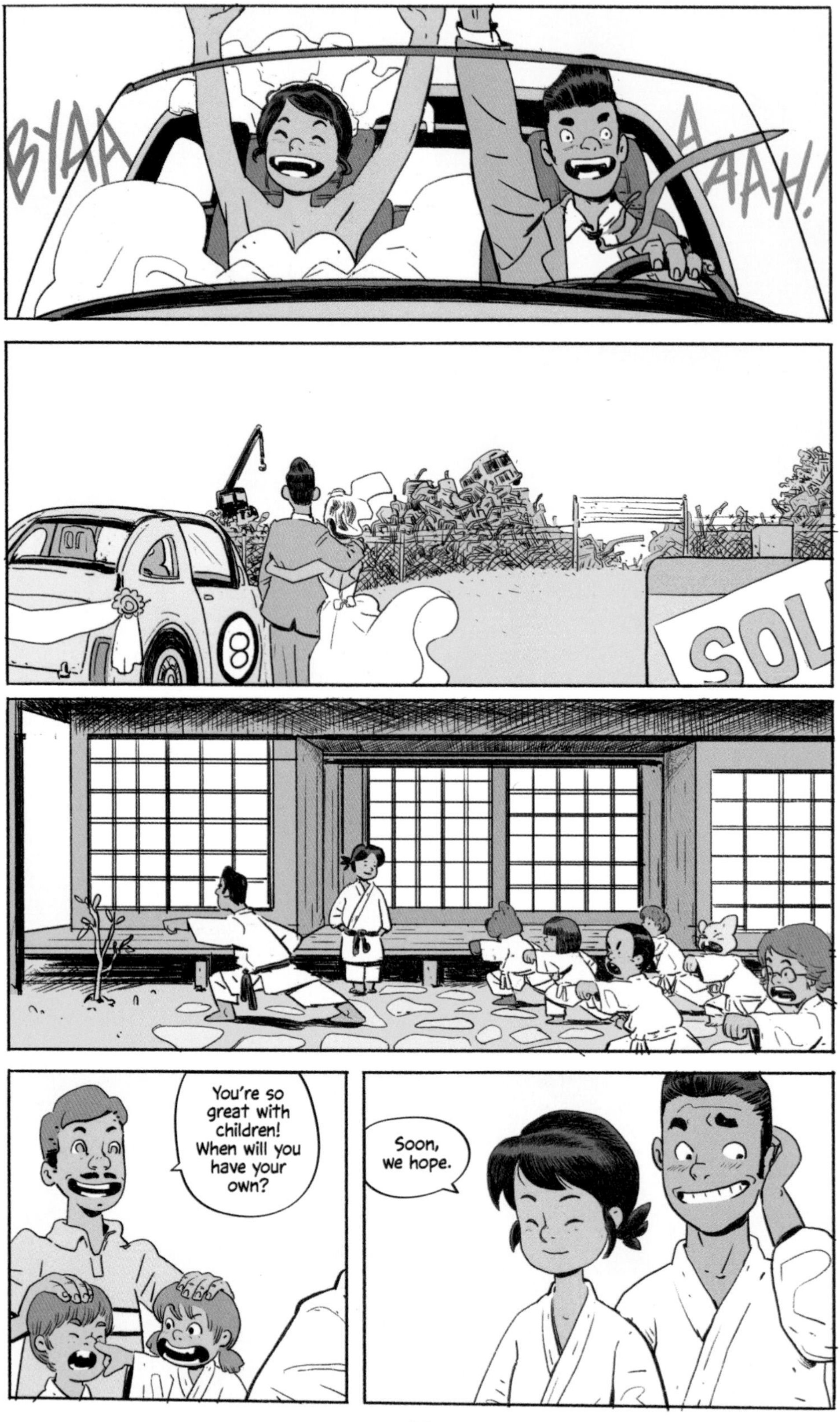
BYAA
AAAH!
SOL
You're so great with children! When will you have your own?
Soon, we hope.

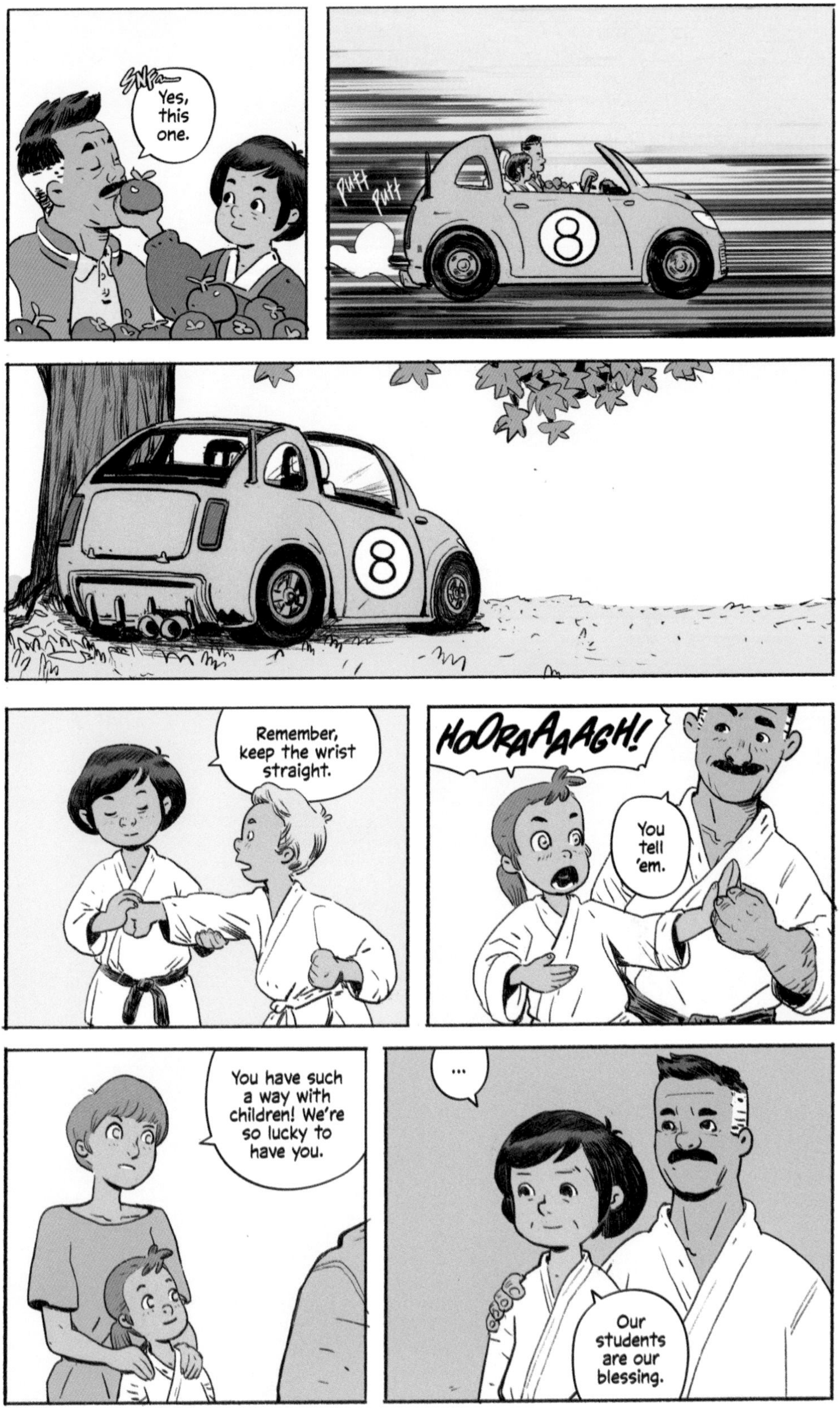

SNFa
Yes, this one.
Putt putt
Remember, keep the wrist straight.
HOORAAAAGH!
You tell 'em.
You have such a way with children! We're so lucky to have you.
...
Our students are our blessing.

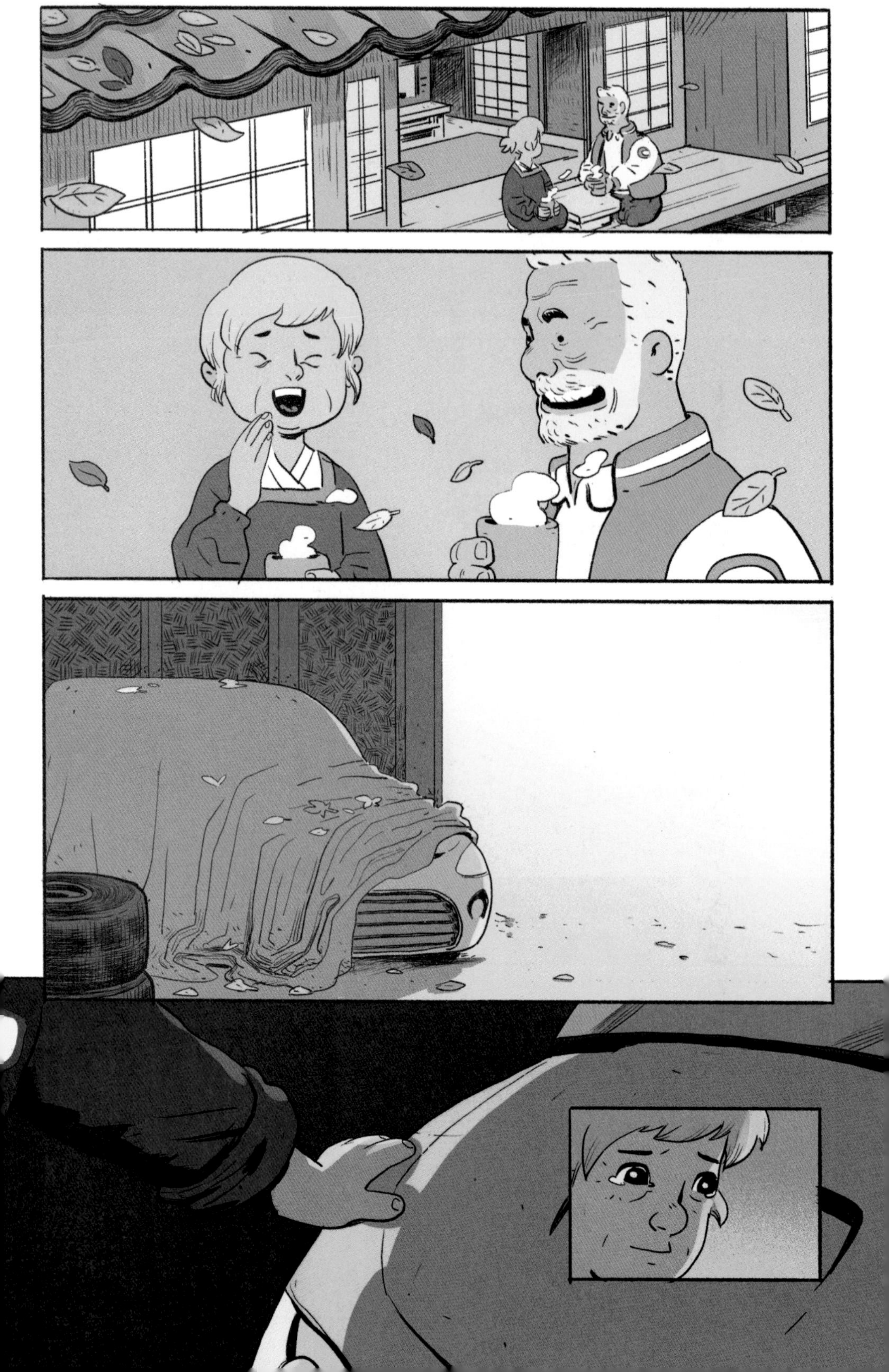

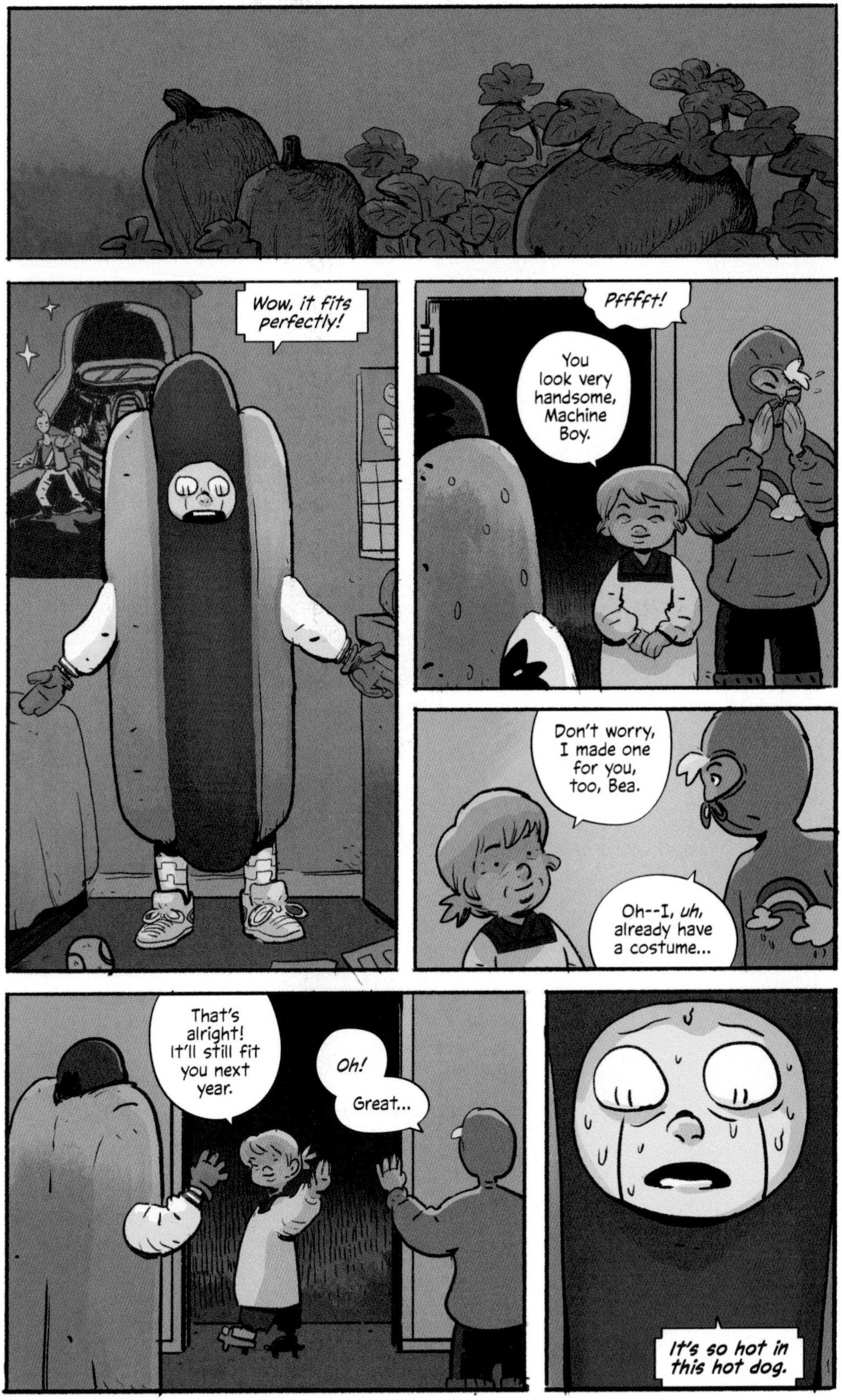
Wow, it fits perfectly!
Pfffft!
You look very handsome, Machine Boy.
Don't worry, I made one for you, too, Bea.
Oh--I, *uh*, already have a costume...
That's alright! It'll still fit you next year.
Oh!
Great...
It's so hot in this hot dog.

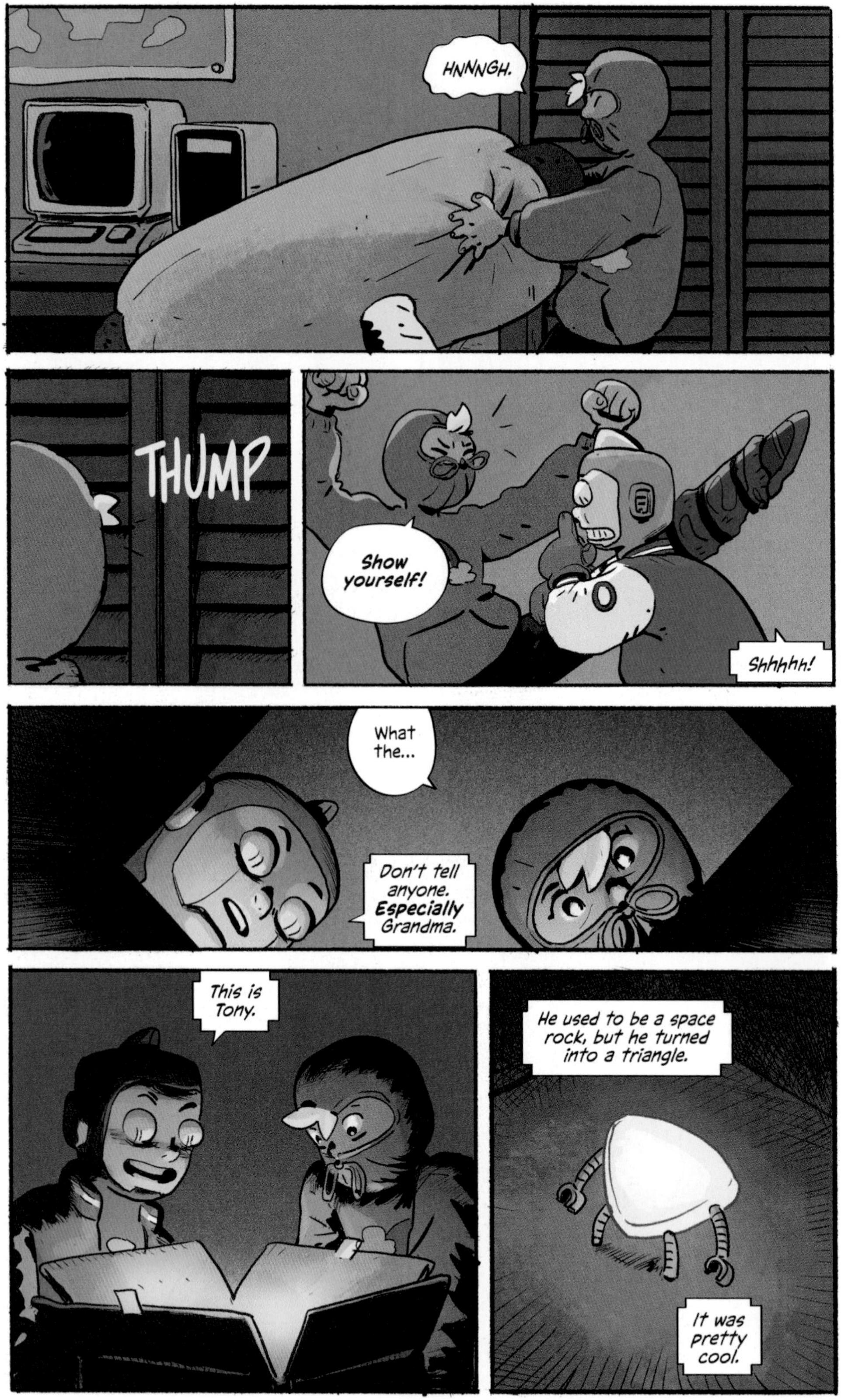
HNNNGH.
THUMP
Show yourself!
Shhhhh!
What the...
Don't tell anyone. **Especially** Grandma.
This is Tony.
He used to be a space rock, but he turned into a triangle.
It was pretty cool.

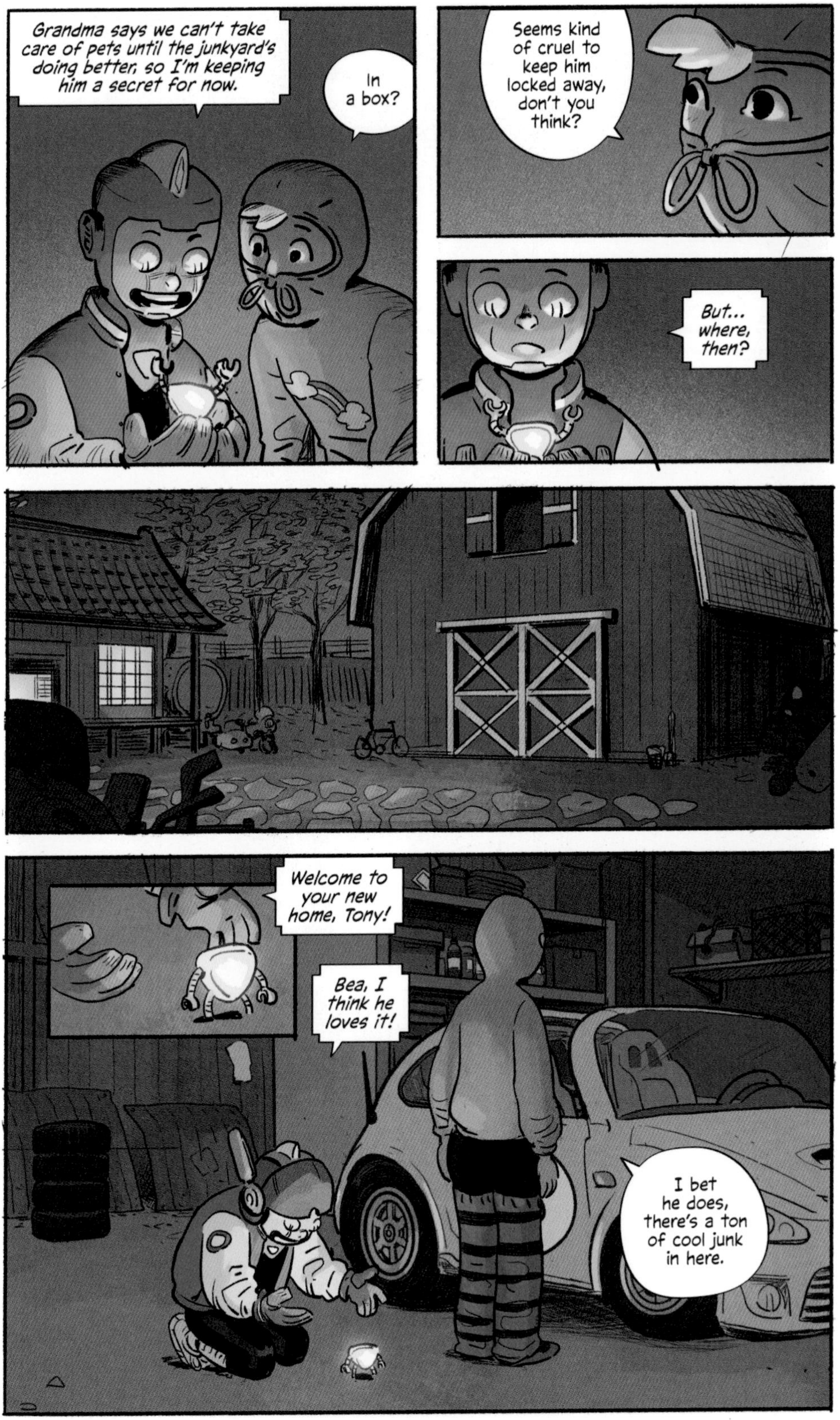

Grandma says we can't take care of pets until the junkyard's doing better, so I'm keeping him a secret for now.
In a box?
Seems kind of cruel to keep him locked away, don't you think?
But... where, then?
Welcome to your new home, Tony!
Bea, I think he loves it!
I bet he does, there's a ton of cool junk in here.

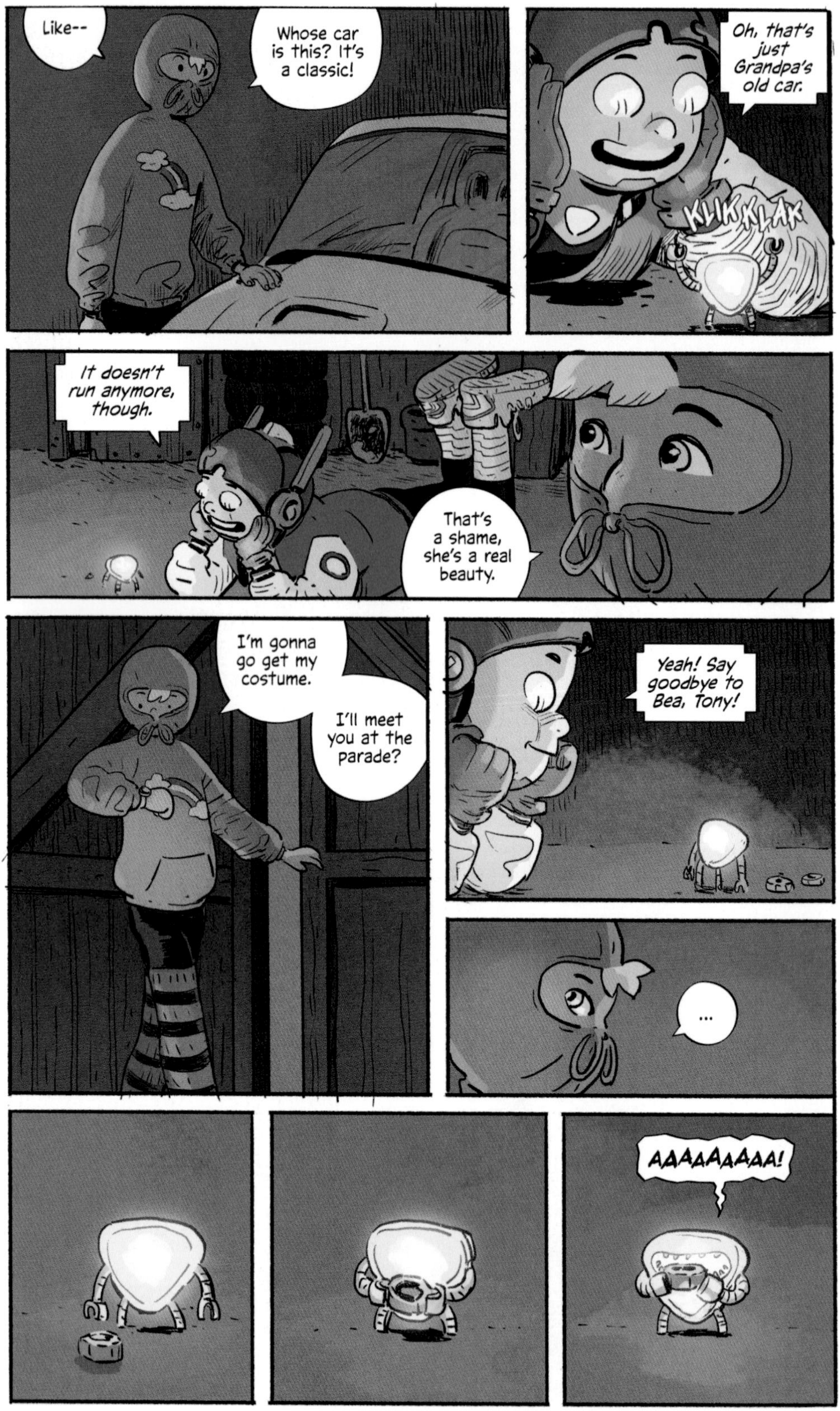
Like--
Whose car is this? It's a classic!
Oh, that's just Grandpa's old car.
KLIK KLAK
It doesn't run anymore, though.
That's a shame, she's a real beauty.
I'm gonna go get my costume.
I'll meet you at the parade?
Yeah! Say goodbye to Bea, Tony!
...
AAAAAAAAA!

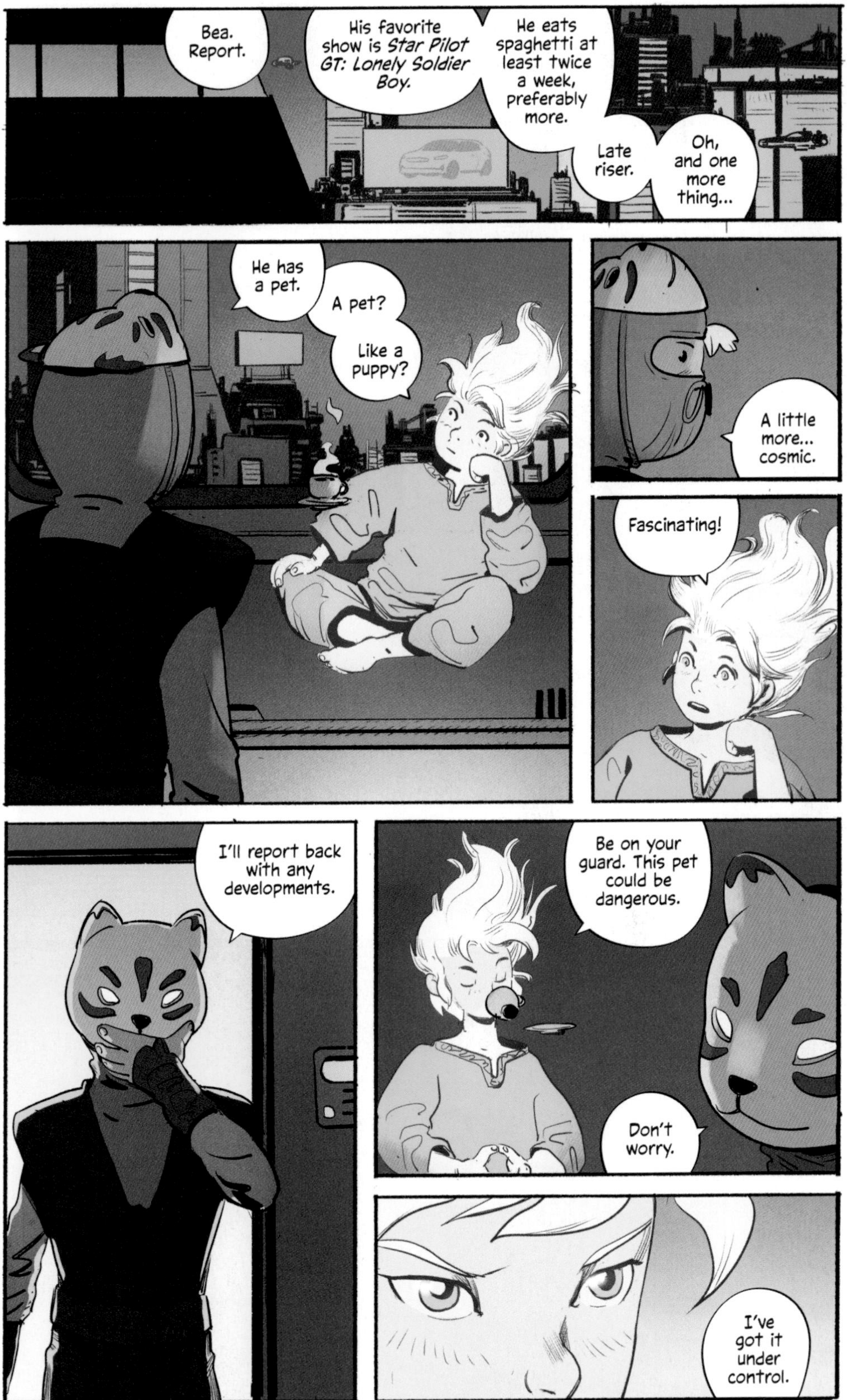

Bea. Report.
His favorite show is *Star Pilot GT: Lonely Soldier Boy.*
He eats spaghetti at least twice a week, preferably more.
Late riser.
Oh, and one more thing...
He has a pet.
A pet?
Like a puppy?
A little more... cosmic.
Fascinating!
I'll report back with any developments.
Be on your guard. This pet could be dangerous.
Don't worry.
I've got it under control.

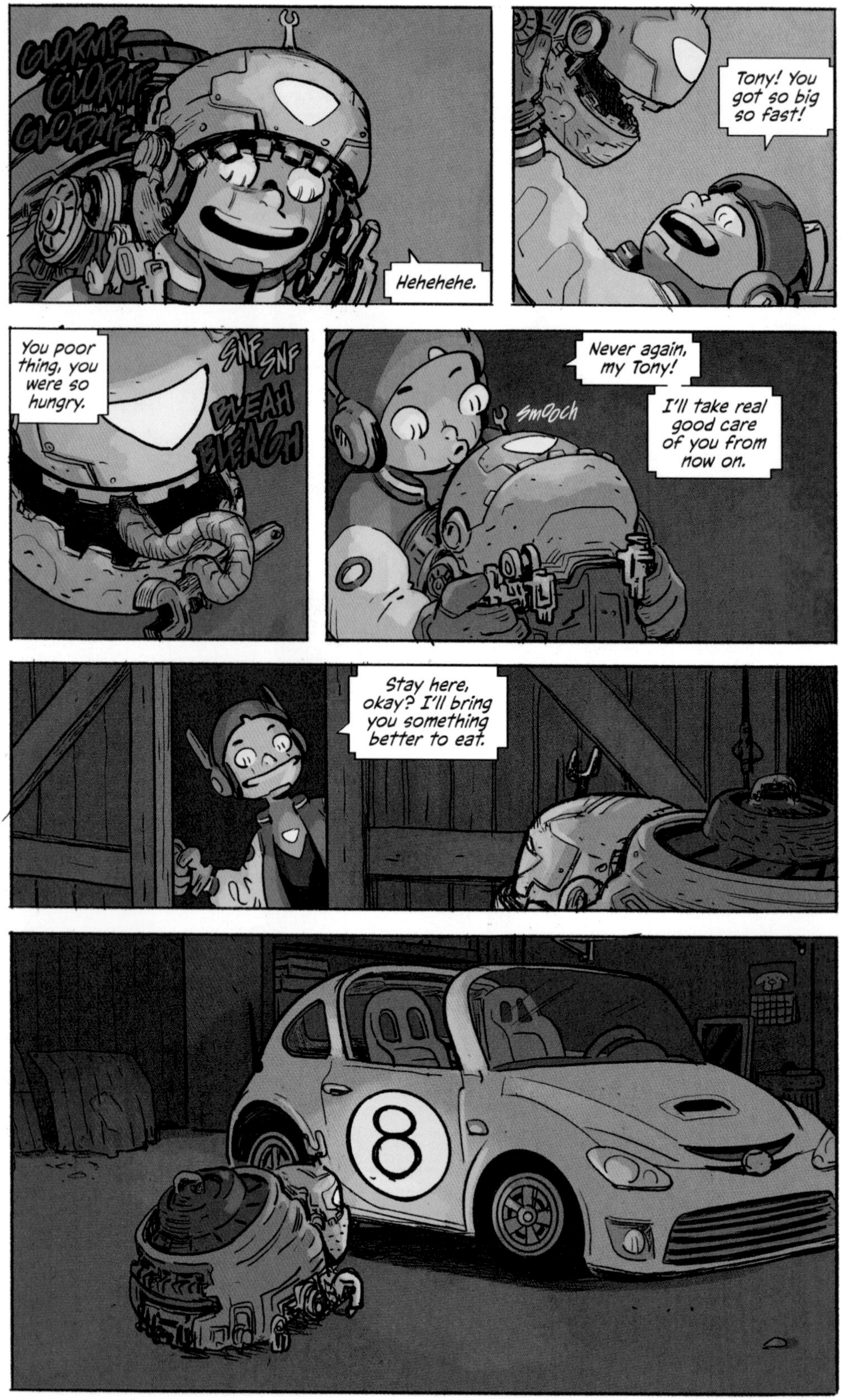
GLORMF GLORMF GLORMF
Hehehehe.
Tony! You got so big so fast!
You poor thing, you were so hungry.
SNF SNF
BLEAH BLEACH
Never again, my Tony!
SMOOCH
I'll take real good care of you from now on.
Stay here, okay? I'll bring you something better to eat.
8

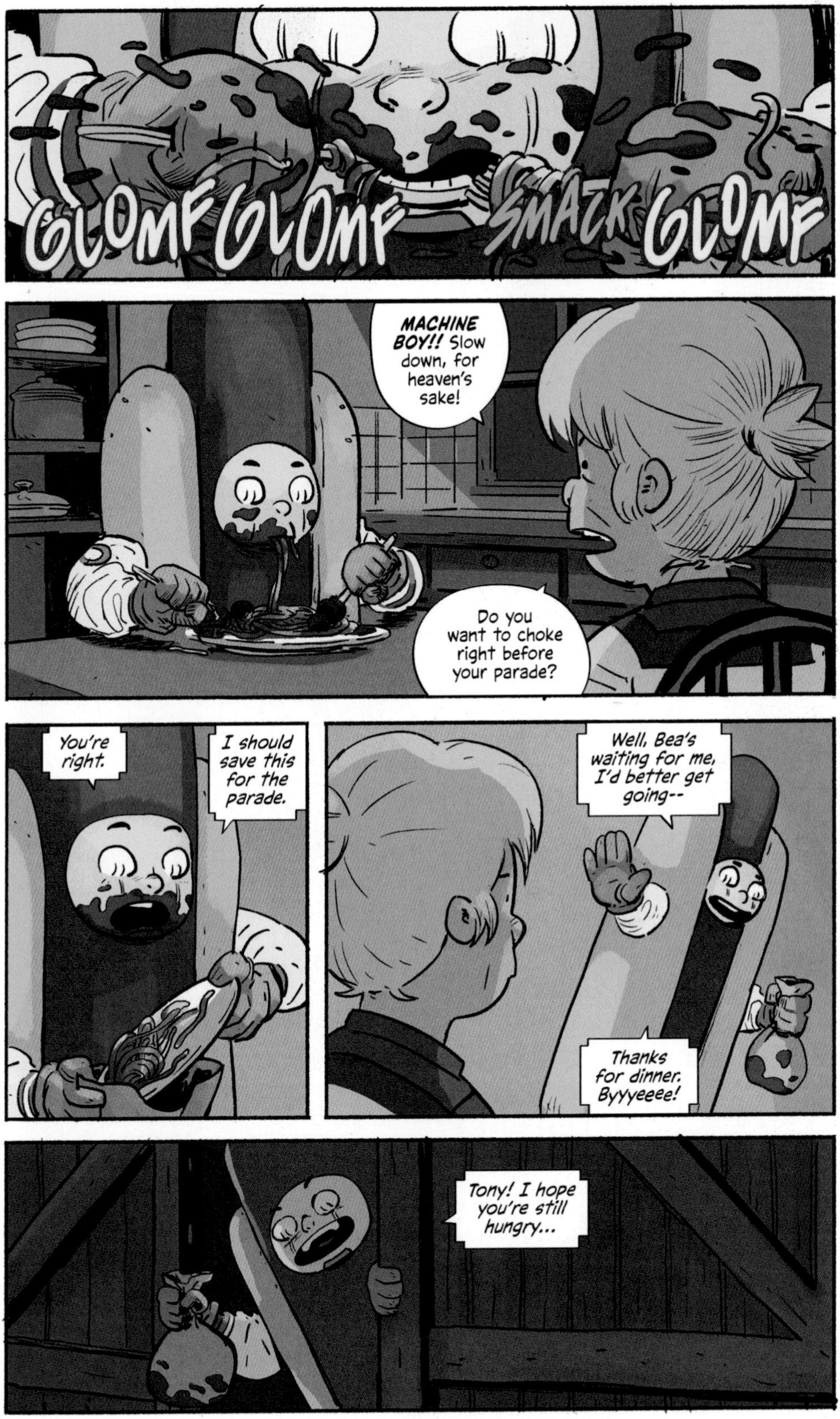
GLOMF GLOMF SMACK GLOMF
MACHINE BOY!! Slow down, for heaven's sake!
Do you want to choke right before your parade?
You're right.
I should save this for the parade.
Well, Bea's waiting for me, I'd better get going--
Thanks for dinner. Byyyeeee!
Tony! I hope you're still hungry...

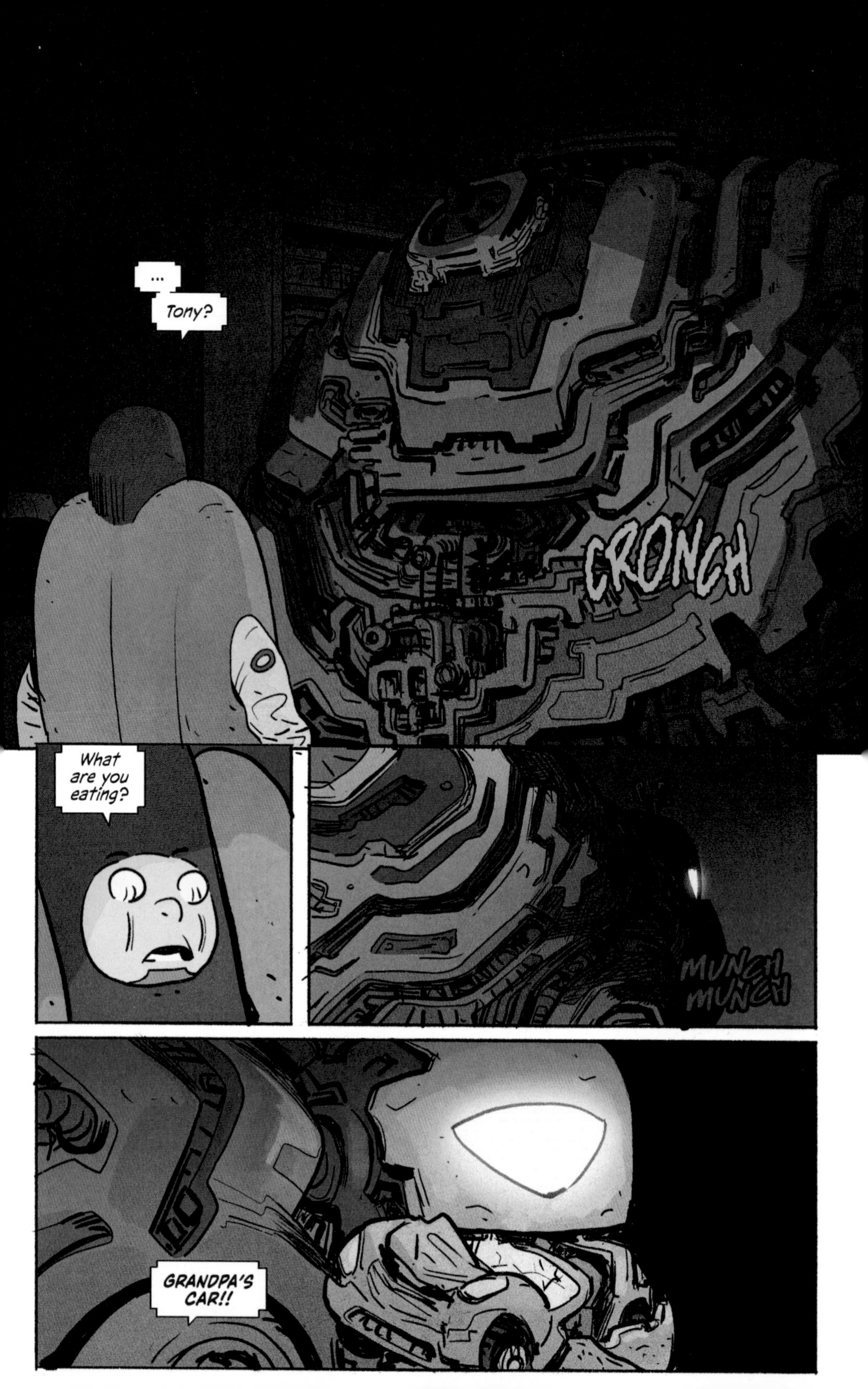
...
Tony?
CRONCH
What are you eating?
MUNCH MUNCH
GRANDPA'S CAR!!

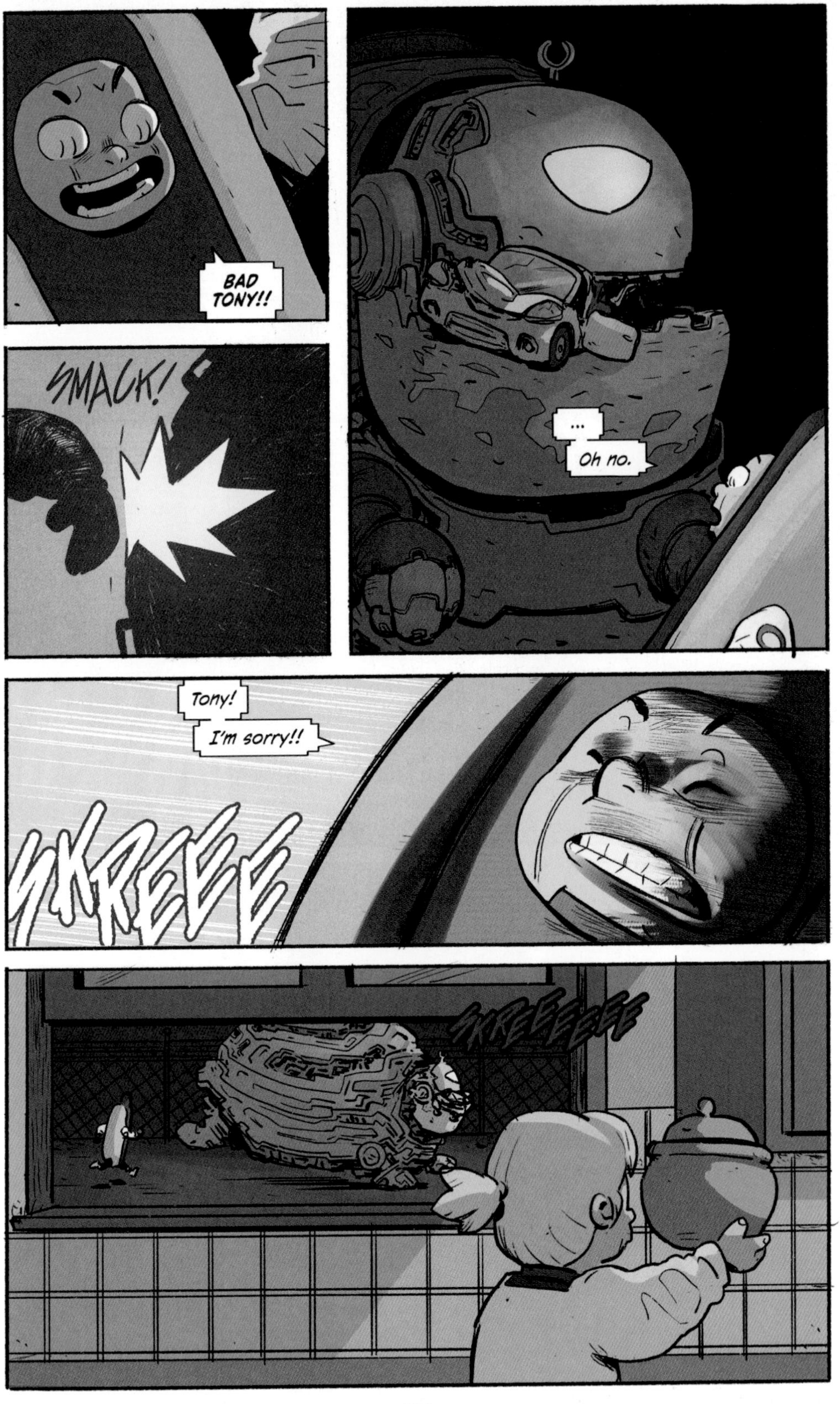

BAD TONY!!
SMACK!
...
Oh no.
Tony!
I'm sorry!!
SKREEE

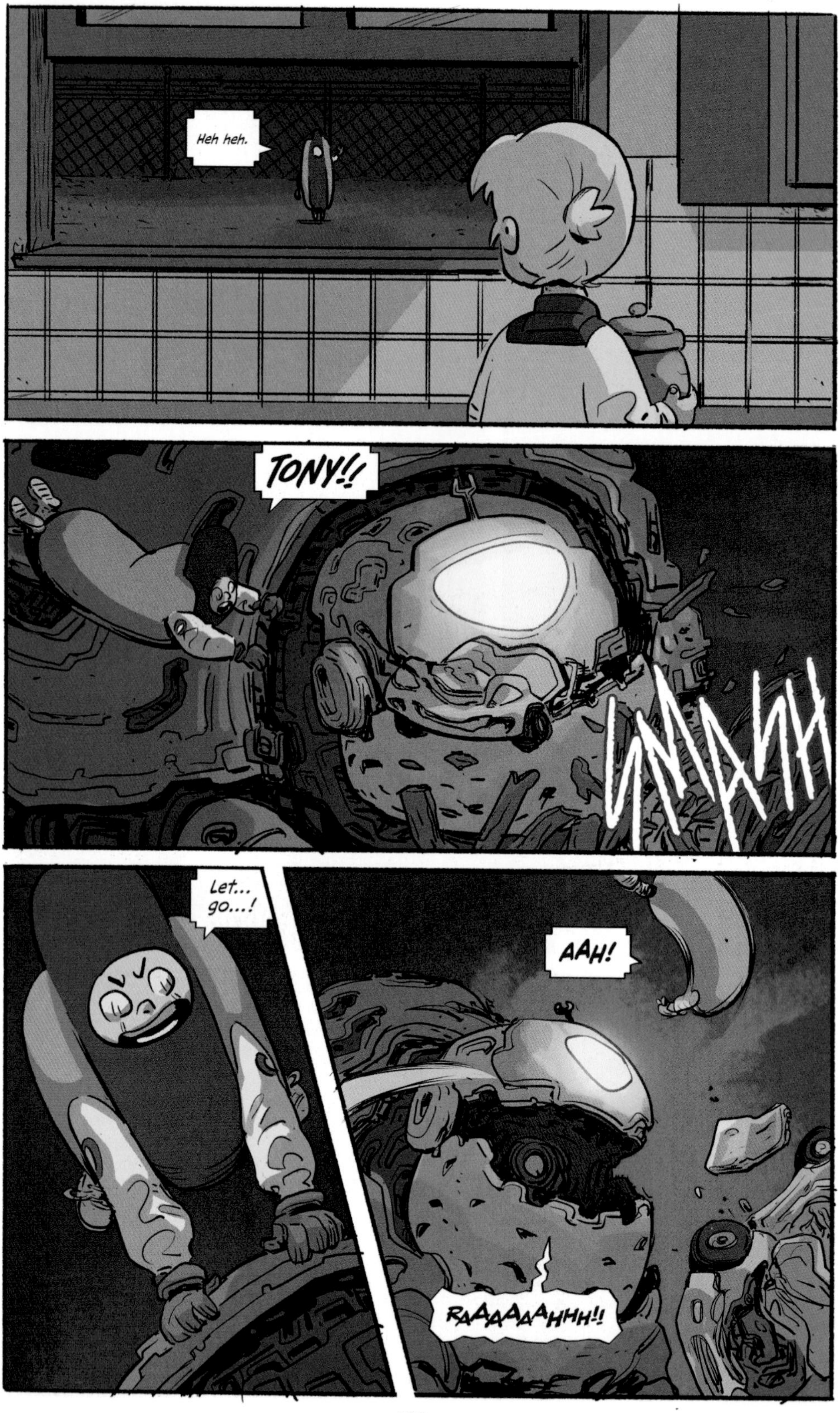
Heh heh.
TONY!!
Let...
go...!
AAH!
RAAAAAAHHH!!

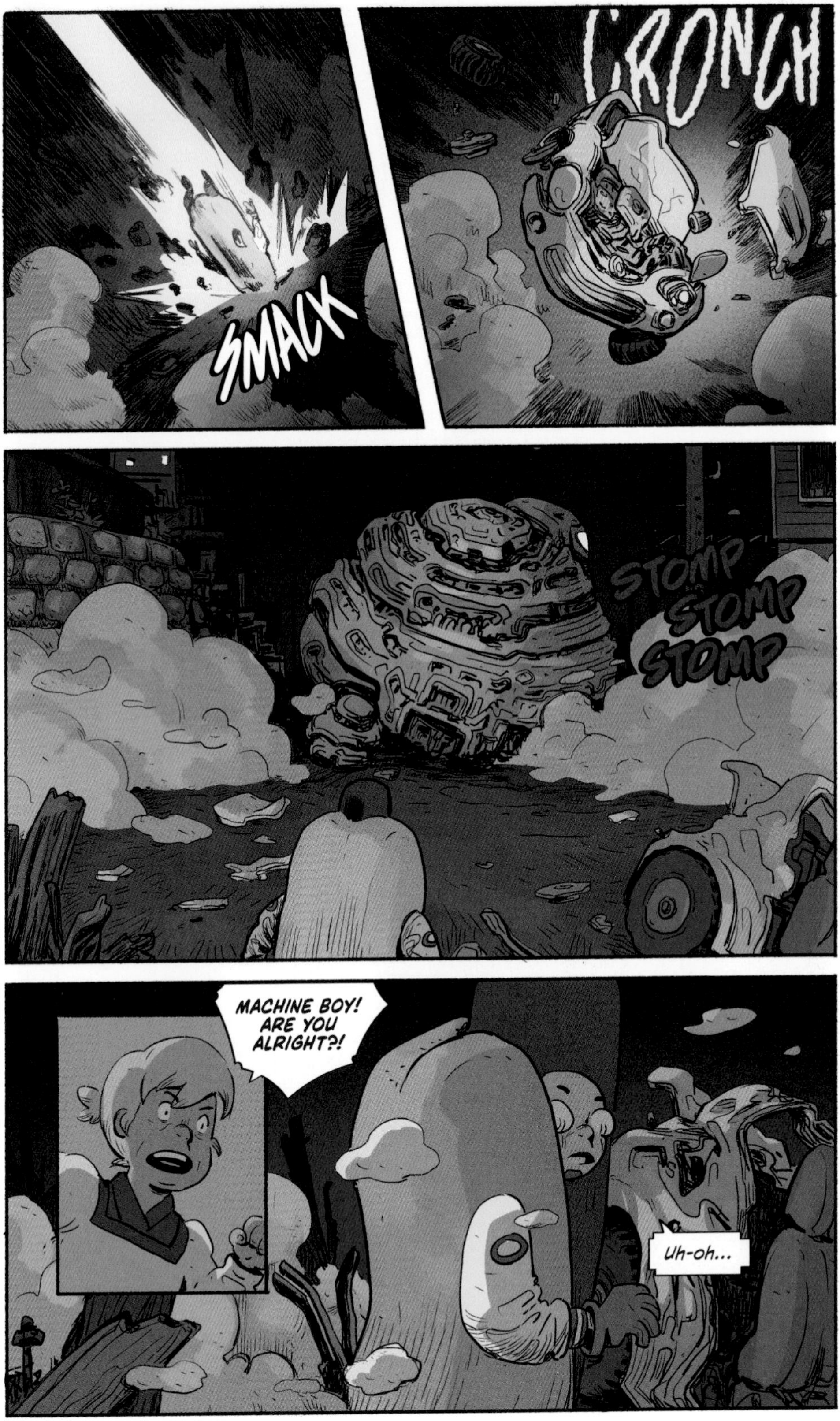
SMACK
CRONCH
STOMP
STOMP
STOMP
MACHINE BOY! ARE YOU ALRIGHT?!
Uh-oh...

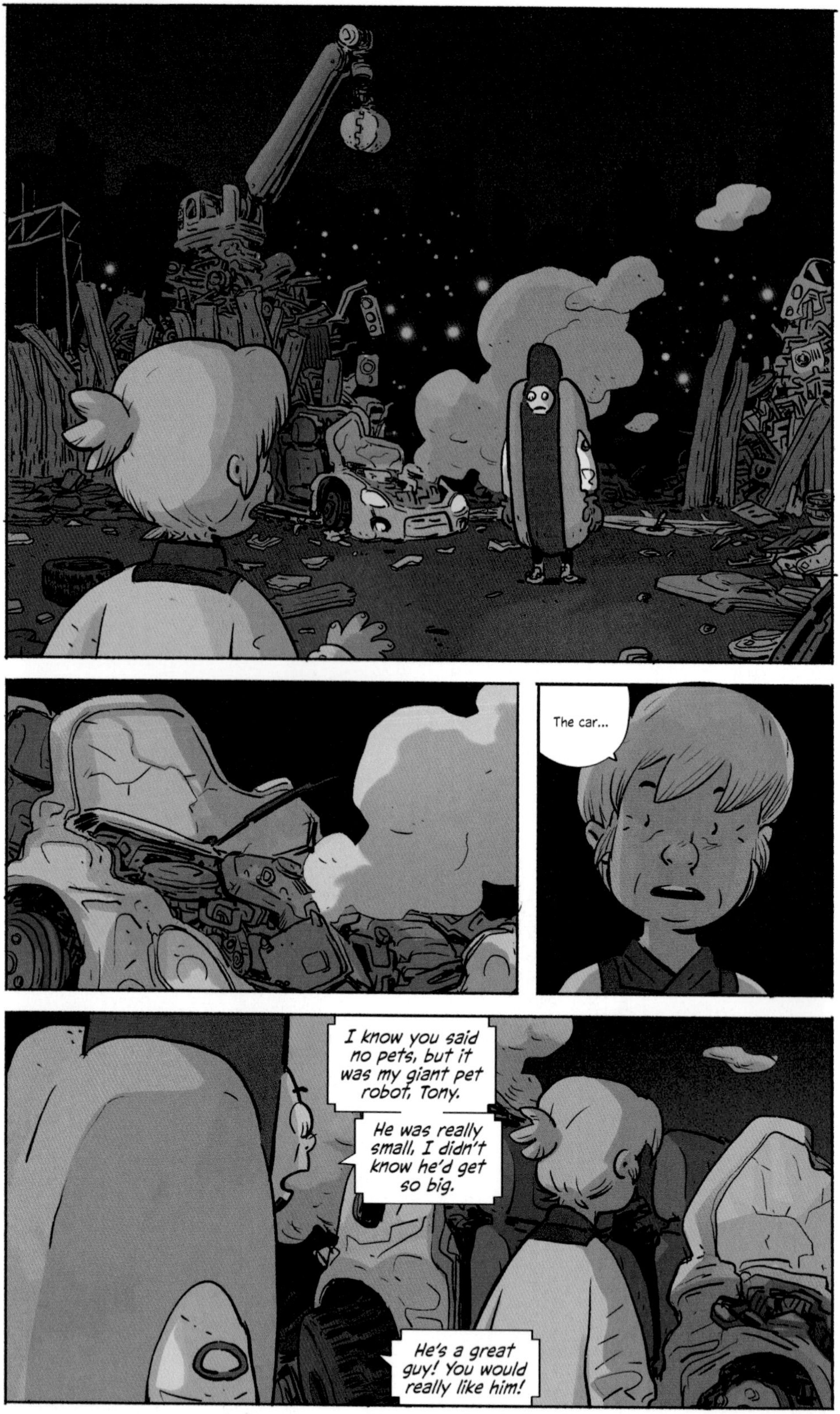
The car...
I know you said no pets, but it was my giant pet robot, Tony.
He was really small, I didn't know he'd get so big.
He's a great guy! You would really like him!

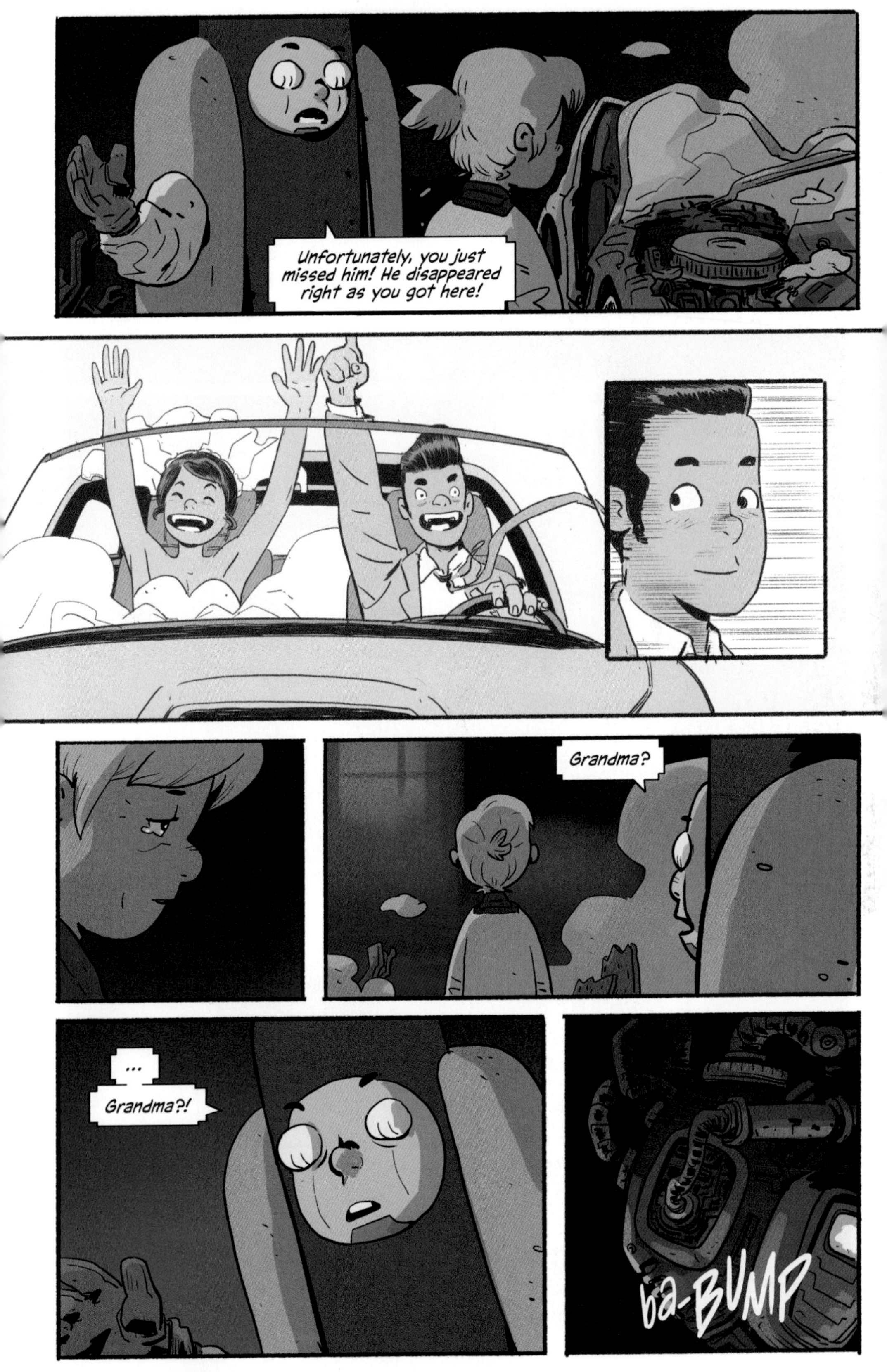
Unfortunately, you just missed him! He disappeared right as you got here!
Grandma?
...
Grandma?!
ba-BUMP

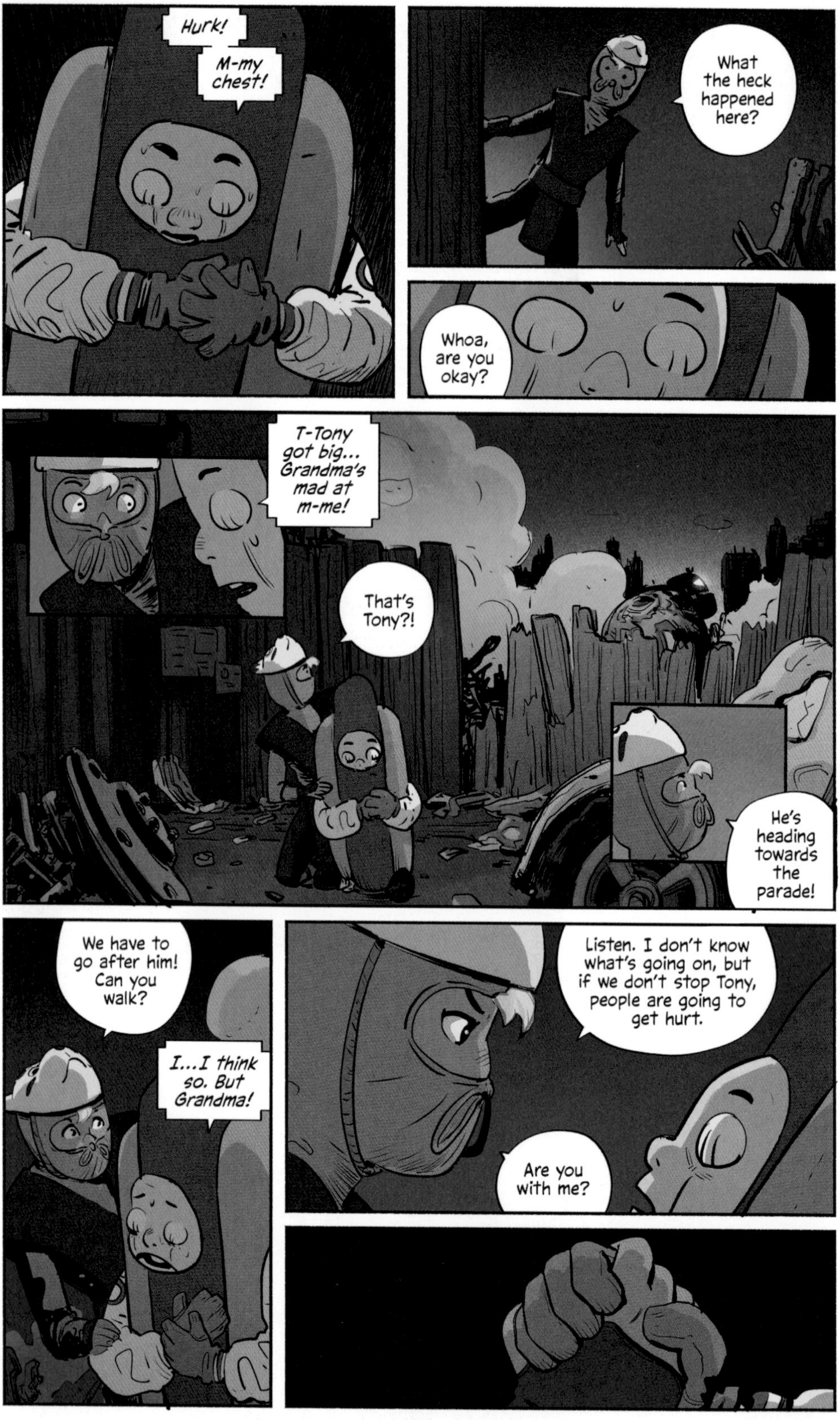
Hurk!
M-my chest!
What the heck happened here?
Whoa, are you okay?
T-Tony got big... Grandma's mad at m-me!
That's Tony?!
He's heading towards the parade!
We have to go after him! Can you walk?
I...I think so. But Grandma!
Listen. I don't know what's going on, but if we don't stop Tony, people are going to get hurt.
Are you with me?

Happy Halloween, MEGA 416! Are you ready to get mashed?!

This party's gonna be--

Monstrous...

We're not gonna make it down there in time!

We need speed.

AAAAA!!

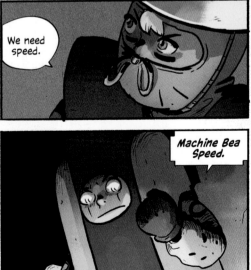

Machine Bea Speed.

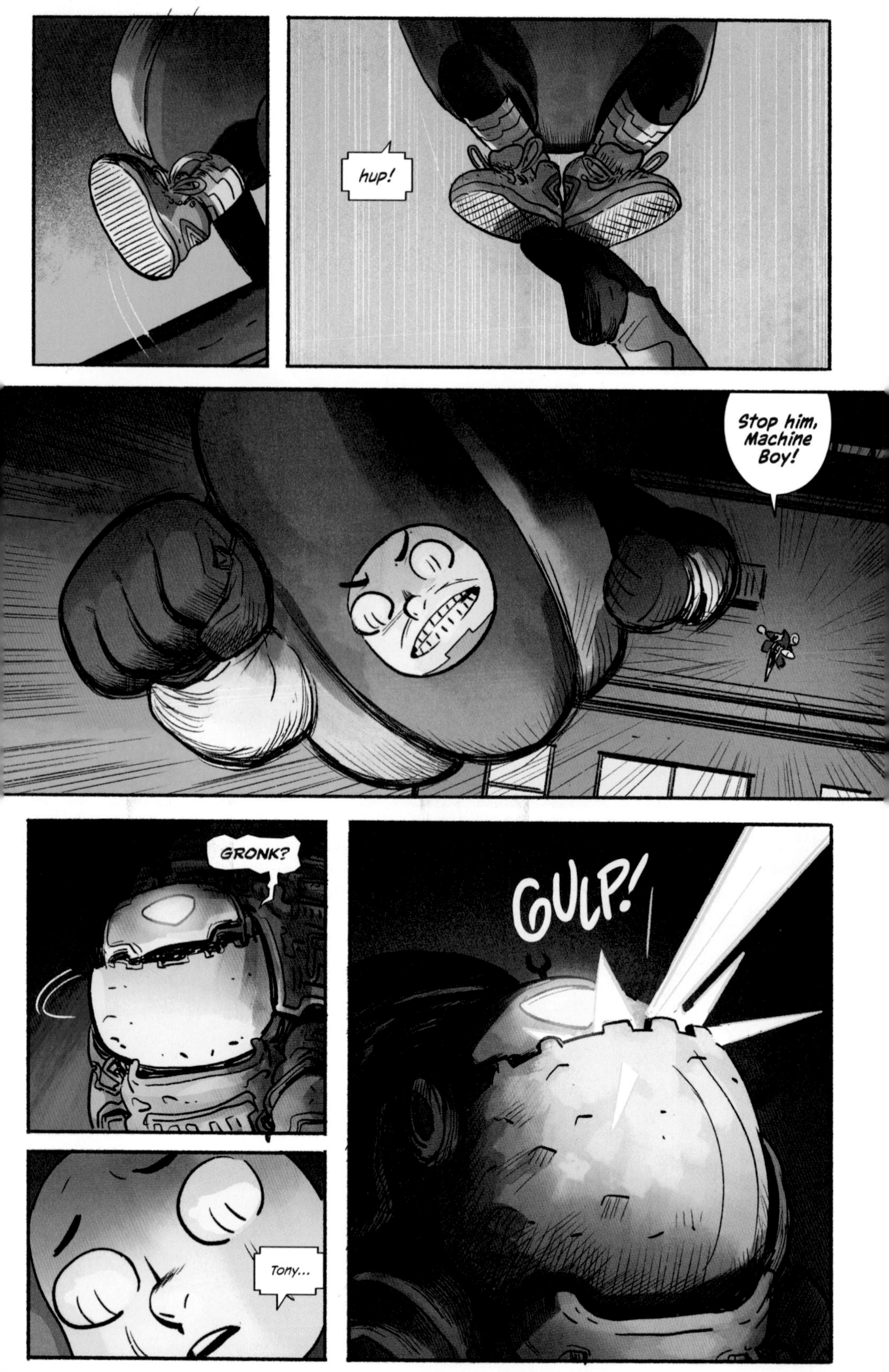
hup!
Stop him, Machine Boy!
GRONK?
GULP!
Tony...

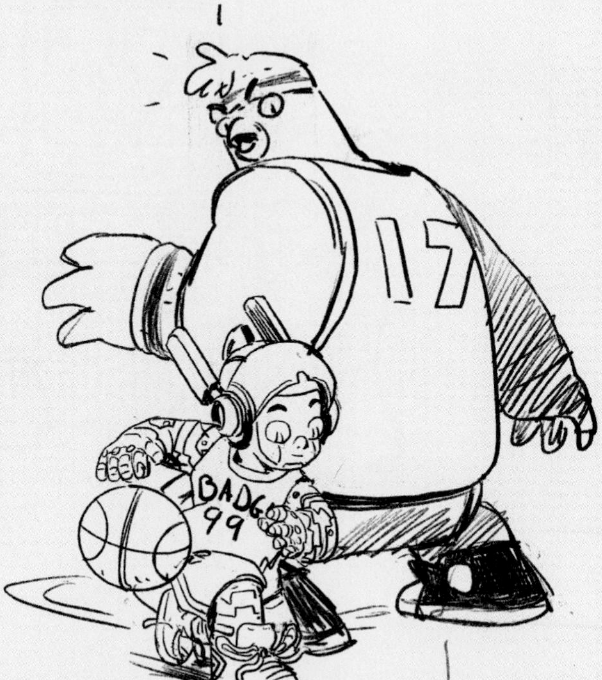
17
BADG
99

CHAPTER 6

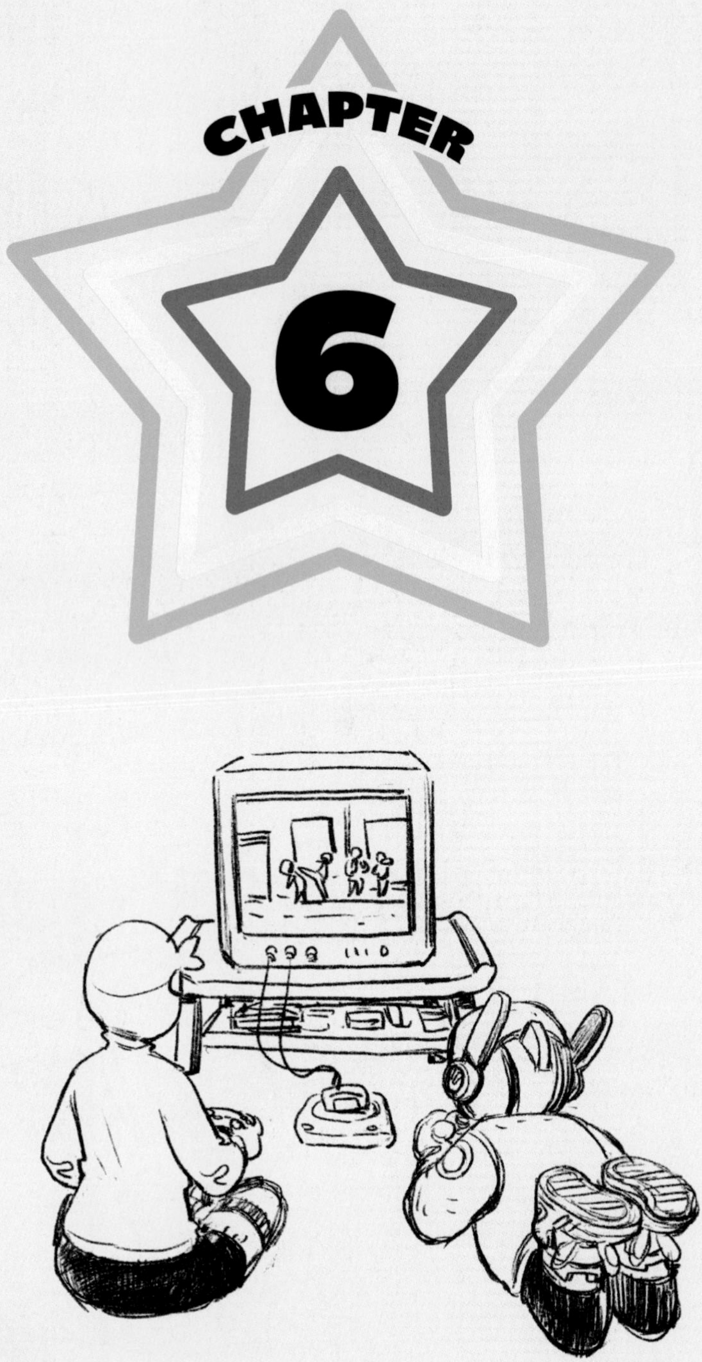

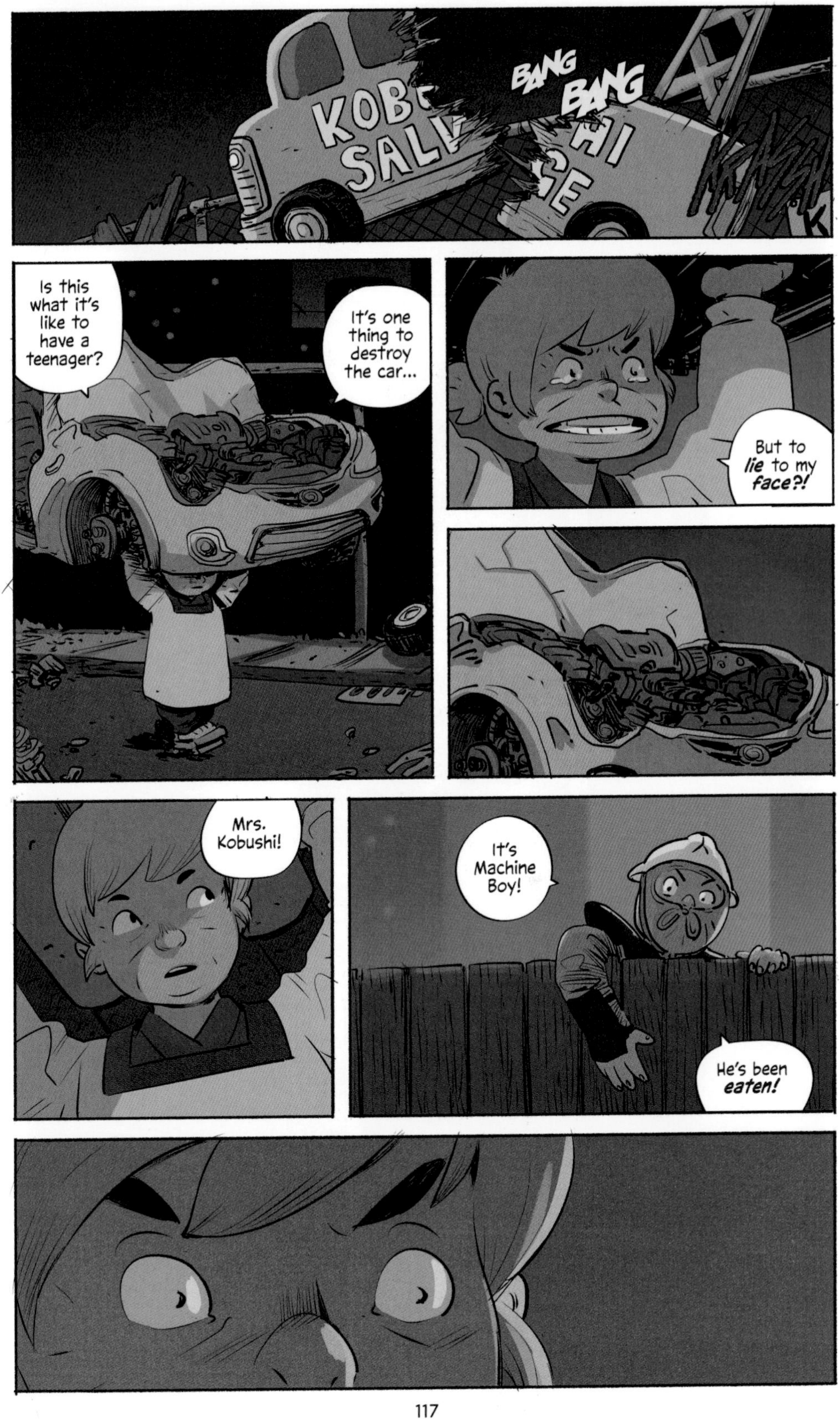
BANG
BANG
KRASSH
Is this what it's like to have a teenager?
It's one thing to destroy the car...
But to *lie* to my *face?!*
Mrs. Kobushi!
It's Machine Boy!
He's been *eaten!*

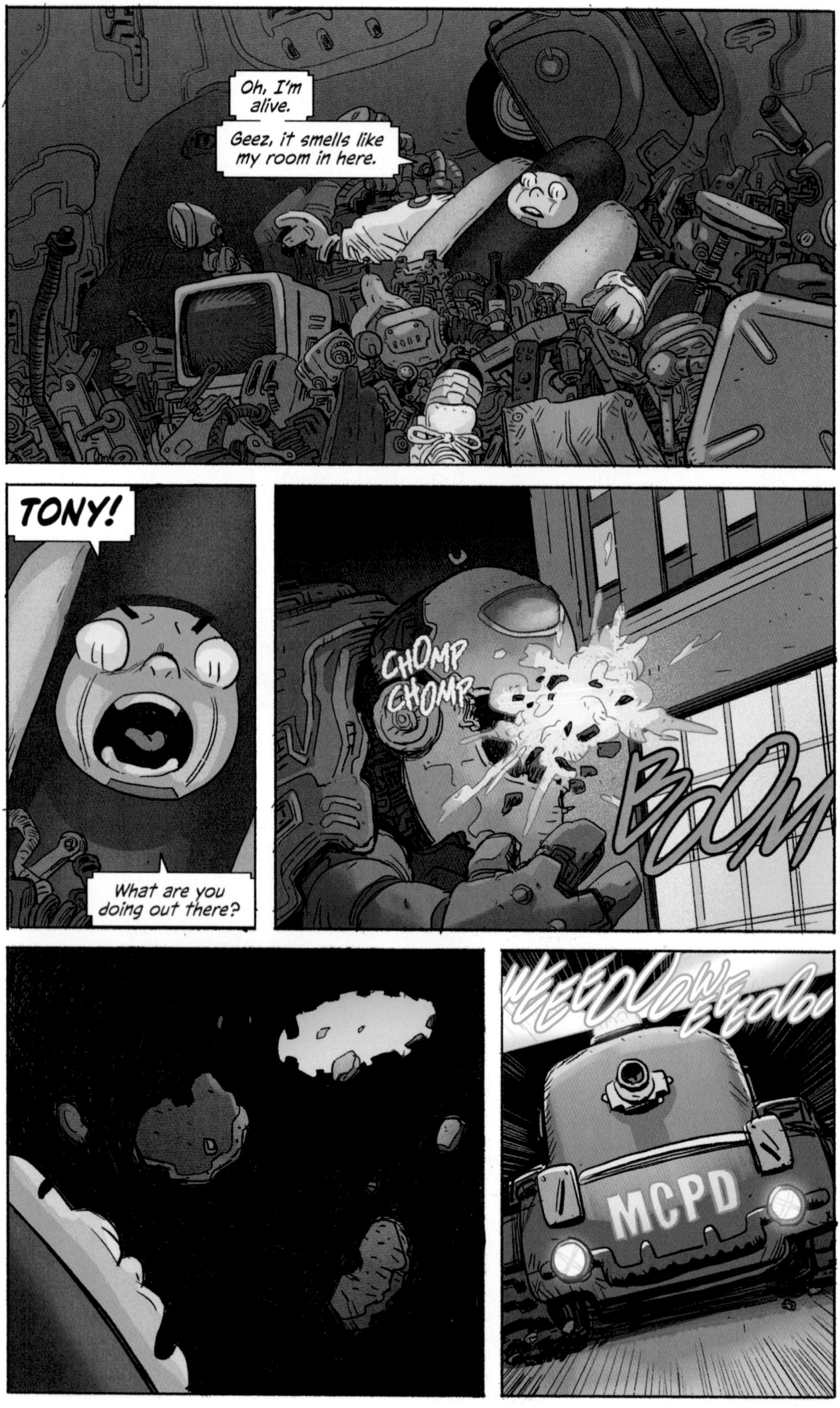
Oh, I'm alive.
Geez, it smells like my room in here.
TONY!
What are you doing out there?
CHOMP CHOMP
BOOM
MCPD

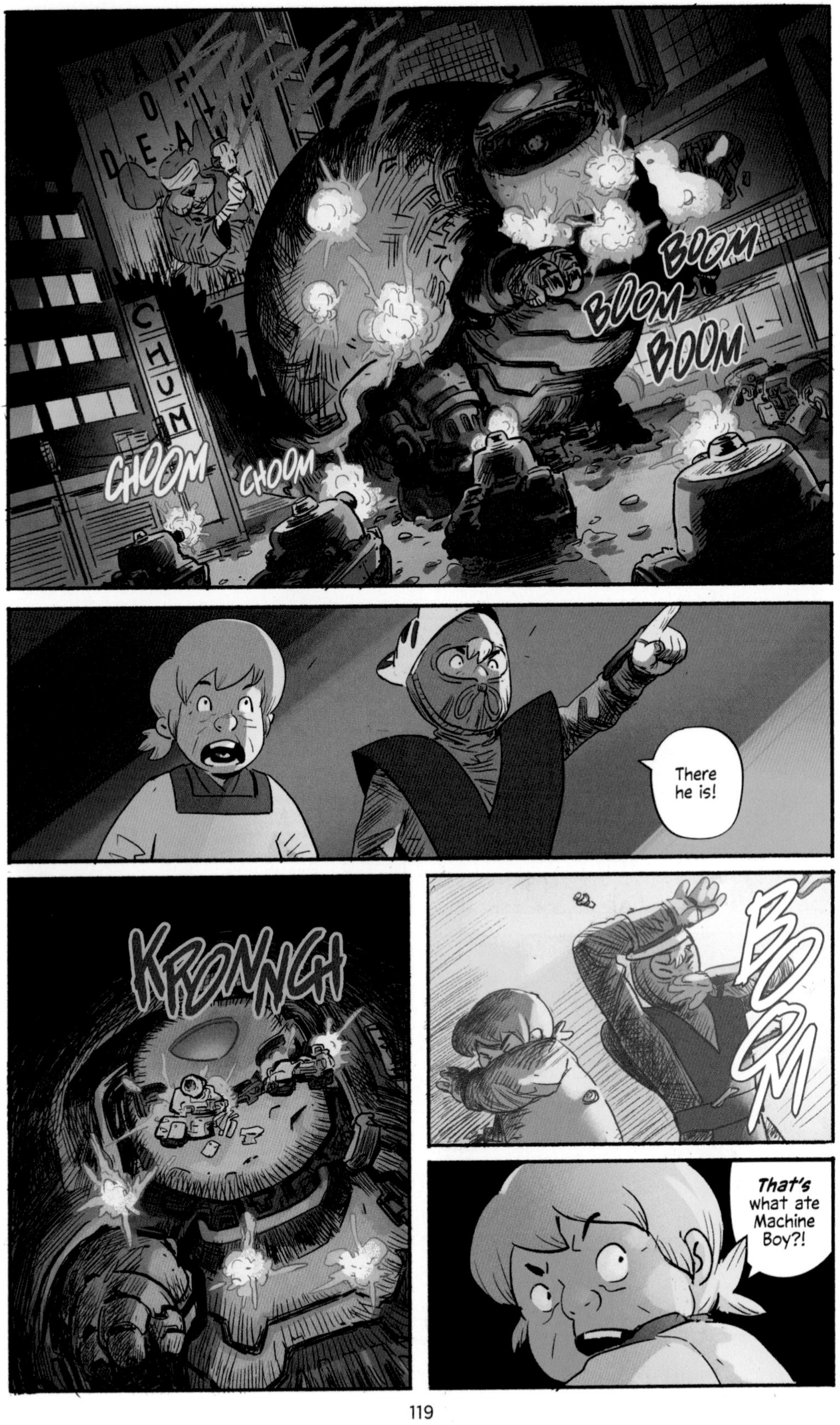
CHUM
BOOM
BOOM
BOOM
CHOOM
CHOOM
There he is!
KRONNCH
BOOM
That's what ate Machine Boy?!

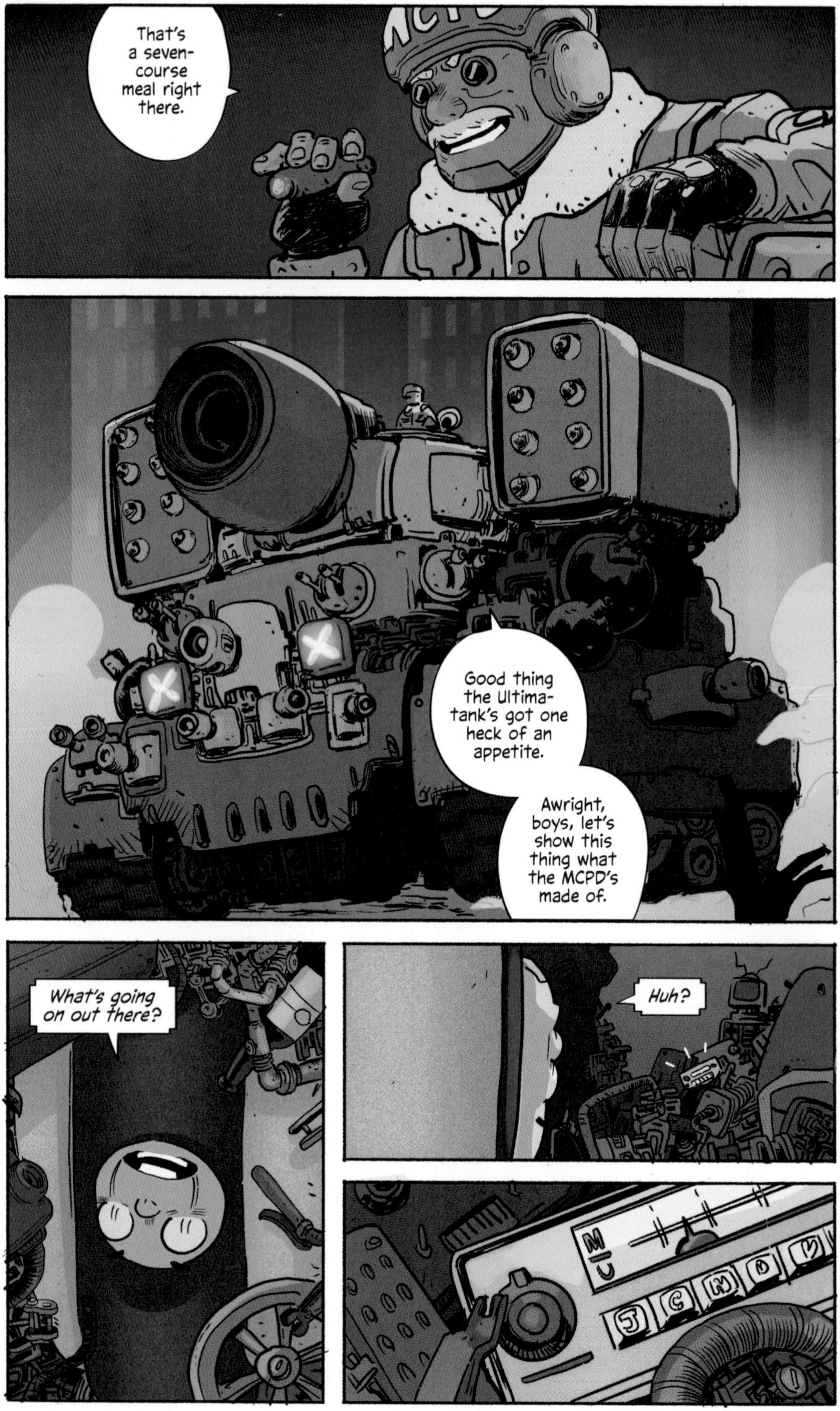
That's a seven-course meal right there.
Good thing the Ultima-tank's got one heck of an appetite.
Awright, boys, let's show this thing what the MCPD's made of.
What's going on out there?
Huh?

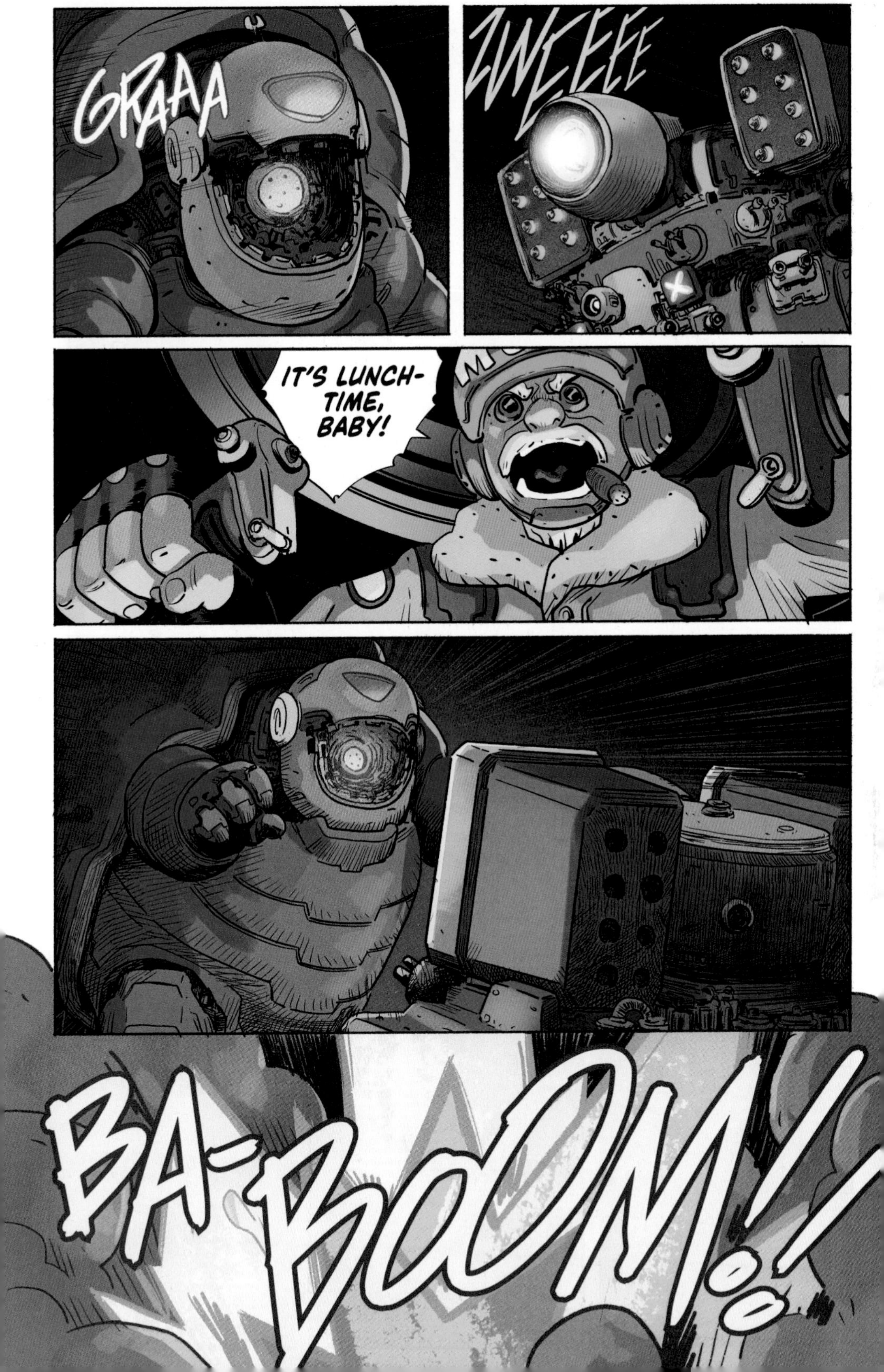
GRAAA
ZWEEEE
IT'S LUNCH-TIME, BABY!
BA-BOOM!!

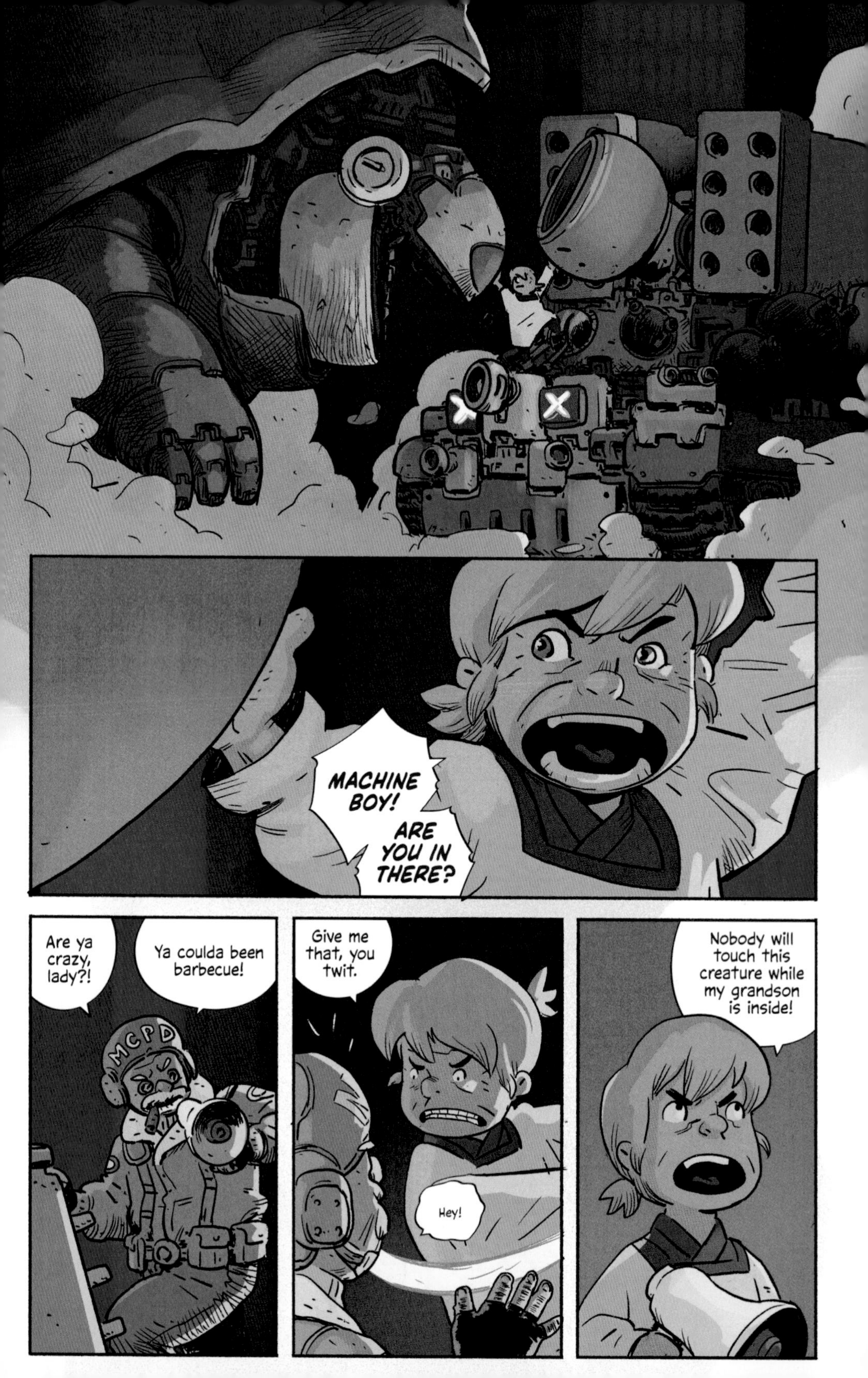
MACHINE BOY!
ARE YOU IN THERE?
Are ya crazy, lady?!
Ya coulda been barbecue!
Give me that, you twit.
Hey!
Nobody will touch this creature while my grandson is inside!

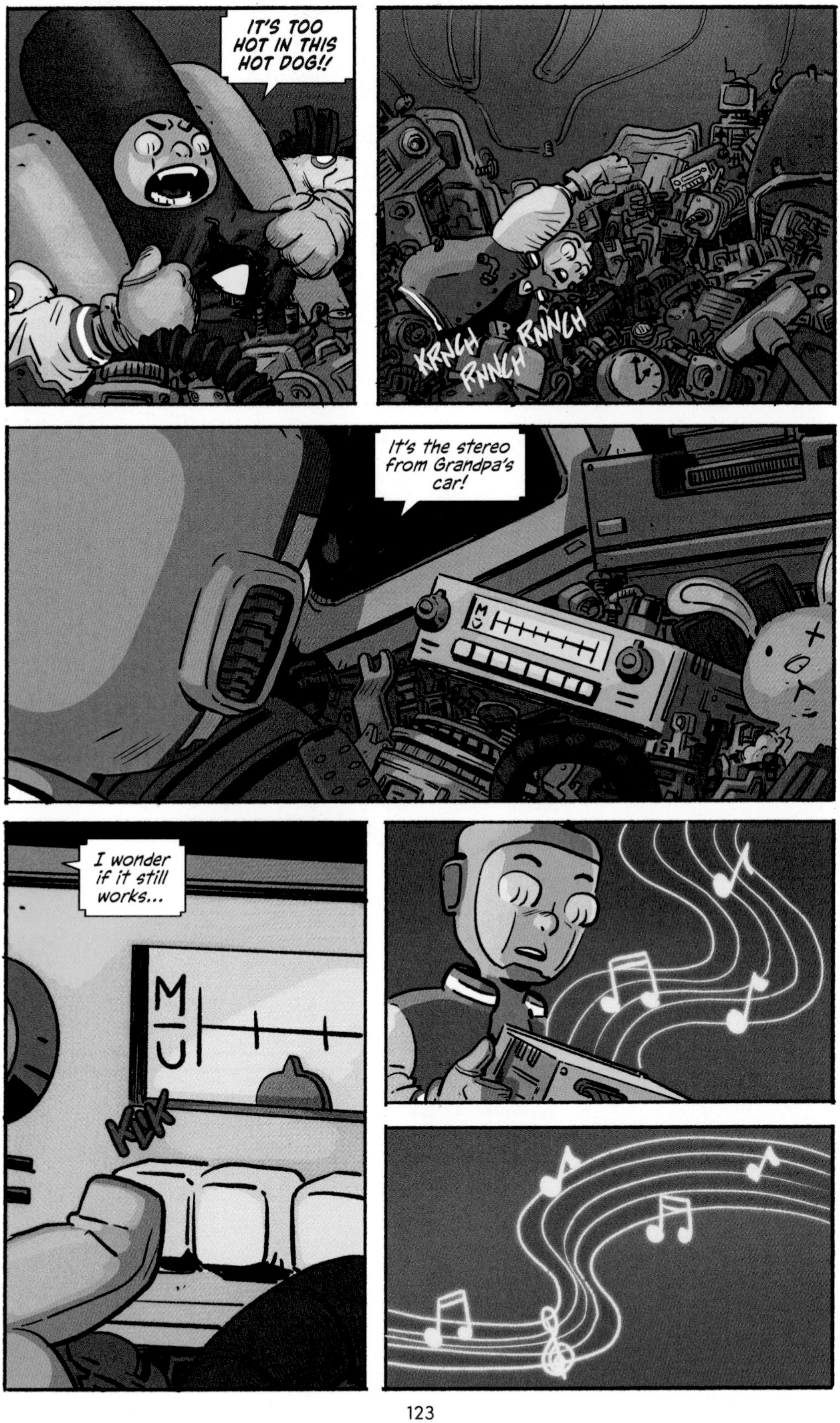
IT'S TOO HOT IN THIS HOT DOG!!
KRNCH
RNNCH
RNNCH
It's the stereo from Grandpa's car!
I wonder if it still works...
KLIK

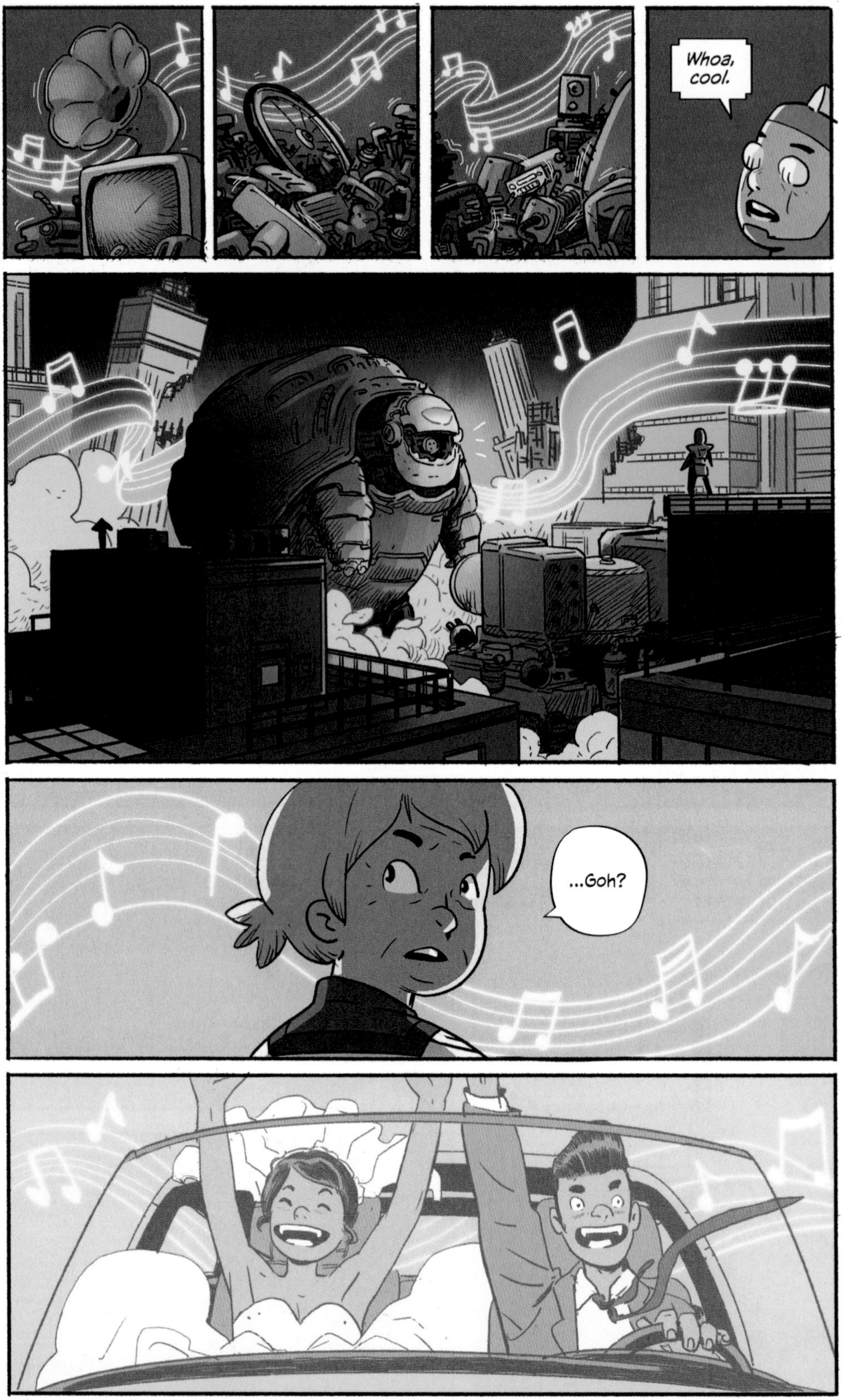
Whoa, cool.
...Goh?

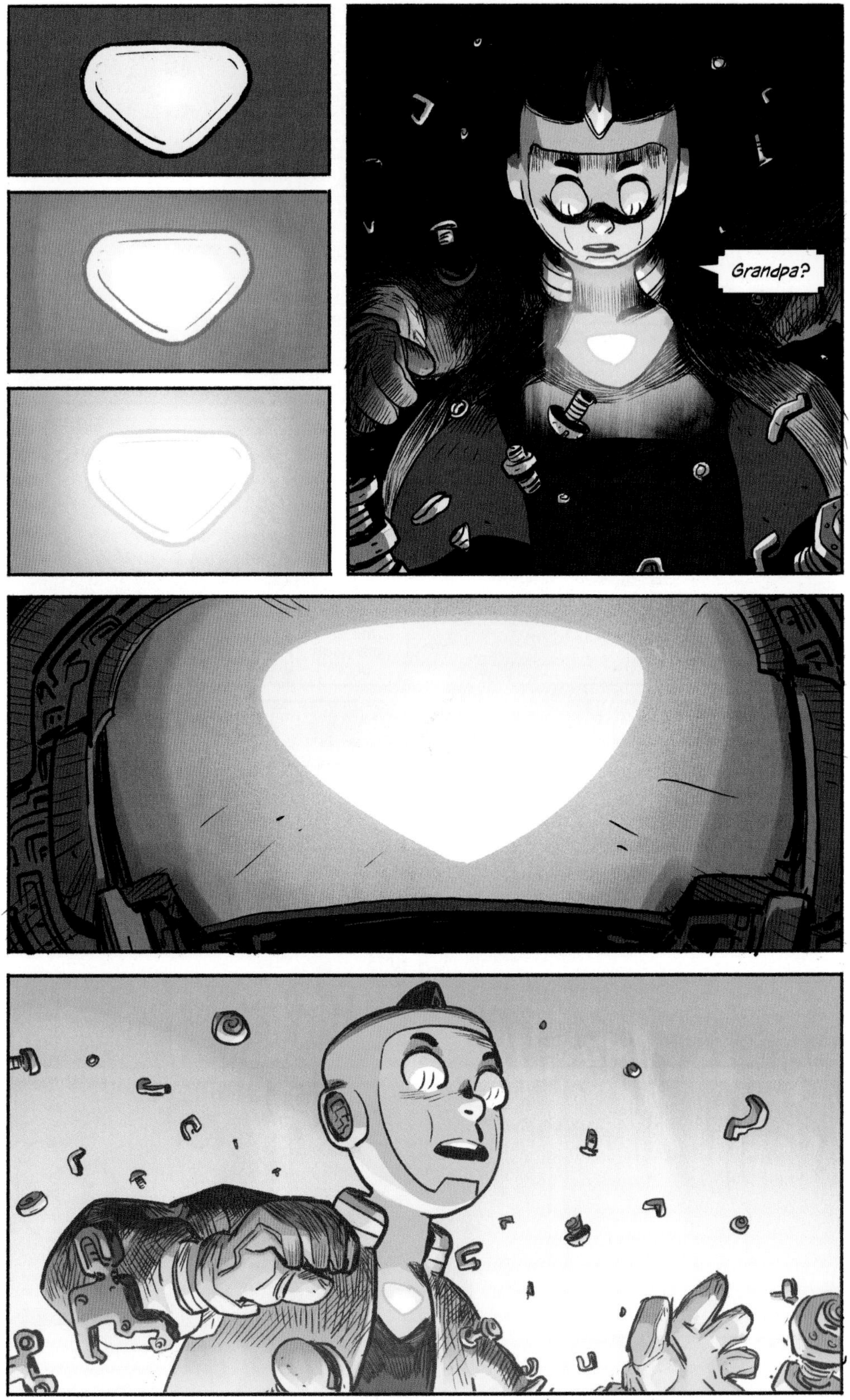
Grandpa?

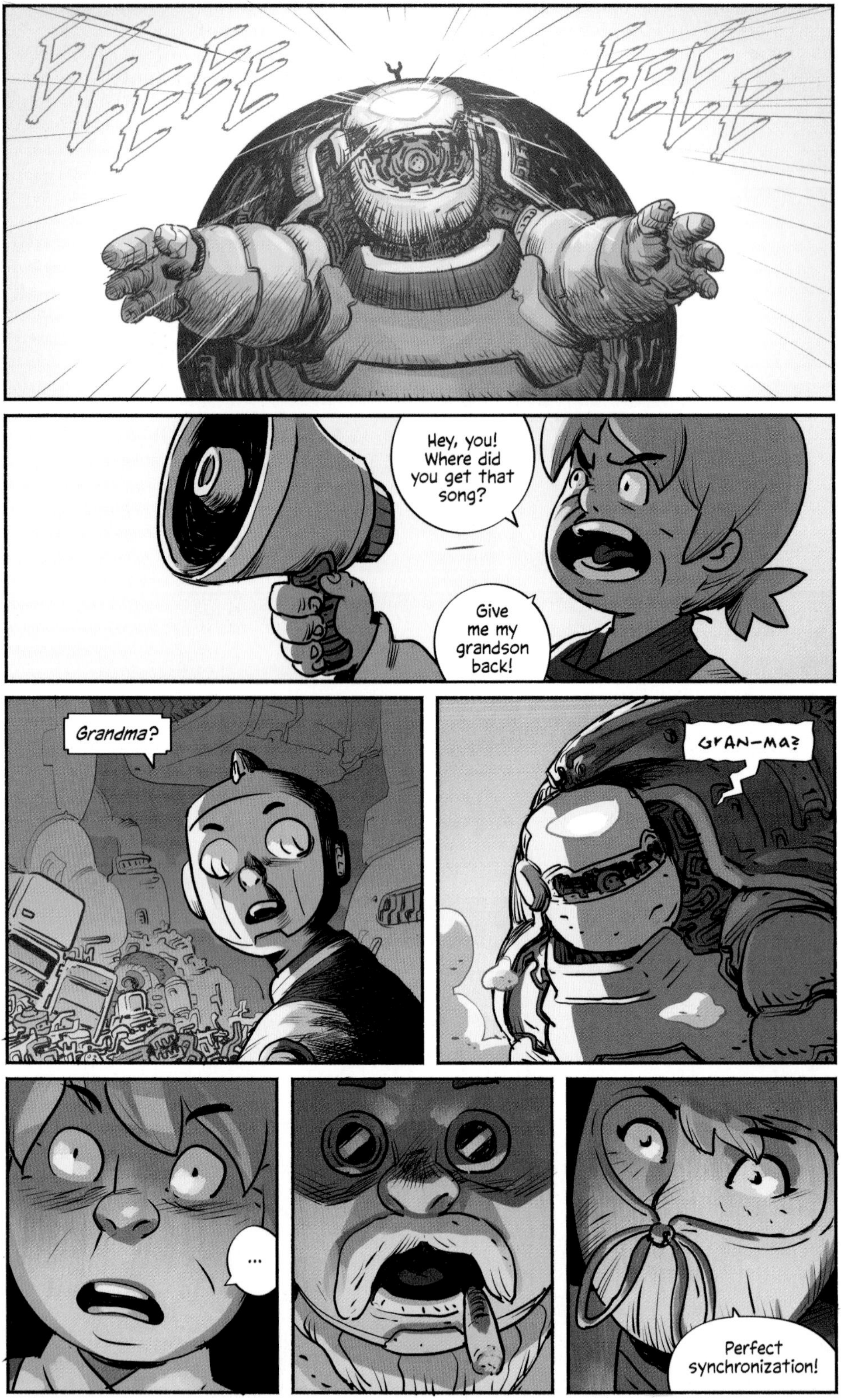
EEEEEE
EEEE
Hey, you! Where did you get that song?
Give me my grandson back!
Grandma?
GRAN-MA?
...
Perfect synchronization!

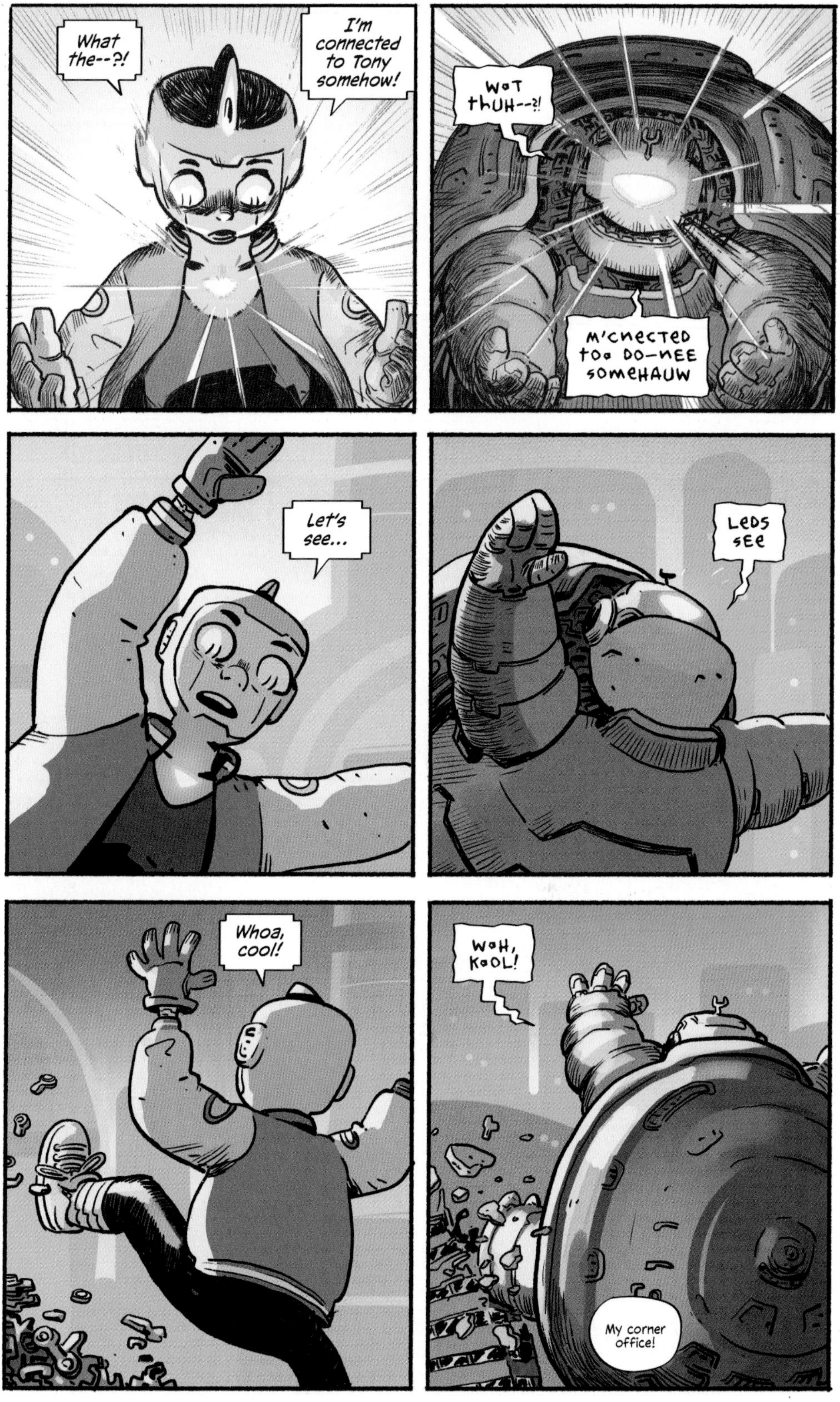

What the--?!
I'm connected to Tony somehow!
WoT THUH--?!
M'CNECTED TOo DO-NEE SOMEHAUW
Let's see...
LEDS SEE
Whoa, cool!
WoH, KoOL!
My corner office!

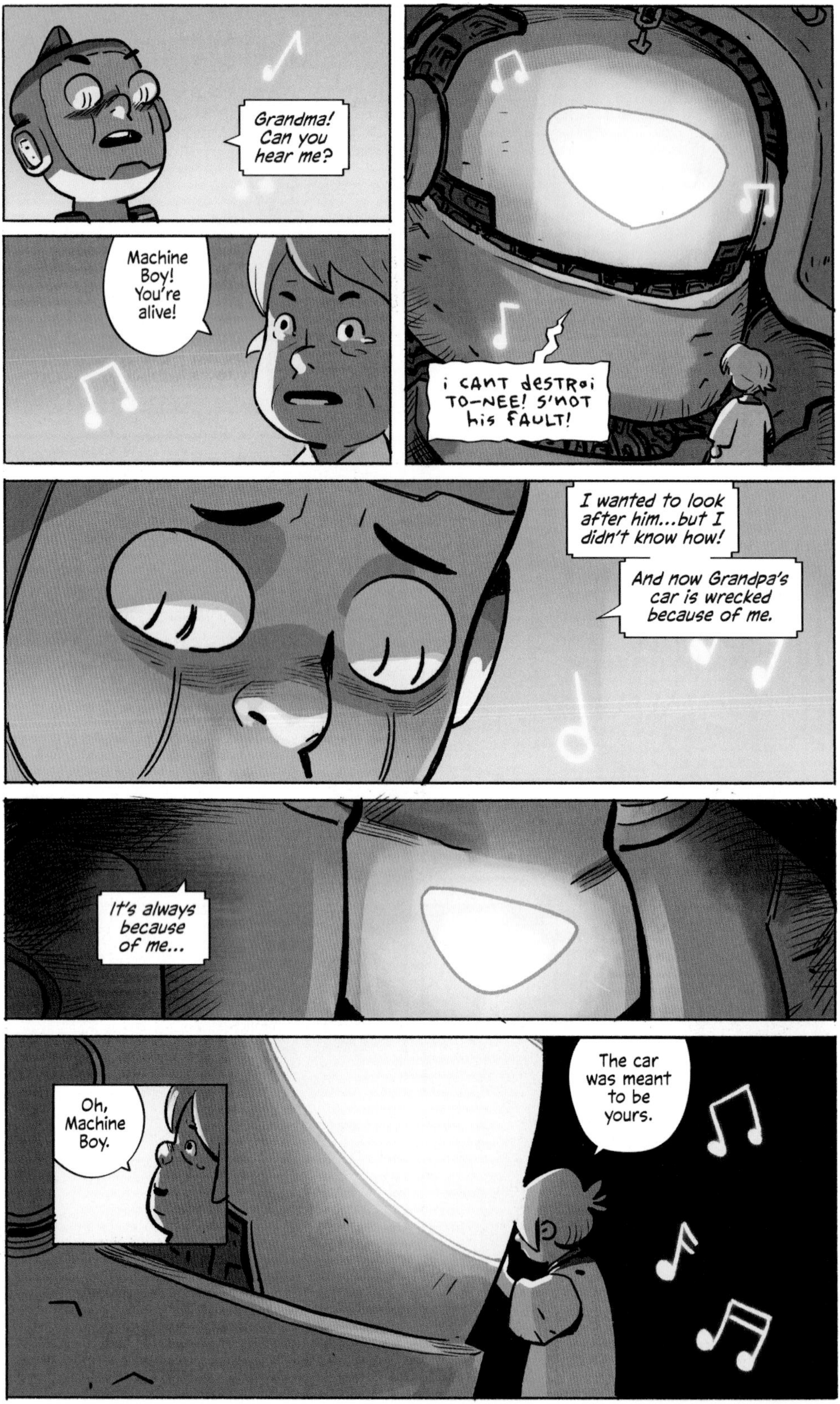

Grandma! Can you hear me?
Machine Boy! You're alive!
i CANT destroi TO-NEE! S'NOT his FAULT!
I wanted to look after him...but I didn't know how!
And now Grandpa's car is wrecked because of me.
It's always because of me...
Oh, Machine Boy.
The car was meant to be yours.

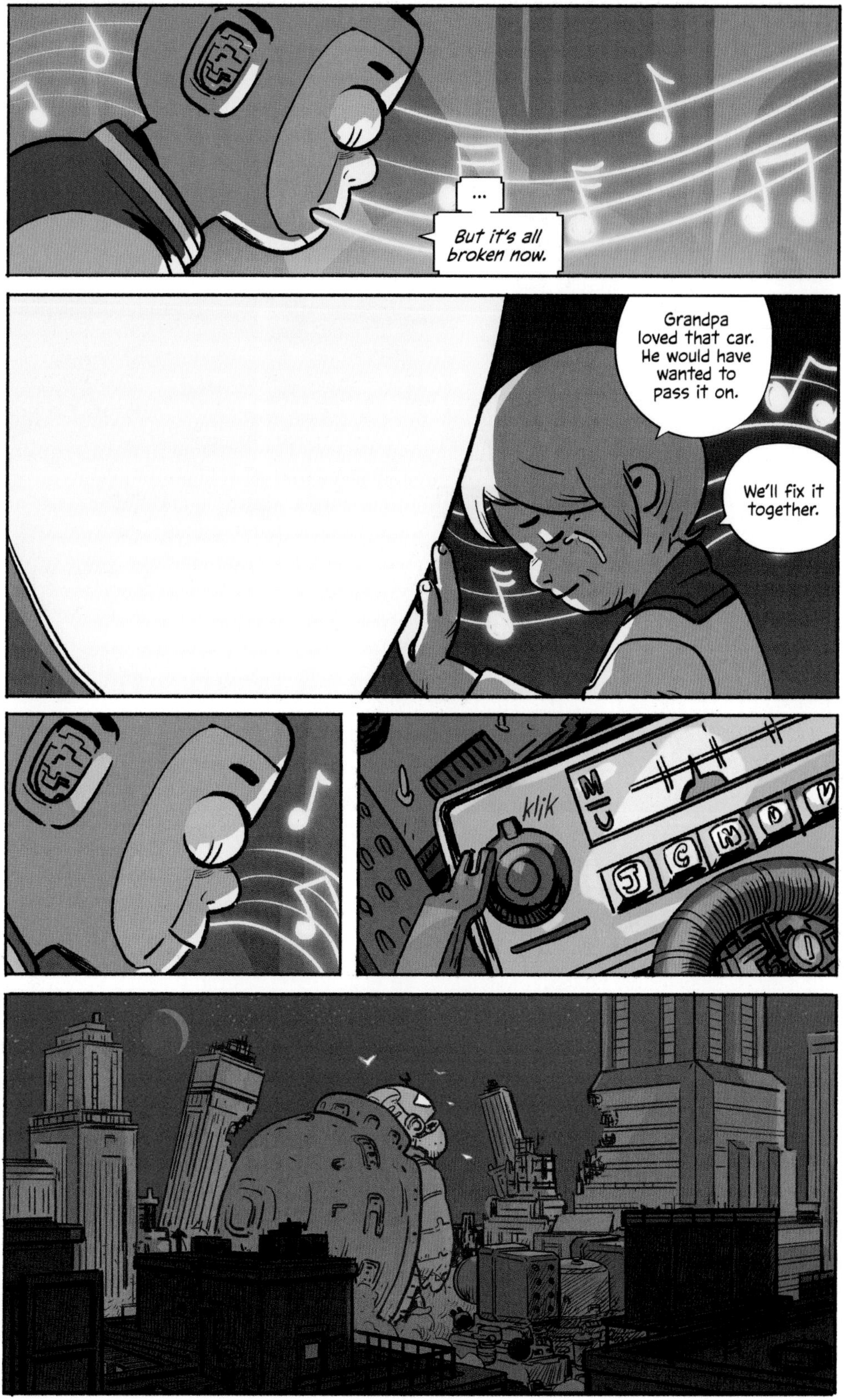

...
But it's all broken now.
Grandpa loved that car. He would have wanted to pass it on.
We'll fix it together.
klik

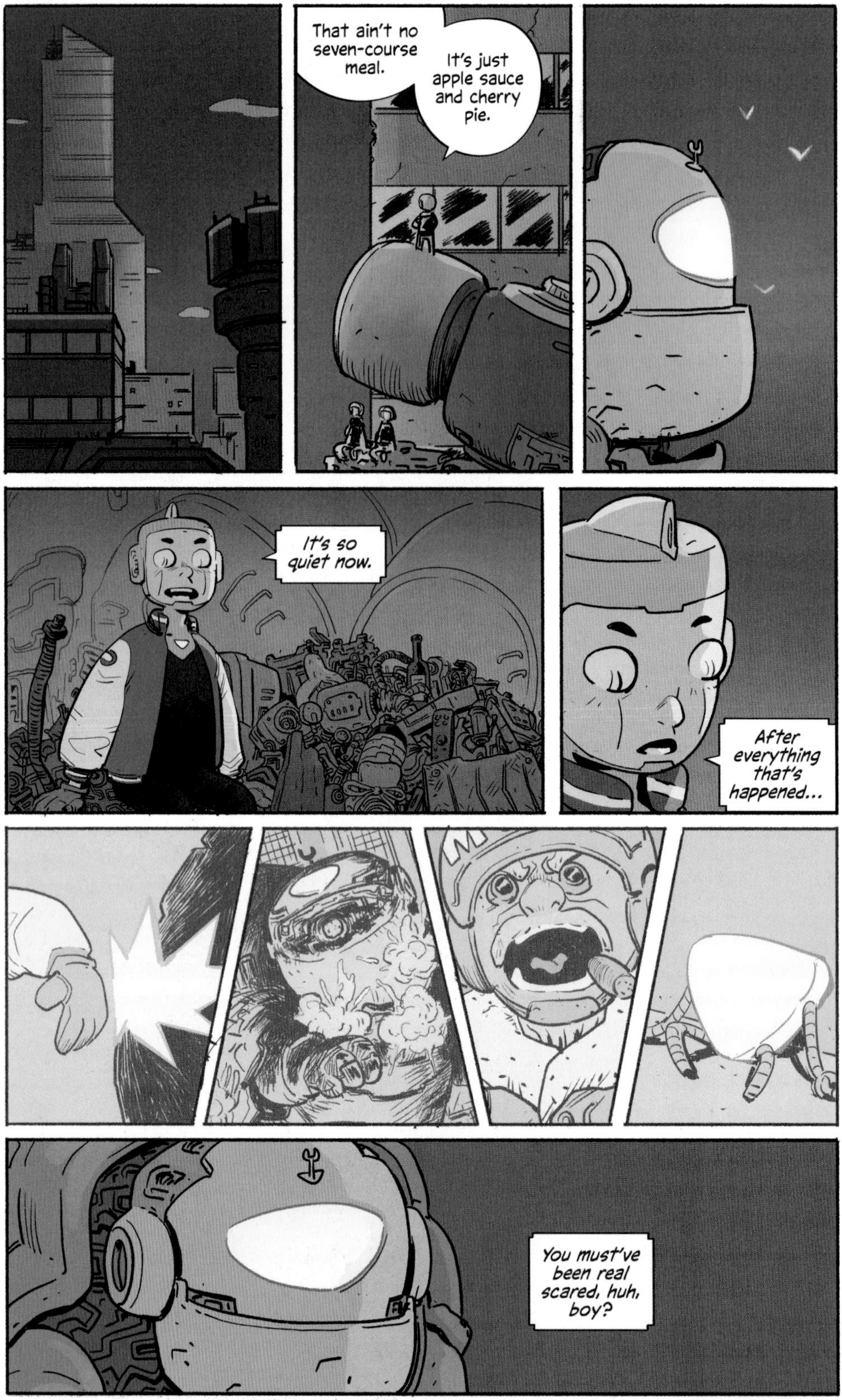
That ain't no seven-course meal.
It's just apple sauce and cherry pie.
It's so quiet now.
After everything that's happened...
You must've been real scared, huh, boy?

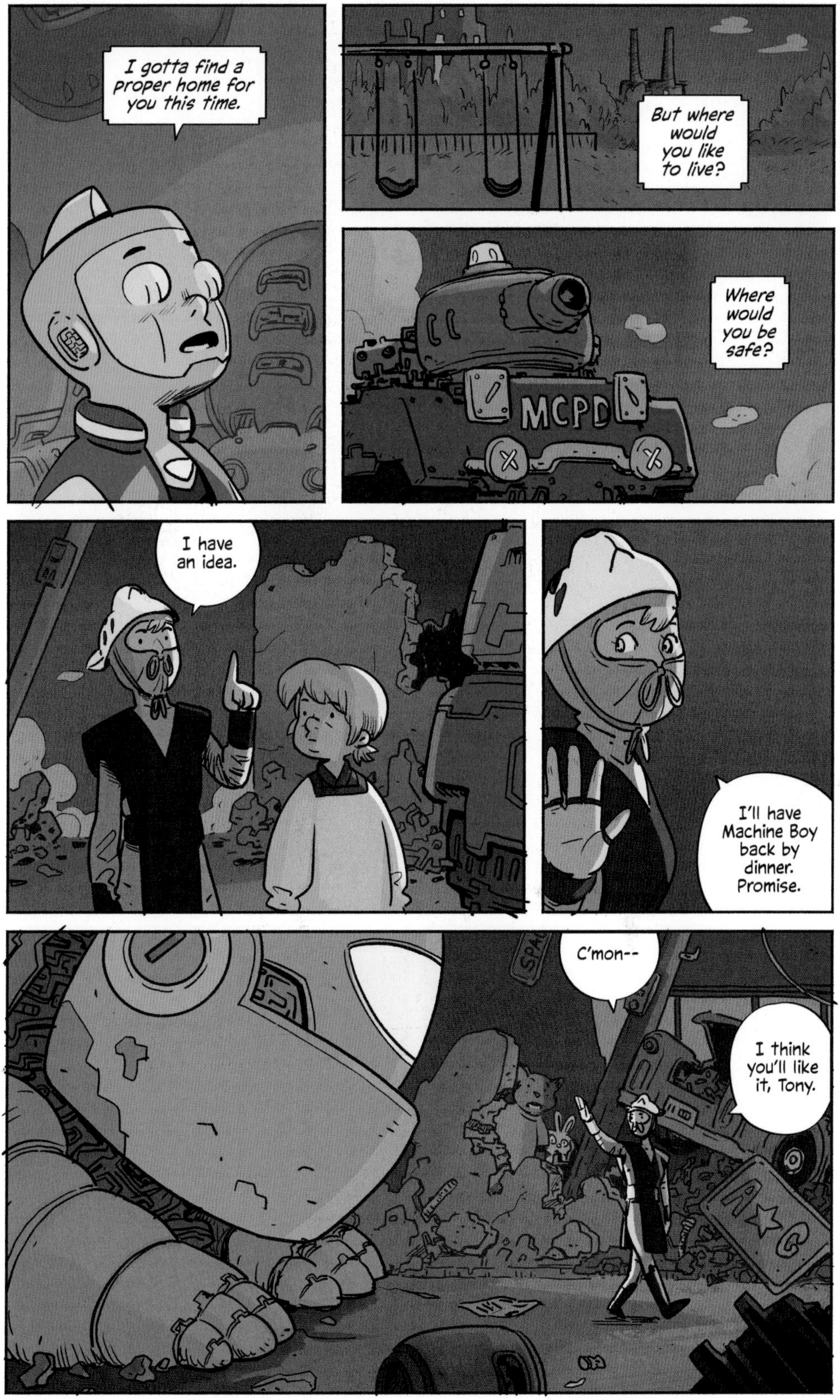

I gotta find a proper home for you this time.
But where would you like to live?
Where would you be safe?
MCPD
I have an idea.
I'll have Machine Boy back by dinner. Promise.
C'mon--
I think you'll like it, Tony.

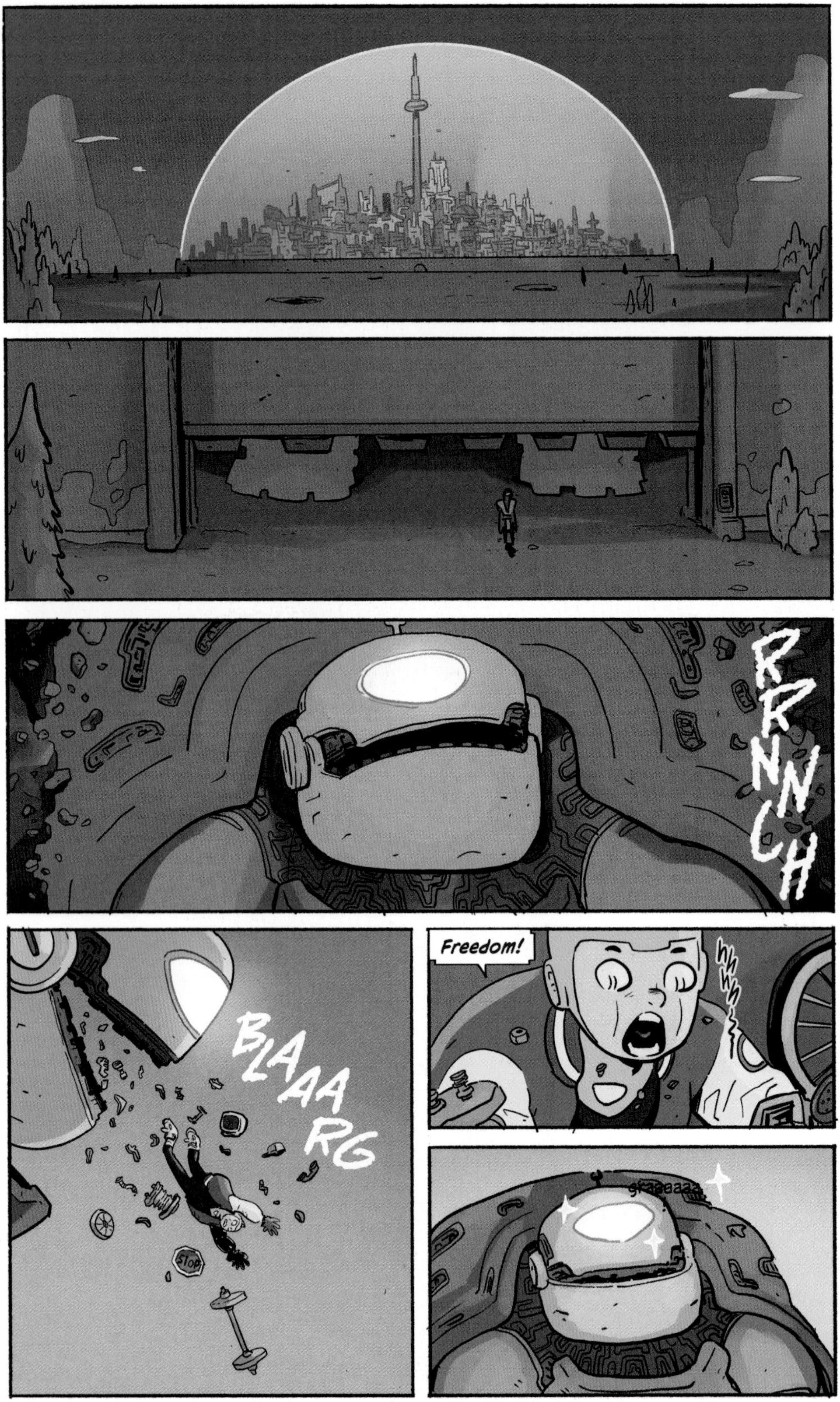
RRNNCH
BLAAAARG
Freedom!
graaaaaa

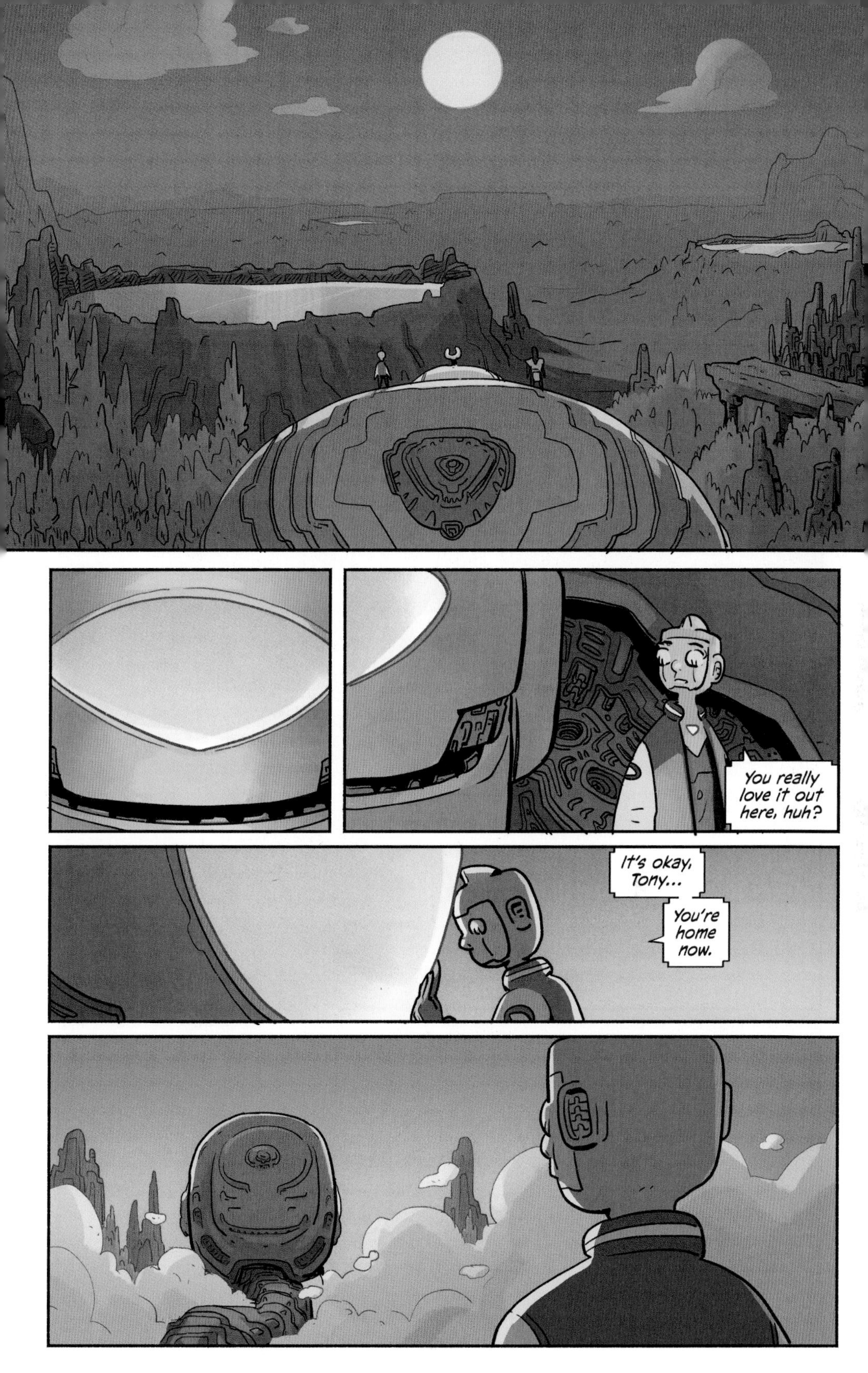
You really love it out here, huh?
It's okay, Tony...
You're home now.

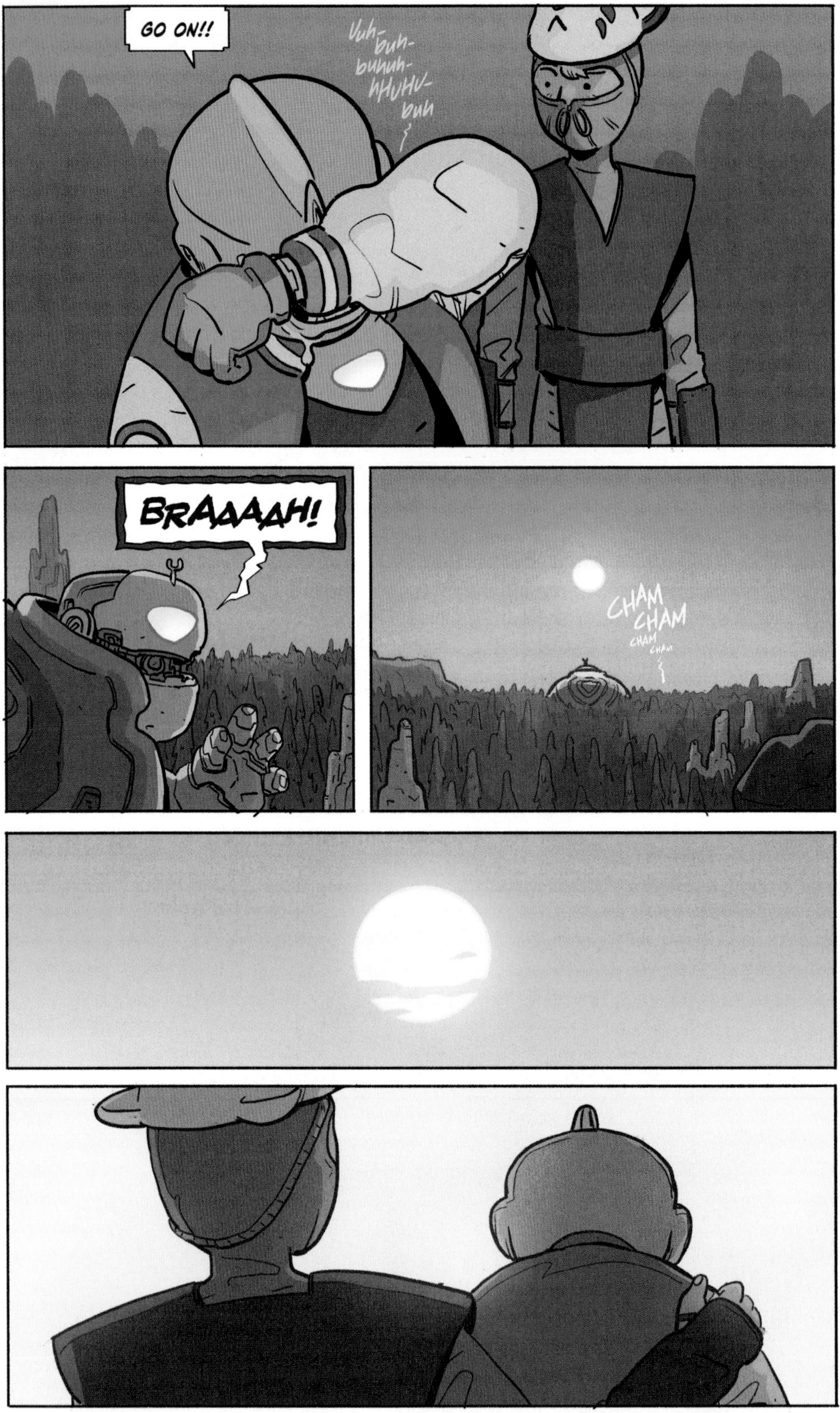
GO ON!!
Vuh-buh-buhuh-hHUHU-buh
BRAAAAH!
CHAM CHAM CHAM CHAM

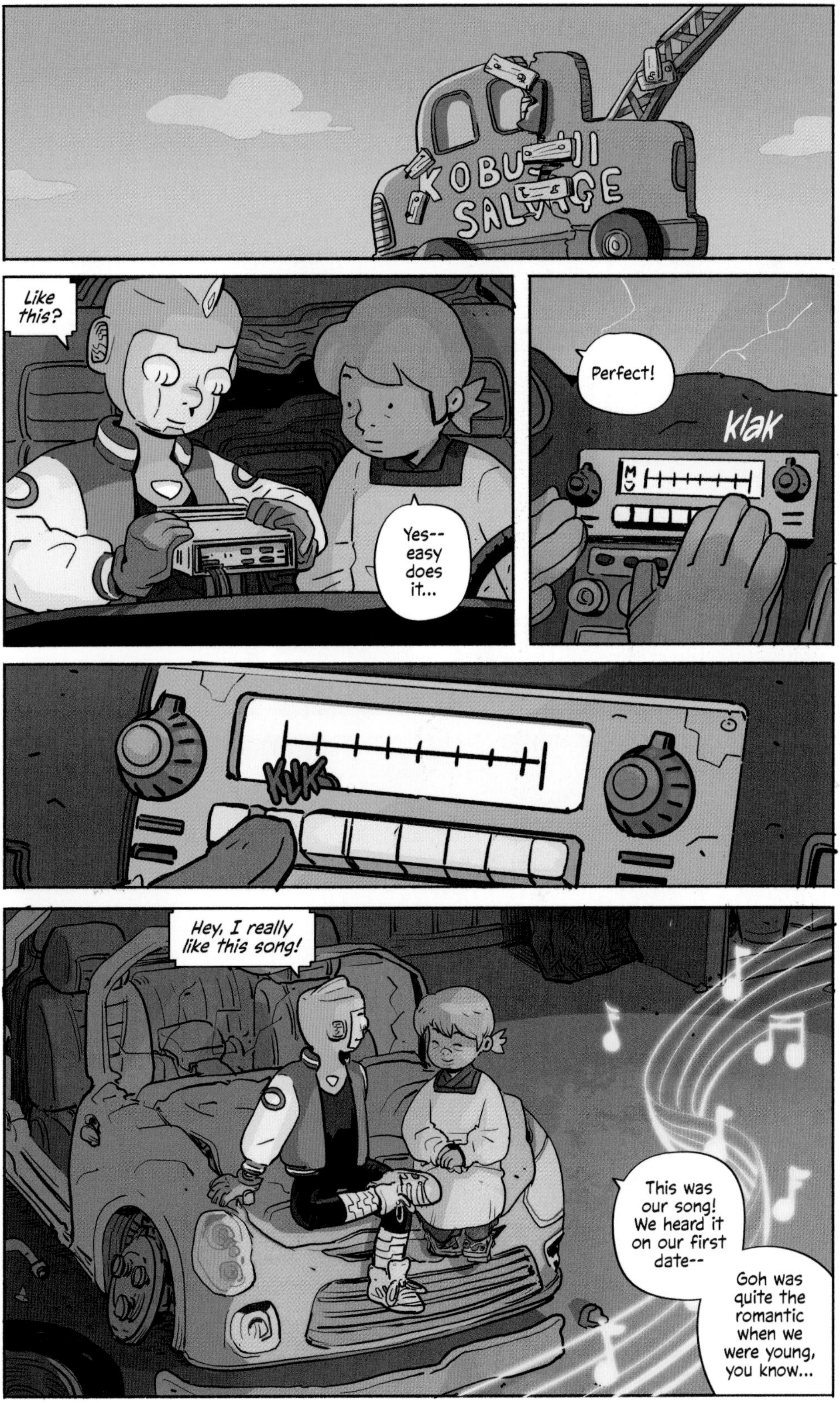
KOBU-HI SALVAGE
Like this?
Yes-- easy does it...
Perfect!
KLAK
KLIK
Hey, I really like this song!
This was our song! We heard it on our first date--
Goh was quite the romantic when we were young, you know...

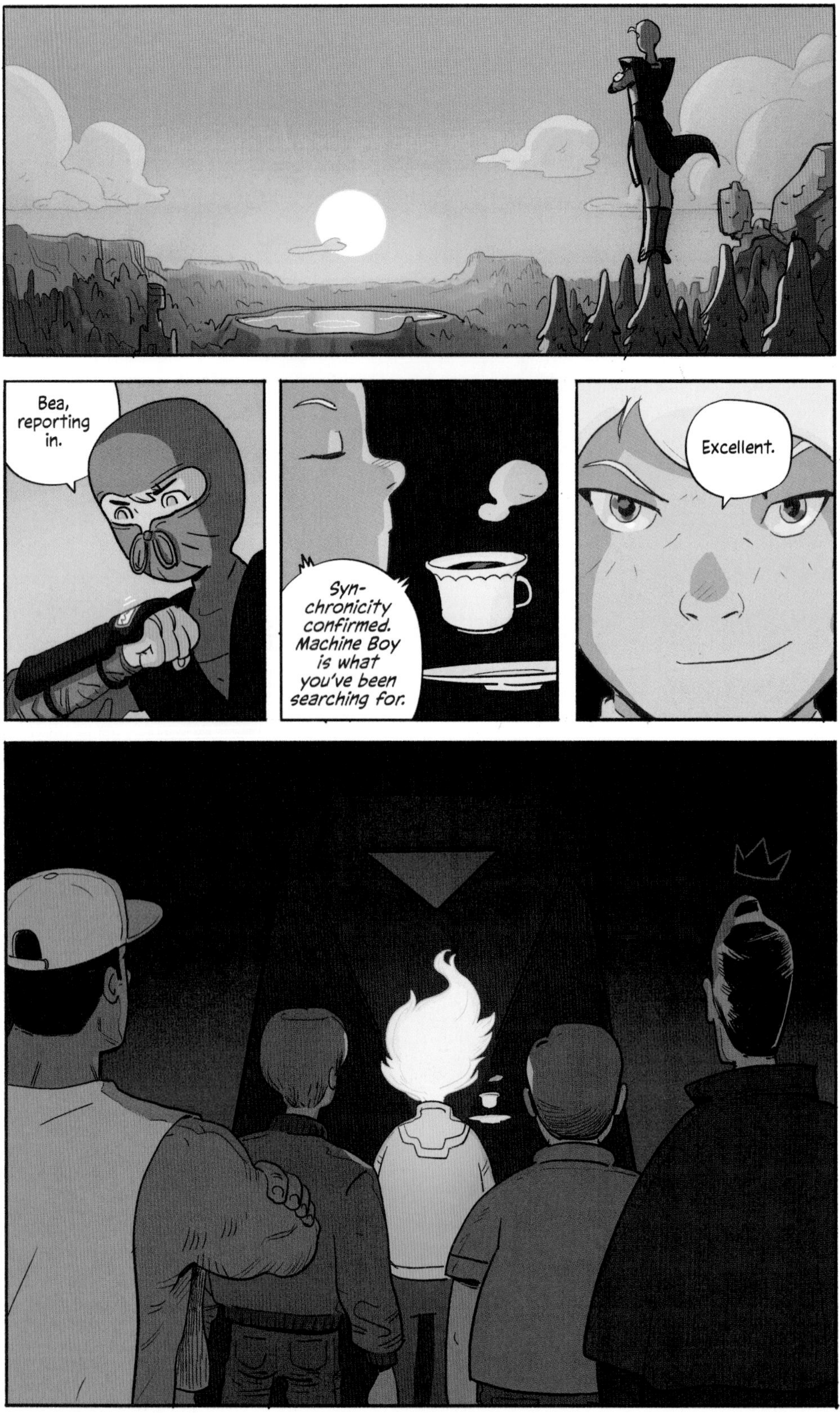
Bea, reporting in.
Syn-chronicity confirmed. Machine Boy is what you've been searching for.
Excellent.

CHAPTER 7

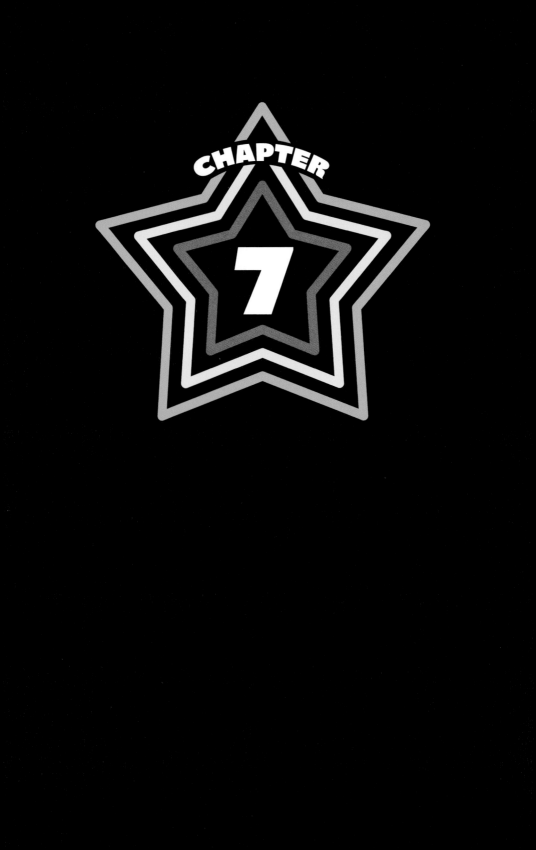

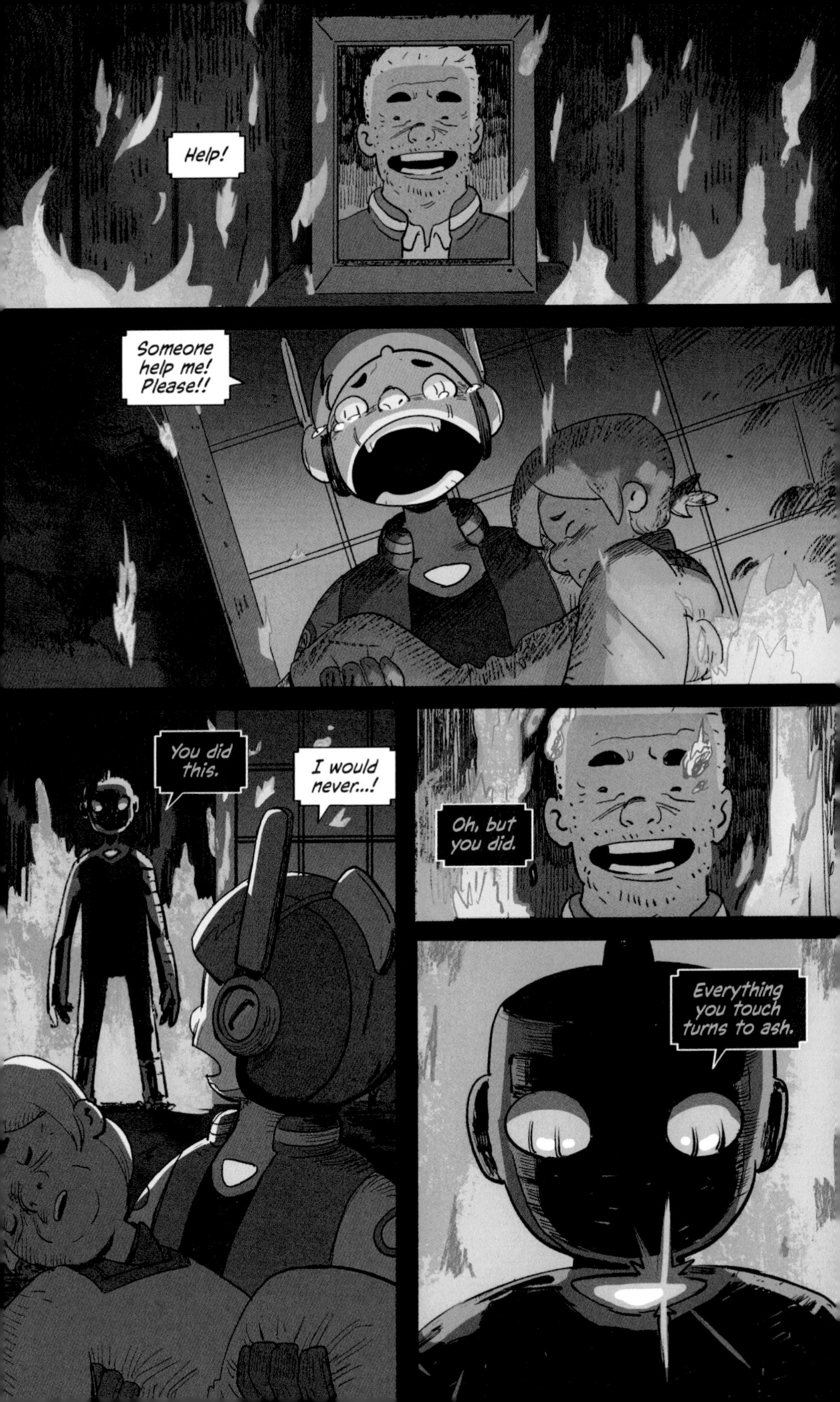
Help!
Someone help me! Please!!
You did this.
I would never...!
Oh, but you did.
Everything you touch turns to ash.

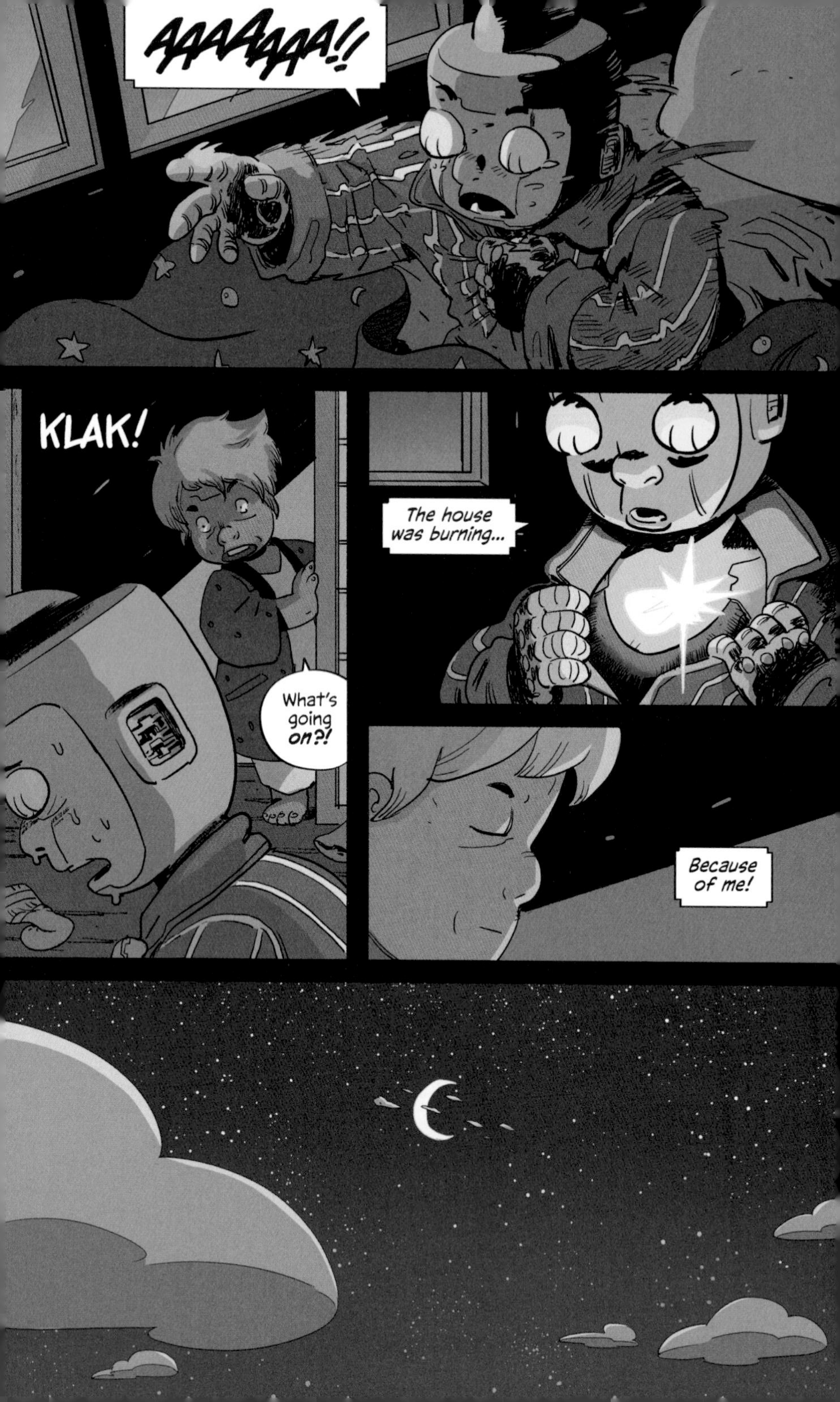
AAAAAAAA!!
KLAK!
What's going on?!
The house was burning...
Because of me!

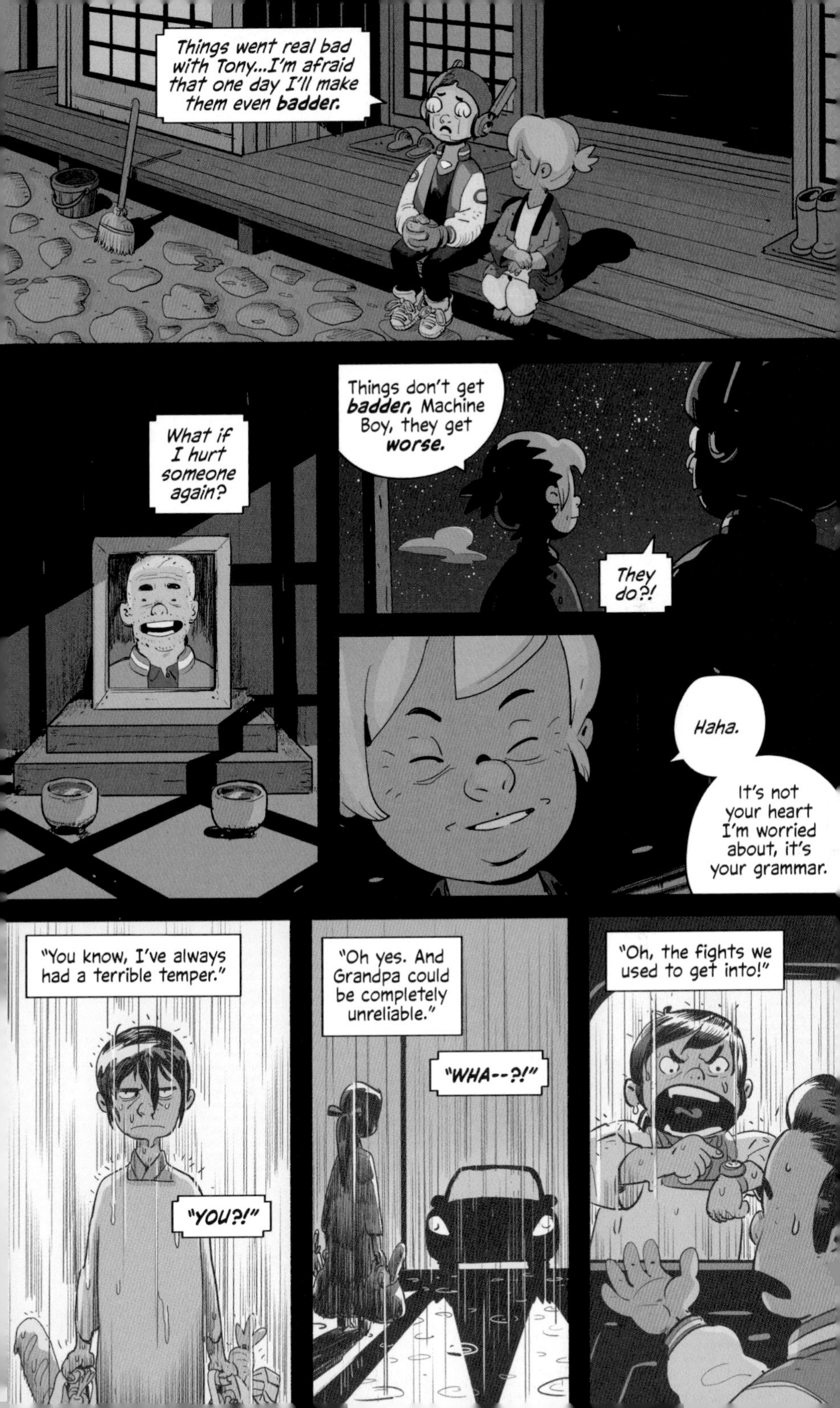
Things went real bad with Tony...I'm afraid that one day I'll make them even **badder.**
What if I hurt someone again?
Things don't get **badder,** Machine Boy, they get **worse.**
They do?!
Haha.
It's not your heart I'm worried about, it's your grammar.
"You know, I've always had a terrible temper."
"YOU?!"
"Oh yes. And Grandpa could be completely unreliable."
"WHA--?!"
"Oh, the fights we used to get into!"

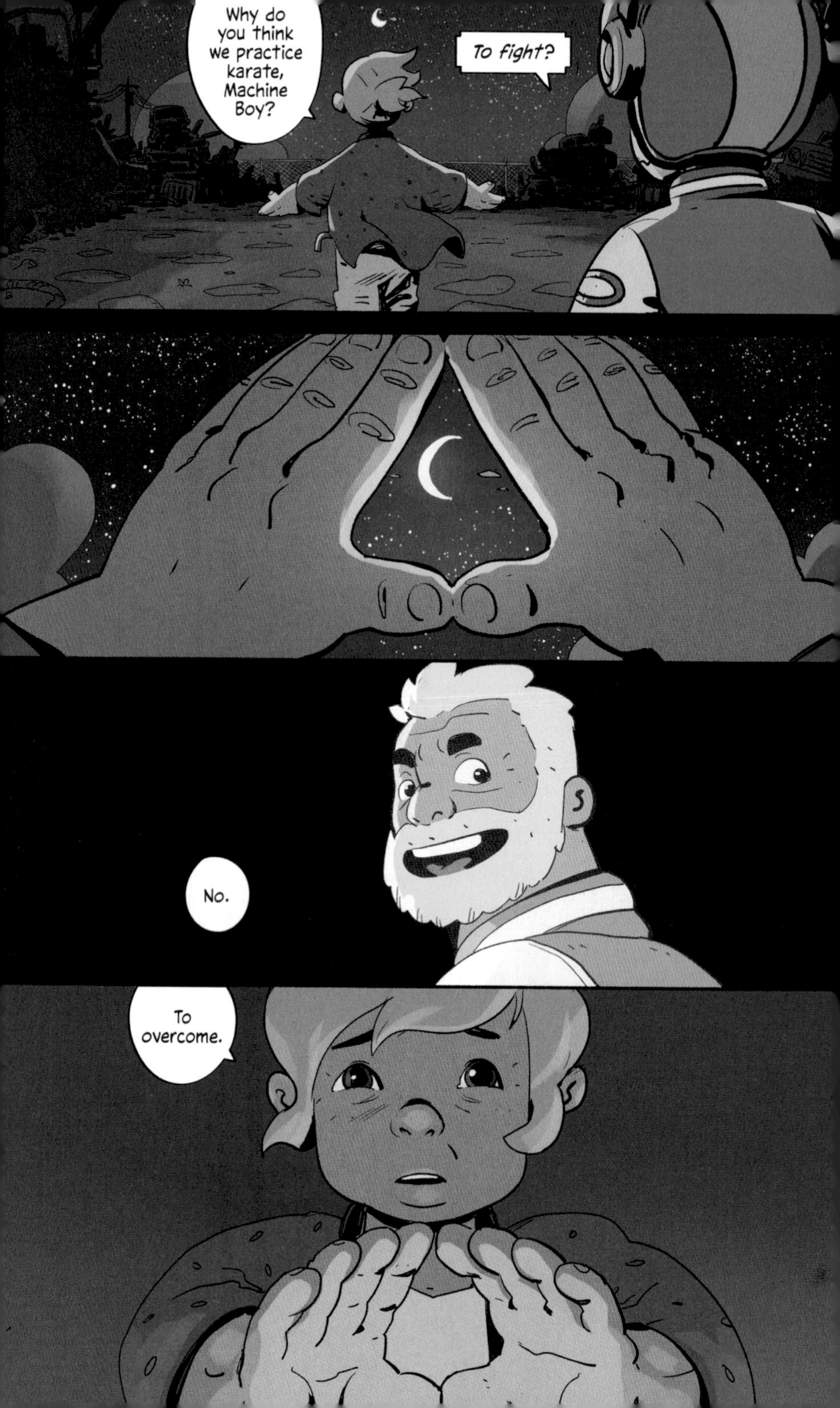
Why do you think we practice karate, Machine Boy?
To fight?
No.
To overcome.

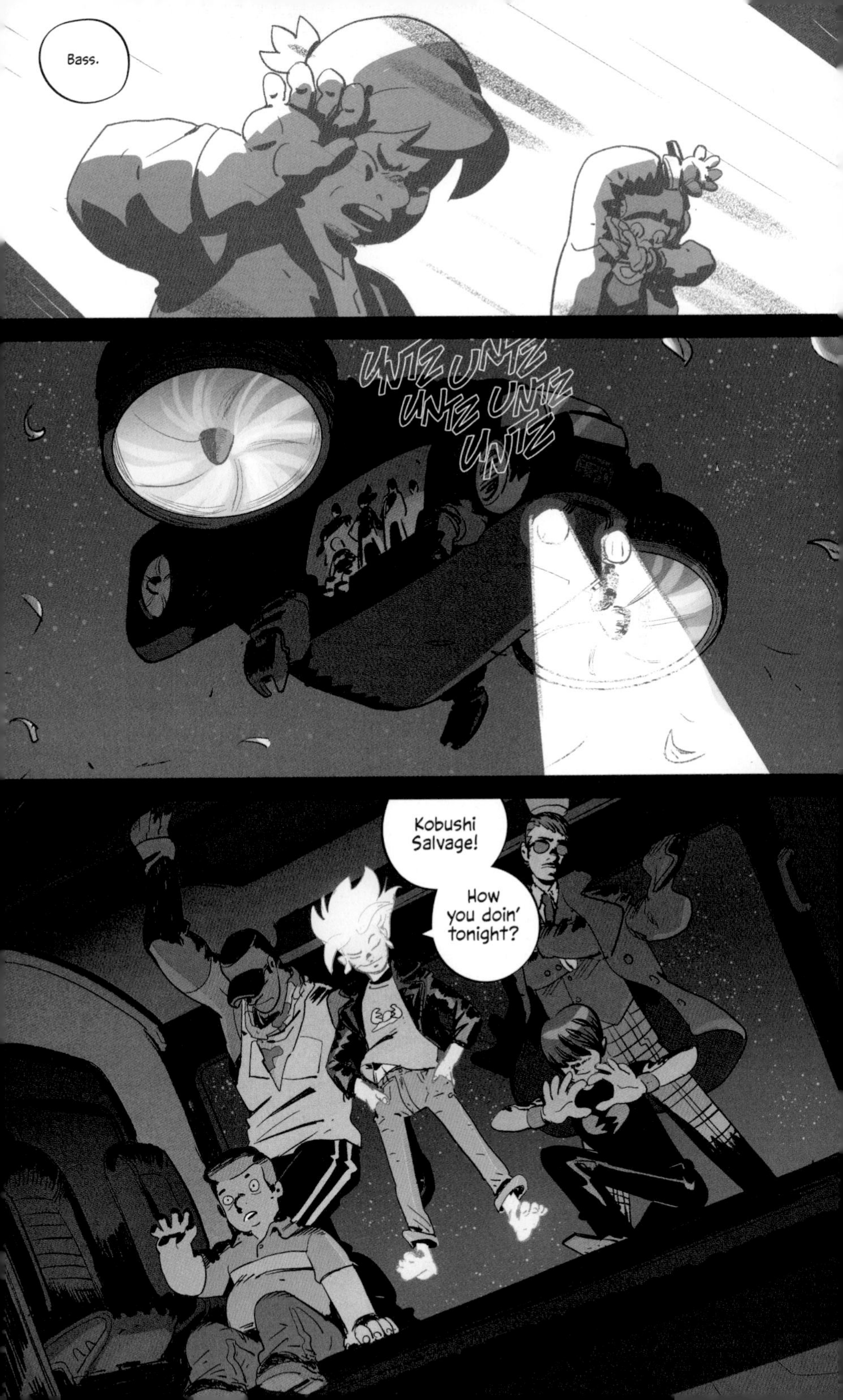
Bass.
UNTZ UNTZ UNTZ UNTZ UNTZ
Kobushi Salvage!
How you doin' tonight?

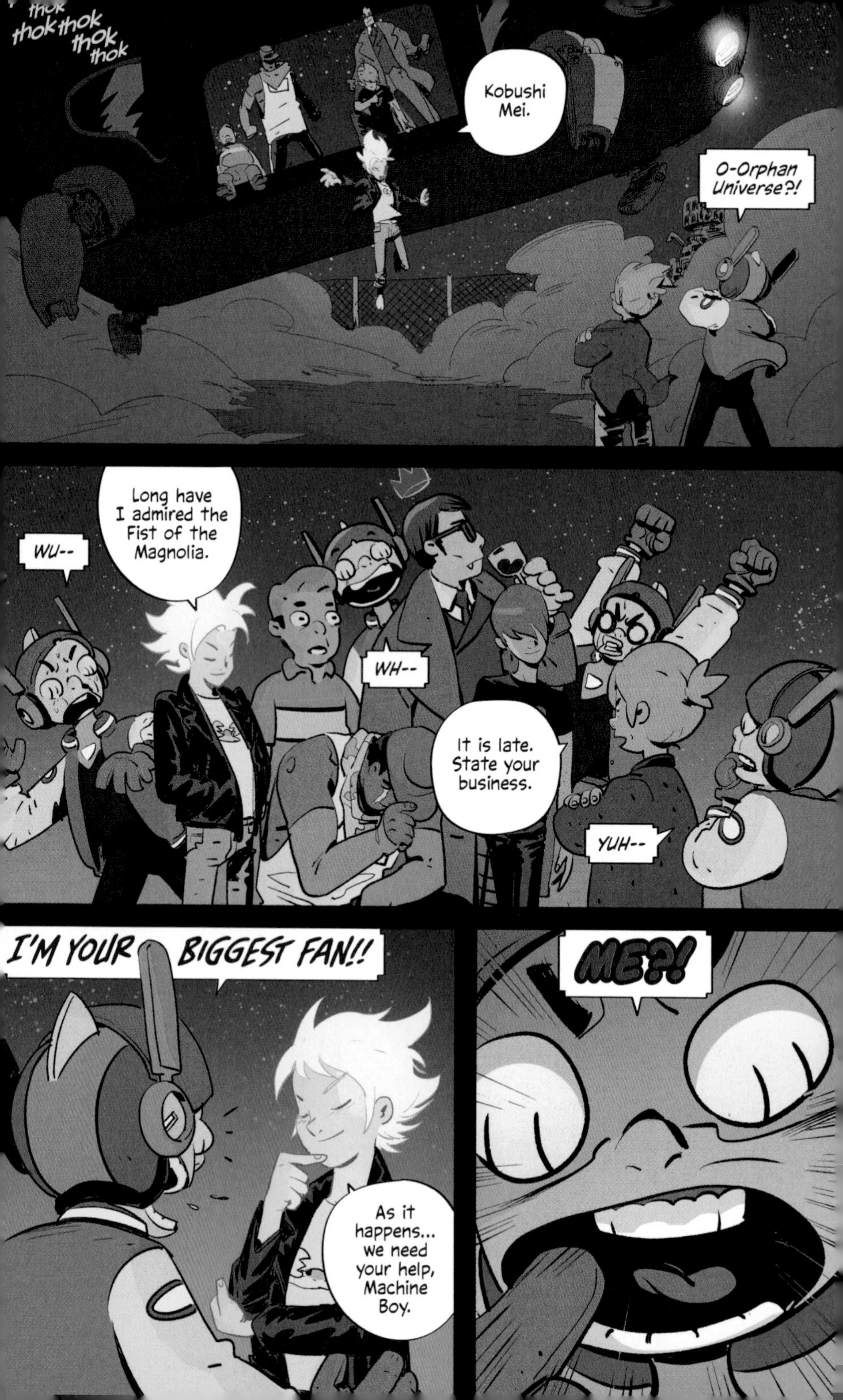
thok thok thok thok thok
Kobushi Mei.
O-Orphan Universe?!
WU--
Long have I admired the Fist of the Magnolia.
WH--
It is late. State your business.
YUH--
I'M YOUR BIGGEST FAN!!
As it happens... we need your help, Machine Boy.
ME?!

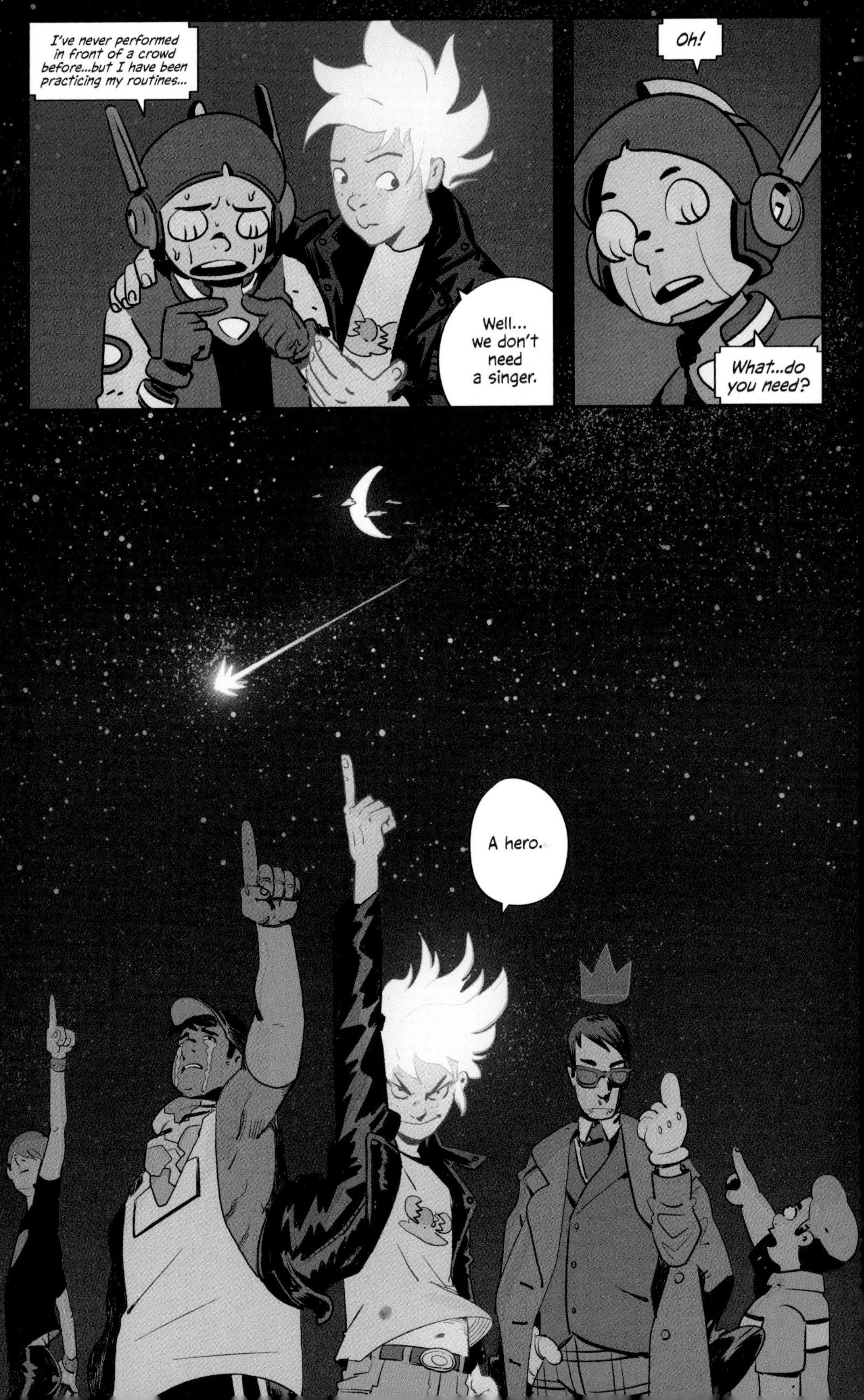
I've never performed in front of a crowd before...but I have been practicing my routines...
Well... we don't need a singer.
Oh!
What...do you need?
A hero.

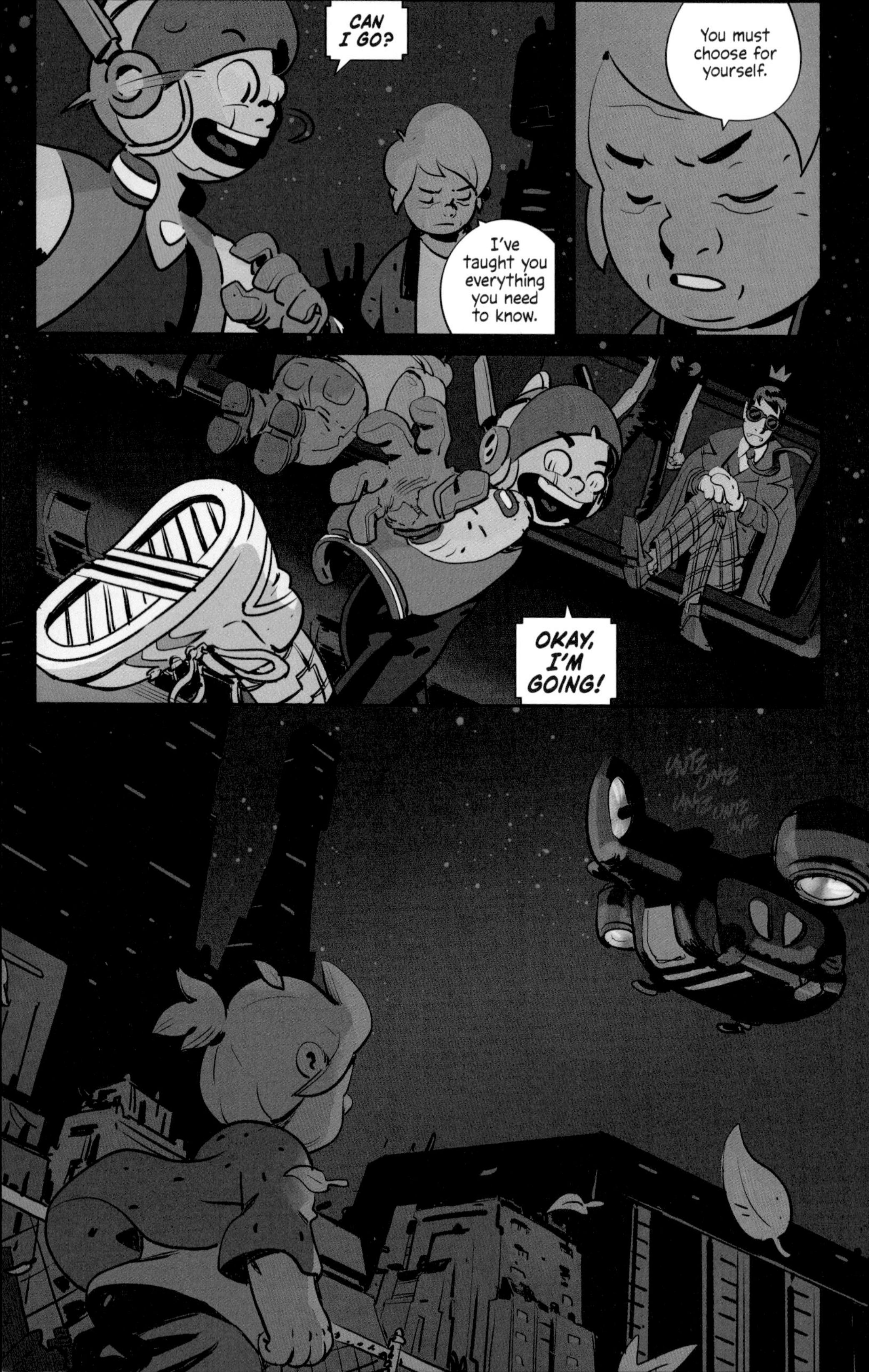
CAN I GO?
You must choose for yourself.
I've taught you everything you need to know.
OKAY, I'M GOING!

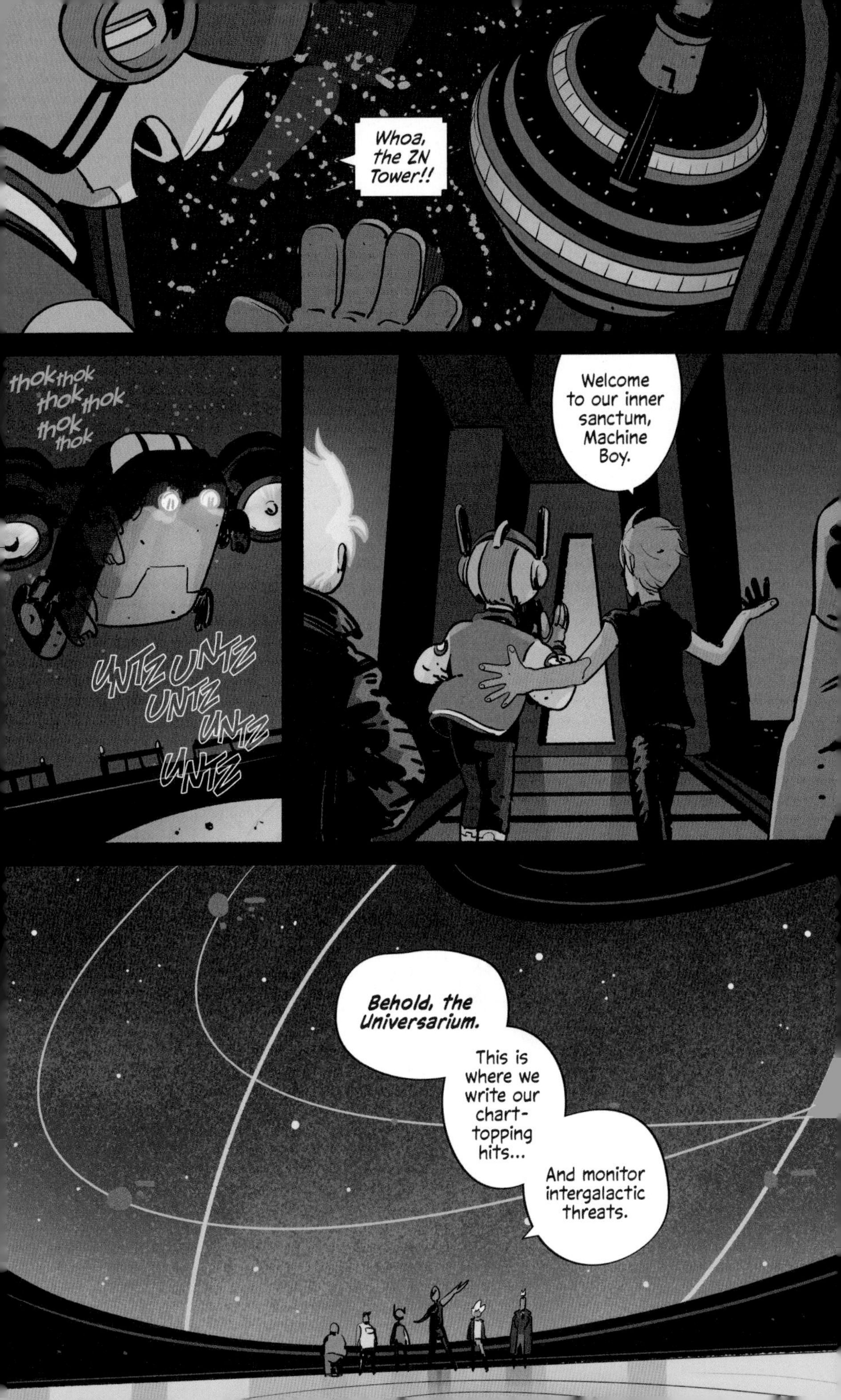

Whoa, the ZN Tower!!
thok thok thok thok thok thok
UNTZ UNTZ UNTZ UNTZ UNTZ
Welcome to our inner sanctum, Machine Boy.
Behold, the Universarium.
This is where we write our chart-topping hits...
And monitor intergalactic threats.

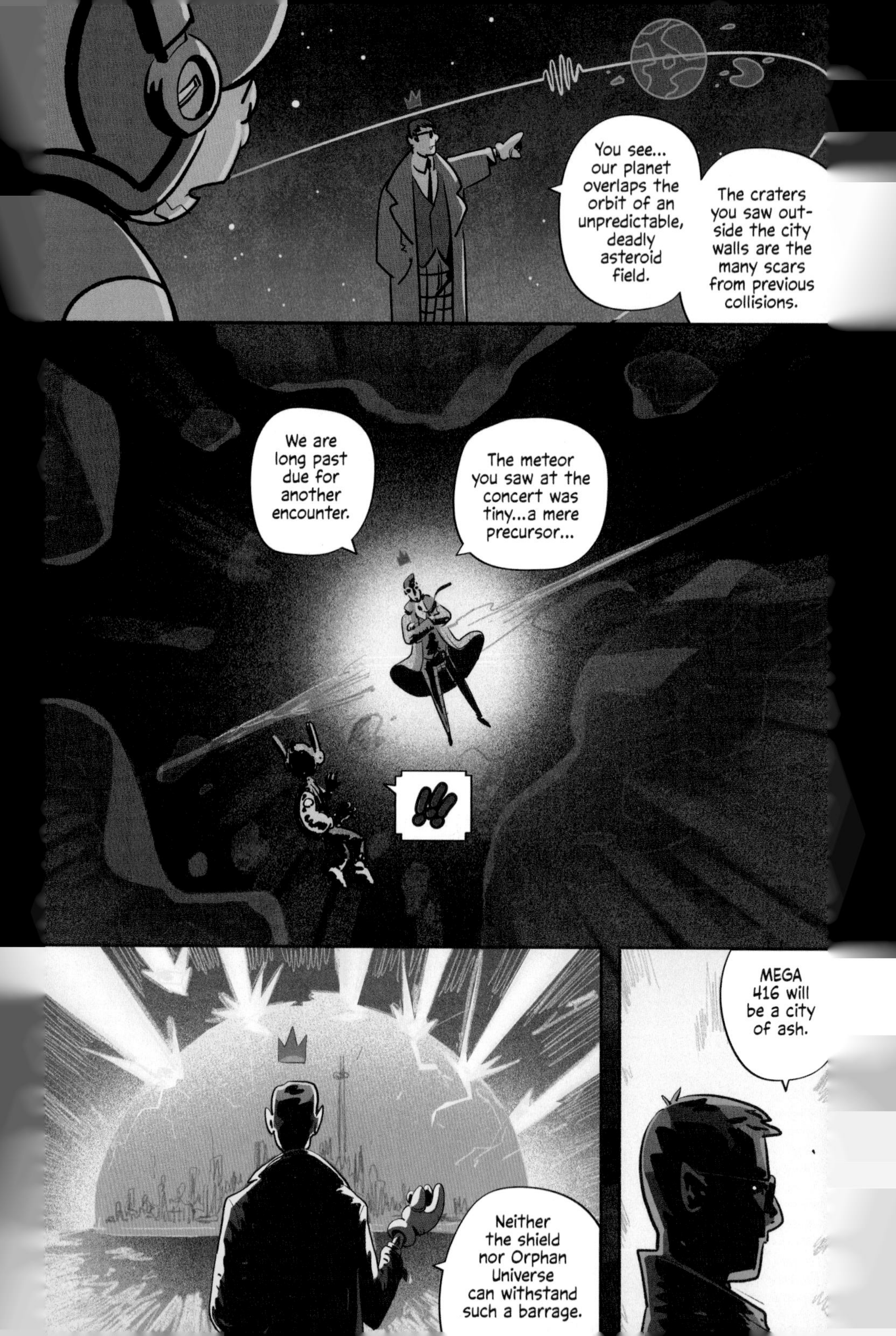
You see... our planet overlaps the orbit of an unpredictable, deadly asteroid field.
The craters you saw out-side the city walls are the many scars from previous collisions.
We are long past due for another encounter.
The meteor you saw at the concert was tiny...a mere precursor...
!!
MEGA 416 will be a city of ash.
Neither the shield nor Orphan Universe can withstand such a barrage.

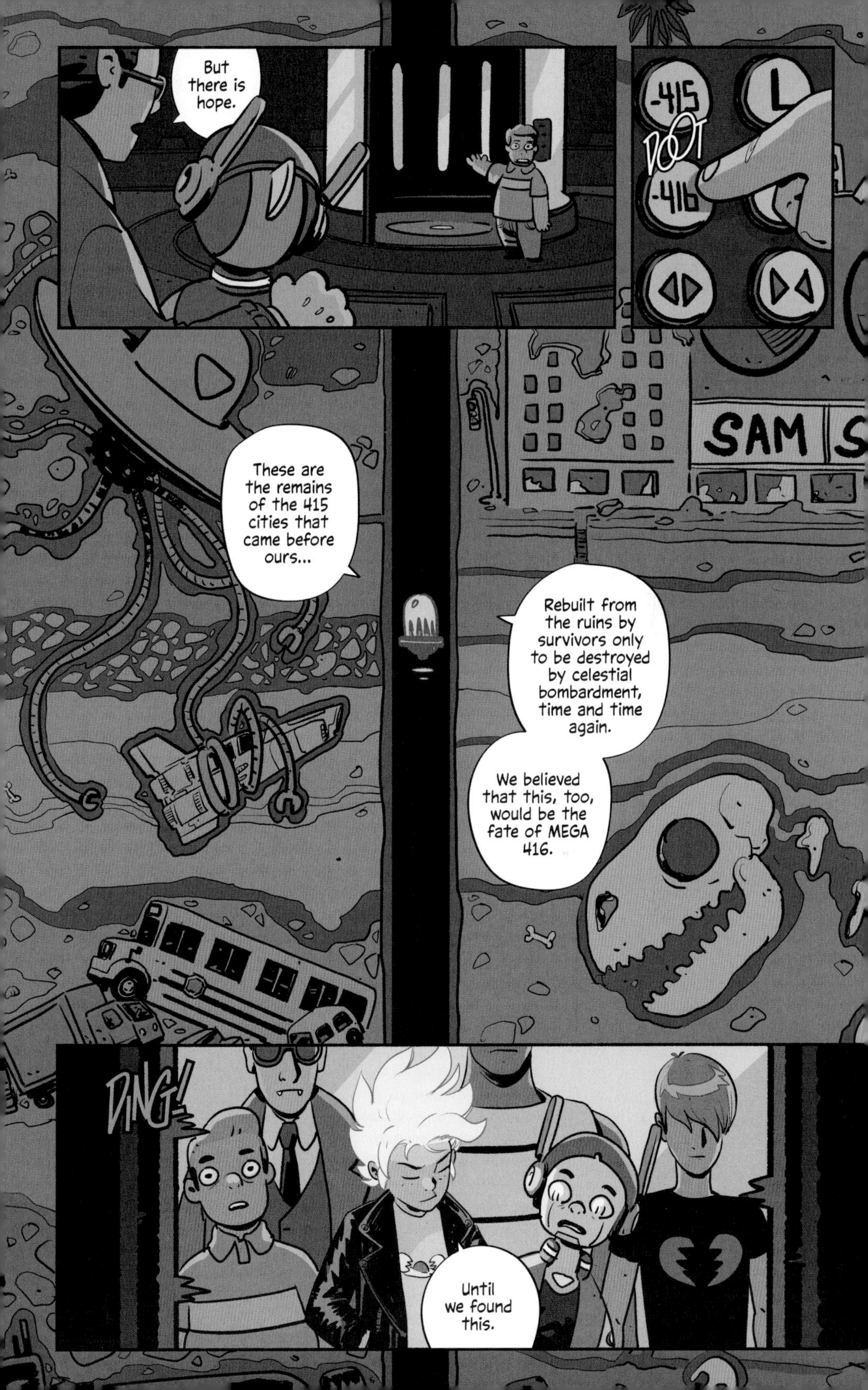
But there is hope.
-415
L
DOOT
-416
These are the remains of the 415 cities that came before ours...
Rebuilt from the ruins by survivors only to be destroyed by celestial bombardment, time and time again.
SAM
We believed that this, too, would be the fate of MEGA 416.
DING!
Until we found this.

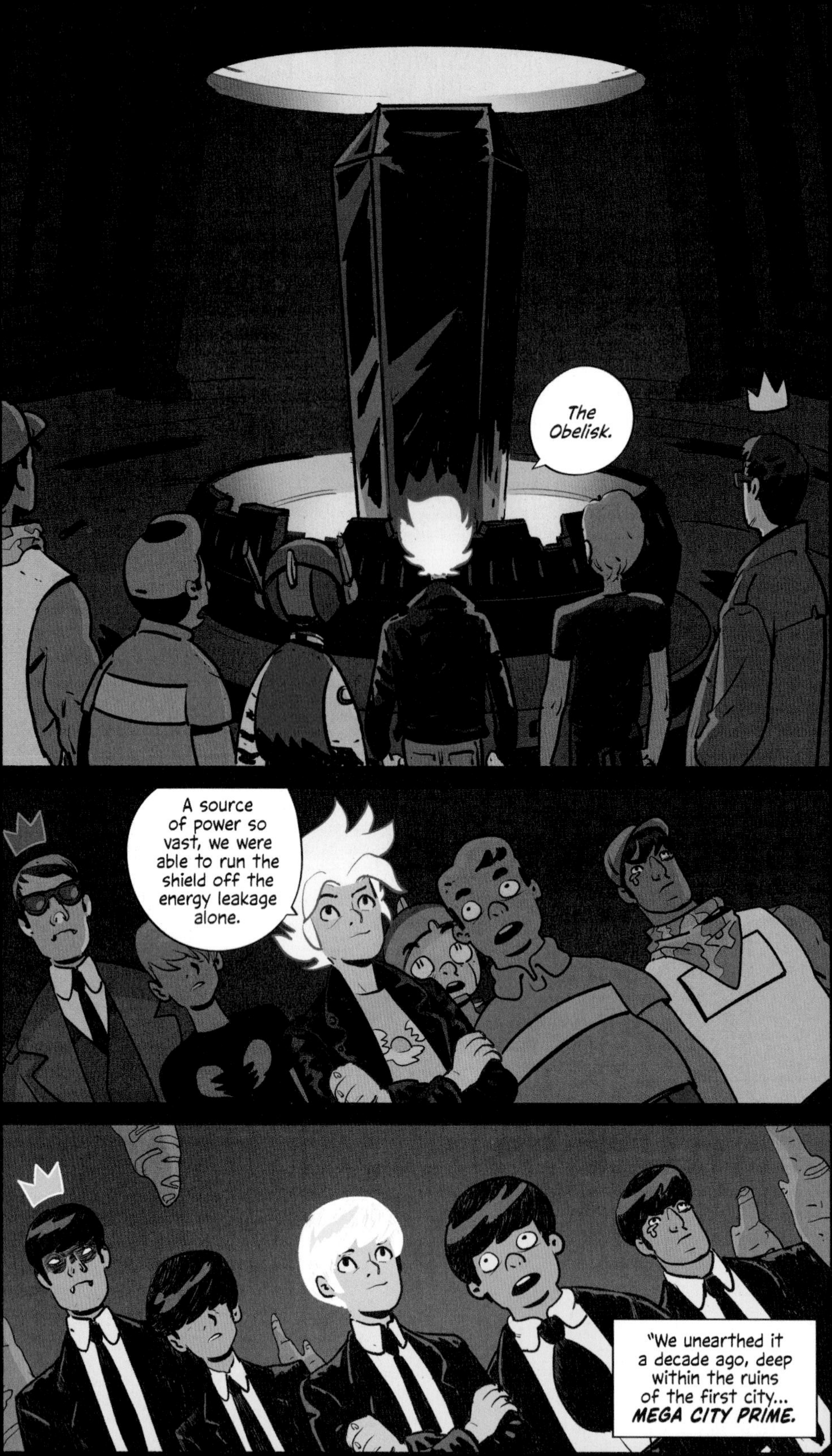
The Obelisk.
A source of power so vast, we were able to run the shield off the energy leakage alone.
"We unearthed it a decade ago, deep within the ruins of the first city... MEGA CITY PRIME.

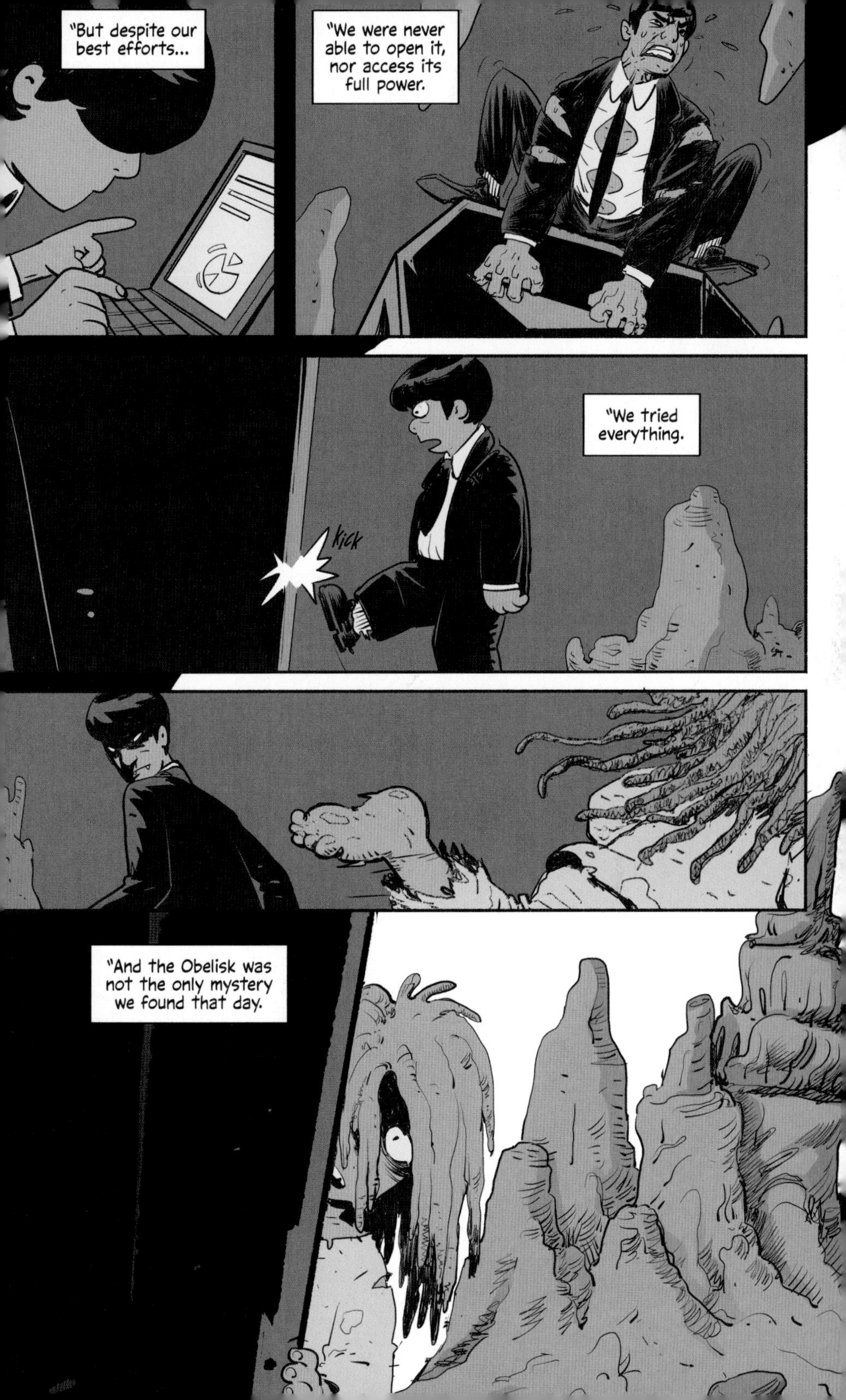
"But despite our best efforts...
"We were never able to open it, nor access its full power.
"We tried everything.
KICK
"And the Obelisk was not the only mystery we found that day.

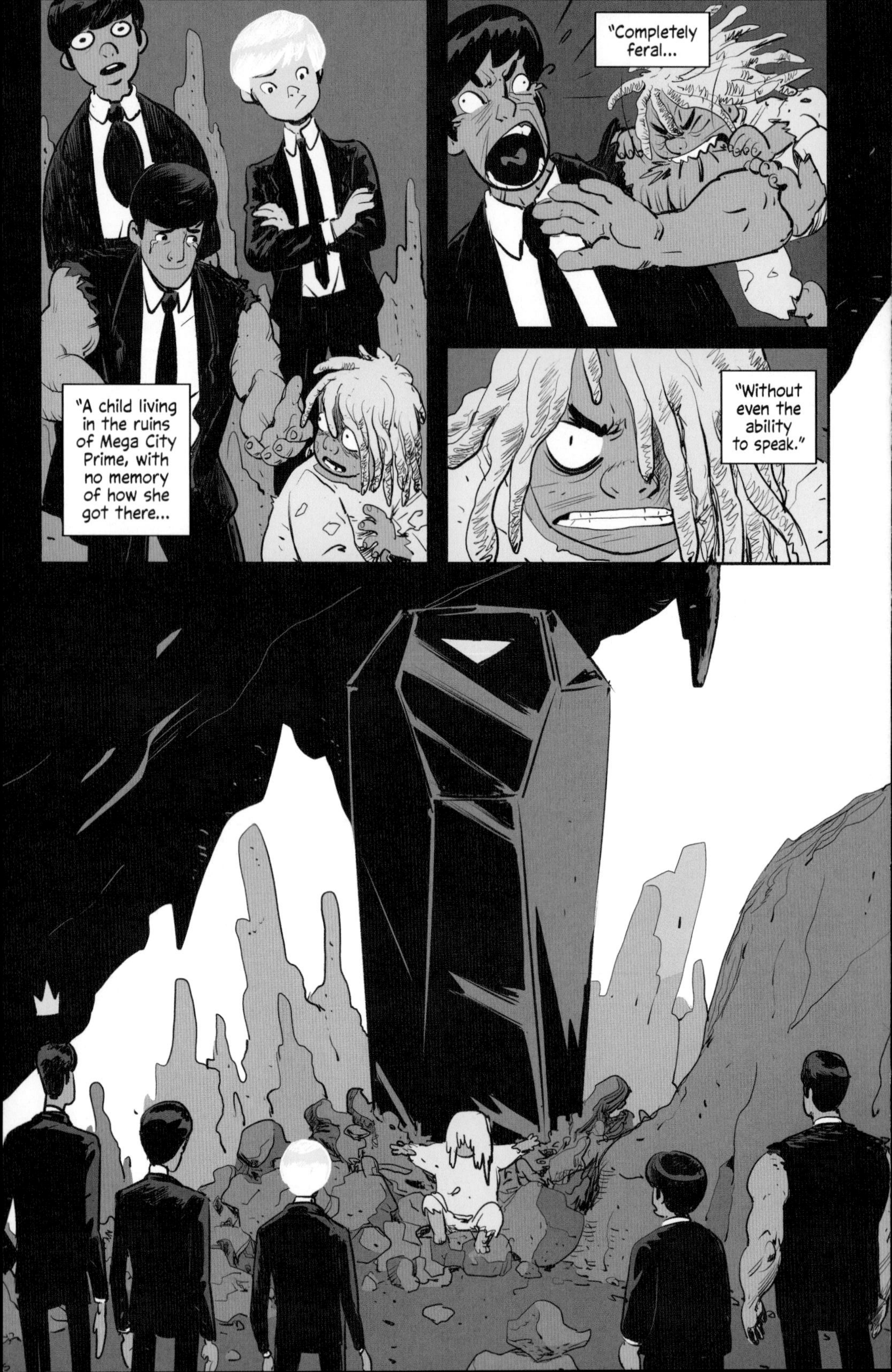
"A child living in the ruins of Mega City Prime, with no memory of how she got there...
"Completely feral...
"Without even the ability to speak."

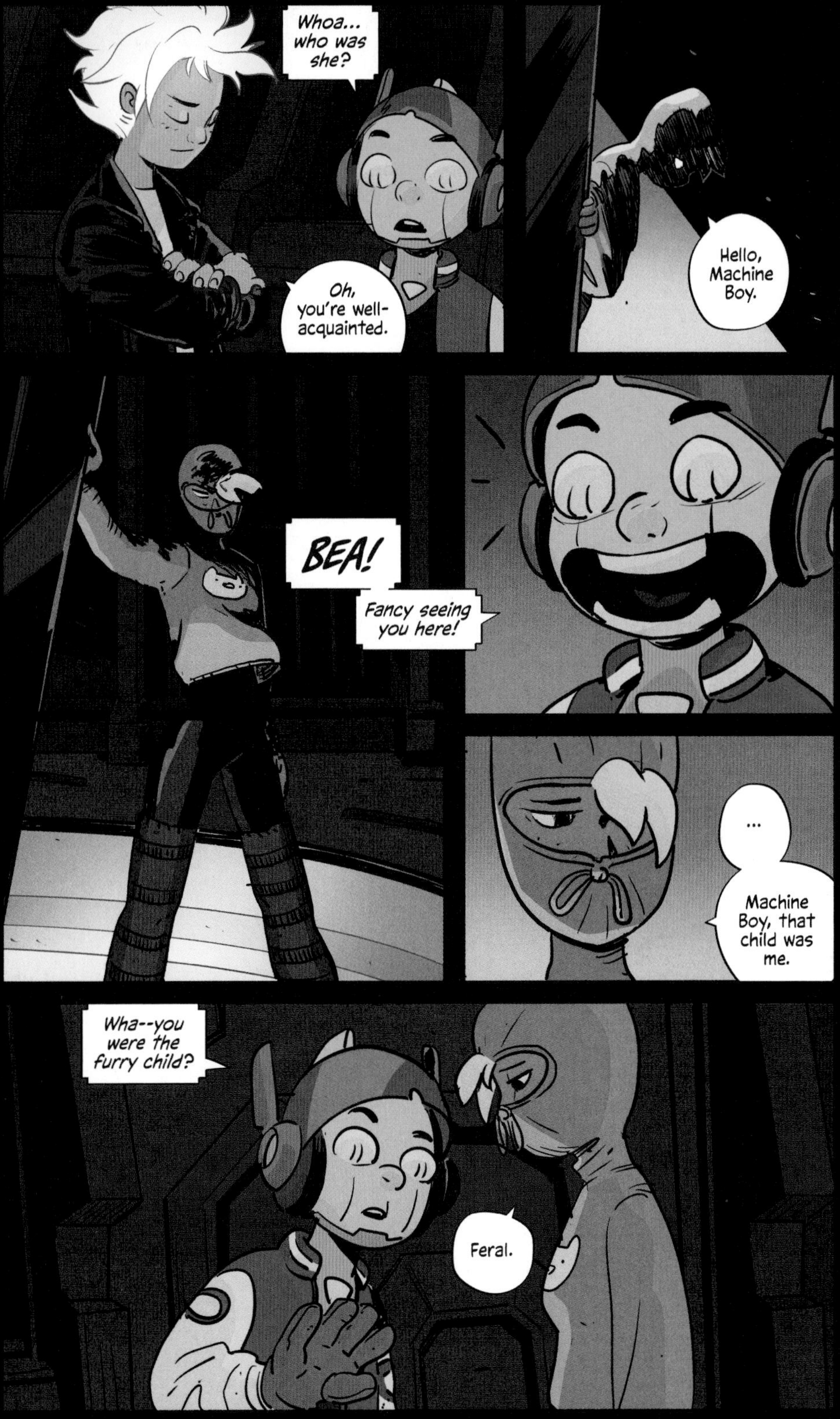
Whoa... who was she?
Oh, you're well-acquainted.
Hello, Machine Boy.
BEA!
Fancy seeing you here!
...
Machine Boy, that child was me.
Wha--you were the furry child?
Feral.

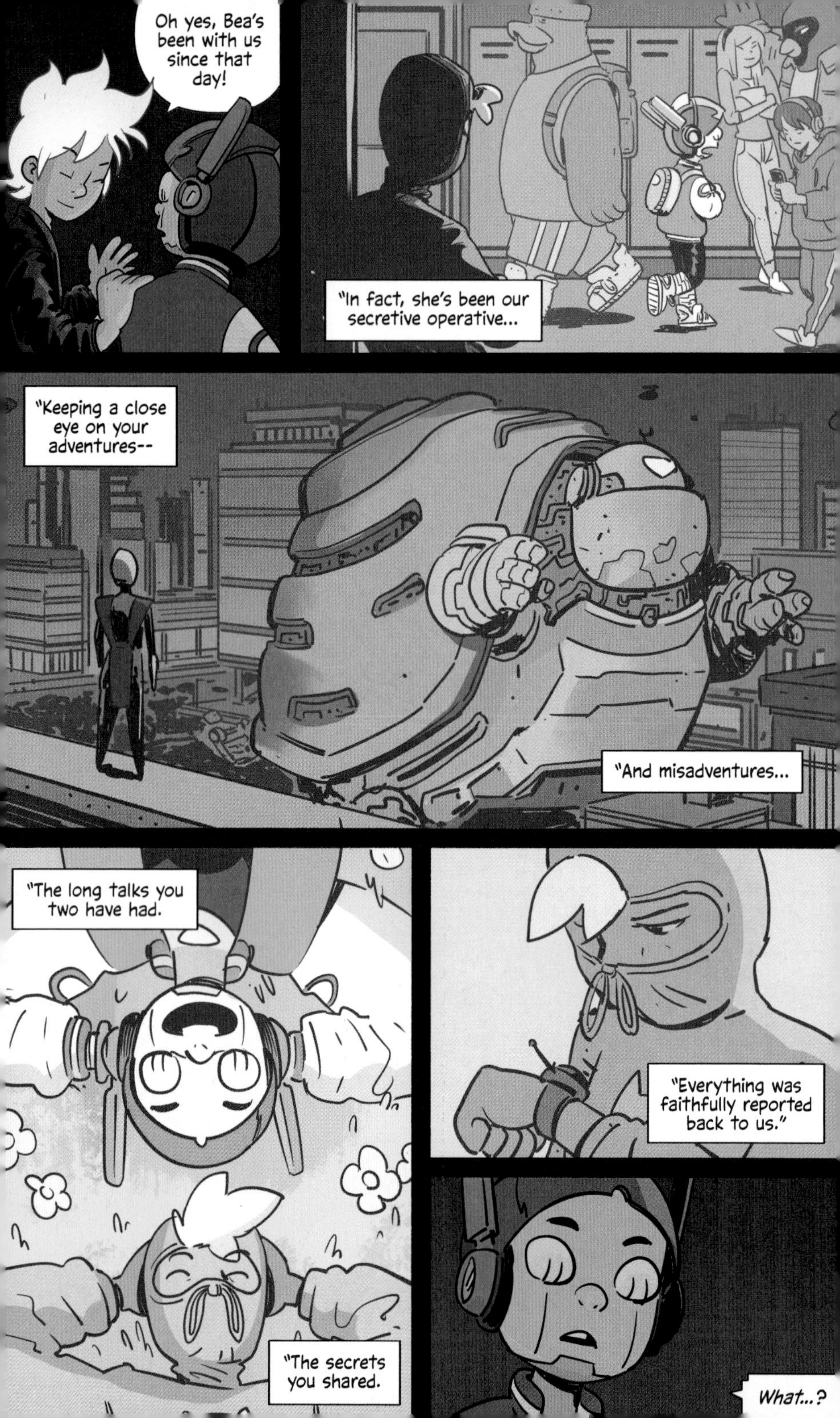
Oh yes, Bea's been with us since that day!
"In fact, she's been our secretive operative...
"Keeping a close eye on your adventures--
"And misadventures...
"The long talks you two have had.
"The secrets you shared.
"Everything was faithfully reported back to us."
What...?

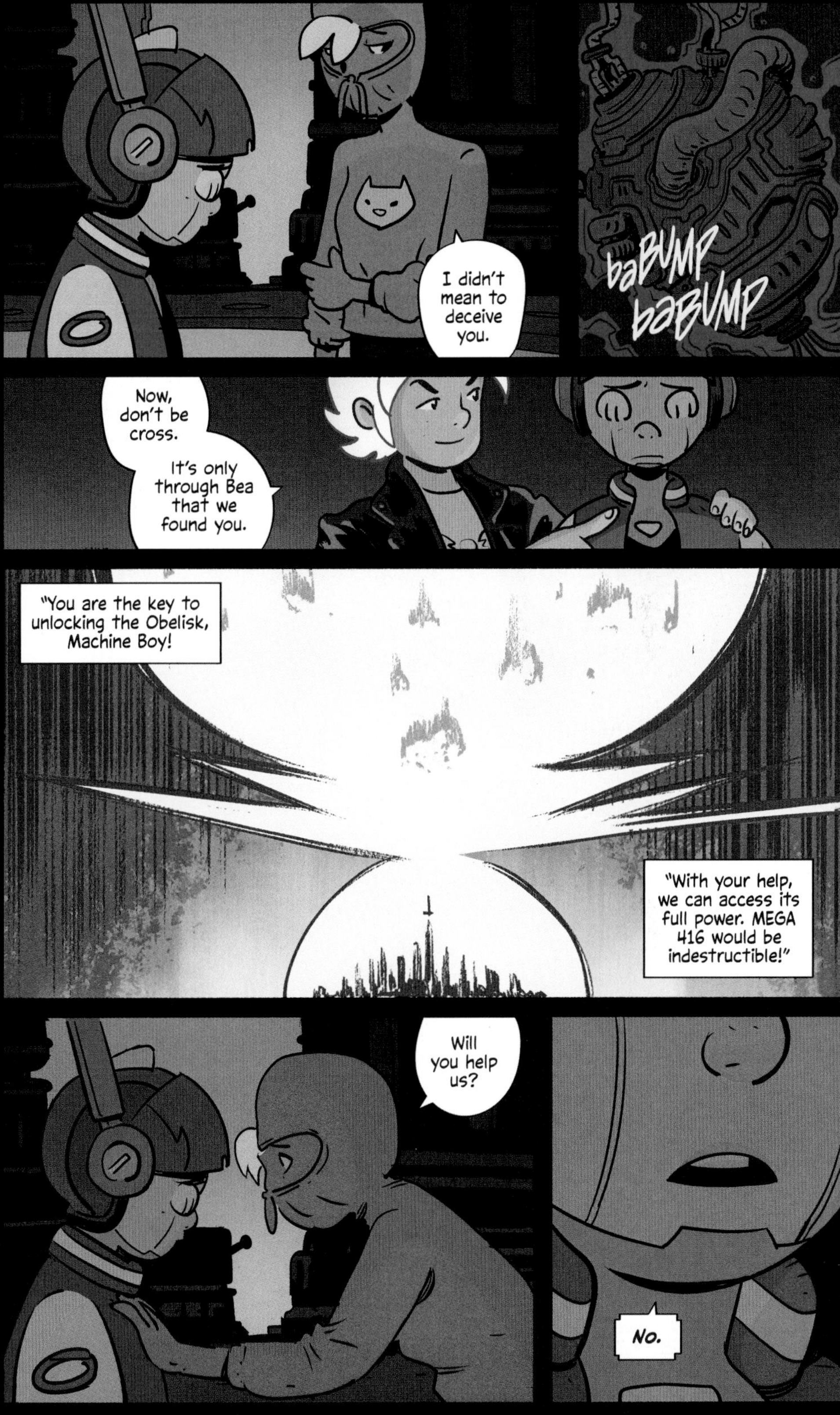
I didn't mean to deceive you.
baBUMP babUMP
Now, don't be cross.
It's only through Bea that we found you.
"You are the key to unlocking the Obelisk, Machine Boy!
"With your help, we can access its full power. MEGA 416 would be indestructible!"
Will you help us?
No.

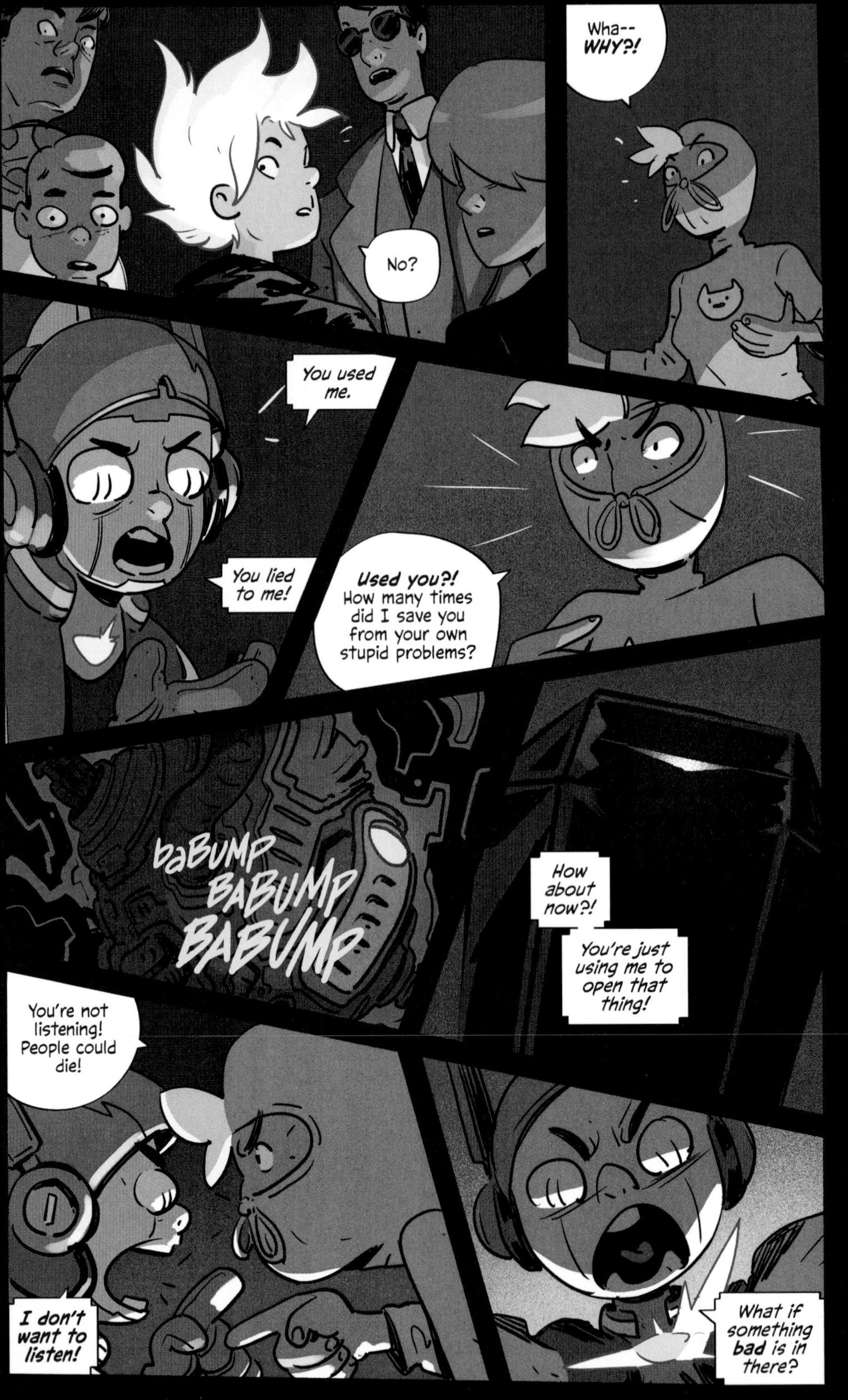

No?
Wha-- WHY?!
You used me.
You lied to me!
Used you?! How many times did I save you from your own stupid problems?
baBUMP BABUMP BABUMP
How about now?!
You're just using me to open that thing!
You're not listening! People could die!
I don't want to listen!
What if something bad is in there?

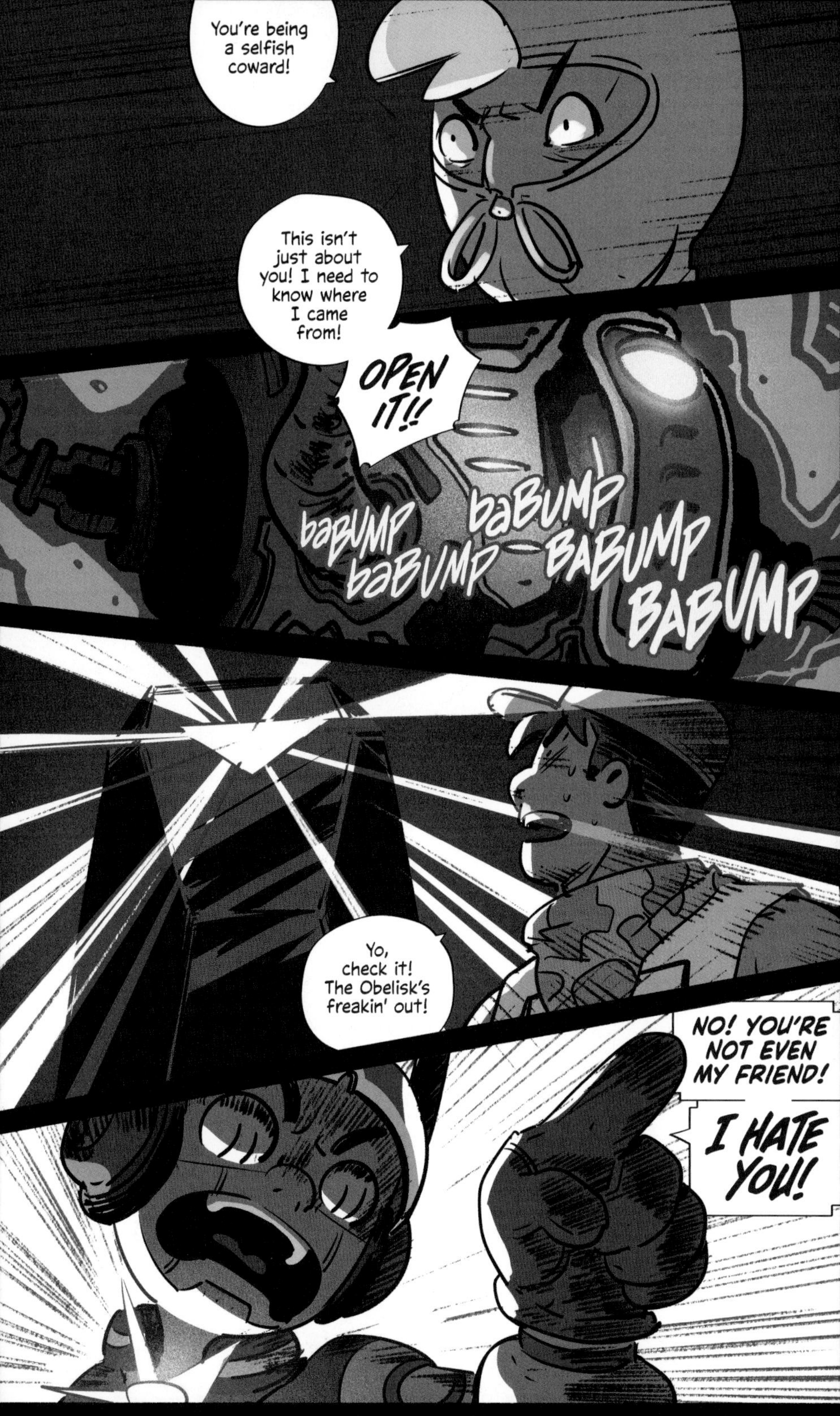

You're being a selfish coward!
This isn't just about you! I need to know where I came from!
OPEN IT!!
baBUMP baBUMP baBUMP BABUMP BABUMP
Yo, check it! The Obelisk's freakin' out!
NO! YOU'RE NOT EVEN MY FRIEND!
I HATE YOU!

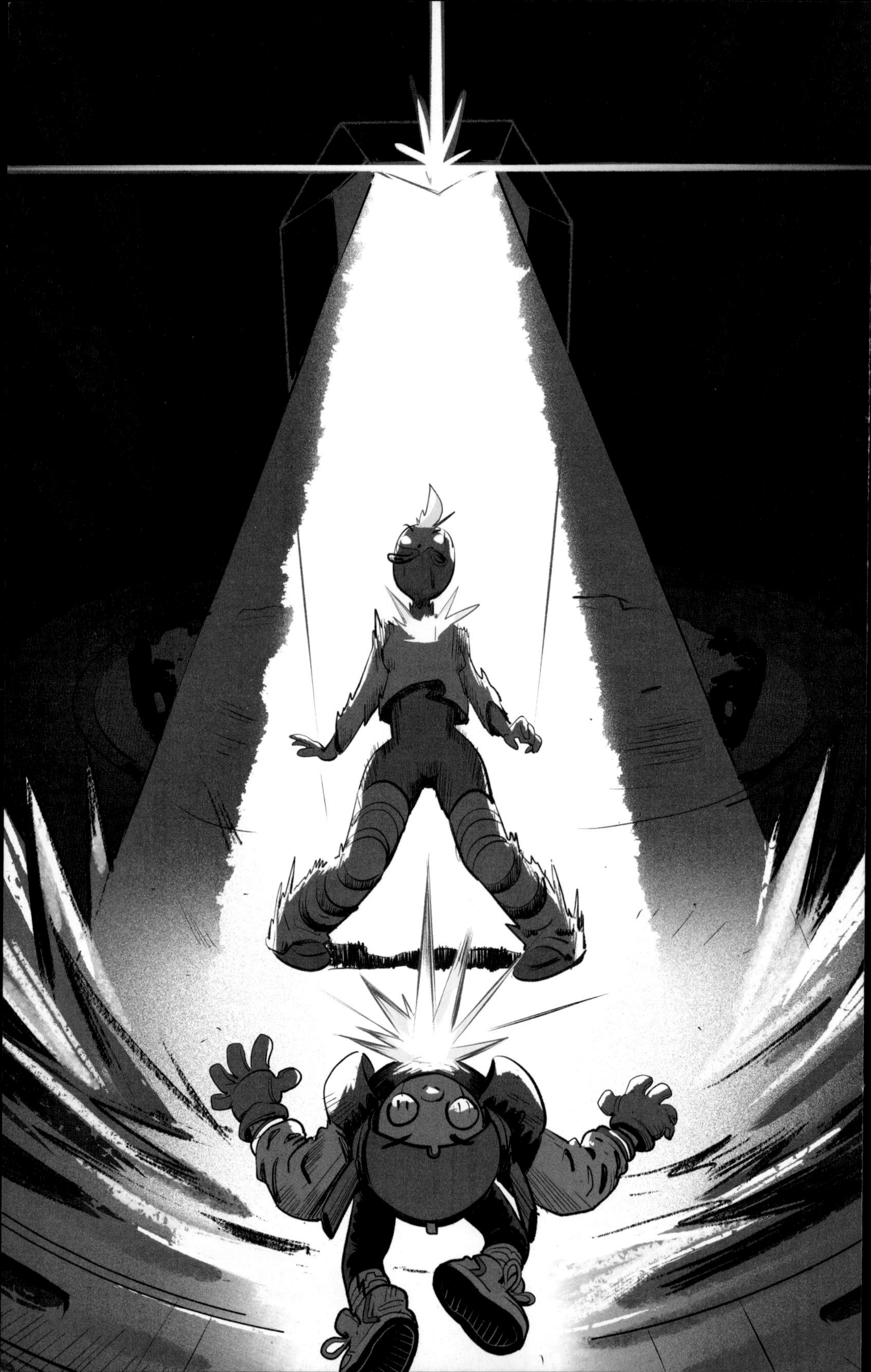

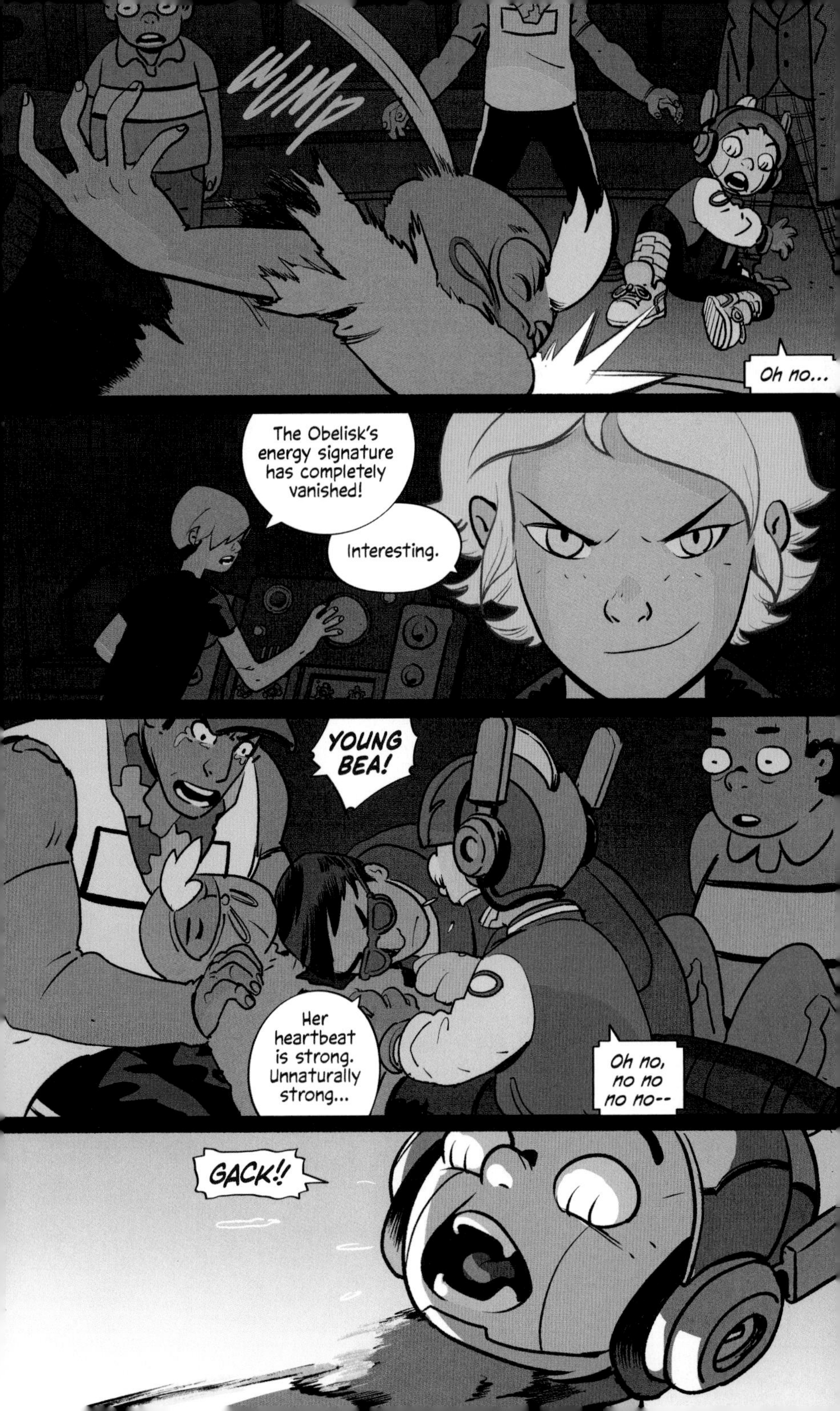
WUMP
Oh no...
The Obelisk's energy signature has completely vanished!
Interesting.
YOUNG BEA!
Her heartbeat is strong. Unnaturally strong...
Oh no, no no no no--
GACK!!

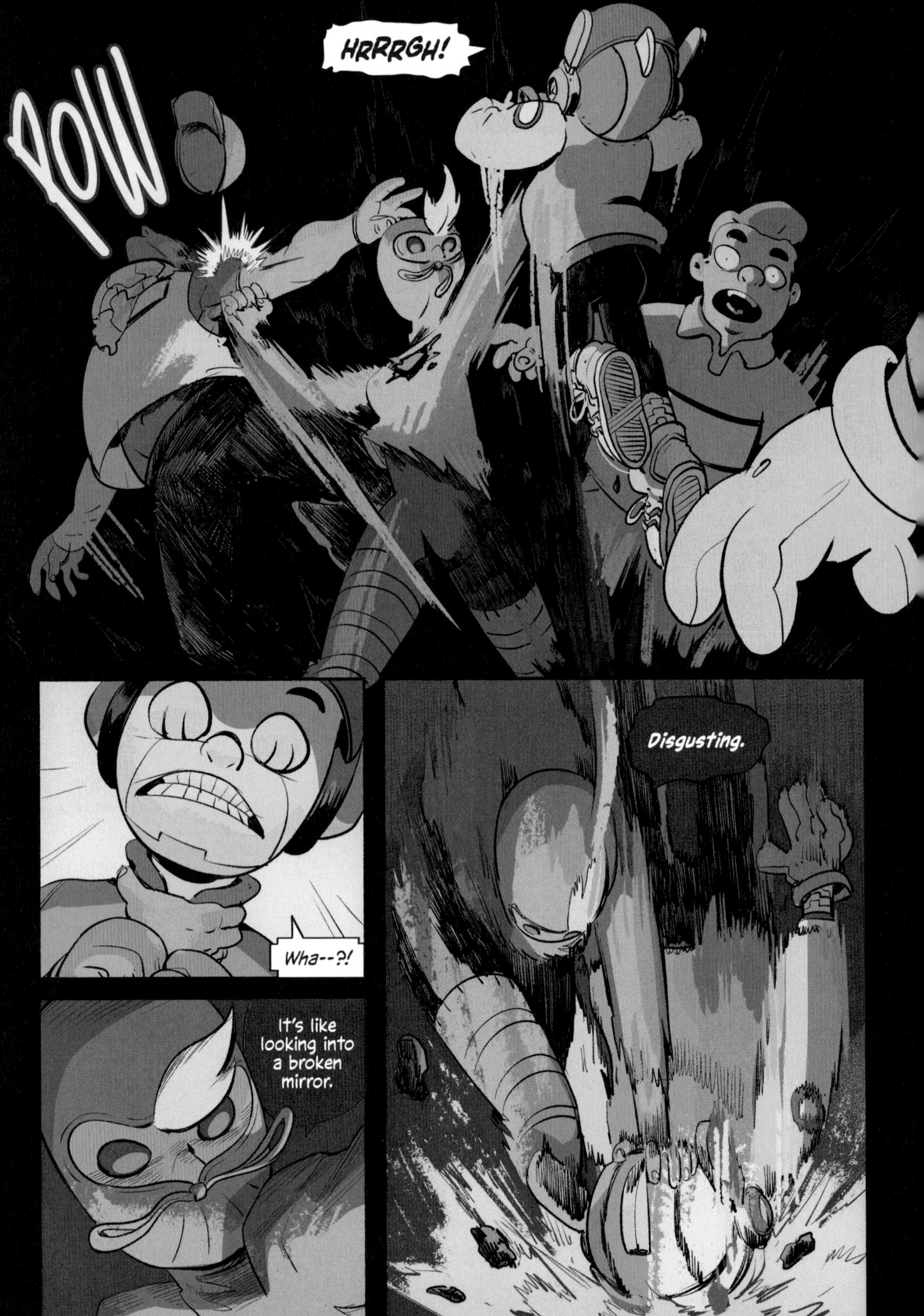
POW
HRRRGH!
Wha--?!
It's like looking into a broken mirror.
Disgusting.

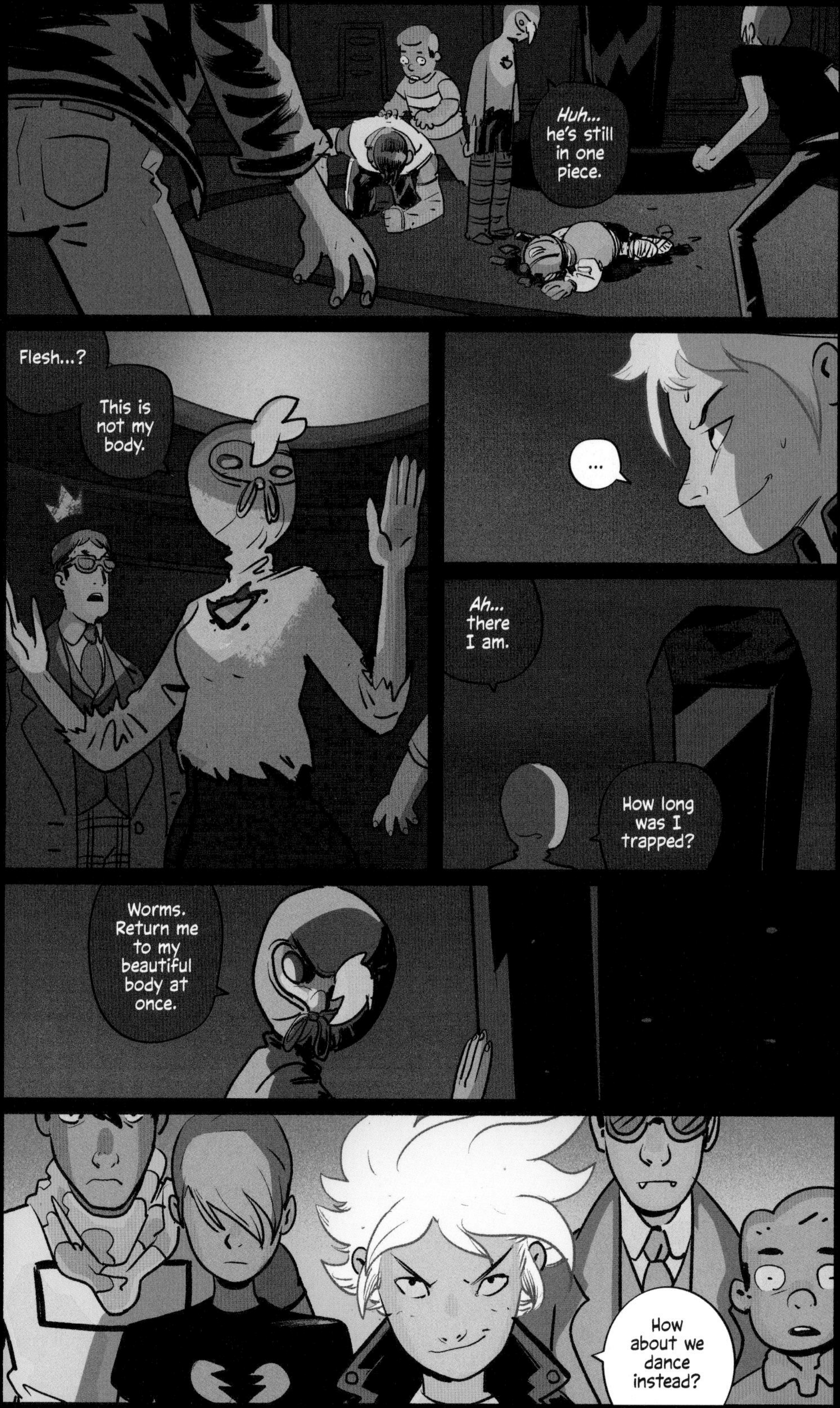
Huh... he's still in one piece.
Flesh...?
This is not my body.
...
Ah... there I am.
How long was I trapped?
Worms. Return me to my beautiful body at once.
How about we dance instead?

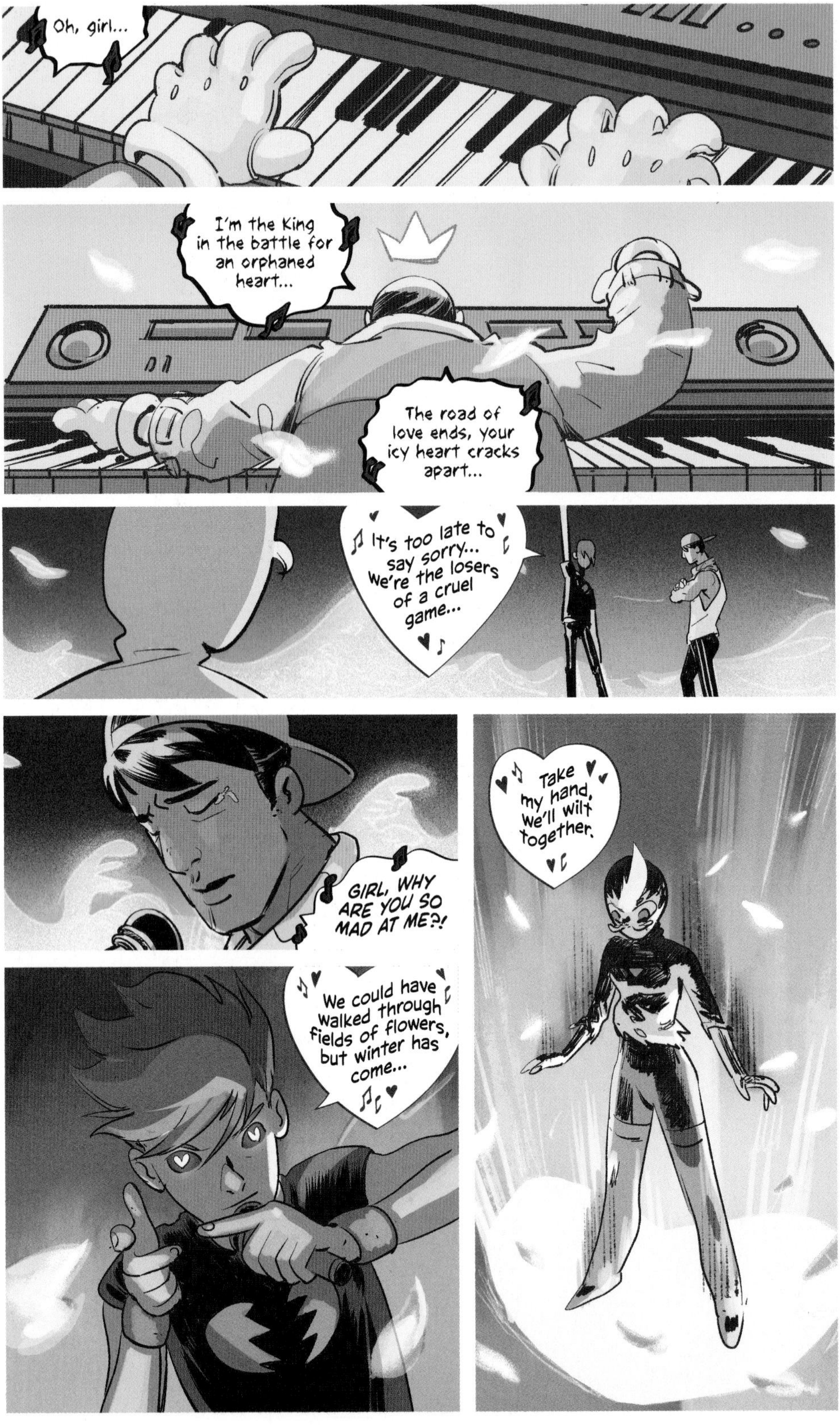
Oh, girl...
I'm the King in the battle for an orphaned heart...
The road of love ends, your icy heart cracks apart...
It's too late to say sorry... We're the losers of a cruel game...
GIRL, WHY ARE YOU SO MAD AT ME?!
We could have walked through fields of flowers, but winter has come...
Take my hand, we'll wilt together.

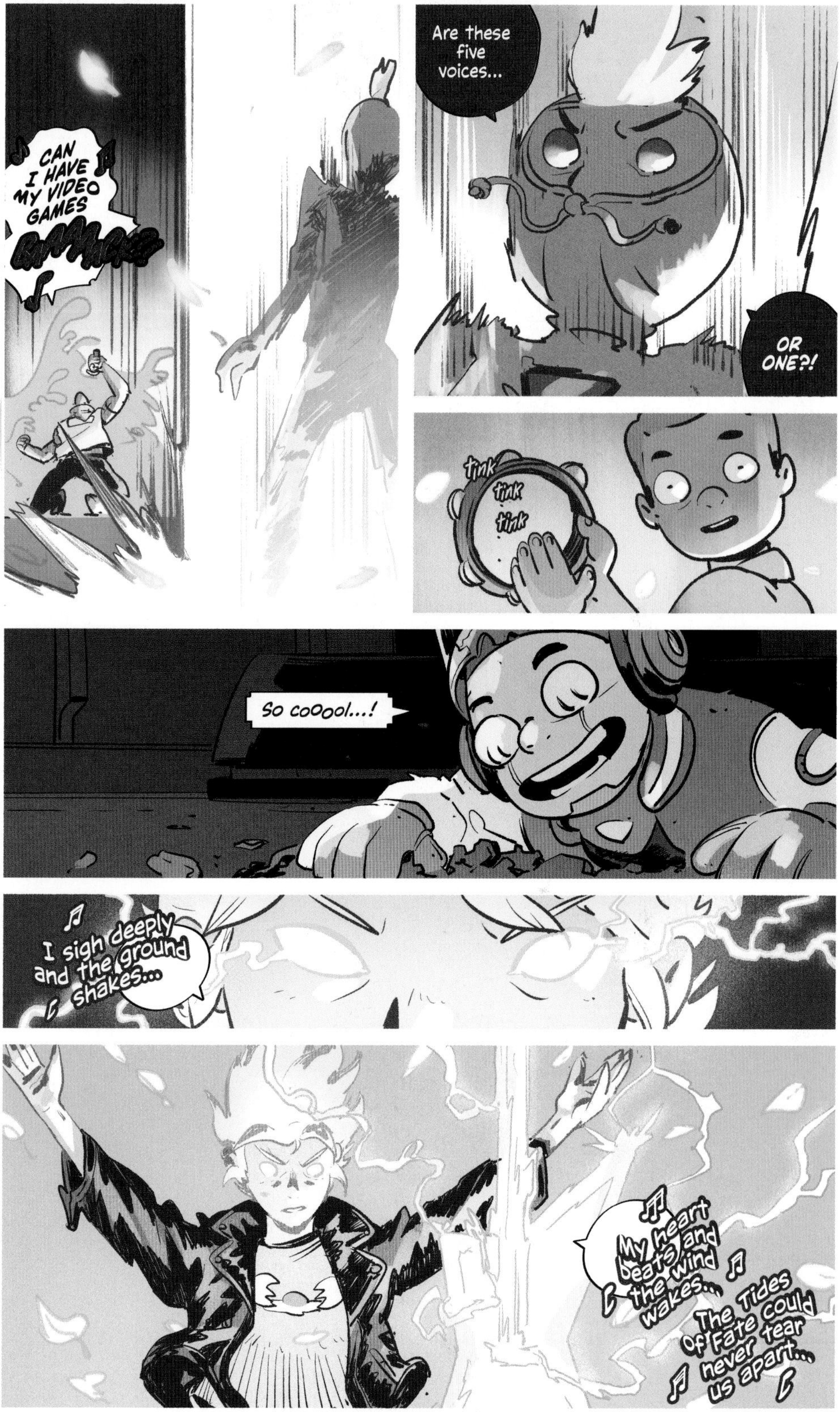
CAN I HAVE MY VIDEO GAMES BAAACK!!
Are these five voices...
OR ONE?!
tink tink tink
So coOool...!
I sigh deeply and the ground shakes...
My heart beats and the wind wakes...
The Tides of Fate could never tear us apart...

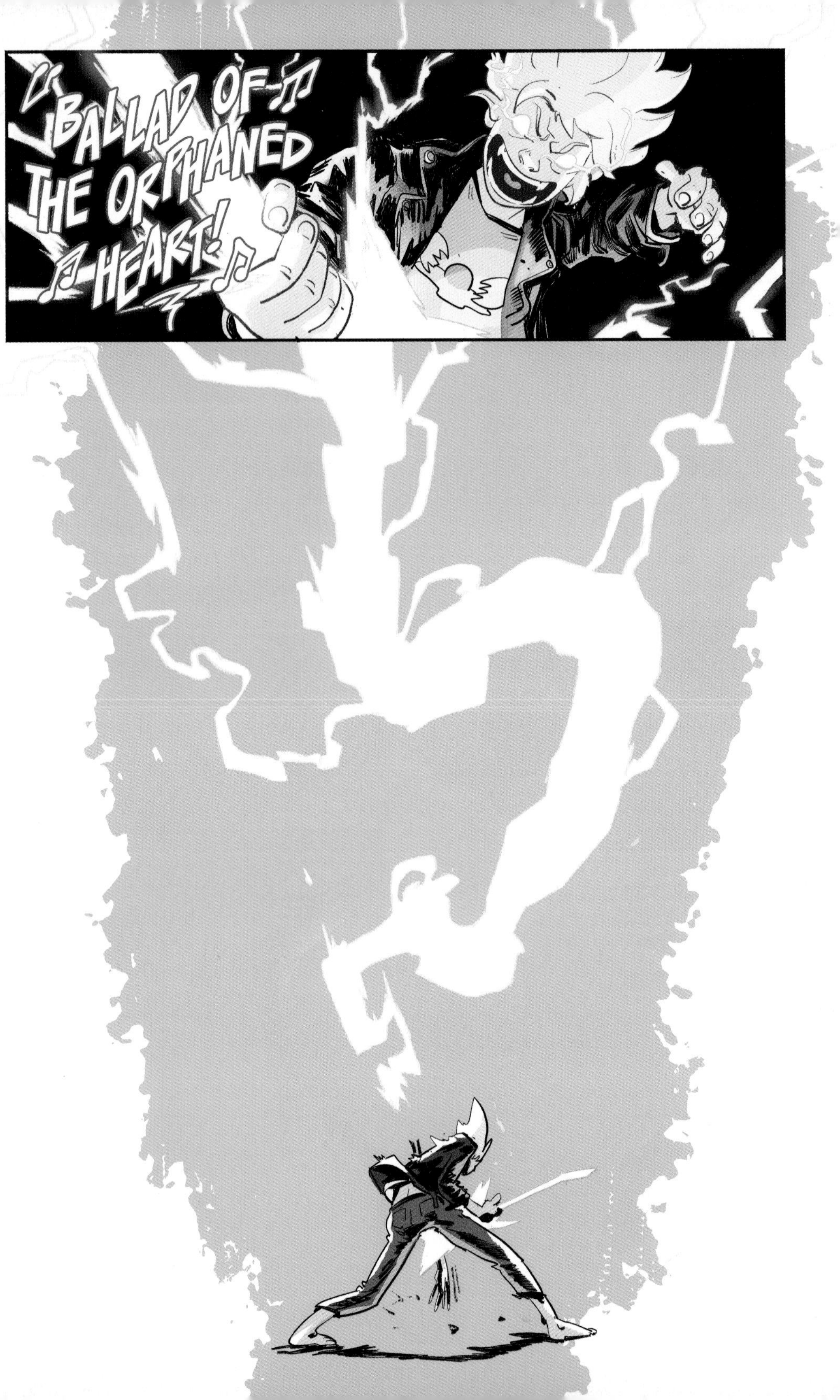
♫ BALLAD OF ♫ THE ORPHANED ♫ HEART! ♫

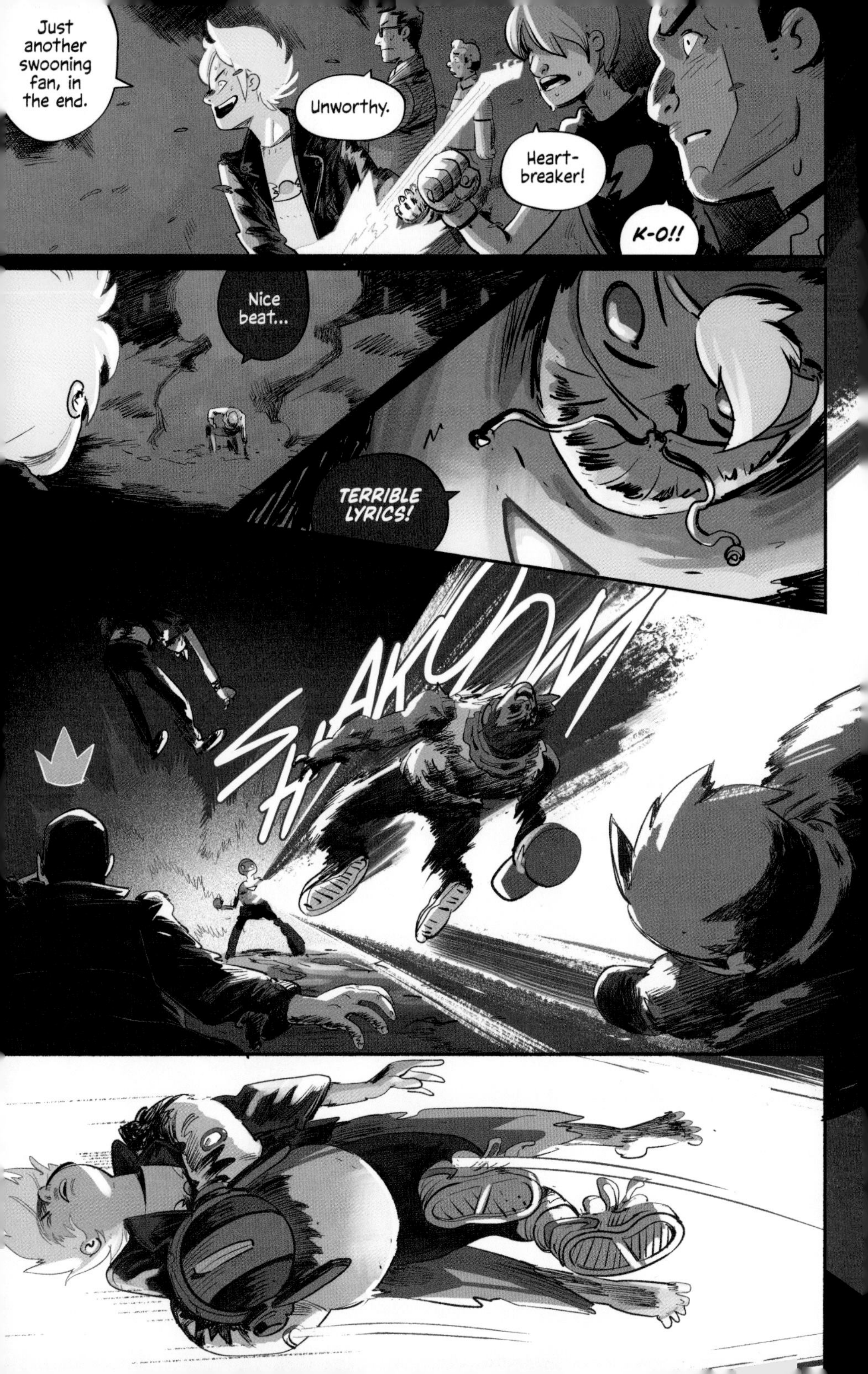
Just another swooning fan, in the end.
Unworthy.
Heart-breaker!
K-O!!
Nice beat...
TERRIBLE LYRICS!
SHAKOOM

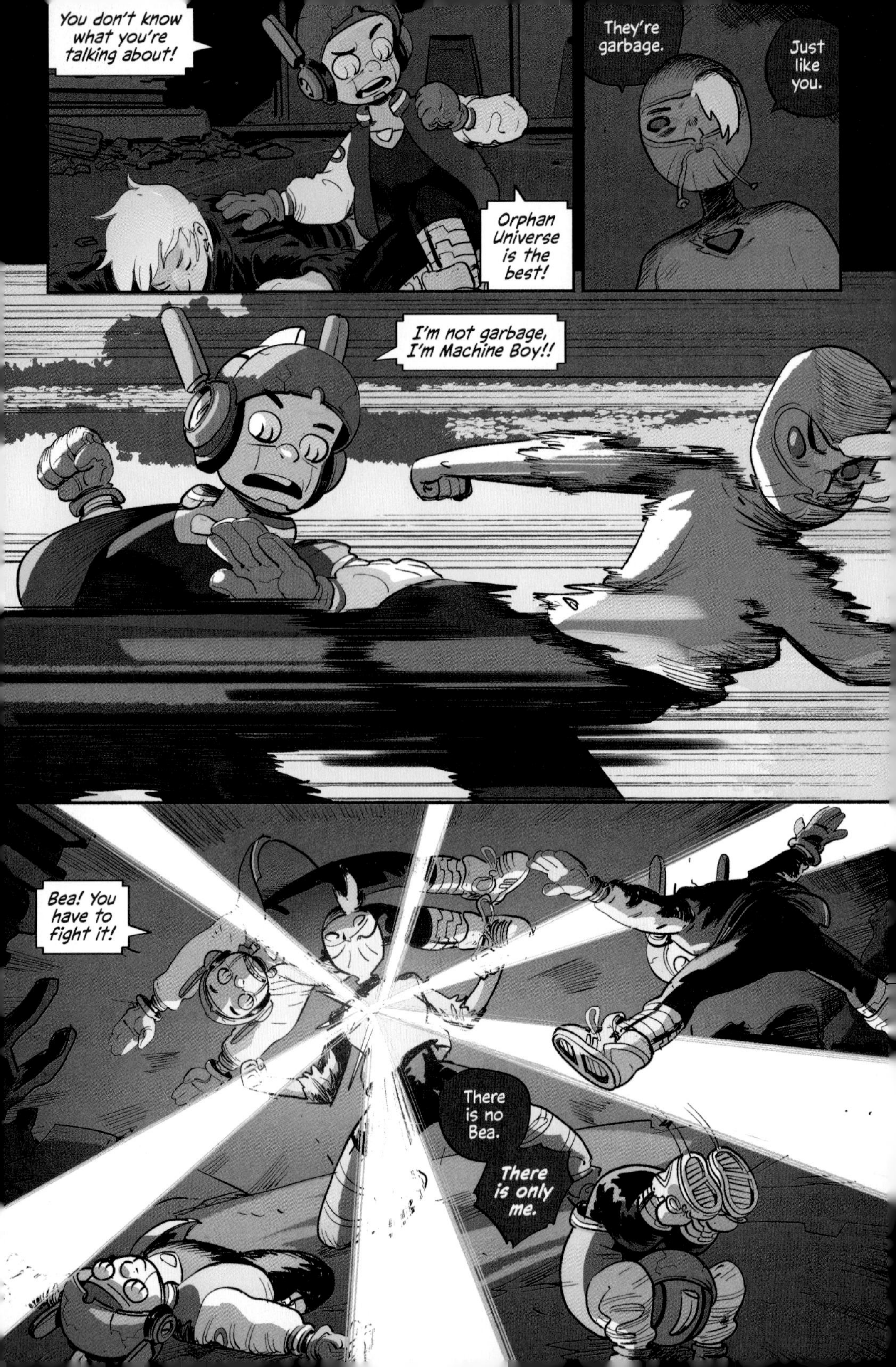
You don't know what you're talking about!
Orphan Universe is the best!
They're garbage.
Just like you.
I'm not garbage, I'm Machine Boy!!
Bea! You have to fight it!
There is no Bea.
There is only me.

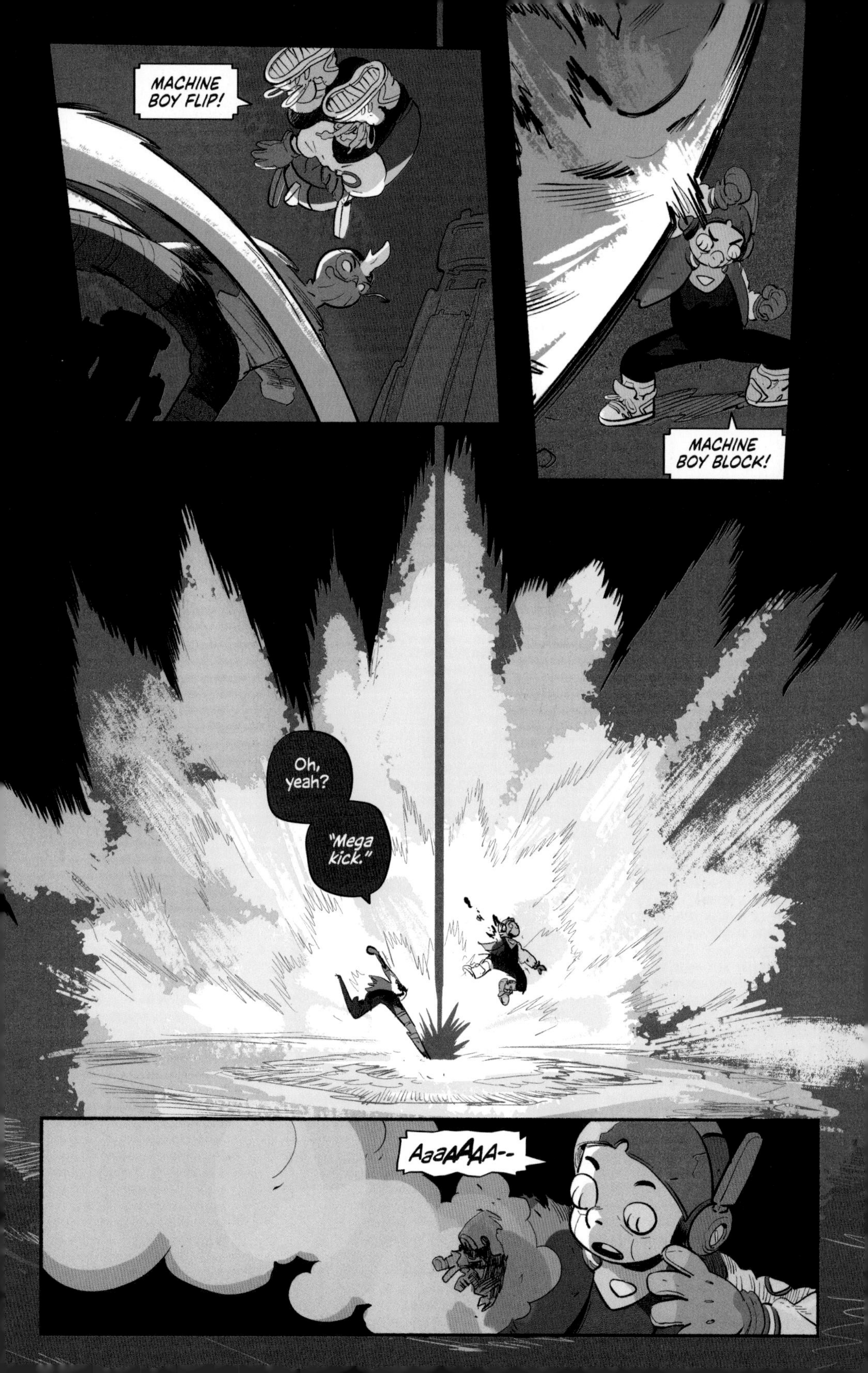

MACHINE BOY FLIP!
MACHINE BOY BLOCK!
Oh, yeah?
"Mega kick."
AaaAAAA--

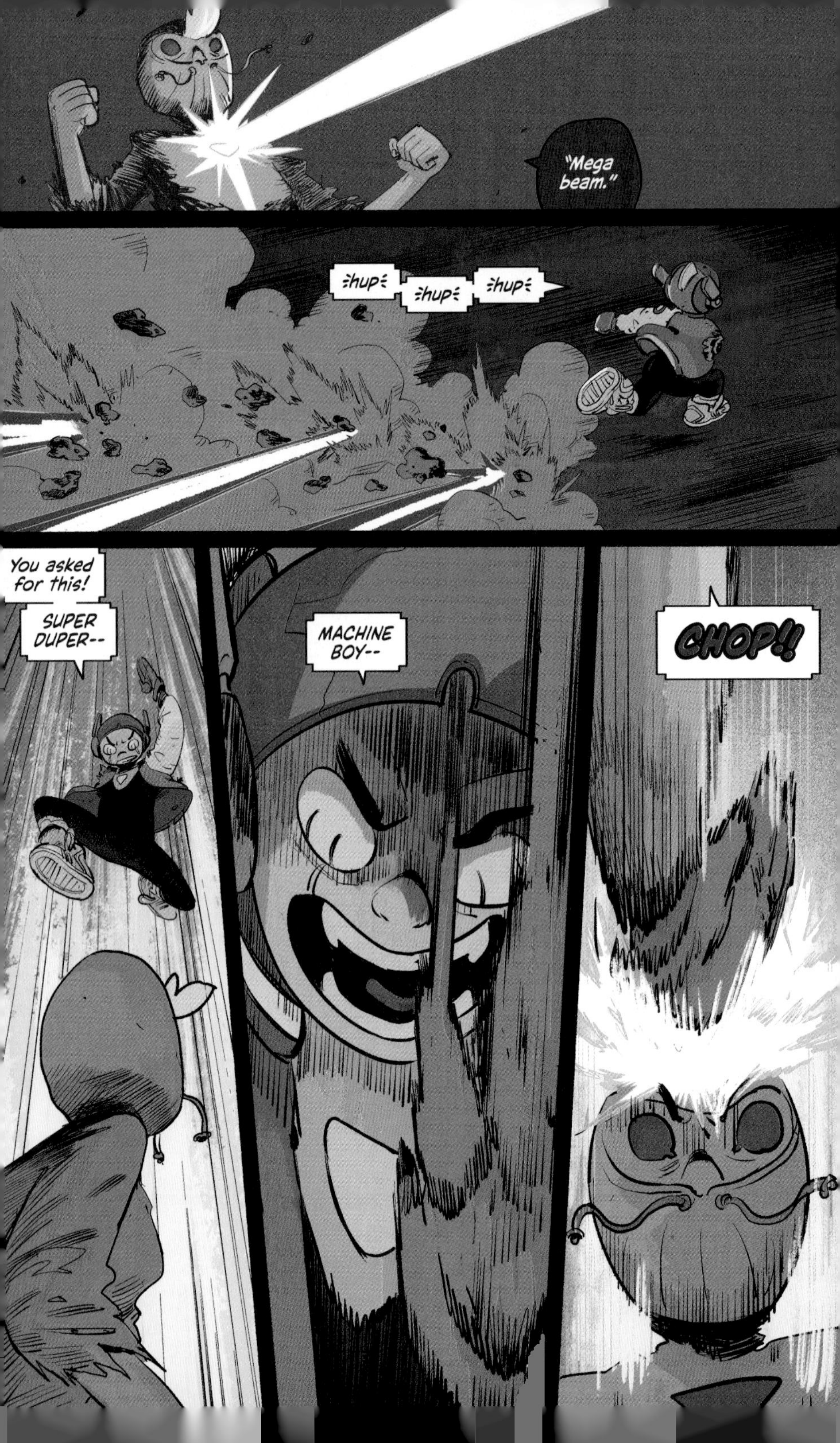
"Mega beam."
hup
hup
hup
You asked for this!
SUPER DUPER--
MACHINE BOY--
CHOP!!

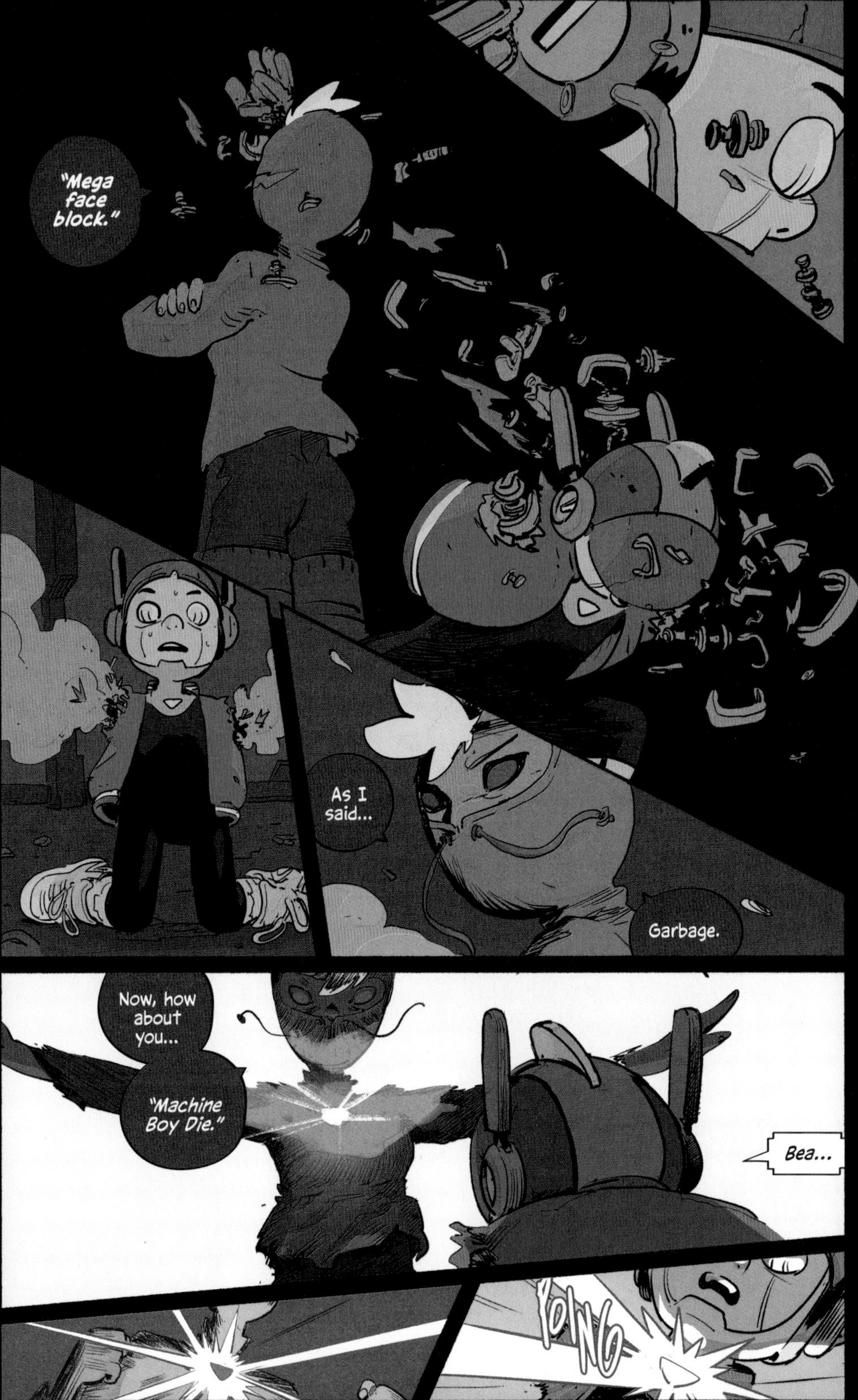
"Mega face block."
As I said...
Garbage.
Now, how about you...
"Machine Boy Die."
Bea...
YOING

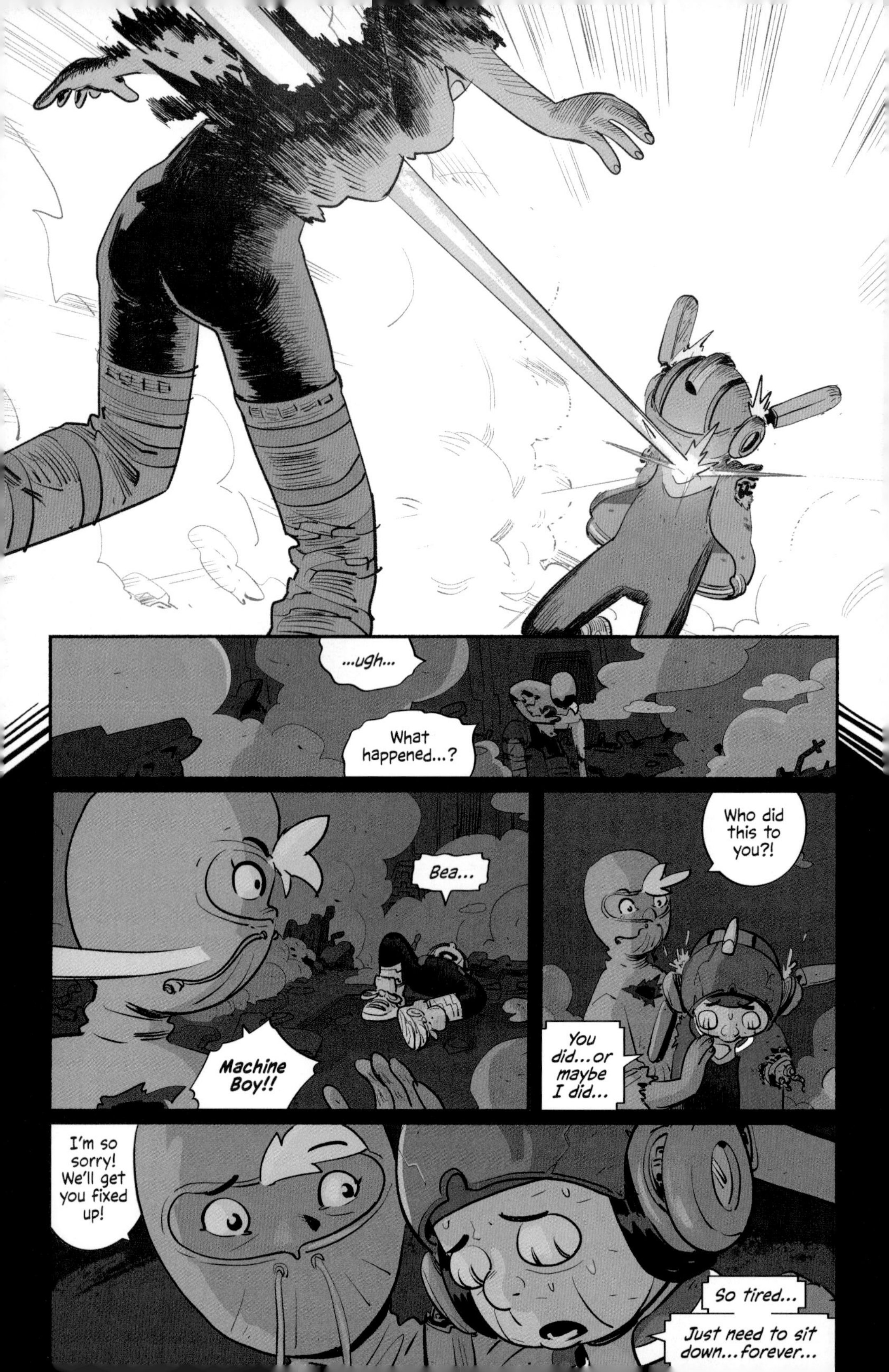
...ugh...
What happened...?
Bea...
Machine Boy!!
Who did this to you?!
You did...or maybe I did...
I'm so sorry! We'll get you fixed up!
So tired...
Just need to sit down...forever...

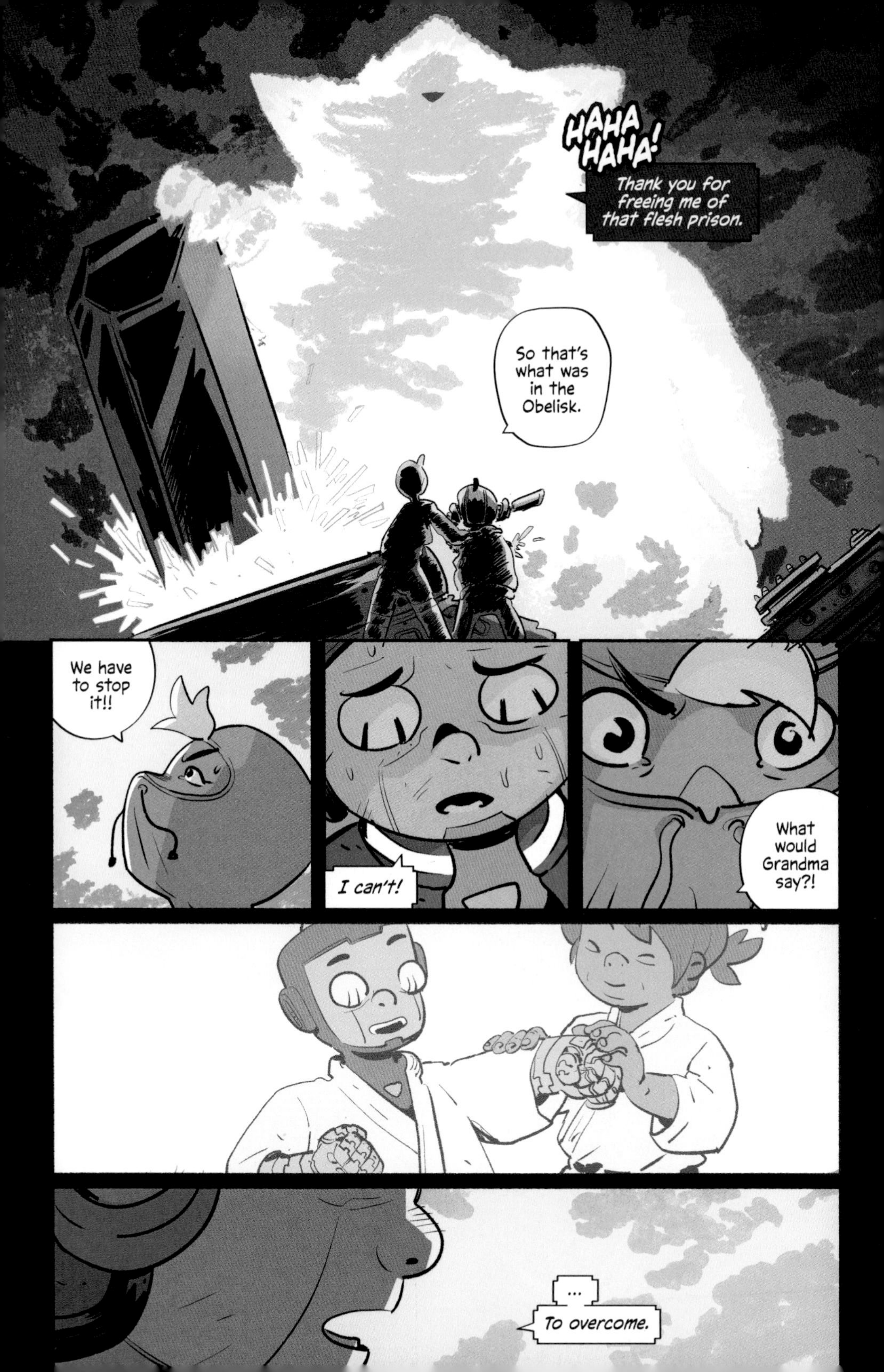
HAHA HAHA!
Thank you for freeing me of that flesh prison.
So that's what was in the Obelisk.
We have to stop it!!
I can't!
What would Grandma say?!
...
To overcome.

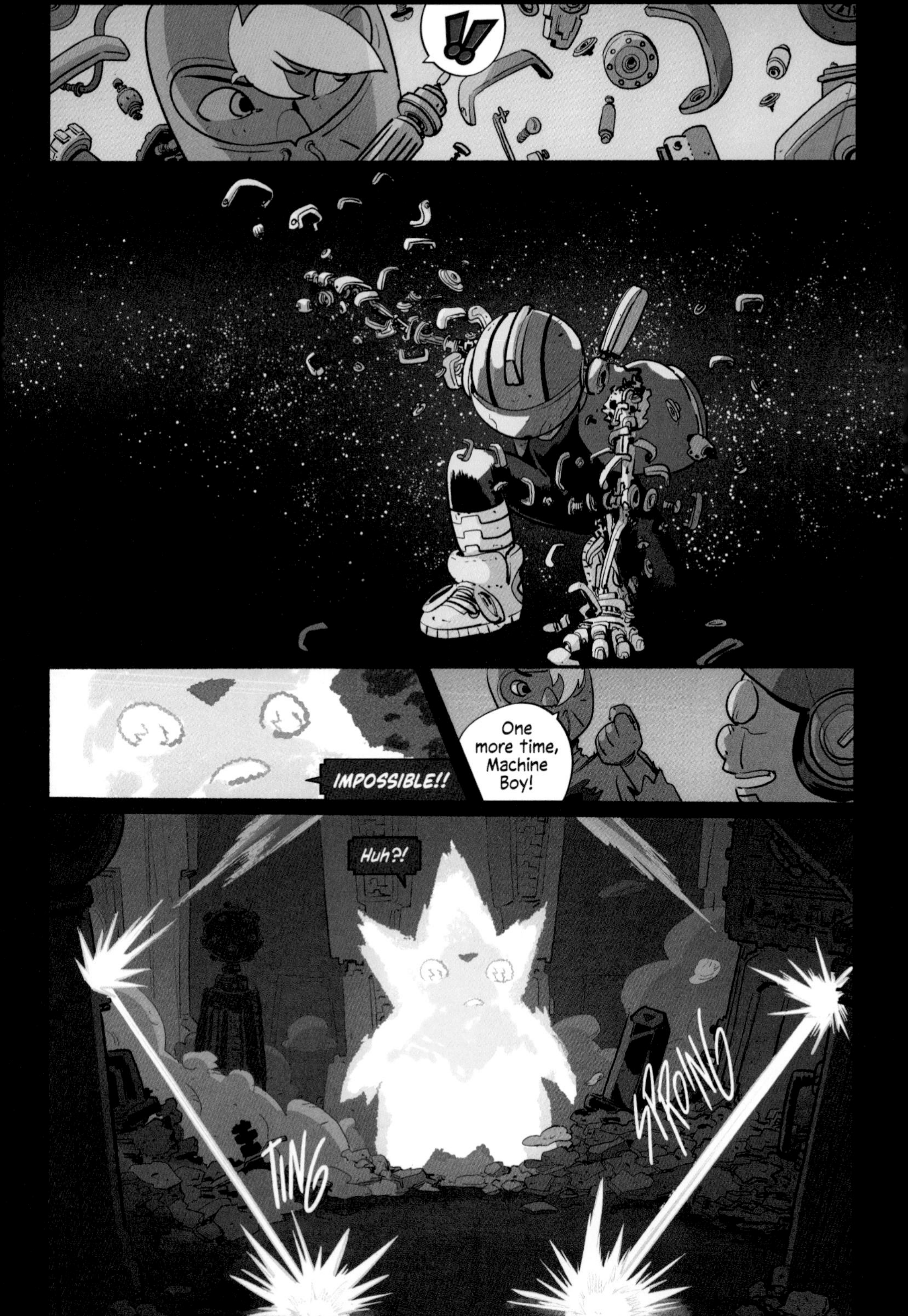
!
IMPOSSIBLE!!
One more time, Machine Boy!
Huh?!
TING
SPROING

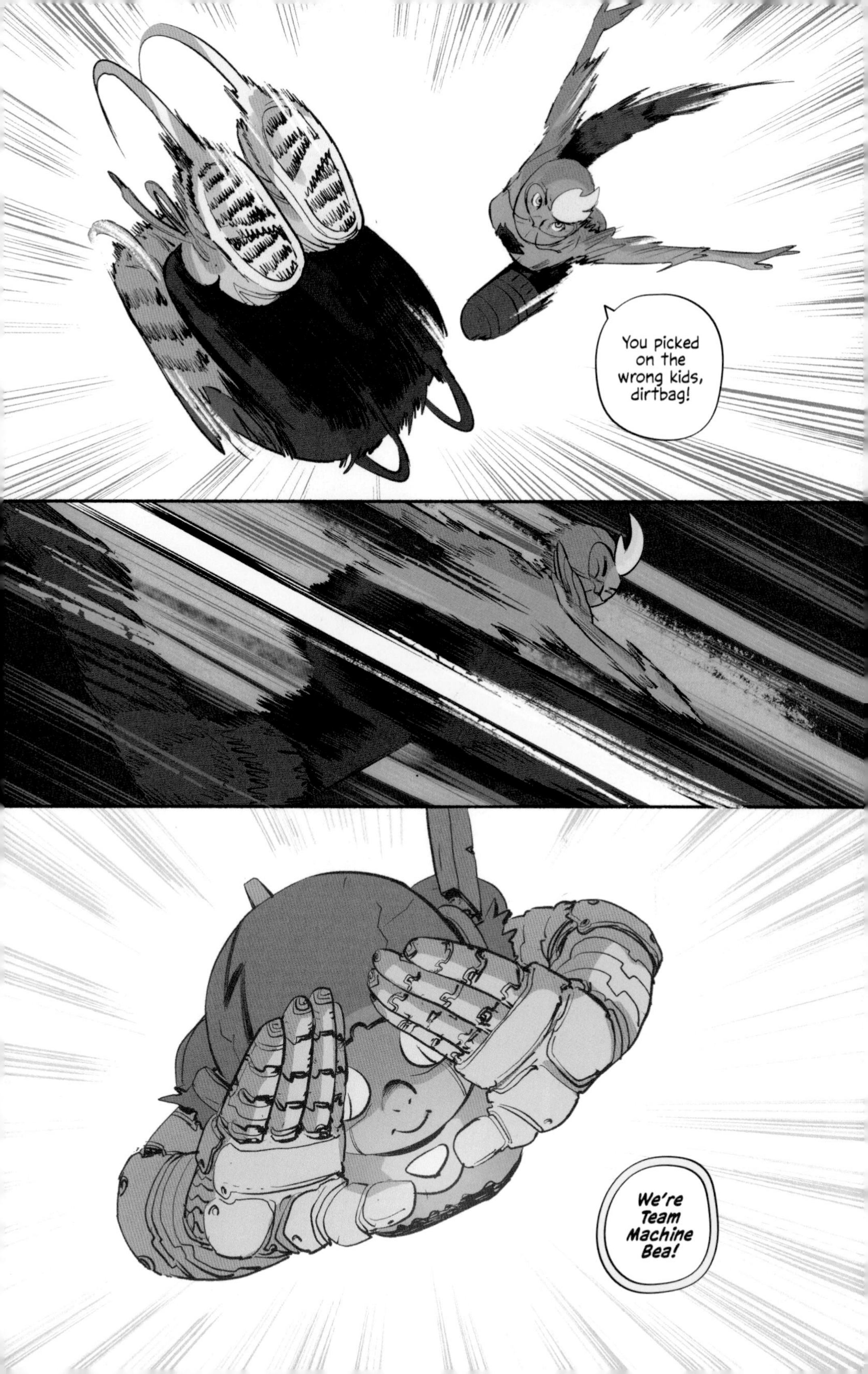
You picked on the wrong kids, dirtbag!
We're Team Machine Bea!

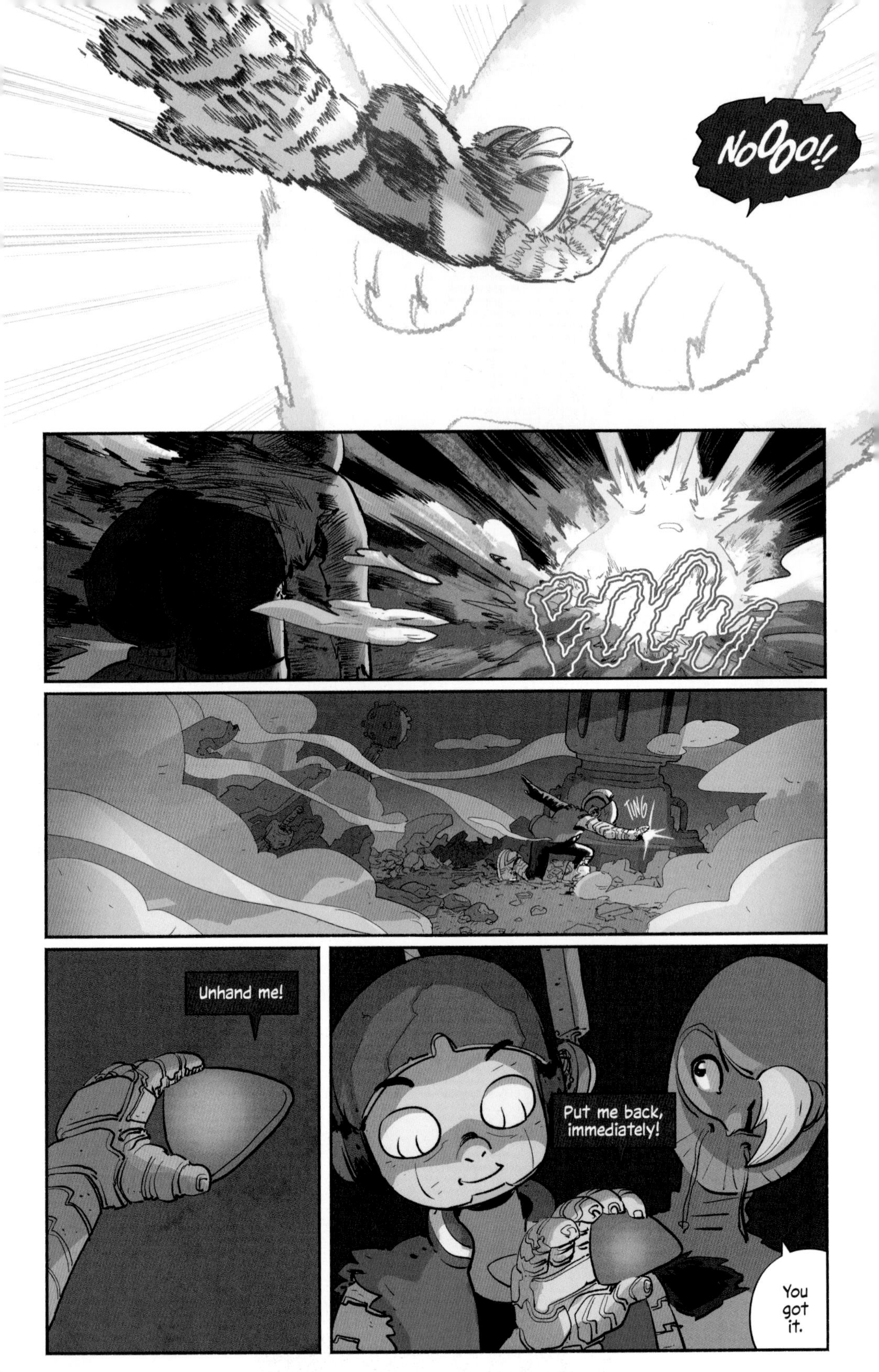
NOOOO!!
BOOM
TING
Unhand me!
Put me back, immediately!
You got it.

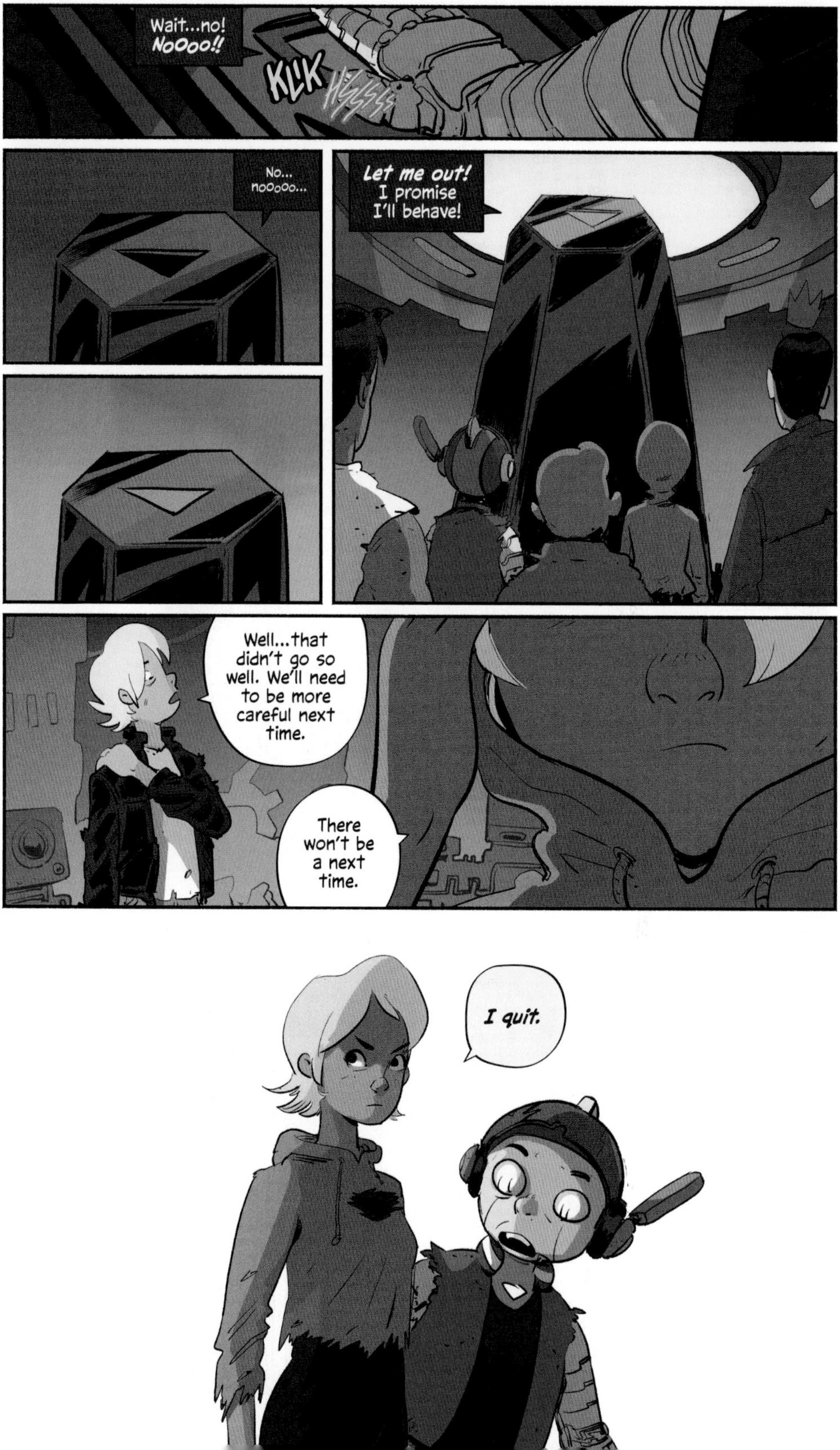
Wait...no!
NoOoo!!
KLIK
HISSSSS
No...
noooooo...
Let me out!
I promise
I'll behave!
Well...that didn't go so well. We'll need to be more careful next time.
There won't be a next time.
I quit.

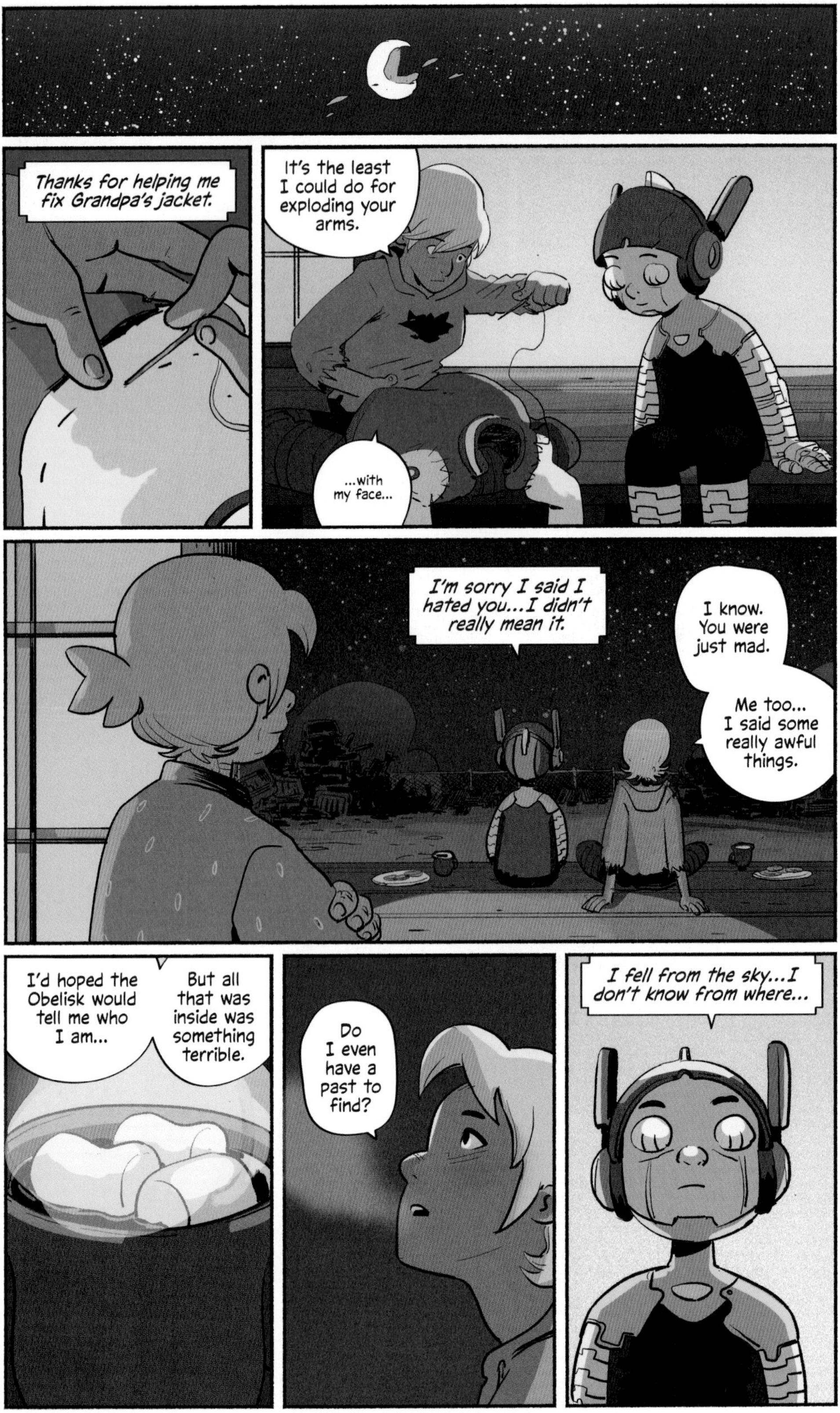
Thanks for helping me fix Grandpa's jacket.
It's the least I could do for exploding your arms.
...with my face...
I'm sorry I said I hated you...I didn't really mean it.
I know. You were just mad.
Me too... I said some really awful things.
I'd hoped the Obelisk would tell me who I am...
But all that was inside was something terrible.
Do I even have a past to find?
I fell from the sky...I don't know from where...

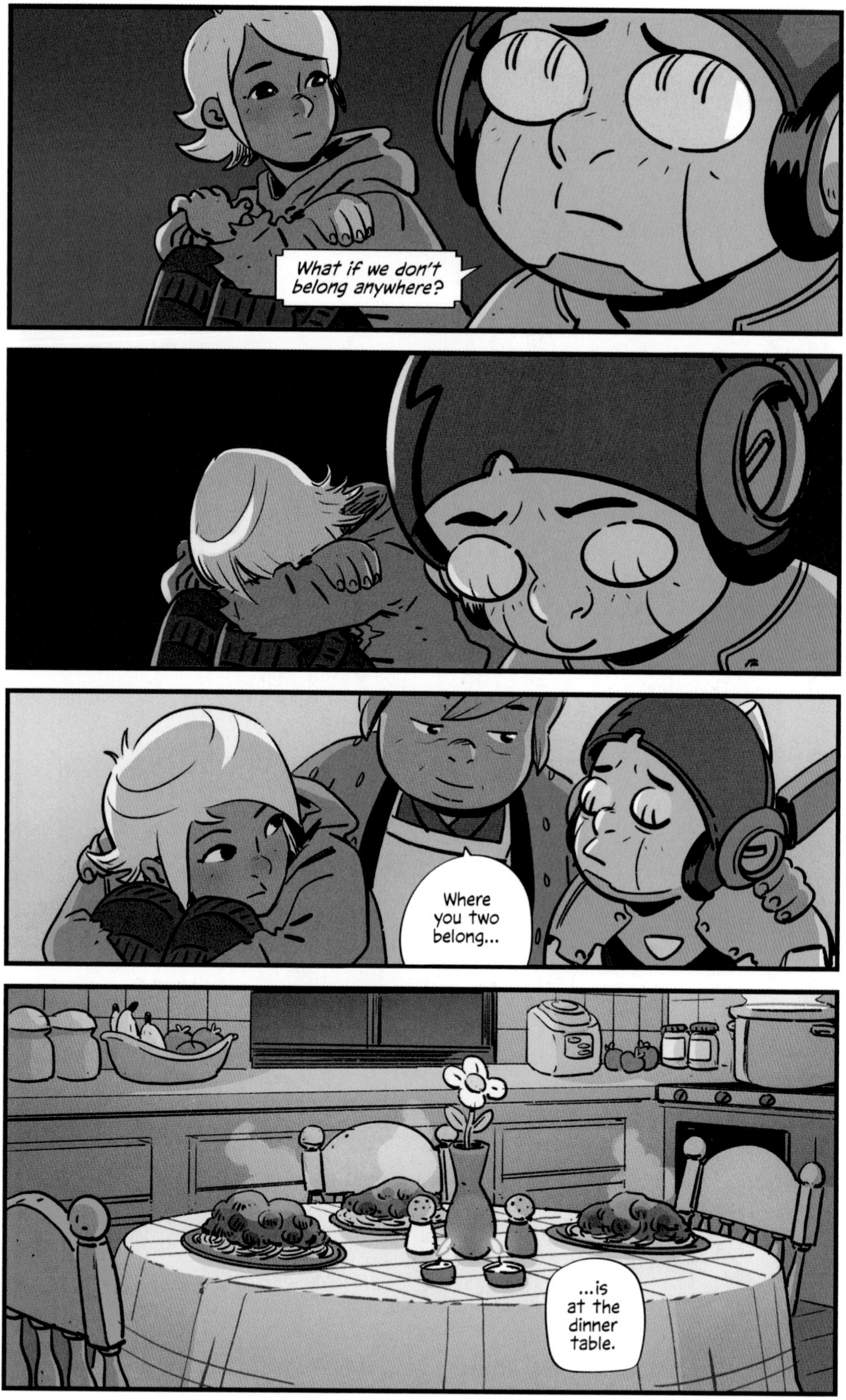
What if we don't belong anywhere?
Where you two belong...
...is at the dinner table.

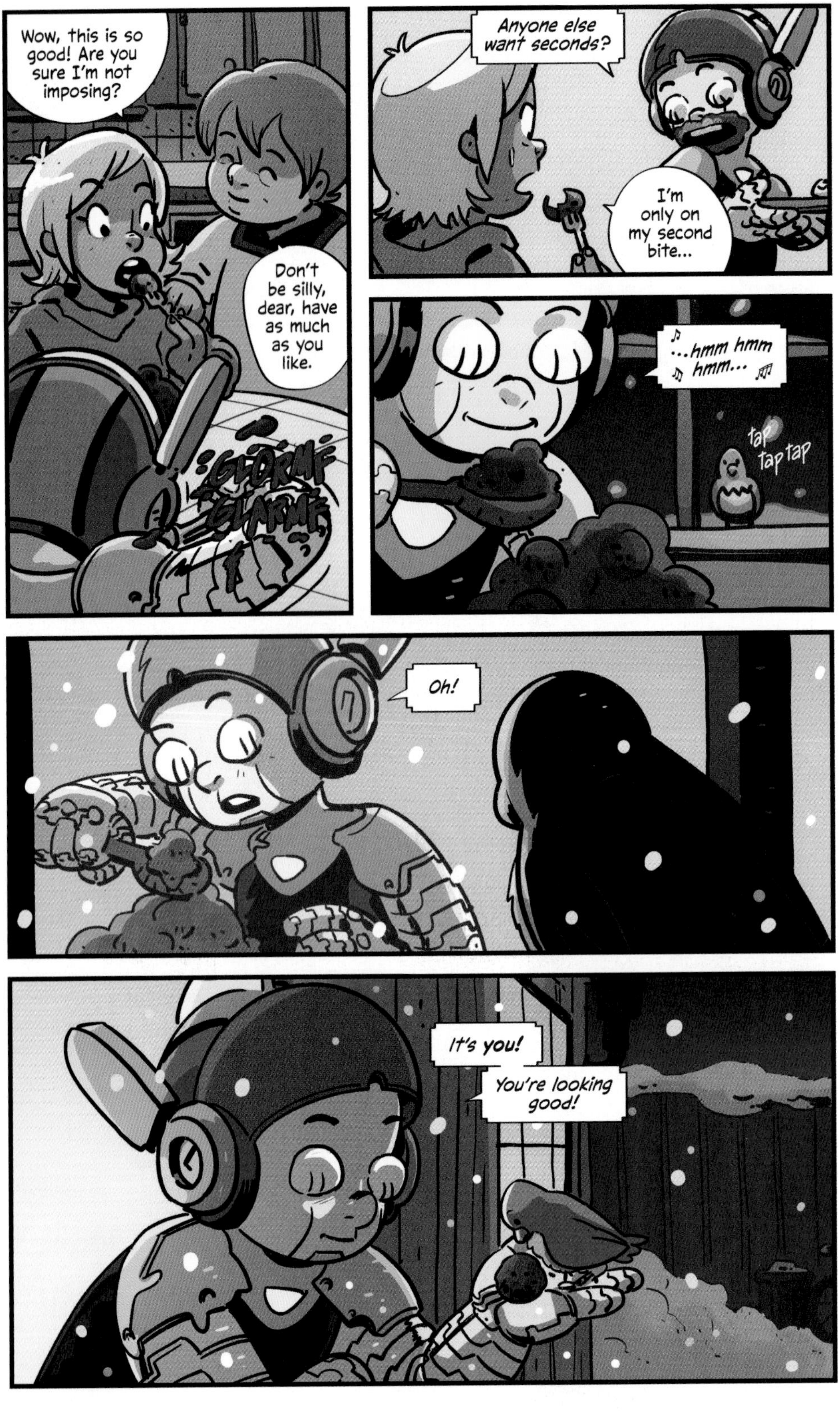
Wow, this is so good! Are you sure I'm not imposing?
Don't be silly, dear, have as much as you like.
GLORMF
GLARMF
Anyone else want seconds?
I'm only on my second bite...
...hmm hmm hmm...
tap tap tap
Oh!
It's you!
You're looking good!

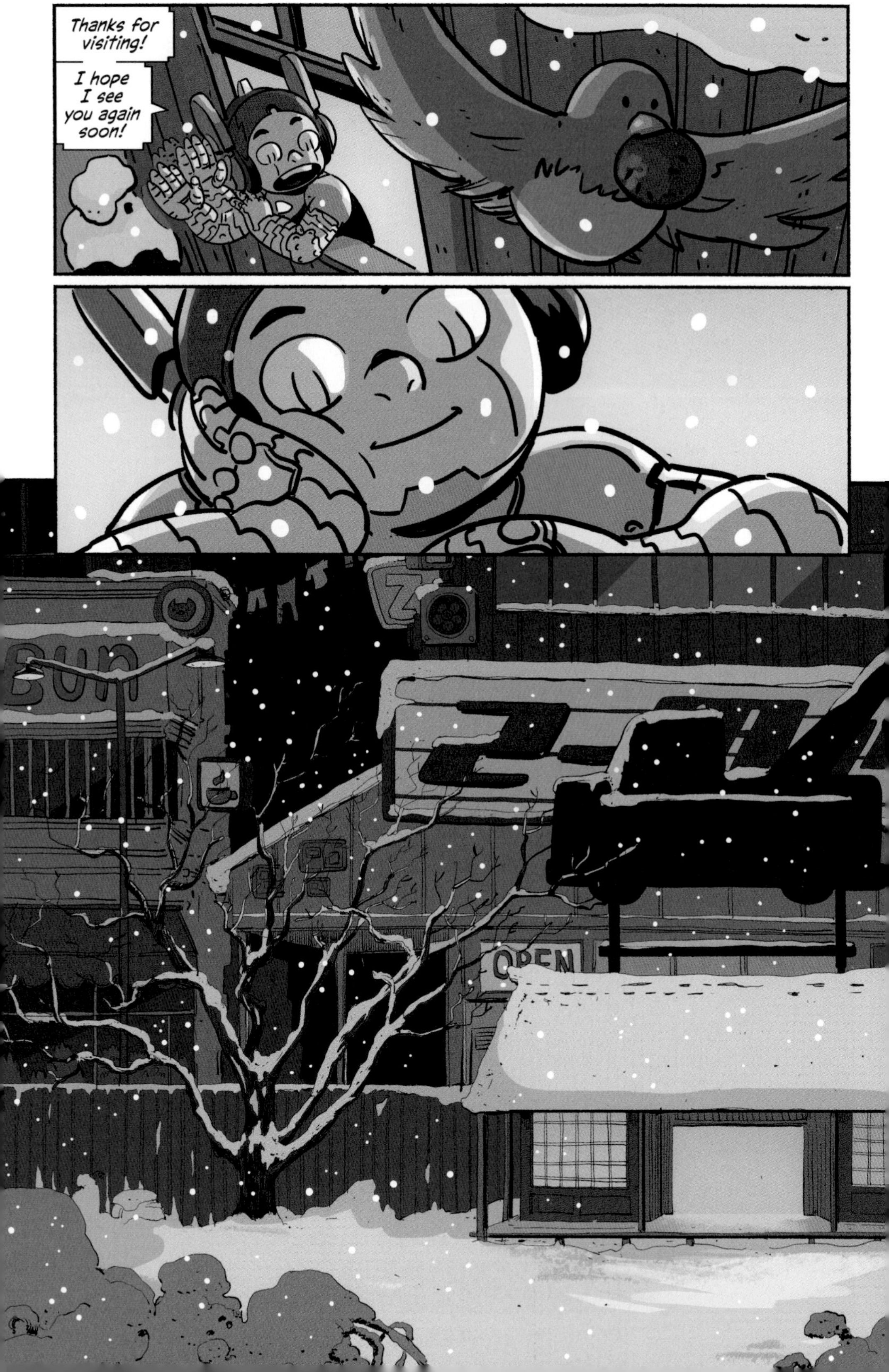
Thanks for visiting!
I hope I see you again soon!
BUN
OPEN

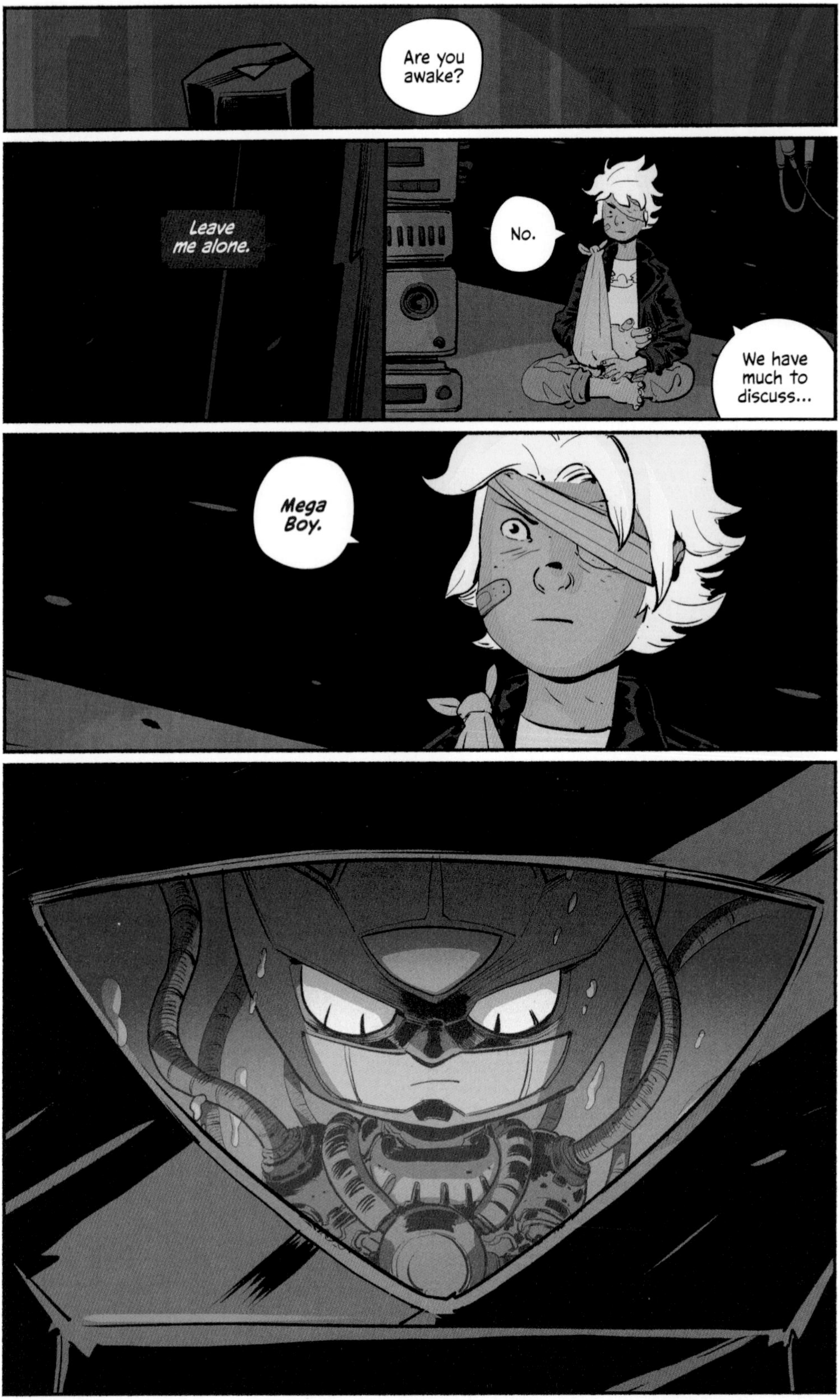

Are you awake?
Leave me alone.
No.
We have much to discuss...
Mega Boy.

ACKNOWLEDGEMENTS

We'd like to acknowledge Arielle Basich first and foremost - without you this book would never have existed. Thank you for believing in us and helping bring the world of Machine Boy to life. Thank you to Aditya Bidikar for translating the world of Machine Boy into lettering that lives and breathes. Thank you to Alex Antone, Sean Mackiewicz, Carina Taylor, Arune Singh, and the entire Skybound team for guiding us through the process of bringing a book into the world. A huge thanks to Becka Kinzie and Jukie Chan for your hard work flatting pages. Thank you to our friends, studiomates, pets and families for supporting a life making comics. Irma would like to specifically thank Charles Tigner for his patience and support.

Tri Vuong: *Creator, Writer, Artist*
Irma Kniivila: *Creator, Writer, Colorist*
Aditya Bidikar: *Letterer*
Arielle Basich: *Editor*
Carina Taylor: *Book + Logo Design*
Andres Juarez: *Book Design + Production*

Teaching guide by Creators, Assemble Inc. | Lexile Measure: GN290L

EVERYDAY HERO MACHINE BOY. FIRST PRINTING. 978-1-5343-2130-4
Published by Image Comics, Inc. Office of publication: PO BOX 14457, Portland, OR 97293.

PRINTED IN THE U.S.A.

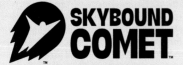

TRI VUONG is a comic artist and writer based out of Toronto, Canada. He is the creator of the popular comic *The Strange Tales of Oscar Zahn* on Line Webtoon and the author of LEGO® NINJAGO®: GARMADON from Skybound Entertainment. He is a veteran of the video game and animation industry whose list of clients include Ubisoft, Corus Entertainment, C.O.R.E Digital Pictures, Koei, and Capybara Games. His work on *Bubble Guppies* and *Clash of Heroes* has won multiple awards.

IRMA KNIIVILA is a Toronto-based cartoonist and illustrator. She has worked with Penguin Random House, Marvel, Boom! Studios and IDW, and her illustration work has appeared in *The Globe and Mail, Reader's Digest* and *The Walrus,* among others. For more, visit irmaillustration.com

GRANDMA MEI'S
SPAGHETTI & MEATBALLS

INGREDIENTS:

- 1 onion, peeled & diced
- 2 tablespoons olive oil
- 3 cans (28 oz. each) whole peeled tomatoes
- 4 cloves garlic, peeled & minced
- basil
- 1 cup breadcrumbs
- 2 lbs ground pork, veal & beef mixture
  (or your favorite meatless substitute!)
- 2 large eggs
- ½ cup freshly grated Parmesan cheese
- salt & pepper to taste

DIRECTIONS:

1. Sweat onions in oil until soft and golden, 6-7 mins. Add garlic and cook until golden, ~1 minute.
2. Pass tomatoes through a blender and pour them in.
3. Bring to a gentle simmer. Add basil, salt & pepper to taste.
4. Cook for ~30 minutes, stirring occasionally. Adjust seasoning, if necessary.

While the sauce is simmering, make the meatballs.

1. Add breadcrumbs & two eggs to a bowl of ground meat.
2. Add grated cheese, herbs, and salt & pepper to taste.
3. Mix it with your hands. A twisting claw-like motion helps make sure the meatballs aren't too dense.
4. Roll them up. At this point, you can brown them in a pan with oil, or toss them right in the pot of sauce.
5. Simmer for an hour.
6. Mangia!

READING GUIDE

IMPORTANT SETTINGS

- Mr. Hound's Grocery
- Mega 416 (city)
- Mr. Hound's greenhouse
- Kobushi house
- Bathurst Secondary
- Universarium

NOTABLE CHARACTERS

- "Karate Grandpa" Goh Kobushi
- Grandma Mei Kobushi
- Machine Boy
- Mr. Hound
- Bea Sharpe
- Orphan Universe members:
  - Petit Dejeuner
  - Doki Doki Doki
  - King
  - KO
  - Chad

KEY THEMES

- Spaghetti
- Family
- Community
- Personified animals
- Martial arts
- Grief and loss
- Sense of belonging
- Friendship
- Self esteem

DISCUSSION QUESTIONS

1. Who or what would you say is responsible for Goh's death? Was it the actions of one or more characters? Was it something that was destined to happen that day?
2. What did Mr. Hound's reaction to Mei Kobushi say about his character? What about how people respond to the death of one another's loved ones?
3. Discuss the symbolism of the bluebird throughout the book-from Machine Boy's first appearance, to the greenhouse, to the end. How does the bird make you feel and what do you think the symbolism is here?
4. What do you think "Don't rob tomorrow to feed today" means when Mei says it?

5. Osu is the Japanese word for "push" or "to endure." Discuss the significance of this word and concept throughout the story.
6. The bullies say that Machine Boy is "not even a legit person" (page 87). Do you agree? At what point do you as a reader start to "forgive" Machine Boy for the chaos that takes place around him?
7. Discuss the concepts of loss and grief throughout the story: How do we see each of the main characters dealing with loss (of grandpa, of the car, of Tony, etc.)?
8. Grandma Mei says she and grandpa Goh do karate "to overcome." What activities do you turn to when you are facing stress or negative feelings?
9. When Machine Boy finds out Bea was an operative and not his friend the whole time (page 155), he initially says he won't help save 416. Is he being a "selfish coward" like Bea says? What would you do in that situation?
10. What does the story say about the concept of "family?" We see the Kobushis never had a child of their own. How does Mei and Goh's treatment of their community, including their students and Machine Boy, show their feelings on what family means?

ACTIVITY IDEAS

1. Design your own robot, including a costume. Give it a name and some characteristics.
2. What's your favorite food? Ask your family for an old recipe for it, or find one online.
3. Write your own song lyrics/poem inspired by the book.

SCURRY

MAC SMITH

**SKYBOUN
COME**

PART I

LINGERING LIGHT

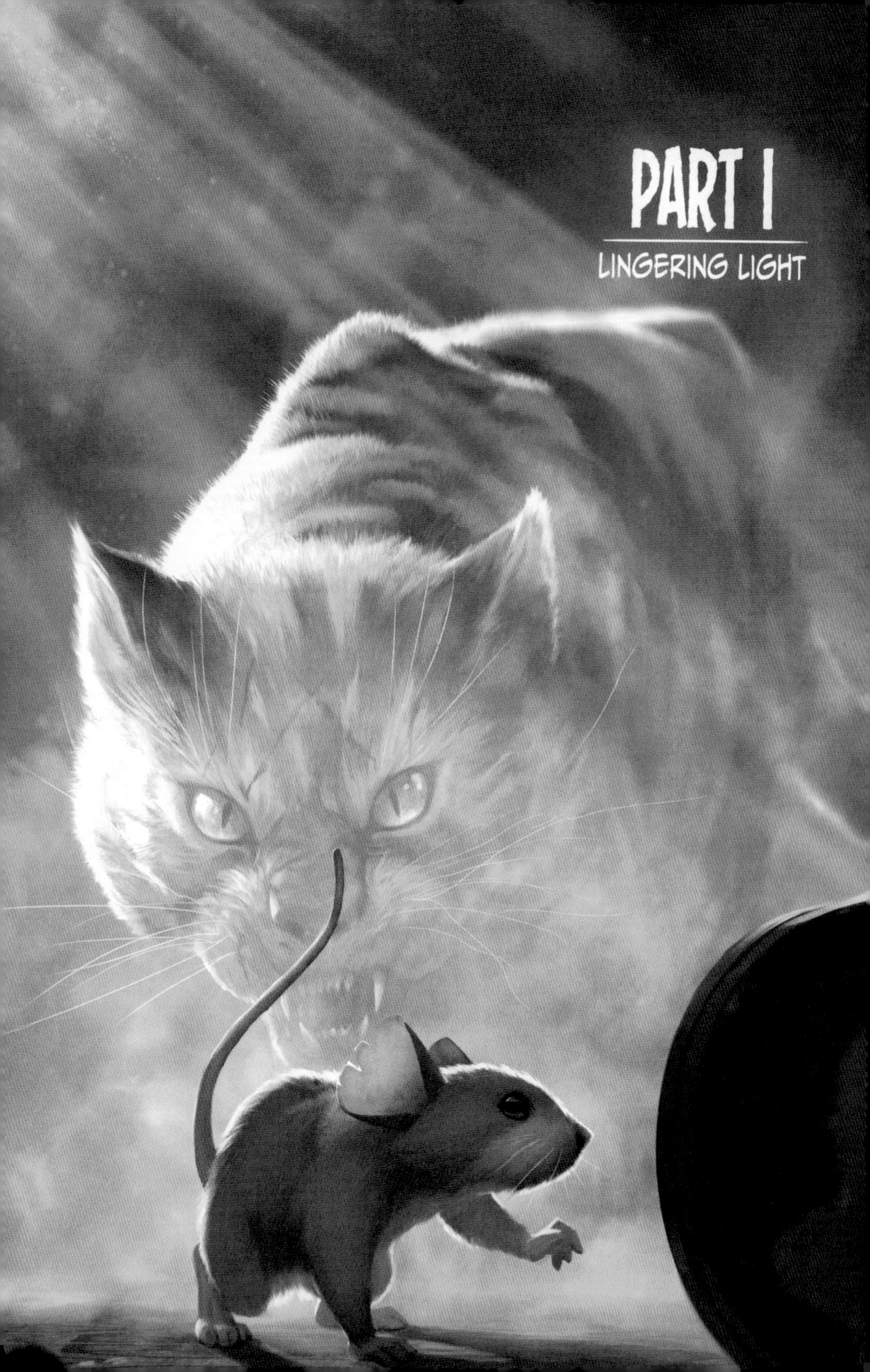

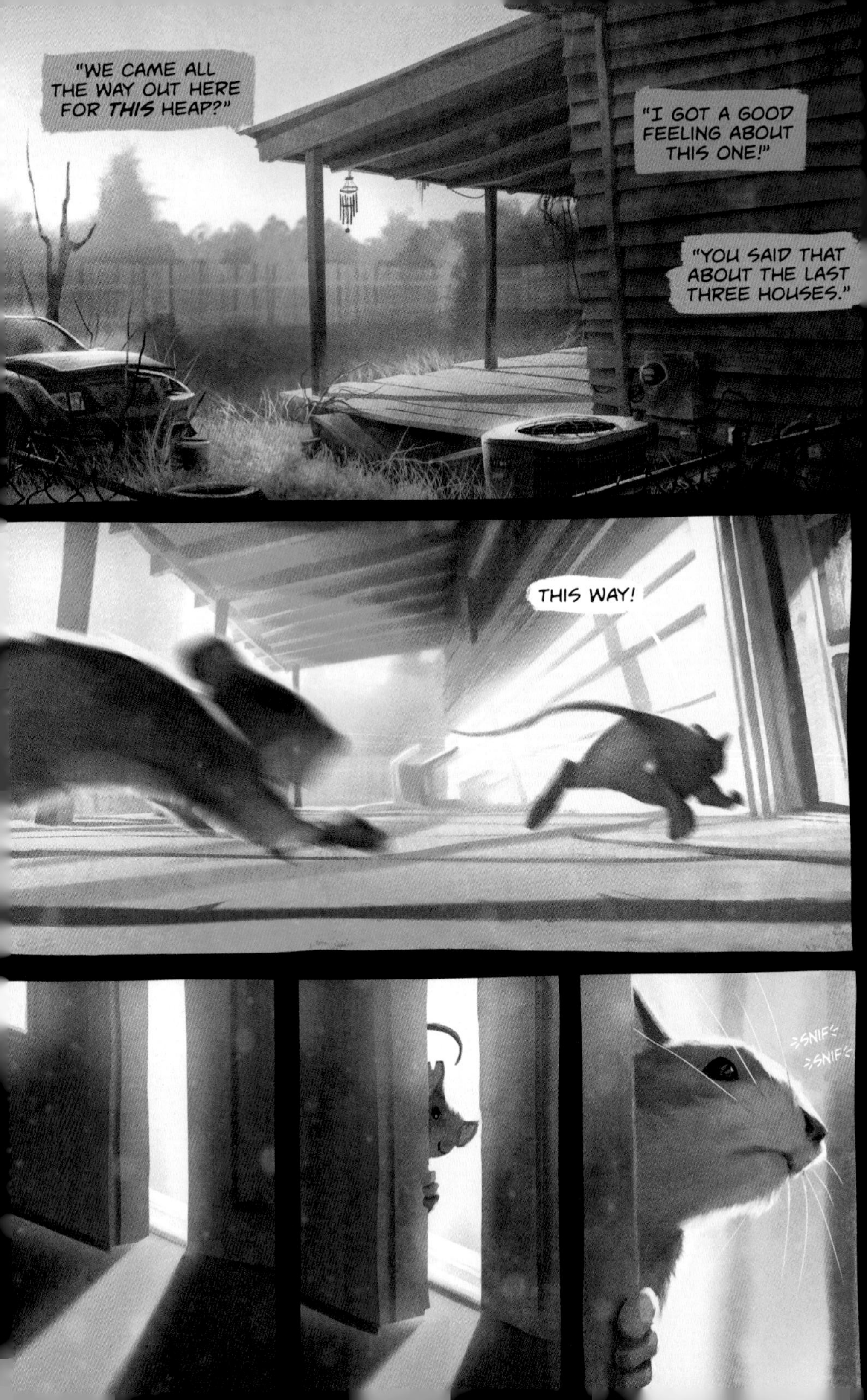
"WE CAME ALL THE WAY OUT HERE FOR THIS HEAP?"
"I GOT A GOOD FEELING ABOUT THIS ONE!"
"YOU SAID THAT ABOUT THE LAST THREE HOUSES."
THIS WAY!
SNIF
SNIF

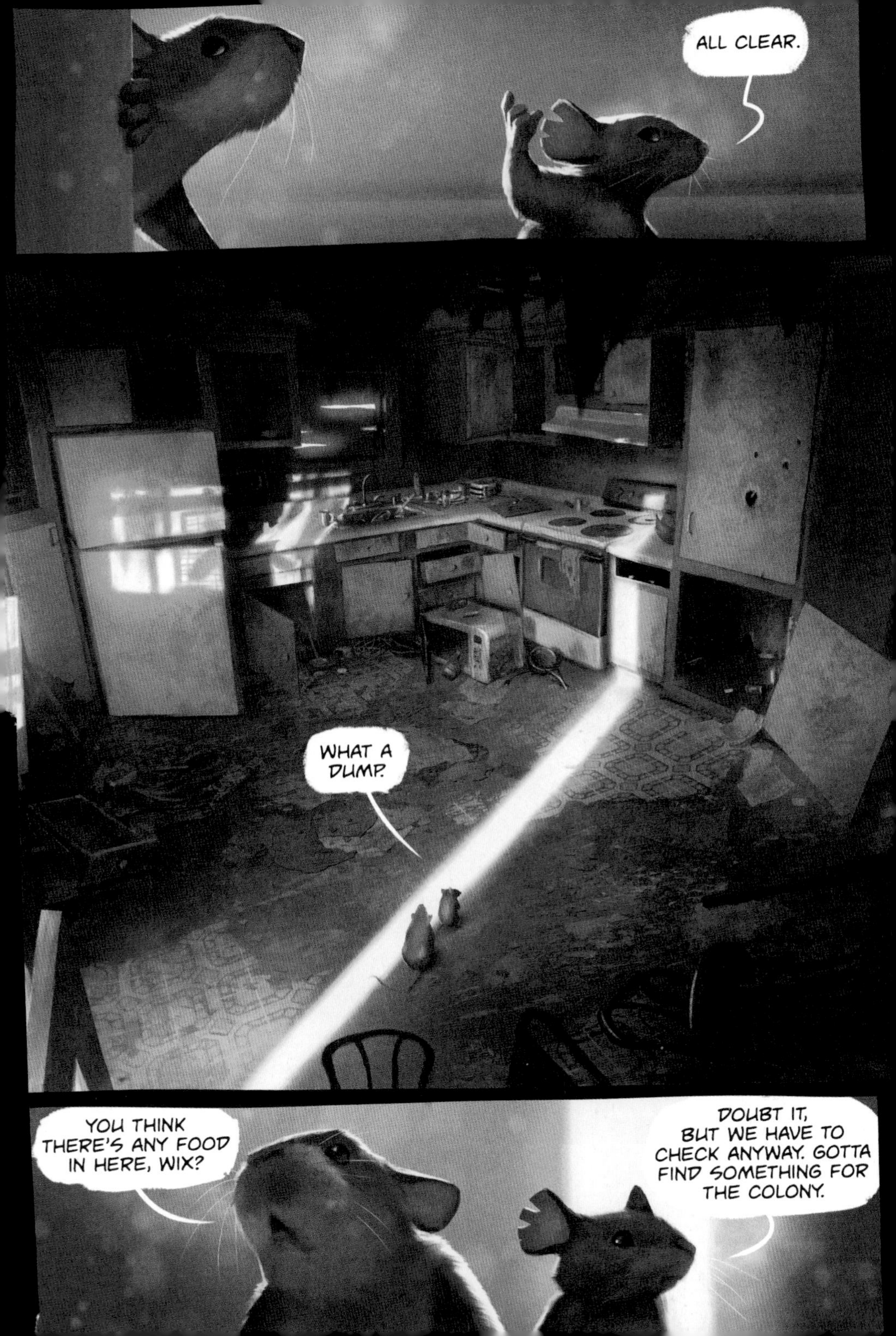
ALL CLEAR.
WHAT A DUMP.
YOU THINK THERE'S ANY FOOD IN HERE, WIX?
DOUBT IT, BUT WE HAVE TO CHECK ANYWAY. GOTTA FIND SOMETHING FOR THE COLONY.

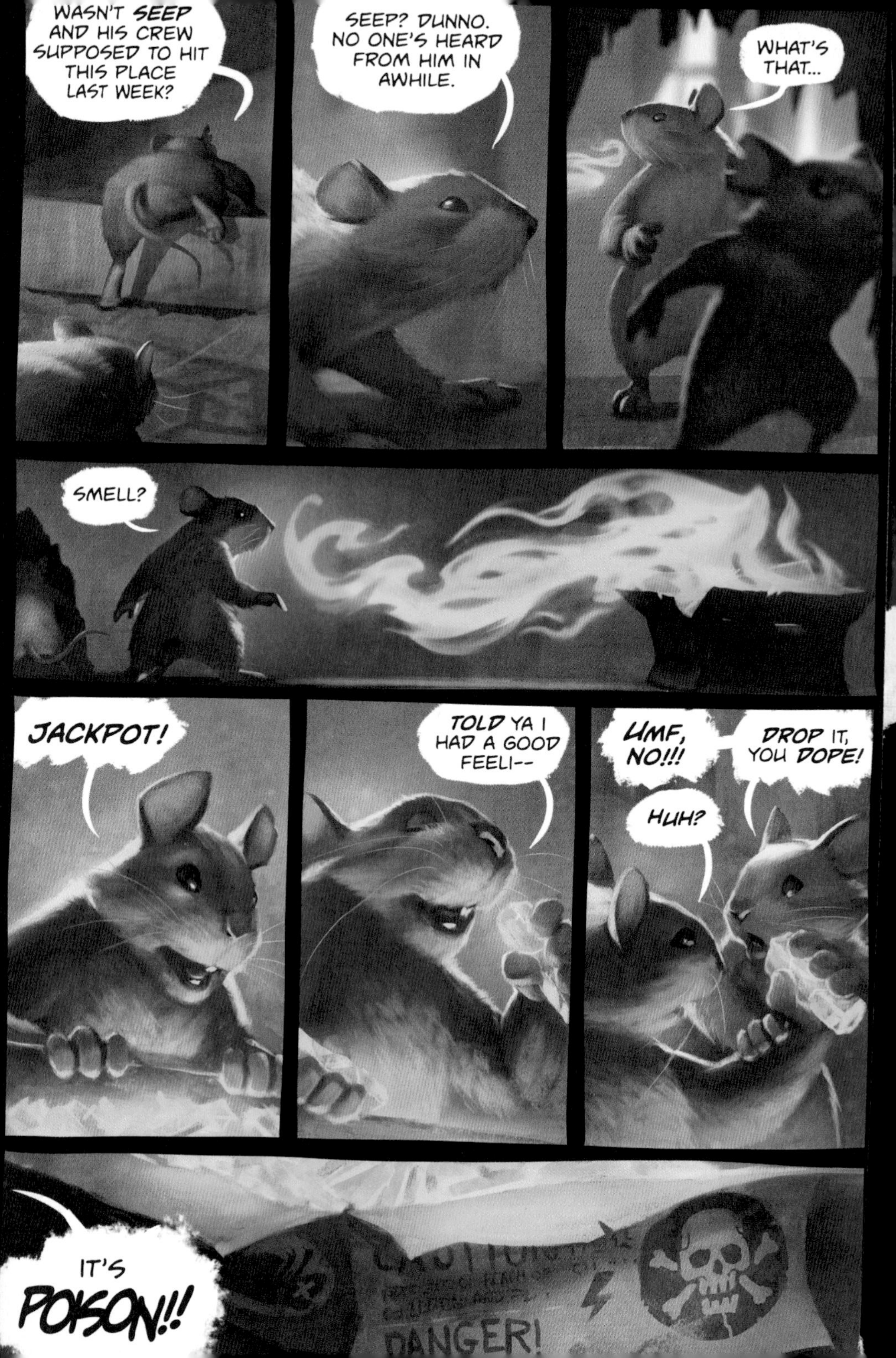

WASN'T SEEP AND HIS CREW SUPPOSED TO HIT THIS PLACE LAST WEEK?
SEEP? DUNNO. NO ONE'S HEARD FROM HIM IN AWHILE.
WHAT'S THAT...
SMELL?
JACKPOT!
TOLD YA I HAD A GOOD FEELI--
UMF, NO!!!
DROP IT, YOU DOPE!
HUH?
IT'S POISON!!
DANGER!

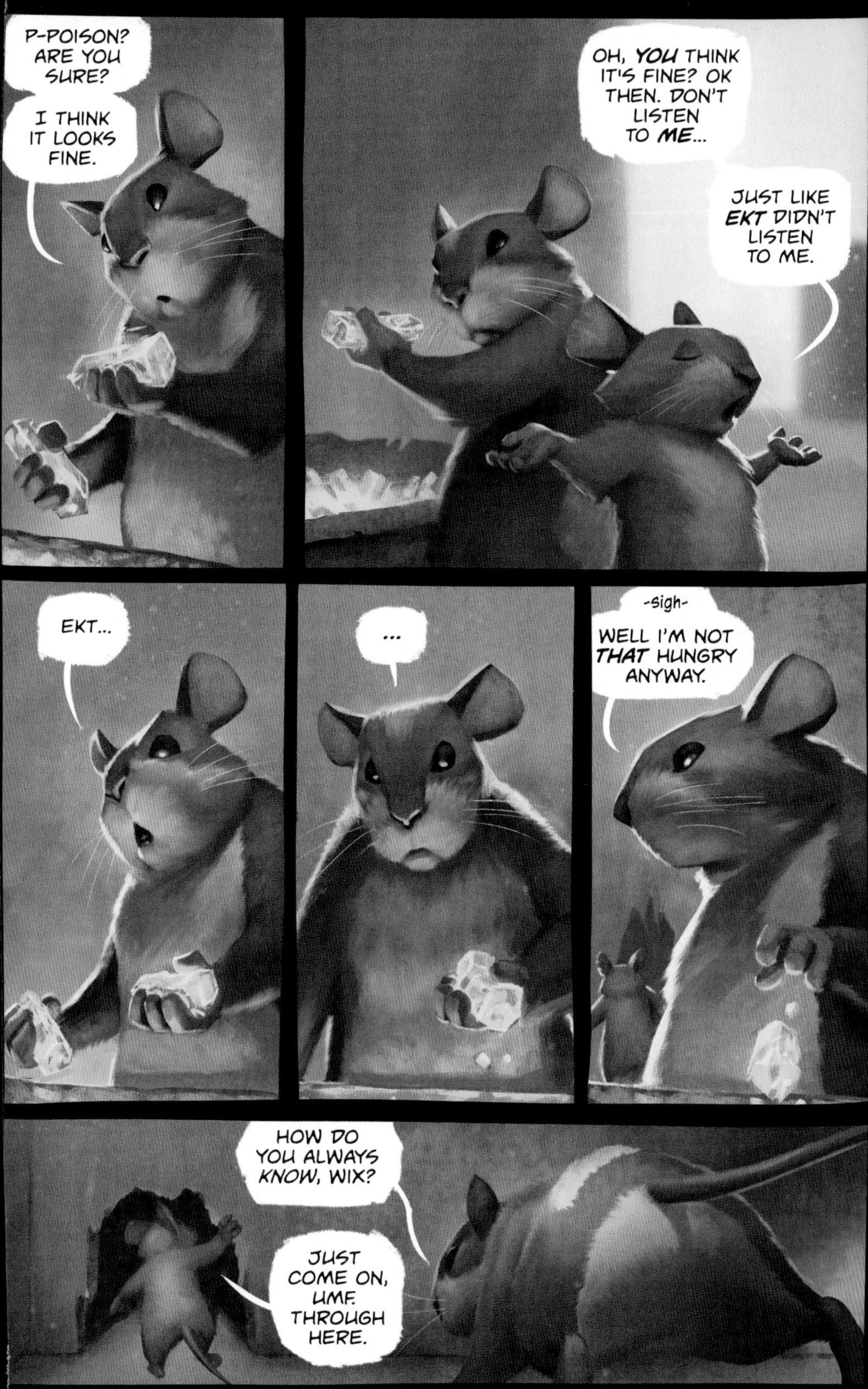
P-POISON? ARE YOU SURE?
I THINK IT LOOKS FINE.
OH, YOU THINK IT'S FINE? OK THEN. DON'T LISTEN TO ME...
JUST LIKE EKT DIDN'T LISTEN TO ME.
EKT...
...
-sigh-
WELL I'M NOT THAT HUNGRY ANYWAY.
HOW DO YOU ALWAYS KNOW, WIX?
JUST COME ON, UMF. THROUGH HERE.

TO BE CONTINUED IN SCURRY

EXPLORE NEW WORLDS
For Middle Grade Readers in SKYBOUND COMET